Harriet Grace grew up in Inkpen, Berkshire. She has grown-up children and stepchildren and now lives in London. *Cells* is her first novel.

To hank and Tass

with love June

Harry xx

Cells

by

Harriet Grace

This first edition published in Great Britain in 2008 by
Four O'Clock Press - a Discovered Authors' imprint

ISBN13 978-1-906146-67-2

Available from Discovered Authors Online –
All major online retailers and available to order through all UK bookshops

Or contact:

Books
Discovered Authors
Roslin Road, London
W3 8DH

0844 800 5214
books@discoveredauthors.co.uk
www.discoveredauthors.co.uk

Printed in the UK by BookForce Distribution
BookForce policy is to use papers that are natural, renewable and recyclable
products and made from wood grown in sustainable forests wherever
possible

BookForce Distribution
Roslin Road, London
W3 8DH
www.bookforce.co.uk

For Charlie

ACKNOWLEDGEMENTS

With thanks to and in memory of Charles Runge who first suggested I should write, and Bill Stanton who helped me realise I could write fiction.

Enormous thanks to Jane Rogers for her assistance throughout the book, Jo Pestel and Penny Faith (fellow MA graduates of Sheffield Hallam University), my Friday writing group, and Jo Field, my editor; to the Guardian newspaper for allowing me to spend an afternoon on the Features Floor, and particularly to Roger Alton and Sarah Marshall; to Discovered Authors for discovering me; and to Charlie Grace for his unwavering and loving support throughout all the years we have known each other.

ONE

MARTHA

It was ten to seven and something was wrong with one of the terminals on the Women's Desk.

'Where the hell's Liza?' The Women's editor seemed to have disappeared. Martha strode past the flickering screens feeling as if she could hit something. Pain was creeping into her scalp. Her boots thudded on the lino floor as she swerved round the Obituary island.

'Martha!' A voice from *Weekend Review*.

'Not now!'

'Martha...!' Another voice. The phones rang. People shouted to each other across the room.

She reached the Women's corner and stared at the blank screen. Daisy's feature on grandmothers in the city had vanished. Strands of hair stuck to the girl's tear-stained face. 'I've – I've lost it, haven't I?'

'No, you haven't.' Martha's shirt clung to her. The place was like a sauna today – they never got the heating right. She punched the power button. Jab, jab, like the darts of pain in her head. Flicker of light. Nothing. 'You sure you haven't sent it down-line already? Didn't you keep a hard copy?' But the girl was covering her face with her hands, and Martha would have to put an arm round her and dredge up some sympathy when all she wanted to do was to walk away.

'You'll remember it, Daisy. You'll remember what you wrote. Come on, let's find a free terminal.' But she didn't say that last sentence because as Daisy pulled back her chair, the room gave a long sigh and expired into silence.

For a few seconds Martha thought she was expiring too, a curious not unpleasant feeling – the quietness, the peace... everything cutting out suddenly. Her headache seemed to lift, the tightness loosening. She put her hand to her forehead

1

thinking, thank God, it's going, and reached out to Daisy's thin shoulders, wanting to comfort her now, make up for the harshness. But then there was a burst of noise as everyone shouted in protest and leapt up from their terminals, and the sparks of pain returned.

Mercifully, Dave from Maintenance was still in the building and was summoned upstairs. He hunched over Daisy's screen before scurrying off in search of other terminals – or to some main terminal – to the heart of it anyway. Martha wasn't into any of that. Her job was to make stories out of the mess that is the world, stories that looked as if they existed before she made them, as if they were there already, whole, in the ether, and not the botched up cutting and pasting reality that was second nature here. She steadied herself against Daisy's chair. People were back in front of their blank computers, scribbling notes on their pads, or talking to each other, or on the phone. One or two had got out their laptops. She pulled the chair away from the desk and sat down.

It must have been then that she noticed him. In profile at first – a tall man, in jeans and a slightly grubby T-shirt, not much more than a boy; dark long hair. She had seen him before, delivering parcels and taking coffee and sandwich orders, but not close to. He was standing next to Daisy chatting to her and he turned and glanced towards Martha as if he sensed her attention, his eyes meeting hers before he looked away; dark, wide-set eyes, pale skin. There was a kind of calm in his face that made her want to sit back and gaze at him. He doesn't know he's got it, she thought.

'Martha, are you alright?' Daisy's hand was on her arm. 'Martha…?'

It was the man who took her arm in a warm, firm grip through the sleeve of her shirt, guiding her back to her desk. Their skins touched as he handed her into her chair, and then he was gone and there was a cold space on her skin.

Daisy ordered a taxi, dry-eyed now and recovered it appeared. Martha could see Liza returning to the Women's corner. Tony arrived, grinning and dumping some papers on her desk. 'Dear oh dear, Martha...' He pulled up a chair, scraping it along the floor and pushed his rimless glasses up onto his head.

'Noise, Tony!'

'What – ?'

'I can't stand noise –'

'Are you alright, Martha?'

'It's a headache, that's all. Just take over for this evening, will you?'

'Of course.' He nodded slowly, and glanced at Daisy, winking at her. 'We'll manage, won't we?' He looked back. 'Go home, Martha, and get properly better.'

'I'll be here in the morning, Tony!' He was looking too happy. He was after her job.

The young man was there again, standing the other side of her desk. 'Excuse me, please.' His dark eyes moved from hers to Tony's. 'I think Dave needs to talk to one of you.'

Martha watched the two men go, the younger one half a head taller. 'Who's Jesus?'

Daisy removed the red band from the nape of her neck and shook out her hair. 'Jesus?'

'What's his name?'

'That's Jon!' Daisy giggled. Her hair was being scooped up again. 'He's one of the editorials. You know, a messenger.'

'I know what an editorial is.' Martha pressed her fingers into her forehead. The girl was too confident for her own good.

All weekend she lay in bed nursing her aching head. Tony would be doing the Monday edition having done the Saturday and Friday editions, and at this rate would be doing the Tuesday edition too. She didn't know how quickly the

3

technical problem had been solved, or what features had got into Friday's edition. Had Daisy's made it? Had any features been included? If anyone had rung her, Grant hadn't told her. And she'd felt too ill to ring them.

Grant brought her Saturday's edition with a bowl of consommé, but she turned on to her other side and the paper slipped off the bed unopened. The pain lodged itself behind an eye or throbbed in the top of her neck, or lay like a hot, tight bandage across her forehead stopping her from reading or working. The headaches during the treatment had been like this. She tried to sleep, tried not to think about the treatment. A memory of headaches returned to her, a memory of herself as a child curled up in her darkened bedroom longing for Daddy, praying that the animal in her head, as she called it then, would go away, praying that Daddy would be in the mood to come and see her. He would prop the pillow behind them and swing his legs onto the bed so that they were lying next to each other. He would put his arm around her. The warm skin of his hand always found the bare skin of her arm or her hand. The books he read were the books he was teaching in class: 'The Hobbit', 'Wind in the Willows', 'David Copperfield'.

She dropped in and out of sleep, took more analgesics, lay in a bath, tried to read, got back into bed, closed her eyes. For weeks, months, she'd managed not to think, but now the images came back: Mr. Shorn avoiding their eyes across the wide polished table and looking down at his notes and then lifting his head and shaking it; Grant, that night, moving up behind her and pressing his body against hers, warm breath on her neck, and making her turn towards him, making himself go into her.

The next day she'd plunged back into work and tried to put the whole business behind her. She'd urged the editorial team to find more stories, think of new ways of saying them. She'd reminded them of the constant pressure to produce more –

more pages, more sections, larger sections. What are our bench marks? How can we be cutting edge? She initiated a new column called 'The Professionals' and roped in Grant to be the first professional. Sometimes at night she stretched a hand down to arouse him though she knew he was tired. Sometimes as he slipped into her, she thought *now we've given up maybe it'll work*. At least there were no more treatments, no more dashing out of the office, no more awkward questions, no more of Tony's questions: 'Out again?'... 'Looking a bit peaky?'... 'Leaving early?' Annoyingly, he made tears come to her eyes. Now Mr. Shorn had given her and Grant the thumbs down, at least she wouldn't have to hide anything.

She shifted herself up to a sitting position and stuffed the pillows behind her back. Through the window the poplar tree swayed, the last leaves clinging to its branches. Beyond, the brown water of the Thames stretched to the Twenties mansions and the recently built single-dwelling homes on the opposite bank. If she could pretend, as she had when she was a child, that the animal in her head wasn't there it might slink away.

On Sunday, Grant appeared with the bundle of Sunday papers and told her he was calling the doctor.

'I don't need a doctor.'

He stared at her, the line digging into his forehead.

She leaned against the pillows. 'Not that sort.'

'Oh Martha...' He dropped the papers on to the floor, sat on the bed and pulled her towards him.

She felt herself go stiff, rigid. 'Unexplained infertility – it's such a stupid phrase!'

'Let it go.'

'I can't.'

'Please...'

'I want to try again.'

'Let it go, honey. We've decided.'

5

Martha shifted away from him. He was ten years older than she was and looked it today. The lines at the corners of his eyes, which she usually loved, seemed taut, ugly. '*You don't have to.*'

'What?'

'Well, donor sperm might…' Her shoulders lifted.

'Martha, unexplained infertility – it's the *both* of us.'

'I know.'

'Are you going to consider donor egg?'

'I don't know.'

'Oh, for Christ sakes.' He stood up, making the bed shudder.

She glanced out of the window. The sky was grey. Spots of rain splattered the glass. 'You don't *mind*, do you?'

He placed his hands on the wooden bed end, his mouth working, little dents in his cheeks.

She reached for the glass of water on her side table, unable to bear the look.

His hands lifted. 'Of course I mind! Oh what the hell. Let's forget it. Let's try and forget it.' He moved over to the door. 'If you don't need a doctor, I'm going to take a walk.'

She nodded. The glass of water felt cold in her hand. Through the window the poplar shivered against the sky. His footsteps thumped on the stairs. The front door banged.

In the kitchen the cafetière, a bowl, a plate, a knife and a spoon had been washed up and stacked on the draining board. The dishwasher lay idle mostly; it took too long to fill and then smelt of stale food. They had decided years ago to use it only when they had guests, which wasn't often; there never seemed to be time. Martha pressed the kettle button and carefully opened the fridge not wanting to jar her head. Grant's stuff was neatly lined up: natural live yoghurt, decaf coffee, cooked lentils, sliced rye bread, sugarless apricot jam. Further back was her stuff: a packet of salami (past its sell-by date probably

– she didn't bother to check) and some peanut butter. Life without Grant – she tried to imagine it… white bread and peanut butter and sugar-full jam, caffeine-swollen coffee and tea. Where the hell was he? It was at least two hours. At least her headache was on the wane.

There was no tea, so she poured boiling water onto an apple-and-mango teabag, made a peanut butter on rye and sat down at the table. The phone rang. She jumped up, certain it must be Grant, tripped over her dressing gown and knocked her knee on the table leg. It was one of his patients.

She limped into the sitting room and stared out through the French windows. The thick high hedges on either side made the garden like a tunnel. The poplar leaves carpeted the grass and needed raking up. He wouldn't have his mobile. He liked hiking as he called it, and often went off for whole days, exploring the London parks or driving to the Chilterns or the South Downs, and never took his mobile. Not that he would be hiking today. She sank into the sofa and reached for the remote, but then was on her feet again wandering about the empty house imagining all the space hers. She pushed open his door and stood taking it in: bare walls, neutral colours, armchair in its analytical position, couch…

'It's like a cell,' she'd told him once.

'Exactly; a safe cell.'

She'd laughed. 'You sure you don't mean a soft sell?'

He'd frowned, not getting it.

There were some typed notes on his desk. She picked them up: *'We must at all times be alert to the clues the person does not know they are revealing…'* He was so into his work – his patients, his teaching, his writing. So was she, of course. 'Brilliant at plucking out the stories behind the stories and identifying the unique angle' – who'd said that? Someone… probably that journalist writing the piece about editors; she'd kept the quote. Something was running down her leg. She let go of the notes. A clot of blood had landed on his pale, off-

7

white carpet – a dark, glistening, magenta clot. She stared at it a moment as if it was a work of art, and then bunched her night-dress into her crotch and ran for some cold water.

The shower poured over her, beating onto her face and soaking into her hair. The treatment had stopped months ago, but she still hoped. She was only forty-one. Friends of hers had got pregnant at forty-five, forty-six. She rubbed in shampoo and massaged her head. She was early this time so there hadn't been time to hope, in theory. Sometimes she was late. Her periods were irregular. It was difficult to know when to start hoping.

She towelled herself dry, stuffed in a Tampax and pulled on some clothes. At least nothing hurt now, and her energy was returning – the energy to tackle what she knew – and that was what she had to focus on. Look forward; don't look back. It was like a mantra she must keep repeating. She tugged the sheets off the bed, picked up the newspapers, lugged everything down to the kitchen, jammed the sheets into the washing machine, tipped away the remains of the cold apple-and-mango tea, brewed a decent caffeinated mug of coffee, and sat at the table trawling through the *Observer*, the *Independent* and the *News of the World*.

She left a message on Tony's answer phone: 'Much better, Tony. Back tomorrow. See you at the morning conference, unless you'd like a lie-in after your overworked last few days. New idea. A male column. Something in between diary and letters. Fragile male ego threatened by self-sufficient woman. You know, the whole woman can do everything on her own thing. Even have babies.'

Grant was obviously making a day of it. She got her anorak from the cupboard under the stairs, shoved on her Wellingtons, went out by the front door, glanced up and down the road in case he might be coming home, and then stamped down the path at the side of the house. She raked up the leaves into the bonfire pile at the end of the garden. Too sodden for a fire now. Indoors again, and the answer phone was flashing.

'Tony here. Don't worry about the conference tomorrow morning. Ease yourself slowly back. Interesting idea. Need someone who's had that experience – unless you think all men are having it – ' A guffaw. 'What would you call it – male impotence, metaphorically speaking? Redundancy, perhaps? Glad you're better.'

She flopped onto the sofa in front of another showing of *The Last of the Mohicans.* A long-haired Daniel Day Lewis reminded her of the Jesus guy she'd noticed when the terminals crashed – his hair anyway... not so much the face – the Jesus guy wasn't as good looking as that... was he? She couldn't quite remember... She dozed off and dreamed she was meeting Grant for the first time, except that this Grant had lots of dark hair and was offering her a job. She was grateful and flung her arms round him. Grant had never had much hair even when she'd first met him. She could distinctly feel his hair falling forward onto her face and tickling her skin.

Then it was the real Grant, helping her off the sofa. The television was making *Newsnight* noises, although there wasn't *Newsnight* on a Sunday.

He led her upstairs and helped her to undress.

'Grant, get into bed too. Please.'

'You shouldn't have been up.'

'You've been away hours.'

He nodded slowly.

She reached for his hand. 'Where've you been?' It seemed unreasonable now, scary – he'd been out so long.

'Walking.'

'Walking? It's the middle of the night. You could have rung.'

'I didn't take the mobile. I'm sorry, Martha.' He dragged off his clothes, laid them over his chair and went into the bathroom.

9

She heard him pee and then brush his teeth. Water gurgled down the plug hole. The shower door creaked. She kicked off the duvet and swung her legs out of bed.

But he had come back into the room and was standing naked in the doorway and looking at her intently, the line back in his forehead. 'I don't know what I'd do without you.'

She ran and put her arms around him. His body felt hot as if he had a fever. 'Poor love, where have you been?'

TWO

GRANT

He woke in the night and stretched out a hand to feel the rise and fall of her sleeping body, wanting her. And then remembered, and rolled onto his back. The sheet was hot under his body. He shifted trying to find a cooler spot. They had not made love. It might have helped. The duvet lifted. Martha stirred and gave a little groan. Perhaps she would wake and they could talk and he could tell her what he did yesterday, how he went up onto the footbridge over the river and gazed at the water. How he took a train from Putney Bridge station to Wimbledon, walked on the common in the rain and sipped a cup of tea in a plastic mug in the Windmill Café. How he found a movie in Wimbledon to stop himself from going over and over in his mind what she had said. But he never talked to her about these things and could not imagine how they might start. Perhaps she would wake – or he could wake her – and they would talk about normal, everyday things and the need would dissipate, or they would make love.

The duvet had settled. They were not going to talk, or make love. He stuck a leg out from under his side of the duvet. The air was icy on his skin. He could see the pale rectangle of the heavily curtained window and imagine the right-hand side opening outwards letting in the raw night air off the river. Martha liked the window open on the coldest of nights. It reminded her of her childhood in the Brecon hills, cosy in bed under the blankets and eiderdown. Nowhere was cold here in comparison to those winters he had spent in New England. There was a squawk from the river. A vehicle droned – an all-night truck on the Putney Bridge Road probably, driving through the night; or a plane perhaps, one of the sixteen night flights. He slid his legs over the side of the bed, reached for his

11

reading glasses next to his book and crept out of the room. Grabbing the duvet from the map room, he carried it downstairs to his consulting room, picked up his lecture notes from the desk and settled himself on the couch. *'We must at all times be alert to the clues the person does not know they are revealing: the physical ticks – the visual, the aural, the tactile…'* The words he had written seemed relevant suddenly. Watch your wife, they seemed to say, take note of any tiny changes she is revealing, but is not aware she is revealing. He pushed the duvet back, feeling hot again. He was overreacting. Her comment about donor sperm had come out of desperation and a headache. The muscles in his lower back ached. He stuffed one of his patients' cushions behind him, and glanced down at his notes. But the light stung his eyes; he sank down further and rested his head against the side of the couch.

Teaching was what had kept him going in that earlier part of his life. At the Institute, they would watch a family group through the one-way window. He would instruct his students to lower the sound and watch the silent tableau, taking particular note of what their bodies were saying. There would be a guffaw or snigger. But he would keep it serious. 'Observe how they sit; cross their legs; fold their arms; use their hands. Which one of them leans forward? Why does that one blink so much?' He would turn up the sound. 'What do their voices *sound* like? What words do they use – battle words, soft words? Do they cough or clear their throats?' 'Or fart?' some smart-ass student added. But Grant didn't care. The tougher those students were the more effort he had to put into them, allowing him to forget that outside the classroom he was begging Ruthie not to leave, begging her not to take Christopher away.

His heart raced even now as he thought of Christopher. On one of his weekends he had taken the child to the sands at Cape Cod; the place where he had ridden horse-back with Ruthie two or three summers earlier, before Christopher was born. It was a perfect day – gentle breeze, sparkling light – and he'd covered the child in sun cream and slipped off his diaper, dangled his feet in the sea and thrown him in the air and caught him – up into the air and back, up into the air... until Christopher was choking with laughter. The tide was coming in and they built a sand castle, Grant digging out a moat, although the little boy was too young to appreciate the sea flooding into it or feel frightened that their castle would sink under the waves. He banged his spade on his bucket, 'Mom, Mom, Mom...' Grant removed the spade. 'Dad, Dad, Dad...' The small face crinkled and broke into sobs; a hand reached up. Grant returned the spade to his son's dimpled fist and enclosed it in his own so that they were banging the bucket together. 'Dad, Dad, Dad... Mom, Mom, Mom...'

He remembered how on the Sunday the car seemed to drive itself upstate and into New Hampshire. If he'd had any sense he would have let it continue into Vermont and up into Canada. But he stopped when he reached the ranch-style lodge overlooking a lake and mountains. At about the time that he should have been returning Christopher, he dialled Ruthie's number.

'For God's sake, Grant!'

'Please, Ruthie... ! I just want to be with him, get to know him. Just for a week. It's vacation. I haven't got classes now.'

'That's not what we agreed.'

'I'm his father, Ruthie.'

She started shouting. 'I want him back! Bring him back!'

He must have been shouting too. Christopher woke and began crying. He had to pick him up, rock him.

'Is that him?' she called. 'Christopher – ! Oh God…!'

'It's alright. Please, Ruthie. It's alright.'

She went quiet. 'Oh, Grant…' Her voice was soft. 'Grant, I know you love him. You love him, don't you? I understand. But bring him home, huh? Bring him home tomorrow.'

She made it sound as if she would let him come home too. He pictured those night-time feeds, lying in bed together in the soft glow of the low wattage night-light that he'd bought specially. They took turns to give Christopher his bottle. Later Ruthie got too tired to get up and groaned sleepily at his cries and turned away. Grant fed Christopher in his little bedroom so as not to disturb her, sitting in the small chair by his cot grateful that Ruthie was unable to breastfeed and that he could be so involved.

For twenty-four hours after the phone call he could not let go of the child. He lay on the bed cradling him in his arms, stroking his skin, smelling it, kissing his fine, blow-away hair. Through the window the mountains flushed pink as the wispy clouds turned vermillion. The lake became a pale replica of the sky. When the colours had dissolved and the sky was a deep, dark blue, he tucked his body round the warm sleeping form of his son and feeling the tiny lift of his breathing, allowed himself the luxury of relief: his instinct to take this drastic measure had been right; it had done the trick.

At breakfast, the little guy on his lap, he ordered porridge for two.

The waitress smiled down at them. 'Sir, wouldn't you like a high chair?'

Grant shook his head. He spooned porridge into the child's mouth and imagined – as he often had, before things deteriorated with Ruthie – Christopher as a toddler; Christopher as a sporty seven-year-old; Christopher as a wild teenager. He hated having to lose the physical contact as he fastened him into the car seat. He drove south, glancing frequently at his son in the rear view mirror and reaching an arm behind to squeeze his small, plump leg or podgy foot.

Ruthie's voice was so welcoming through the voice box at the entrance to the apartment building. He smiled as he walked along the corridor to her door, Christopher on his hip. Felt quite horny if he was honest... the thought of her long, smooth, hairless thighs and the fuzz of her pubic hair. But her boyfriend was waiting for him like a bouncer at a party. He snatched the child and slammed the door in Grant's face. Grant could hear the screams of the child, 'Dad! Dad!' But maybe he imagined that. He was screaming himself, banging the door, kicking it.

One or two doors opened in the corridor and the Janitor appeared and told him that unless he quit now, this instant, he would call the police. Some jerk behind him said he already had, and Grant was led out of the building by two large policemen while trying to explain that it was his child in there, his child behind that locked door.

The following day when he pressed the buzzer against their apartment number there was no reply. It was probably broken; Ruthie was hopeless with anything technical. He tried the Janitor's buzzer and spoke to him through the voice box. 'I've come to see Mrs Weber. Number 8. They're not –'

'They've gone, Sir.'

'What?'

'You were here, yesterday, huh?'

'Yeah.'

'They've gone.'

'Gone? '

'That's what I said.''

'How could they have gone?'

'They're not here, huh?'

'But it's my child. They've got my child.'

'I can't help you. Like the policeman said last night. See your lawyer.' The machine clicked off.

Grant stared at the solid, wooden door and the white strips of the buzzers next to the apartment numbers. He pressed the Janitor's buzzer again. It had a stupid, flat sound.

A few days later, a letter arrived, written by Ruthie from her Mom's address in Virginia, apologetic, quite sweet. It crossed his mind that the boyfriend had made her write it.

Dear Grant, I've treated you bad. I'm sorry to say he's not yours. Little Christopher is not yours. You must leave us alone.

He did not believe her. That little body, warm next to his, how could he be someone else's? He refused to think of dates, of birth dates, conception dates. He was married to Ruthie, for heaven sakes. He had paternal rights. Christopher had his family name. He spent days it seemed writing and rewriting a letter to Ruthie, knowing that he should be contacting his lawyers. But just the idea of lawyers, of legal machinery crashing into such tender places, had him starting out on his letter to Ruthie again, had him searching for ways of negotiating this thing...

The notes were slipping off his lap. Grant came to with a start and placed them on the floor. There was a crick in his neck. He wriggled his shoulders, slid down into the couch, pulled up the duvet, and remembered his hot shame. So dumb! He'd spent weeks away from Ruthie on that course in California and never thought to calculate that Christopher could not possibly be his.

THREE

JON

The girl on the telly had the same hair as Daisy – what his ma would call ash blonde, Jon mused, leaning back in his armchair and crossing his legs over the arm. She was getting out of a car on a beach and letting her hair blow in the wind. It was a shampoo advert, though it could just as easily have been a car advert. He reached for his can of Foster's and took a pull.

Daisy's hair was longer though, not quite that colour – more yellow than blonde. Sometimes she lifted her hands off the keyboard, pulled her hair all together, enclosed it in the hole made by her finger and thumb and twisted one of those coloured stretchy bands around it; then he could see the white skin of her neck. He would pass her way a bit later with more deliveries and her hair would be flowing over her shoulders again, like the girl in the advert.

Daisy had talked to him that evening. She'd been crying, her blue eyes full of water. The computers had gone down; she'd lost her story about grandmothers in the city, whatever that was about. He'd hung around near the computer bloke, knowing he should be continuing the deliveries, but wanting to be close to her. A teardrop shone on her cheek. He'd wanted to put out a finger to soak it up. The boss woman, Martha Morgan, had arrived and sat in Daisy's chair. He'd caught her looking at him. She had eyes that stared through you.

Another can. Finger in the ring-pull. Click…. Flashing tinsel stars exploded onto the screen. Reindeers leaping over snowy cartoon mountains. *'Christmas comes but once a...'* The phone was ringing. He swung his legs down and reached over the chair arm across the cans of lager to where he'd left it on the floor.

Pete's voice. 'You fucking wanker!'

'Wha– ? Christ, Pete – sorry!' he pushed himself to the edge of the chair and jabbed the mute button on the remote. 'Where are you?'

'Where do you think?'

'Wha–?'

'In the fucking *Spit and Polish* as we arranged.'

'Sorry!'

'I'm going back to Shirley's.'

Jon's heart gave a little lift. 'Isn't Shirley with you?'

'If you think I'm inflicting this fucking pub on Shirley...'

'Pete, I'll be there in ten minutes. Ten minutes.' Jon scrambled to his feet and glanced around for his jacket.

'Are you so fucking busy?'

Pete knew he wasn't. Where was his jacket? If Shirley wasn't with Pete he wanted to be there. These days Pete usually meant *Pete and Shirley*, and it was difficult to motivate himself to get there on time. The jacket was on his bed. 'I want to see you, Pete. I've met this girl.' It sounded more on than it was, but Christmas was coming and he wanted to buy Daisy a present. With Pete on his own he could talk about that, weigh up his chances with Daisy. He hitched the phone under his chin and inserted his arm into the sleeve of his jacket. 'This girl – she's called Daisy.' He switched the phone to the other shoulder. 'Pete, are you there?'

'Alright but fucking get here!'

'What about Shirley?'

'She's here!'

'I thought you said she wasn't.'

'I was pissed off.'

'Okay, okay...'

Jon pressed the off button and stared out of the window of his tiny basement flat. The street light shone down the outside steps, showing up the greasy window panes. Could he be arsed to go, with Shirley there? It was never the same with her; he could never talk to Pete properly. He closed the curtains, checked in the inside pocket of his jacket for his money and switched off the television. Wasted evening probably, but he went out of the door and headed up the road to meet them.

Next morning, same as every morning, he set off on a voyage across London. He could do it by boat if he had the time. He both lived and worked near the Thames. Where he lived the river was narrower. He could walk along the Portsmouth Road to the Royal Promenade, see the trees on the other side – and all that space beyond with no houses – and imagine he was on the edge of the country. Some days – on summer evenings when the trees were black shapes, but the sky was still light – he could pretend he was on the edge of the world. At work, the Thames was everywhere, bright and sharp between tall buildings, and further away the whole mass of it swept past the Millennium Dome, which he could see in the distance.

It was dark now when he got up. He liked the walk through the cold, lit streets white in the frost or shining in the rain, up the slight incline to the station, looking forward to the yellow fug of the train and a corner seat facing the engine. At that hour, he and the regulars were spoilt for choice. He varied the sides to get a different view, although now it was only his reflection he saw in the window. When he had started in this job it had been light in the mornings. He had gazed at the streets and houses from safe inside the train and it had felt like the beginning of something. If Pete or Shirley, or one of his other friends, or people in the office – or, heaven save him, his dad – had asked him why it felt like that he couldn't have explained it. It was only on days when Dad wasn't telling him that by twenty-six he should have settled down to a regular job, or Pete wasn't drawing up the ideal career plan for him, that he could *think* it.

19

Shirley had given him *London Connections: Rail and Underground Services* – she worked in the City. 'Pete told me you're not good at finding your way.' Sounded naff the way she said it; and Pete had no right telling her. She'd offered to go with him, but he didn't want her looking over his shoulder. She and Pete had also given him a hard cover book, *The Greater London Street Atlas,* as if he hadn't got the message. He spent one Saturday afternoon flicking through the pages trying to work out how the river got from his place to Canary Wharf, and then realised that it was all there on the large map with the squares, in the front of the book. The map went right down to Leatherhead where his ma and dad had moved. But he was hopeless at maps. He put it away. He could get it out again when Pete and Shirley made their promised visit. If they ever did. With Shirley around, they probably wouldn't.

By the time he noticed Daisy it was dark in the mornings. He could do the journey with his eyes shut, and now the picture he made in his head was prettier than the one through the window. He saw himself, like in a film, arriving at work, hanging up his coat on his peg in the Mail and Communications room, sorting the letters and newspapers, piling them on to the trolley, checking how he looked in the small mirror, and heading for the Features Floor. There would be a close-up of the slow revolving of the trolley wheels as he got to the floor and approached her desk, and then the camera would lift to her face and stay there. He took orders for drinks and snacks. Hot chocolate and a croissant for Daisy. He liked to watch her put the croissant into her mouth, and see the little brown flakes get caught in the damp corners of her lips.

One morning he saw Martha Morgan at Waterloo heading for the underground. He'd overheard Daisy call her a bloody cow when she stopped Daisy's article, the one that got lost when the computers went down. He didn't understand how Martha Morgan could stop it if it had got lost, until Daisy explained that she had written it again a few days later, which made him appreciate what a cow Martha was. *Iniquitous*! The word burst into his brain like those kinds of words did – words that he'd read somewhere, *head* words not talking words. People talked too quickly, getting their words in before him. Except Pete. With Pete, he could use words he didn't know he had: *chauvinist... philistine...* usually referring to his dad.

Martha Morgan moved on into the crowds, and he dawdled at the top of the escalator not wanting to get on the same train as her. When he emerged into the open space of Canary Wharf, blinking in the light – it always felt bright after the underground, even when it was raining – someone clasped his arm and he swivelled round thinking some silly bugger was trying to steal something and then, for a second, thought it was Daisy – he should be so lucky.

Martha Morgan had short hair, bits of grey in it, and weird eyes, pale blue with yellow specks like a marble he'd owned as a kid. She took her time to let go of his arm. He tried to think what the fuck he'd done.

Her mouth was widening into a smile; clean, white front teeth straight along the bottom. 'I thought it was you.'

'Oh...' he couldn't think what to say.

'You saved me the other day, remember? When the computers crashed.'

'Oh... oh, yeah.'

She laughed. 'I wanted to thank you. You got me back to my desk. I had a migraine. It's Jon, isn't it?'

They plodded along the pavement towards the office. Normally he liked to take a detour and go via the footbridge over the water, feel the air swirling around, glance up at the high buildings, see what the sky was doing, hear the thud of the pile driving – he loved all that. He was glad he didn't have to look at her. She was the sort who made him want to stare at the ground. He remembered walking her back to her desk. She had brown boots on that day, same as today. He had done it to impress Daisy, show her that he was cool.

21

They stopped to cross the road at the traffic lights and Martha's face swung round. 'Where do you live?'

Her eyes drilling into his he came up with the stupidest answer. 'Two squares up from Leatherhead–'

She laughed, a whiff of minty toothpaste putting him off his intent to complete what he'd started, '...on – I mean, in *The Greater London Street Atlas.*'

Her hand came down on his arm. 'Brilliant! Where the hell's that?'

'Surbiton.'

The green pedestrian sign was flashing and they ran to get across before it turned red.

She glanced at him. 'Do you always get here this early?'

'Yeah, usually...'

'How far do you have to come?'

She'd already asked him that...

'Do you like working for us?' Questions, clip clip with her brown boots on the pavement, her brown leather brief case swinging in her hand. As they went through the swing doors she asked him to bring her a tea and two croissants. Bloody cow, he remembered.

Daisy had been having lattes recently. That day he didn't manage to get her a latte. Steve, head of Mail and Communications, grabbed him by the arm and told him that nursery school had finished now and today was the day Jon was going to flex his muscles and go on an adventure to Watford.

Watford? Another word exploding in his head. People got transferred to Watford. He stared at the piles of newspapers to be distributed, the sacks of post to be sorted.

'The print works.' Steve tugged at his elbow. A special piece of equipment for the printers was to be delivered. 'Take you half a day.'

It felt like he was going for ever. The Docklands Light Railway was alright but once he got on to the Central Line it felt like he was being banished into exile. Gritty winds blew around the corners and along the passages. At the foot of a steep escalator, a busker strummed on his guitar. A piece of holly lay amongst the coins in the guitar case like an omen warning him that he wouldn't be at Canary Wharf at Christmas; he would be in the frozen fucking north, miles away from Canary Wharf and Christmas presents and Daisy. He landed up at King's Cross and had to ask the ticket officer how to get to Euston and then persuade him to let him through the barrier with his ticket that didn't allow for detours. He'd have gone home if the bulky parcel didn't seem like a time bomb. By the time he reached the Print Works at Watford he was handing in his notice. Watford was way off his circuit.

But the foreman thanked him for delivering the parcel so quickly and directed him towards the canteen, 'Long journey. Doesn't close 'til two,' so that he was smiling on the journey home, settling back into his seat with a can of coke and enjoying the view. By then the office seemed like home. Watford was a little excursion, no problem. He gazed out of the window and watched the fields and trees flash by until they turned into buildings and streets and he could see the taller buildings in the distance. Across the aisle a roll of glittery green and red Christmas paper stuck out of a bag of shopping. He pictured himself handing Daisy a present, wrapped in the shiny, colourful stuff opposite, her glancing up, their fingers touching...

'And what time do you call this?' Steve strode out of his office and into the foyer.

Jon took a step back, aware of people walking past him towards the lifts. 'Sorry, mate– '

'It's the middle of the bloody night!'

Jon pulled at his sleeve trying to see his watch. 'It's twenty to five –'

'Phone, boy. Haven't you got a mobile?'

'Look mate, I'm not a boy –'

'No? So where was your mobile then?'

'I left it at home.'

Steve moved nearer. 'You've just wasted half a day.'

'You can't do it in half a day.'

'You shouldn't be here!'

He was going to fucking lose the job, and Daisy. Goodbye to those shampoo adverts and dreams about Christmas presents. 'I'm alright round here! I'll be alright to Watford now.'

Christ! Who took you on?'

'I promise you. It's been perfect up to now.'

'Shut up, man!'

And then Martha Morgan appeared, heading towards them from the lifts. 'Everything alright?'

It was all he needed with her short hair and those pale blue eyes with yellow specks.

'What've you done, Jon? Stolen the crown jewels?'

Steve was making a face. 'That would be a hanging offence. Can't be that bad surely?'

Why couldn't she shut up?

'He's just spent all day getting to Watford and back.'

'Perhaps the train was delayed.'

'Please, Miss Morgan! I'm trying to do my job.'

'Of course you are. I shouldn't interfere.'

Steve nodded slowly, his lips hardly moving. 'Go home, Jon. I'll see you in the morning.'

Jon turned away. His hands were clenched – he stuffed them into his pocket. Fucking talking about him as if he wasn't there.

She was behind him, calling his name. He whirled round, almost knocking into her, stepped back and bumped into someone coming through the swing doors. 'Sorry, mate.'

She was looking at him with her pale blue eyes. 'Don't worry about it.'

'Wha–?'

'Steve will be fine in the morning. Come and have a drink.'

And now she was leading the way through the swing doors and out on to the pavement, and he was following her.

FOUR

MARTHA

They left the building and crossed the road; neither of them saying a word, she slightly ahead of him looking for somewhere off the normal run. It was a cold evening, the street lights competing with the crimson sky, people already at the end of their day trickling out of offices and making for the station. They dodged around a group of girls, stepping out into the road and back to the pavement. Martha delved into her bag for her mobile. 'Sue,' she held it to her ear. 'Something's come up. I'll be about half an hour.' She pushed open the door of a wine bar, aware of Jon behind her. Dark, leather upholstered benches lined the walls. There were small tables, a bar in the corner; enough people to preserve anonymity. She turned back to him, 'Okay?' He nodded, his gaze sliding past her. Martha made for an empty table next to the wall.

'I'm just going to the toilet,' he mumbled.

'What are you drinking?' she called after him.

'A Foster's.'

She sat down on the leather bench and glanced round the room for anyone who might know her. A skinny girl, skirt half-way up her thighs, came to wipe the table and took her order. The coffee machine whirred, steam fizzed. The man at the next table was reading *their* paper, flicking through the pages, scanning a column here and there, folding it. All that industry and energy to produce it, read so casually. She leaned back against the leather remembering her recent phone call...

'Mr Shorn please.' She'd hoped to be put straight through, but the secretary had to be reminded who she was and wanted to know what the call was about. All around her the decibels were rising. It was at the point in the afternoon when deadlines had become visible – everyone concentrating on copy, phones ringing, people shouting across the floor – no one would hear her. 'I want to discuss…' she had struggled to find the right phrase, 'donor…'

The secretary had got it immediately. 'Ah, for that kind of appointment you and your husband will both need to attend. You will also be required to attend a counselling appointment at the clinic.'

'But I want to talk to Mr Shorn on his own.'

She must have raised her voice. Sue, her assistant, picked up her pad. 'Everything alright?' Eva was looking up from the Health desk.

She had nodded, terminated the phone call without making an appointment, and in need of a few moments' fresh air had left the floor.

The wine bar was filling up. A group of women had collected by the bar and were talking in shrill voices. A couple of businessmen were sitting down at the table on the other side of her.

For the last two weeks Martha had thrown herself into her work and refused to think about babies. She tested herself against her colleagues; turned down ideas; stopped stories, proving to herself, if to no one else, who was in charge. She set herself up against Tony, disagreed with him over issues, made sure that he backed down. Her confidence returned. Then, at lunch time today she had gone to the mall under the station to start some Christmas shopping and been assaulted by mothers and toddlers. She had fled back to the office, confidence draining out of her.

The man reading *The Chronicle* was turning to the sports page. The paper crackled. She watched him meticulously press the folds and lay it on the table next to his drink.

Perhaps she would try Mr Shorn again and insist that she talk to him.

Jon was walking back now, a loping easy movement, skirting round the tables, hands in his pockets. He was thin, lean was a better word, waist caving in under a worn leather jacket, belted jeans hanging loosely from his hips; that thinness looked good at his sort of age. For a second she imagined her fingers touching those hips, feeling the bone through his skin.

She gestured towards the chair. 'You probably would've preferred a pub. They've only got Beck's. I hope that's okay.'

He pulled out the chair and sat about a foot away from the table.

Come nearer, she nearly said. 'So you were at Watford?' It sounded hearty. 'Took you longer than you expected – or rather Steve expected.' She laughed. 'His bark's probably worse than his bite.' Why was she talking like this?

The bridge of his nose had become criss-crossed with lines; she could picture how he might look in twenty years' time, skin courser, lines etched. 'You think I should leave.'

'Sorry?'

'Leave the job.'

'No, of course I don't.'

'Tha's why you asked me here.'

'No...'

His dark eyes shifted.

She looked away, grateful that the skinny girl was heading their way. 'I just thought you needed a drink.'

A small circular tray was lowered onto the table, the glasses carefully placed in front of them. He reached for his beer and took a swig, broad, strong fingers curling round the glass.

She swallowed a mouthful of wine. A Chilean Sauvignon Blanc, just dry enough, but nice and cold. 'Was the train delayed, in fact?'

'Wha'?'

'The train to Watford.'

'Na.' He lifted his shoulders, the worn leather creaking faintly, and placed his glass back on the table, the level of beer lowered by about an inch. 'Didn't think Watford was part of the job.'

'Didn't you?'

The question seemed to encourage him. He glanced up and shook his head, friendlier. 'Wasn't in the job description.'

She laughed. 'Wasn't it?'

'Na...' his eyes paused on hers. He took another swig of beer and wiped his mouth with the back of his hand. 'Steve makes up the rules.'

'I bet he does.'

'I'm not good at finding places. Local's okay.'

Why are you in the job, she wondered, but she was laughing and wondering whether he knew he was funny, or whether he meant to be. She hadn't thought about herself for at least five minutes. 'You'll be alright then.'

'Wha'?'

'You've been to Watford now. You'll know it.'

'Wouldn't bank on it.'

The lines had returned to the bridge of his nose. She had an urge to put her fingers there and ease the lines away. The rest of his face seemed to be without lines. She wondered what it would feel like next to hers, and whether his hair would tickle as it fell forward. What remained of Grant's hair was cropped close to his head. The comparison made her want to laugh again. The wine was going to her head. She probably seemed old enough to be his mother. 'So what's your next step?'

'Wha'?'

'After this job. Where are you aiming at?' It was a silly interview sort of question, and irrelevant.

The lines were back. 'Why do I have to be aiming anywhere?'

'You don't.'

'People always want to know where I'm going.'

'It's alright, you don't.'

'I'm happy here.'

'That's great.'

He nodded slowly and ran his hand through his hair, tucking the right side behind his ear. His mouth widened into a smile. 'Fucking Watford!'

Laughter burst out of her. She took another sip of wine.

The skinny girl arrived with roasted dry peanuts and spicy Chinese nibbles and left two small bowls on the table. He nudged the bowls across to Martha, took a fistful of nuts for himself and washed them down with more swigs of beer.

'I was certain you were going to tell me to leave. Daisy thinks you're a bloody cow.'

'What...?'

'Fuck, sorry!' His eyes widened, staring into hers a moment. He lifted his glass and put it down again. 'Fuck, I didn't mean to say that. I don't know why I said it.'

She lifted her shoulders. 'Don't worry. It goes with the territory.'

'Wha' –?'

'I have to make unpopular decisions and people don't like me. Are you and Daisy...?' A numbness was spreading through her.

'I say all the wrong things. You're a nice lady.'

'Don't worry about it. Have another beer.'

His hands were on the table, raising himself to his feet. 'I don't know why I said it.' He tapped his forehead. 'I've had it up to here today.' He pushed the chair under the table. 'Sorry.' He swung away.

She watched him move through a crowd of people who had just come in, his dark head visible above the other heads until he reached the door. When he'd gone she sank back into the leather bench. How fucking stupid... what was the matter with her? The girl was a couple of tables away. She lifted her arm and ordered another glass of wine.

When she returned to the office there was a note on her desk from Eva: something about a feature on Alzheimer's... Eva had gone home early. She poured herself a mug of iced water from the water cooler, swilling it around in her mouth. Things appeared to be happening in the Women's corner but when she slid into the edge of the crowd, they were discussing nothing more urgent than the Features Christmas party.

Liza took Martha's arm. Her funny, quirky face usually made Martha smile, but she found it hard to take in what Liza was saying; the words washed over her: 'We're postponing the first of *'The Professionals'* to... We've got Mary's piece on ... and there's a piece Daisy is investigating on the effects of the Holocaust on the second generation...'

Liza wants my job too, Martha thought – and she could do it; better than Tony. 'Fine Liza,' she nodded. The two glasses of wine mixed with the iced water were making her feel dizzy.

'Of course,' her arm was squeezed, 'it's Grant, isn't it? He's the first *Professional*. Do you mind?'

'Why should I mind?' She'd forgotten for a moment that she'd asked Grant to be part of the series.

Everyone was dispersing, as if she was causing it, glancing at her, 'Hi, Martha,' but moving away. Liza was smiling. 'I meant that it's being postponed 'till the New Year.' She laughed. 'Daisy suggested we should do you.'

'No thanks.'

'The last in the series perhaps. A nice coda: the Features Editor.'

Daisy was sitting at her desk staring at them as Martha looked her way. She thinks I'm a bloody cow. Martha glanced round to see if Jon was in the department. But why would he be there?

She pushed her key into the lock of their front door hoping that it wouldn't require turning and that Grant would be home, but it did. She switched off the alarm and dumped her stuff in the middle of the hall, feeling tired. There was a smell of furniture polish. Catrin must have been.

The figures 9.25 glowed momentarily from the oven clock before the kitchen light flickered on. So late! Their working hours never fitted well. She was often hyped-up until one in the morning, while Grant, an early riser, had clients to see only a few hours later – as early as seven sometimes. He would be home within the next hour, having lectured or run an analytical group or maybe having gone to a lecture himself, and would come into their immaculate house, poke his head round the sitting room door where she would be settled in front of 'Newsnight' and vanish again. If she returned after him he might be sitting on the sofa reading. He rarely watched television and would go to his room if she wanted to watch something. They had learned to fill their evenings independently – their mornings too; they didn't even get up together.

None of this had mattered until recently. She sat down on the stool and stared at her reflection in the glass oven door, a forty-one-year-old, infertile woman in her tastefully designed kitchen. Tonight, she couldn't stand the thought of herself in this kitchen with its hand-made units and gleaming surfaces. She glanced round for the phone, but friends asked her how she was and she couldn't bear that question.

She poured herself a glass of wine. In the fridge there was a jar of artichoke hearts and a plastic container of black olives. She unscrewed the jar and dipped her fingers into the oil, clasped the pale white-green artichoke between thumb and finger and put it into her mouth. She was starving. Her fingers fished for another. In the fridge door was a packet of Parma ham; on the second shelf some fresh noodles only a day past their sell-by date.

Soon, a pastel greeny-pink mixture heaved in the pan. She turned it with the wooden spoon and added black olives. She crushed two cloves of garlic watching the white flecks melt into the mixture. Thin French beans would be perfect, but there weren't any. She glanced at her watch – too late even for the deli. Fruit... a pudding. Grant loved puddings. There were three Golden Delicious apples, an orange with its tiny label from South Africa, and a spotty-skinned banana. She chopped them up and poured over some Kirsch. And why not a starter? She had to top up the simmering water, add olive oil to the mixture in the pan. She found some mild goat's cheese, and dabbed in blobs of that. She laid the table while she thought about starters – decided against it. Searched out napkins, washed and pressed, and untouched since the last – whatever... supper party, lunch party - months ago, years ago... no, Philip and Kathleen had come with their three kids only a few Sundays ago. There was a new packet of candles in the usual place.

She didn't hear him come in and when she turned, his face was illuminated by the candles, and she loved the way surprise slowly registered in his eyes. 'Wow, Martha!'

'You haven't eaten?'

The creases at the corners of his eyes crept into his hairline as he smiled and shook his head, and she loved those too tonight. She leaned against him feeling his arms around her.

He found a bottle of Chardonnay and she ladled out the freshly cooked noodles glistening in the artichoke sauce. There was a small, hardened block of parmesan at the back of the fridge and she held the cheese and the grater over his plate, but he said it was perfect as it was. They tucked in as if they were ravenous and downed the wine, hardly saying a word. She got up and fetched the fruit salad and he put out a hand and grabbed her wrist pulling her towards him, both hands now round her wrists. 'I want you.'

'Do you?'

He nodded, his thumbs lightly rubbing the soft insides of her wrists.

'Do you really?'

'Very badly.' He released her hands and took her arm. 'Come on, let's go upstairs.'

Perhaps this is alright, she thought, as she followed him up to their bedroom. Perhaps this is – perhaps this will be enough. For a second the image of Jon pushing through the wine bar crowd as he left, lit up in her mind.

They reached their room and she closed the door and stood not moving while Grant turned on the sidelights and drew the curtains. She thought he might suggest a bath first – they did that sometimes. But he took her hand and tugged her over to the bed and hardly seemed to have enough patience to pull off her clothes and take off his own.

FIVE

JON

Martha Morgan was looking across the floor towards him as he had a quick chat with Daisy. He lifted his arm, friends now… and then remembered the wine bar. *Daisy thinks you're a bloody cow.* How could he have said that? He turned away feeling hot. Daisy's blonde head was bent over her pad, hair loose today, shiny and clean. He'd planned on asking her out for a beer, but he hesitated.

Liza, head girl of the women's department, was talking to Peter from Books. She glanced up and pushed her chair away from her desk as if she was about to get up. Purple-Hair, the secretary, was staring at him. Her lips pouted round her pencil – suck, suck. Piss off, he wanted to say. He put off saying anything to Daisy. Have the weekend first, he thought, contenting himself with a grin and an 'Okay, Daisy?' She gave him such a sweet smile that he sailed out of the department feeling he could fly. Her lower lip was bigger than the upper one – fleshy pink, swollen sort of – didn't need botox. He would store the smile in his mind over the weekend, let it sink in through the pores of his skin – and any other orifices… *Orifices!* The word detonated in his head, and then he couldn't think of anything else.

All Saturday her smile and that word, and other words, jerked off like… *jerked* – Christ! He couldn't think without another word exploding. I'll make the flat nicer, get better *equipment*… I'll blast out the neighbours with heavy metal when she *comes*… I'll think *hard* about how I can progress at work… His thoughts and the words erupted in his head sending hot lava through his body.

At one point he ran up the basement steps, stood on the pavement and let the cold, raw, Saturday afternoon blow through his jersey and T-shirt. Nasty wind and it made him shiver. Hot one minute, cold the next. He went and fetched his jacket and took himself off to the library to look up about computers.

'You'll need to look in the careers directory.' The librarian peered at him through ugly, large, round glasses reminding him of Ma's new ones, which was a sure way of cooling down his feelings. 'Under IT – Information Technology.' As if he didn't know what IT meant.

He lugged the huge book onto one of the tables, found the IT section and saw that there were columns about it. IT for Christ's sake. Pete, on one of their career discussions, had recommended he become PC literate. 'You can type with two fingers, can't you? Find a class, for fuck sake.' Him and classes didn't go together, Pete should know that. Perhaps he would buy a computer and teach himself. Learn how to mend them, like Dave from Maintenance. Learn how to mend computers for Daisy.

At home, he dragged a four-can out of the fridge and settled into his armchair with the Yellow Pages. 'Complementary medicine' – Shirley was into that, in a small way. 'Rescue Remedy'… dripping little beads of it on to her tongue whenever Pete or her job were causing her hassle. 'Nux Vom'… for when she was feeling sick after a hangover. 'Compost'... 'Compressors'... He licked his finger and turned the page. 'Computers'...

Sod computers, he could be looking for a Christmas present for Daisy. He broke off a can and pulled at the metal ring. He would have to ask her out before he could give her a present. His heart gave a little whirr. He took a swig, and a thought swirled in with the warm beer slipping down his throat. He would ask Daisy if it was possible to buy a discarded second-hand computer from the office. She wouldn't know, but it would be an opener, 'Who do you think might know?' Then he could drop in the idea of a drink after work to discuss it.

By Sunday the smile in his mind had faded. The words had quietened too. As he had known they would by a Sunday. He hadn't been to his folks for a few weeks and he could feel his fists clenching as he plodded off to the station. It being Sunday he had to change at Wimbledon and Epsom. He ran through his usual thoughts: Leatherhead isn't home. You moved out of the family home a couple of years ago. Ma and Dad moved out. The place doesn't exist. No 29 Andrews Road, New Malden, does not belong to you any more. You don't have to walk into that hall, smell the cooking and Dad's cigarettes – or whatever it was that was so familiar. You don't have to step into the lounge, see Dad glued to the telly, hear Ma crashing around in the kitchen and be fucking back there stuck in front of that same telly not daring to move.

Limitless telly had been the envy of his school mates. He hadn't been able to concentrate for thinking what he'd do with himself if he wasn't watching. 'Stop skulking around your mother. Find something to do!' had been Dad's frequent cry. If he could've helped Ma in the kitchen, washed up the saucepans, peeled the potatoes – done something to snuff out those little groans from her throat as she rushed from one thing to the next – it might have filled up the dangerous space beyond the area of the telly. He knew how to help. He'd watched Ma do things when Dad wasn't around. He could have done it. Shown Dad he wasn't lazy. But those things were women's work, forbidden to him and Dad. 'Your room's stacked with toys,' his dad would shout up the stairs. He would sit on his empty bedroom floor and stare at the closed cupboard. Inside were boxes of toys he had mostly grown out of and never much played with, tidied away by his mother.

He sat on the train now and went back to the scene when he kicked the cupboard – kick, kick until the thin door panel broke away from its frame. He wished his dad had come up

37

and hit him, thrown him against the wall, shouted at him, told him not to damage the furniture. Then he could have fought back, kicked him, kept him there, got out his toys and asked how he should play with them. But his dad didn't want to come to his room even then, when he'd made such a noise kicking the cupboard door. His dad said he was a lazy, good for nothing who didn't concentrate and didn't take things in however much he explained. Jon couldn't remember him explaining anything, which proved what Dad was saying: he was lazy and didn't concentrate, and therefore he didn't take things in and remember. He stood on that landing outside his bedroom door all those years ago and waited, and suddenly Dad was shouting, screaming, 'You're useless! Useless!' Excitement flared up. Jon had started down the stairs, running, stumbling, clinging on to the banisters, hurtling down, nearly at the bottom. But then the kitchen door banged, that final kitchen door sound so that he knew it was the kitchen door, knew – and a sicky gunk rose into his throat – knew the words were for his ma. He ran back upstairs and banged his bedroom door, once, twice... swallowing hard, swallowing the gunk in his throat; the door shuddered on its hinges, things fell off the hook... three times, four, louder and louder. The sound filled the room – bang, bang, bang – the noise expanded and filled the emptiness – bang, bang, bang...

Arriving at quarter past one, and ignoring his dad's face which said *you're normally here by one,* he did something radical: he touched his dad; put a hand on his shoulder, or rather the shoulder pad of his blazer. And then for consistency's sake – although he never did that now – bent to kiss Ma's cheek as she shuffled out of the kitchen, though his lips didn't reached her skin.

Dad's shoulder jerked away. Ma took a step back breathing quickly, her hand clutching the oven gloves, pushing at the tight curls on her forehead. 'It's... it's nearly ready.'

''Course it is.'

'There's no *of course* about it, son!' Dad did up a couple of the gold buttons of his blazer and glanced round as if the room had become colder. He would undo them in a minute, sit down in his chair and turn off the mute button of the telly.

Jon moved into his dad's line of vision and tried to catch his eye. 'Ma always gets dinner on time, doesn't she?'

'No thanks to you.'

''Course not, it's women's work.' He was smiling, attempting to introduce some humour, if his dad would care to look.

'Pardon?'

'That's what you used to say.'

'What about men's work?'

'That's something different.'

'As if you'd know!'

Oh, fuck off, he wanted to say. His dad was so predictable in his Sunday blazer with its gold buttons and his thinning hair glued to his head. Some Sundays Jon wore his charcoal-grey corduroy jacket and got his hair cut a bit to see if that would make a difference with Dad. It never did. Today he was in the second-hand leather jacket with the patched elbows. His hair had grown at least an inch since his last visit. 'I've got a good job now, Dad.'

'What – a messenger for a newspaper?'

'I didn't want to be a butcher, Dad.'

'You don't want to be anything! That's your trouble.' His father stuck his hands in his trouser pockets and rattled the money inside.

Ma had slipped back into the kitchen. Jon followed her and stood in the doorway. *You've got to be a professional in whatever you do. Doesn't matter if you're a road sweeper or a dustman – do it professionally.* He tucked his hair behind his ears, Dad's words in his head. He could picture where he said them, father and son closing up the butcher shop. It was just after Jon had left school 'bright-eyed and bushy-tailed' as his dad liked to describe him in those hopeful days; it seemed he might follow in Dad's footsteps. He'd washed down the surfaces with the antiseptic lotion – *which killed all known germs* – and was brushing the floor being careful not to miss a flake or speck of raw meat. Hygiene was everything. *Even, you see Jon, sweeping the floor. Do it professionally.* They were not words his dad would say to him today. He swerved back. 'I want to improve myself!'

His father had moved to the picture window and was staring through the glass at the neat square of lawn backing up to the bare fence and the next bungalow. The money rattled. Jon wondered why he bothered. But he always did for some reason. Ma had bent down to open the oven and was pushing her hands into the oven gloves and pulling out the roasting tin. She lifted it at an angle from the oven, swaying slightly.

Her back felt damp as he steadied her with his hands. She was gasping as she banged the dish on to the draining board, fat sloshing over the side of the tin. He got her a plate for the meat and then washed up the stack of pans in the sink. She poured the juices into a saucepan and he took the roasting tin from her. 'Doesn't he ever help?'

'I don't mind.' She spoke in a breathy whisper. He'd spoken quietly too.

'You look all in. Go and sit down for five minutes.'

'I've got to make the gravy.'

'You've made it.' He lifted the saucepan.

His mother was leaning against the draining board, her glasses steamed up. 'He likes it thick.'

'Doesn't matter,' he put a hand on her arm, 'this once.'

'It's late.'

'Late for what?'

She glanced at her watch. 'He's going to miss...'

'Miss what?'

She blinked behind her glasses, took them off, her eyes not focussing.

His father jumped to his feet as Jon returned to the lounge. He sat down again, his hands on the arms of the chair staring at the opening to the kitchen.

Jon lowered himself onto the settee. 'Dad, Mum's going to come and sit down for five minutes.'

'What?'

'Before we start – a rest.'

'What does she want a rest for? It's dinner time.' His gaze would not leave the opening.

'Dad, I want to talk to you.'

But now his mother appeared, wiping her hands on her apron and his dad sprung up. 'Grand Prix in half an hour.'

Jon looked at his mother. 'Just say you want a break.'

She was untying her apron. Her glasses directed towards him, her eyes almost invisible behind them. No words. Just a lift of her shoulders under the brown cardigan and then a hand pulling the loop of the apron over her head.

'Don't you mind?' his fists were clenching.

She folded the apron in half and turned away. 'It's dinner–time, Jon. We're already fifteen minutes late.'

At some point in his career, Dad had worked in a slaughter house. Good grounding, he was fond of telling Jon. 'Need to know the whole animal in the butchery business and I knew I was going into the butchery business, knew what I was doing, which is more than we can say for you.' *They herd them along a passage. They string them up by their legs. Cut their throats.* The images had stayed with Jon. *Apprenticeship* was a word of his childhood, which he thought meant *learning to kill.* Eyes tightly shut as he tried to go to sleep fearful he might dream, he pictured his dad slicing throats in the yard behind the butcher's shop. Once, he thought he woke up hearing the squealing of blood letting.

His ma should have stopped his dad telling these stories. She should have stood up to him. He pressed his fists into his thighs and sat on the platform waiting for the train back to Epsom. His ma had tight permed curls. He hated the falseness of them, their brown, bubbly cheerfulness, when he could see the dullness in her eyes.

Pete was the only person he could talk to about his parents and his crap childhood, and he missed that now that Shirley was around. With Pete he could try to describe why he didn't do things like other people did, why thinking took up a lot of his life and turning that into doing something felt like a waste of time: apprenticeship in his father's butcher's shop; post-room boy at the nearby pharmaceutical company; assistant to the mechanic at the local garage; shift worker at the sugar refinery – these jobs hadn't got him anywhere. His father told him he hadn't got the staying power. But what was so exciting about a leg of lamb, or a bag of sugar, or a post room? He couldn't see the point in these things. He couldn't make them interest him or see how he might progress. Sometimes, as they leaned against a bar swigging their pints, sadness swept through him, so marked seemed the contrast between being there with Pete having this conversation (Pete nodding and seeming to understand), and doing one of those activities. 'You've got to find something where you can use your brain,' Pete had told him often enough, although they both knew he hadn't got the qualifications. He'd been in the same school as Pete, the same class, but he'd not made anything of it, which summed up the difference between the two of them. On one of these evenings he'd placed his beer on the table and shaken his head. 'I'm useless, Pete!' Pete's hand had touched his arm. 'You've just got to find what you like. Something's out there for you, and once you've found it you can work your way up.'

Pete, he pictured himself saying now, saying it on the phone because if they were to meet, Shirley would come too and he wouldn't talk in front of her. Pete, I want to improve myself! There's a point now, a reason! I want to invite Daisy to my flat; I've got to have a proper job.

'No, I don't,' he said out loud, looking round the flat on that dark Sunday evening. I've got a job. I just have to have a place, a nice clean, dry-smelling place. He switched on the light. Yeah, a tidy sitting room; tidy but a bit fuller: there was the armchair, the TV, the video, the portable CD, but if he chucked the pile of freebie newspapers he could get a small table, a bookshelf perhaps, and a rug to cover the mauve wall-to-wall. Was there a whiff of damp? He would have to get rid of those other magazines, although they were well hidden.

He was forgetting what he wished he'd said to his dad: that he did want to improve himself; that he did want to be what Dad so often said to him – a professional. He was a professional now, in his current job as an editorial, which was a smarter job title than messenger; he should have told Dad that. Maybe this job could lead somewhere if he got himself a computer and practised on it. He saw his dad sitting on the edge of his chair, hands on the arms at the ready to stand up when Ma came through the door. Tears pricked his eyes. If only he could make Dad see these things. He picked up the phone; glanced at his watch – too late to ring. He moved into his little kitchen and jammed the empty beer cans into the bin. Something ponged. Dirty plates filled the sink. He lifted them onto the draining board. Sardine scraps and baked beans blocked the plug hole. He chucked them into the bin, turned on the tap and swilled out the sink, filled the washing-up bowl with hot water and aimed a squirt of Fairy Liquid.

He was aware of two things, mid-morning Monday, as he pushed the trolley on to the Features Floor with a late delivery of journals: Daisy's empty desk and Martha's occupied one.

'Where's Daisy?' he asked Purple-Hair. He turned away before he could see Purple-Hair's face, cursing himself for asking the question, and saw Martha Morgan looking across the room towards him.

43

'Excuse me,' Doris from *Obituaries* was trying to squeeze past. The place was a minefield this morning.

'Hey!'

He turned back.

Purple-Hair had tipped her head to one side and was tapping the end of her pencil against her bottom lip, which was nothing like as pretty as Daisy's bottom lip. 'Can't I help?'

'No, thanks.'

'Sure...?' She bit the pencil between her teeth. 'What is it? You sure I can't help?'

'Course you can't, Ginny!' Someone else now. He didn't look to see. 'It's Daisy he wants.'

Laughter swelled like a wave.

'There she is!'

Heat flushed through him.

'Behind you, darling.'

He heard her voice. 'Are they getting at you?'

She was smiling when he looked up, laughing too but in a nice way – lips stretching across her white teeth – which made him feel strong again.

'Want a beer sometime?' He seemed to whisper it and bent nearer so that he could almost smell her skin.

Her eyes continued to smile. She seemed to nod.

He would have floated out of the department happy for the rest of the day, happy for the rest of the week, but Martha Morgan had wandered over. Daisy's skin was turning pink, and he remembered the wine bar and the bloody cow episode. He pushed the trolley on past Obituaries towards the Books corner, his heart thumping, dropped off a thick envelope and glanced back. *Bloody cow...* sodding hell... but it was alright. Martha was showing Daisy a sheet of paper. They were smiling at each other.

He took his time to circulate the floor, aware of a whole bunch of them in the Women's corner and then a little later noticing they had dispersed and that Daisy was safely back at her desk. Would she come out for a beer? His heart was doing a dance. He made for the lift and prodded the lift button, anxious now to get back to the messenger desk before Steve started kicking up.

'How's Steve?'

'Wha' ?'

Martha Morgan had stepped into the lift behind him. He glanced towards the landing willing someone else to arrive. Shiny, empty lino floor, blank wall opposite. The door closed. For a second he imagined the lift getting stuck, just him and her, and the trolley. She was a tall woman, not much shorter than him. Big boned under the light grey trousers. Christ, he was getting a hard on.

The lift gave a jolt and started descending. She stared up at the floor numbers, her head turned sideways. 'Sorted out your differences?'

Small blue blob of the earring on her right ear and the funny little clip thing at the back. 'Oh, yeah… thanks.'

'Getting on alright?'

No mention of bloody cows or Daisy. 'Yeah'.

Full eye contact. 'No more trips to Watford?'

He'd forgotten the yellow bits in her eyes. 'One.'

'Got there okay?'

'And back.'

She laughed, the skin round her eyes cracking into little lines. Not too many lines for her age. Her head turned sideways again, looking at the numbers.

He rested his hands on the handle of the trolley and leaned against the side of the lift. 'Actually, I'm looking for a computer. I wondered… if the office might have a second-hand one I could buy. You wouldn't happen to know if –?' What had got into him? But it was easier than he thought. Strike while the iron was hot, and lift rides didn't last two seconds. The lift door was opening.

45

She glanced at him, quick flash of her eyes. 'A second-hand computer...?' She shifted the bag on her shoulder and stepped out of the lift. 'I'll see what I can do.' She strode off across the marble floor. Clip, clip in classy, black ankle boots. Her boots must cost her a fortune; she probably earned a fortune.

Steve was kneeling down by the large Christmas tree inserting the lighting plug into the socket. He stood up and called Jon over. 'No one lasts long in this place. Not even her. I've got a delivery for you.'

Watford again. He watched Martha push through the swing doors. He mustn't forget his mobile this time. Steve was still speaking.

' – half an hour. South Quay. You'll need a pass. And I got plans when you get back. Rationalisation of the Mail and Communications room. Bit of elbow grease for you and Gerry.'

The Christmas tree lights flashed on and off, stopped for a moment and started again.

Steve glared at them, his stiff eyebrows sticking out. 'Any good at electrics?'

Jon tried a joke. 'Strobe lighting.'

'What do you think this is? A bloody night club.'

They're called *clubs* these days, Jon could've said, but the thought didn't seem worth passing on.

So much water everywhere it seemed to get into the wind and wrap itself around him as he took the footbridge to South Quay. Blue-black clouds raced across the sky. He ran.

Want a beer sometime...?

Daisy, want a beer?

A beer and a present for Christmas.

Want a beer...?

Want a beer sometime?

It was like a song in his head.

He rang Pete at lunch time and tried it out. 'Want a beer tonight?'

'Okay mate.'

'Want a beer?'

'What?'

'Just practising.'

'What!'

'See you tonight, Pete.'

If Pete hadn't been able to make it, he would have tried Darrell, his friend from Matt's Autos, car mechanic days – he lived in New Malden too. Or Dave at his own local whom he had been meaning to see again. He had quite a list to practise on. He just needed to say the words for real so they would become familiar and easy, so that they would trip off his tongue: *Want a beer tonight, Daisy?*

But he didn't feel like going anywhere after he had sweated home that evening, his arms aching from the lifting and shifting in the Mail and Communications room. Pete wouldn't be on his own. They met at *The Bull* and he listened to their plans to move nearer in. He should have guessed that Pete and Shirley would decide to live together. He would never get Pete on his own now.

He drained his first pint and thought about living with Daisy. Didn't seem too unrealistic, the way she'd looked at him today. He grabbed Pete's arm. 'Surbiton's a good place to live. Suit you both. Direct service into Waterloo...' They nodded and smiled as if they would take up his suggestion. The film rolled into his head: Daisy and Pete and Jon, the stars, drinking at their local, the *Spit and Polish*: Jon and Daisy walking home to a little white terrace with roses up the side and a path and a gate, in one of those roads going down to the Portsmouth Road and the river. Pete and Jon on the train to Waterloo in the mornings, sorting out the world. Shirley, a minor character.

'How's Daisy?' Shirley asked.

Mind reader. But he was grinning, thinking of Daisy whose roots didn't show like Shirley's – Daisy probably didn't have roots. He was glad Pete was at the bar.

'Ooh, I've hit the button!' Shirley's head tilted as he got the once-over. 'I do like your hair longer.'

He should've asked: what does Pete see in you? Got her off the subject of himself, though he didn't want to know the answer. Pete was returning with the refills.

Her hand reached over to the sleeve of his jacket. 'When are we going to meet her?'

She was quite a flirt leaning across like that, her boobs over the table. His pants felt tight.

'Have you brought her home yet? You're sweet when you blush.'

But now Pete was close. How the fuck were these two connected?

She stared at him, her spiky fringe pricking the black, sticky eyelashes.

Pete sat down. 'Budge up.' He slid Shirley's vodka and lemon across the table to her. 'Beer,' he looked at Jon.

'Thanks mate.'

He grinned. 'Is she giving you a hard time?'

The second time he'd been asked that today.

Shirley sipped at her drink. 'We were having a nice chat, weren't we?' She nodded at Jon, head tilting again, and glanced at Pete. 'About Daisy – you know, Jon's new girlfriend.' She put down her glass and leaned across the table again, boobs squashed up. 'Jon, have you and her, you know...?'

'Shirley...!' Pete looked at Jon and chuckled as if it was a joke.

Jon tried to make his face into a smile and laugh it off, but he wanted to give Shirley the two fingers. 'What do you think, Shirley?'

Her glass was at her lips. 'Don't know.'

He swigged back his beer and saw the two of them exchange a glance. Pete gave her a wink. He gulped down his beer, burning inside, and made his excuses soon after that telling them he had an early start. Pete stood up and patted his arm. 'Great to see you, mate.' Shirley blew him a kiss. He hated the way Pete looked into his eyes as if he really cared, hated the two of them.

First the jerseys... then his collection of overalls: Matt's Autos, Motsuki Pharmaceuticals – at one time everywhere he worked required an overall... then the Judge Dredd comics and martial arts mags. He chucked the stuff onto his bed and knelt on the floor in front of the cupboard, breathing quickly, the pile in front of him.

The top one? – no... the second...? the third...? Or had he hidden it? He didn't want to fucking search tonight. He took them off carefully, one by one, onto the carpet. He would know the cover of the one, once he saw it. The back of his neck was sopping. How did you make things happen the way you wanted? He couldn't even do this now. He wanted the one – what the fuck had he done with it? – the one with... with her bum, her buttocks, the one with the black vibrator stuck up the hole, stuck up her arse, stretching her. Aah, nicely... perhaps he wouldn't need it. He lay back on the floor, thinking about the vibrator juddering away inside the tart's arse... inside Shirley's arse, inside Martha Morgan's arse, inside... but he didn't get to thinking about it inside Daisy's arse because now lava was scorching through him and he was thinking of it inside his own arse and jerking himself off.

SIX

GRANT

The smell of carpet cleaning fluid lingered in his room after the professional cleaners had visited, especially in the mornings when he forgot to leave the door ajar to let the air circulate. Or he thought it did. He grappled with the lock on the window, pushed it open and gazed at the cold, silvery light, the streaks of pink in the east. He sniffed – was that a whiff of it? Probably not. Martha had come into his room. She was wandering round the house in her nightdress wondering where he'd fled to – that was what she told him, and then her blood ran down her legs on to the carpet. His carpet. His room. He kept the door closed. She would have had to open it.

He remembered the wild panic in the middle of the night all those years ago, the fumbling for the light switch, the feeling that he would burst if he couldn't eradicate the image of himself and Christopher on the sands or in that lodge, or of Ruthie's boyfriend grabbing Christopher from him and then that fucking police guy threatening him. Words like 'mutilation' and 'amputation' came into his mind, words that he'd explored when he'd first gone into analysis and hadn't thought about for years; words that seemed rather pompous now. Once he'd got his divorce and come to England, he made himself forget Christopher and Ruthie. Enough to cope anyway. Martha wasn't interested in the past. They married. He secured a lectureship in the psychology department of London University. They decided they didn't want children. Martha became a journalist, he a psychoanalyst. Then they decided that they did want kids, at least one. But it didn't work, in spite of all the medical intervention. 'You are one of the ten per cent of couples who have unexplained infertility', the consultant told them.

Back at his desk Grant stared at the clean, bare wall in front of him. He just needed to know why Martha had made the suggestion, why she'd said it. If he couldn't face her answer, he would book in for a few sessions with Neville and try and deal with it. Stripes of shadow from the side window made a pattern on the paintwork. The paint was called 'Matchstick', some name like that; he'd felt enthusiasm for the colour when he'd had it painted. He felt tired, too tired to have a kid, let alone someone else's kid if that was what she really meant.

The letter confirming the funding for the book had arrived this morning. Julia would have received the same letter. He skimmed over the words, and the figure which seemed generous enough, and placed the letter on his pending tray. His workload was heavy this year: teaching, lectures, group-work, patients – and he must find a space in his timetable for this new project. He'd wanted to study 'the father' way back in Boston when he still thought he was a father, but that idea had got lost in his efforts to earn a living at the same time as training to become an analyst. It was only now all these years later that he and Julia had been commissioned to write a book about fathers with the working title of 'Paternal Perspectives', an awful title which would have to be changed. At some point he would have to tell Martha and she wouldn't understand. Wearily, he retrieved the letter and slowly folded it and then, in case she came into his room, stuffed it in his pocket. She didn't need to know yet.

He pulled his notes out of the filing drawer and tried to focus on the talk he was preparing for the Institute of Marital Therapy. He had been to a lecture called, *Perfection and the need for flaws*. The lecturer was an elderly man with white hair who spoke with a hesitant, quavering voice which the microphone exaggerated; Grant had sunk into his seat, wishing he was nearer the back of the lecture hall so that he could escape if necessary. But the man had looked up from his papers on the lectern and gazed through thick, black-framed glasses, his voice becoming stronger as he addressed his audience, 'Think of the asymmetrical face that is more beautiful than the symmetrical one, the dissonant chord that enhances the music, the grit in the oyster that makes the pearl. The negative pulls against the positive and makes the positive stronger.'

Perfection versus flaws... Grant had written, and on a new line for each sentence added:

We look at the flaw as being the thing that is wrong.

What if the flaw is the thing holding the relationship together?

What makes a relationship work?

Take the patient who says: our life would be perfect if we didn't have this problem, that problem...

Maybe the problem is the good thing.

Maybe it is the rest of it that we need to consider.

He liked to turn things on their head, say something paradoxical at the beginning, have his students sit up in their seats, have them straight away thinking of questions, challenges. But this was him and Martha. He removed the top from his pen, drew a line through what he had written and stared at the wall again. The shadow patterns had faded.

Only ten minutes now. He shoved the notes back into the file and closed the drawer. He would have to start again, think of a new approach. He pulled out the filing drawer to have one more look, and then pushed the drawer closed again. Look later. He checked in his diary. Christine followed by Jeremy and then Mike, and the Institute in the afternoon. Christine Mirado... he couldn't visualise her. She was a new one. He glanced in her file to see when they had met for the preliminary meeting; it was one of his rules not to look at his notes before seeing a patient. The room felt cold. He got up and shut the window, and considered going in search of the blow heater they had in the cupboard under the stairs, but he might meet up with Martha and that was another of his rules: avoid seeing anyone while preparing for a patient.

He remembered the new patient as he opened the front door to her – dark, glossy hair pulled back in a clip, large steady eyes. She was doing this as part of her counselling training. These were often the most resistant patients because they thought they were doing it for the training not for themselves. There was a creak on the stairs. He held out an arm indicating the entrance to his room, and before he closed his door saw Martha half-way down the stairs mouthing, 'Wow!'

Get close to a beautiful woman – and this one was stunning in her black suit and fuchsia-pink cardigan, though a bit formal for his taste – share her secrets, watch her lying on the couch only feet away, touch her in the metaphorical sense, but never let her touch you. He'd been practising that ever since Ruthie and Christopher. He could stand outside, get involved and not feel it. It was second nature. He'd never let himself get too close to Martha, or thought he hadn't. He lifted his head. The woman was staring at him from under heavy eyelids which probably meant she'd been crying. Perhaps he needed a break, a rest. She shifted in her chair (she'd been reluctant to lie on the couch) and fingered the edges of her cardigan. He never broke a patient's silence, and the habit was strong enough to stop the novel urge to quit the case and show her the door.

The only thing that cheered him that day was Julia's phone call about the book.

'''The Father' has already been used. What *are* we going to call it?'

He managed a laugh. 'Let's write it first.'

'Grant, you are going to update your computer?'

Martha was standing in the hallway when he got home from teaching that evening as if she'd been waiting for him, and he laughed, relief making him light-headed so sure she had been going to say something else.

'Did I say that?' He placed his briefcase on the chair and put out his arms to her; they stood holding each other in the warm, well-lit house, the smell of coffee flavouring the air, the sound of the television muttering in the background, seeming to want each other.

There had been no more candlelit dinners, but often – unlike Martha over the last year – there had been soup or something warmed up. There had been something else too, a feeling jacked up between them. 'Don't do it,' he seemed to be saying. 'I might, I might,' she seemed to be threatening.

And now she moved out of his arms too quickly, and walked into the kitchen. He would like it to have turned into more, for them to go upstairs and fall into bed.

She glanced round, 'I'll get Jesus to come and have a look at it.'

'Jesus?'

'One of the messengers at work. There's some stew if you like.'

'No, thanks.'

She picked up the cafetière. 'Decaf?

He watched her pour the dark liquid into a mug, hand it to him, open the fridge, put back the casserole and get out some milk. 'They're usually boys. Young lads doing their gap year.'

He lowered himself onto the stool and cupped the mug in his hand. 'Why do you call him Jesus?'

She laughed, small lines at the corners of her eyes. 'He looks like him.'

'Like Jesus?'

'Well, not quite *The Light of the World*. The Burne-Jones, you know–'

He nodded. 'I know.'

She poured the milk into a glass and took several gulps and then lifted her face, traces of white at the corners of her mouth.

'Longish hair. He's a bit inept. Says the wrong things. Gets lost on deliveries.' Her fingers wiped her mouth. 'Not very practical probably. In another world.' She chuckled, younger suddenly. 'You'll have to meet him.'

'And you want to sell him my computer?'

'Or give it to him.'

'How about I might want to sell it, Martha?' It was meant to sound jokey but he could hear the edge in his voice.

She drained her glass, turned to the sink and swilled the glass under the tap. 'I thought it might be nice to help.'

He raised himself off the stool and moved up behind her. 'Sure thing, honey. Invite him over.' He enclosed her in his arms and buried his face into her hair, wishing he could melt into her.

He wasn't sleeping well. Sometimes he got up and went down to his room and tried to work. Other times he went to the bathroom and went for a pee and then ran his hands under the tap, staring at his crumpled face in the mirror, gulped down a tooth mug of water and returned to bed. She was inches away from him, the warm, living person he'd known so long. He just had to stretch out a hand, or move closer to hear her light breaths. Surely, she wasn't entering any kind of treatment.

Memories intruded, odd little details, like the feel of the rough sheets on the bottom bunk in the tiny cabin that he'd shared with Rory, art student with an aversion to flying, on the cargo ship crossing the Atlantic; like the blackness of those nights in the cabin, the blind drawn down over the porthole, the blind drawn down over his life. He'd left Boston and his job at the college and had boarded the ship in New York harbour. There were only twelve passengers and the journey took nine days. It was an Italian line. Herb flavoured pasta dishes were served on white plates embossed with the Line's flag, followed by pink veal that divided into two with the pressure of the side of a fork, or slowly cooked *osso bucco* so tender it fell off the bone. There were sweet liquor, spongy puddings and crumbly white Italian cheeses, and tiny cups of thick, black coffee. He gained the pounds that he'd shed during those past few months and leaned against the railings of the ship watching the prow slice through the waves. Occasionally fish leapt from the sea or birds appeared from nowhere.

He had three months left on his visitor's visa when he met Martha. It was at his American friend, Dale's. He'd escaped the party into her scruffy garden. Dale's little girl was playing an electronic game and he put his arm round her while he chatted to her brother about the second Star Wars film, laughing as they disagreed about the title. A woman followed them out of doors – late twenties, perhaps, tall with thick short hair and a determined expression under dark eyebrows; he could see the contours of her shoulders through a pale lilac shirt. Dale's little girl jumped up and down. 'Look, Grant! Look! The monkey's saving the princess!'

The woman stared at the bunch of nettles growing in Dale's unkempt flowerbed. His arm was tugged by the little girl. The boy was pushing her away as he tried to talk. 'Grant! Grant!'

He hushed the children and turned to the woman. 'Are you alright?'

A flicker of a smile that took a second to reach her eyes. 'Too many people in there.' She turned her head away and looked back at the nettles, the tendons stretching in her neck. He told the children he would play with them later – yes, he promised he would before they went to bed – and led her by the arm to the rickety garden bench and sat next to her.

Her hand brushed his arm. 'Have you got a cigarette?'

He glanced down, shook his head. She had clean, straight-cut nails on strong fingers. 'I can go and see –?' What was he saying, he hated smokers?

'I don't want to go back inside.'

'You don't have to.'

'No, please,' her hand was firm on his arm. 'I don't need one.' She explained that she'd got what she needed from Dale, but there was an old boyfriend in there she didn't want to see. 'I'm not going to give him that pleasure,' she said.

Grant laughed. 'Poor guy, what's he done?'

'Don't ask.' She leaned back, the bench creaking.

He sat back too. A breeze rustled the leaves of the tall tree at the end of the small garden blowing an empty crisp packet across the dry, patchy grass. 'What did you need from Dale?'

'Contacts, a job…?' She hunched her shoulders and folded her arms. ''It's freezing out here.'

He lent her his jacket and placed it over her shoulders which felt broader than he'd imagined. Large body, he found himself thinking, but with not an ounce of extra fat. He was not used to tall women. She seemed a mixture of strong and something else he couldn't figure out. He spent the next few weeks trying not to get attached. After Ruthie he was not going down that route.

He remembered standing on the doorstep of the house where she shared a flat and looking into her eyes – such a pale blue with the yellow pigment spots – so tentative about getting involved that she took it as an insult. He put out his arm to shake her hand, not wanting to be caught by those eyes, and she laughed.

'You can kiss me!'

He leaned forward, but she stepped back and opened the door. 'Come up for God's sake.'

He shook his head. 'I won't.'

'Don't you want to?'

'You don't have to sleep with me, Martha.'

Again she was laughing. 'Who said anything about sleep?'

'I meant – as a thank you for a dinner.'

It was the wrong thing to say. His budget was dwindling and he had probably put too much value on the cost of the dinner. He probably wouldn't see her again, probably couldn't afford to. But she rang him about a week later and asked him to a party, and after that they had dinner once a week or went to a movie. Once, they took a trip down the river to Greenwich. He decided he could go home early if he ran out of money. She was about an inch shorter than him – so that he couldn't help looking into her eyes and beginning to fall for their pale blue colour and those yellow pigment spots. He told her he was on a long summer vacation recharging the batteries before going back to teaching. He saw himself returning broke to his widowed mother in San Francisco and finding a job in the psychology department at Berkeley or San Francisco State. His father had spent his last working years as history professor at the University of California at Santa Cruz. His mother would love him to come back and live with her. 'Why did you do psychology and not a proper subject, like your father?' she asked him increasingly on his visits. Same thing, he told her: history of the mind.

One evening Martha refused to leave the table at the restaurant. 'What's the problem? Can't you get it up?'

He had paid the bill and was standing waiting for her. 'Pardon, Ma'am?' The expression slipped out and he could see she didn't like it.

'You heard.'

He pulled his chair nearer hers and sat down again, anger he thought he'd got over welling up. She was striking that evening, terrifying in a way, all in black and with her short hair newly cropped. The blue blob of her earring was the only colour – apart from her eyes. He watched her pick up her empty wine glass, tip the last red drops into her mouth and glance up.

'It's me, isn't it? '

'Pardon...?' That word again.

'You don't want me.'

'No...'

'That's why you don't want to – '

'No, Martha, no…' He felt better suddenly. 'It's… history.'

'History?'

'Yeah… my history.'

'Fuck that shrink thing.'

He reached for her arm and took her hand. 'Martha, I want to sleep with you.'

'Then why don't you?'

'I'm scared of getting hurt.'

She shook her head. 'Oh, fuck you.'

The first time was in the narrow bed in his small room in the lodgings he'd found near Dale's, his place rather than hers because her flatmate hadn't gone away for the weekend. It surprised him that she minded about her flatmate – she had her own room; he suspected she would do it anywhere with anyone. The thought comforted him – no big deal, no commitment, he was just one of many.

He would never forget the feeling that seemed to lift off her long, large-limbed body, like a vapour… so at odds with what he was expecting. He couldn't define the feeling. Loving, yes, she seemed to want him – she clung to him. But a holding back.

'What is it, Martha?'

'It's alright.'

'Did you come?'

'Yes.'

But he couldn't be sure. 'You're so beautiful.' She lay on her side turned towards him, breathing lightly, the sweat on her skin where they had made contact cool and dry when he passed his hands over her. He'd thought: she'll be a good fuck; I'll get back my confidence, and then I'll go home. But after the first time he wanted to return to her. He would lean on his elbow and gaze into her eyes. 'Is it alright?'

'Yes…'

'Sure?'

'I love how it is.'

But she never said it quite right. He wanted her to be clinging to him, moaning. He wanted to be certain that he was satisfying her. 'Is there someone else?'

'No.'

'Sure?'

'Yes.'.

'Are you sure, Martha?'

'Fuck yes! I love you.'

She said it first. And after that there seemed no going back.

They drove down to Wiltshire to meet her mother, and she told him her father had killed himself.

'Killed himself?' He stared at her, amazed at the way she could so suddenly surprise him.

She was behind the wheel. They had passed Stonehenge and were only about ten miles away from her mother's house. 'Got... got himself killed.'

'You mean an accident?'

'Yeah.'

'Hey, Martha... I'm sorry...'

'Don't make a fuss. Mummy's just getting over it and she won't want to talk about it.' Her strong fingers curled round the wheel. The road ran between green rolling hills reaching out to the horizon under a wide sky and dipped into another valley. Her father had gone out one icy, foggy night on the way to a school meeting and driven his car head on into one of the few remaining telegraph poles.

Poor mother, he thought. In denial. British stiff upper lip too, probably. He wondered whether he was going to like her. 'You say it was an accident?'

'Of – of course.'

Poor baby. The slight stammer made his heart turn over. He glanced at Martha again and she looked at him quickly, a faint flush on her skin. She couldn't bear it, could she? It seemed to explain something. He felt a surge of confidence. He would get her through, thaw that frozen part of her.

In the darkness of the middle of the night, he turned towards her, remembering his confidence then, and how it had worked, how he'd seemed to love her enough. He put his hand out to her, across the expanse of sheet between them until it reached the warm skin of her back willing himself to have the same confidence now.

SEVEN

MARTHA

Tony rubbed his glasses with his handkerchief and looked at her across the circle of chairs. 'So who's going to *lead* today?'

She felt her face tighten and hoped it wasn't the start of another headache. What she'd introduced – once getting Daisy to lead the meeting after only a few weeks in the job – was made to seem questionable, laughable even.

'I haven't decided yet.' Tony was *Legal and Financial* but he regarded himself as deputy editor, though the role didn't officially exist, and his 'concern' about her felt worse now she'd stopped having the treatment, now there was no reason for his concern that had never felt like concern. She glanced around the circle of chairs, several empty, feeling him stare at her. The meetings were held in the book corner, the most secluded part of the floor, cut off from the other areas by the large partition of bookshelves. She looked towards the end of the partition willing more people to appear. 'You know why I do it, don't you?'

He placed his glasses on to his nose. 'Do what?'

'Ask different people to lead each week.' Peter from *Books* two chairs away crossed his legs and avoided her eyes. Sara standing in for Eva from *Health* and sitting next to Tony scribbled on her pad. 'It helps me to see the news from a different perspective. That's why, Tony,' Martha nodded.

His chair creaked as he leaned back a little and folded his arms. 'Of course, Martha.'

Thankfully, Liza appeared round the end of the partition, papers in her hand, grinning as she chewed on gum, her latest prop to stave off the nicotine craving. 'Sorry, sorry. Just had David on the phone about the child prostitution story. Couldn't get him off.' She flopped down into the chair next to Martha. 'Don't look at me like that, Tony. It's true.' She laughed. He smiled back at her. She placed her papers on the floor and turned to Martha. 'Everything alright?' And now Matthew from *Obits* was arriving, followed by Daisy.

Usually, Martha loved the weekly meeting. It was what the job was about. She had to plan the in-depth series or ongoing columns, but had to allow for hot, incoming news which could change the plans at a moment's notice. She loved not knowing what the news would bring and the challenge that Features would produce relevant copy under any conditions. She loved that she didn't have to write the stories but had to have the wisdom to know which stories must be written. Each week had its own personality and the weekly meeting was where it was born and shaped.

Liza was leading today. She invited Matthew to talk about his 'obituary' woman who had helped Jewish refugee children. They discussed the woman's silence. Why did she take so long to speak? What was it about being silent after the war that still fascinated us now? Was there enough for a feature? Martha leaned forward and suggested they do it from a wacky angle, not the usual war-women-kids thing, but from *Travel*, say, or *Financial*. She saw Tony pull a face at Daisy, and then take off his glasses and rub his eyes. She laughed, shaking her head. It normally worked – say something off the wall and the energy began to rise. Sara was suggesting it could go in *Health*, and they took it seriously and spent a few minutes discussing how coping mechanisms had changed since then and whether they were more effective now. Tony stared at Matthew and asked why everyone was still so fascinated by a war that started over sixty years ago? Liza nodded. Martha caught her eye and looked round the circle.

'It's a popular subject, and still topical. We've just had Remembrance Sunday.' 'That was a month ago.' It was Tony again. She smiled, 'Exactly!' They moved on to Liza's piece on child prostitution, and then to the more benign Christmas items. Did they really need three pages on shopping in the suburbs and the demise of the toyshop? There were the regulars: astrology, book reviews, childcare chats. Someone wanted to do something on reluctant fathers.

Martha shook her head. 'Too much on kids.'

Tony chuckled. 'Not your scene.'

She should have said, sorry Daddy? Made him feel old. Or kept her mouth shut. But she looked up from her notes. 'What did you say?'

He lifted his hands. 'You and kids.'

'How the hell would you know?' Her laughter sounded forced. She glanced round the circle smiling and trying to get people to join in.

She checked her email, started a search on war silence, made some phone calls, flicked through the post that Sue had opened. On days like this the need to talk to someone was like a hunger. She yanked back her chair and walked over to the water container. The place felt empty as if after the meeting everyone had scattered down their holes like a bunch of rabbits. Sue was getting up from her desk and walking towards the exit, skirting round Liza's secretary coming in the opposite direction. Loo breaks perhaps. Once or twice Martha had nearly taken Sue into her confidence. That was how you tested P.A.s – confidante... confidentiality... the two words so similar. She filled a plastic mug with iced water and held it against her cheek.

Back at her desk she dialled Mr Shorn's secretary, asked for the number of the counselling department and then dialled the number. A voice told her that there was a cancellation for later in the morning if she would like to take it. She twisted her wrist to see the time. An hour in which to pin down who was doing what. She agreed to the appointment and replaced the phone.

When she looked up Jon was standing at her desk, tall and young with his dark, long hair; and the two seemed connected, the phone call and him being there. His trolley was a few feet away and she had the odd notion that he'd hung around because he sensed she needed support.

'I'm doing the sandwiches.'

'Thanks. But I'll be going out.'

He had a hesitant look as if he knew he should say something more.

She nodded. 'Thanks, Jon.' Her eyes were pricking. Beyond him she could see the large figure of Doris from *Obits* trundling across the floor towards her, holding a piece of paper which was probably the obituary of the woman who had helped those Jewish children. 'Thanks for asking.'

The counsellor had a black line for eyebrows and earrings that fell to her shoulders. They sat, miles away from the IVF clinic, in a side room with two low chairs and a window high in the wall that looked on to a dirty patch of sky and the branch of a tree. There was a box of tissues, a clock on a small table and on the wall one picture: of a mountain near a lake with a solitary boat.

'I have to take a few medical details.'

'Endometriosis, low sperm count, cervical mucus antibodies, polycystic ovary syndrome, sub-fertility, infertility... we've tried all those.' Martha pulled her arms out of her jacket and reached for a tissue. 'God it's hot in here. It's making my nose run.' She blew her nose and clutched on to the damp tissue, and then removed her jacket from behind her and laid it on the worn brown carpet. 'Unexplained. They can't explain it.'

'So that's very difficult for you.'

She swallowed, avoiding the woman's eyes. She'd felt as solid as a rock as they'd walked along the corridors but now her eyes were damp. The big hand of the clock juddered and leaped several minutes. She glanced at the wall and tried to concentrate on the picture. A pointed mountain, Chinese perhaps. Who'd paid for it – NHS? Local health authority…?

'I thought perhaps it might work if I tried something different.'

'You're thinking of donor insemination?'

'I suppose so…'

She imagined a piece on NHS expenditure and the dull statistics that would have to be collected to demonstrate the policy behind the hanging of this one picture in this small, sad room. She placed the screwed up tissue on the table, pulled out another one, and told the woman how they should have made several babies, how the little egg and sperm cells fused outside of her body, how they took photos of the embryos and put them back inside, how for months through the different treatments she became obsessed with anything cord-like: the halyards on the *H.M.S. Victory* at Portsmouth when they were doing a feature on sailing ships, the steel ropes on Hammersmith Bridge as she drove to White City for a meeting with the BBC, her own washing line in her Putney garden; everywhere she saw twisting umbilical cords with no babies on the end of them.

'And what about your husband?'

She shook her head. The branch moved in the window.

The woman cleared her throat. 'Was it his sperm before?'

'Yes.'

'Do you want a baby?'

She looked up. The woman was staring at her. She glanced down away from the pitying eyes. The woman had flat shoes with a bar across. Swollen ankles emerged from a long floral skirt. 'I can't bear not knowing why. I thought I could. I thought I'd accepted it.'

'And you would do anything to get what you want?'

This was a waste of time. She pushed herself to the edge of the chair and then flopped back into it. 'Look, I don't know. I don't know if I want a baby. Probably not. I'm probably not suited!'

'So you're trying to find an answer?'

Martha gazed at the wall feeling the beat of her heart. Perhaps the picture was Lake District, Grassmere... The woman had an annoying way of keeping silent. It could be a rowing boat on the lake, Wordsworth's...

'Do you have any thoughts about why you can't conceive?'

'Of course not.' Some of her questions were crap.

'When no medical reason can be found, some women, some couples, blame themselves. They think if they had behaved differently, if something hadn't happened in their life, in the past...'

'No, definitely not.'

'I only mention this because... these things can be very private – but if these beliefs are there, it can help to talk. Sometimes we need to dispel these beliefs before we can move forward.'

'That's not me.'

'I just wanted to check.'

'I'm wasting your time, aren't I?' There was a hot, mucky feeling in the base of her stomach. 'I shouldn't be here. I'm taking up space. All those people who know they want...'

'You are here.'

'But I don't know.'

'That's alright.'

Martha stared at the woman's bulbous feet pressing against the bars of the flat shoes, and heard her quiet voice.

'Do you want to come back? I could see you next week.'

She tugged at a tissue and blew again. 'I don't know.'

The woman nodded slowly. 'What I must tell you is this: if you do decide that you want to try donor insemination, both you and your husband will be required to attend a mandatory appointment. You both have to be there.'

'I would want to see you on my own.'

She nodded again. 'As you've been part of the IVF programme with Mr. Shorn, you can come back for more counselling on your own if you wish.'

Martha was aware of her hand round the damp tissue loosening, surprised at her relief. 'Thank you. I'll need to think about it.'

The woman put away her diary. 'The mandatory session is different. Everyone considering donor insemination has to attend. It's a legal requirement. In that session you'll be given all the necessary information. In the U.K. physical attributes are...'

Martha shifted in her chair. The window rattled. The tree swayed. She looked round for the picture – mountain, water...

The woman had stopped speaking and was handing her some leaflets. For a moment, Martha thought the women might reach out and touch her, but she sat back in her chair and waited for Martha to leave the room.

She took the bus over London Bridge and watched a man and his daughter striding along the pavement, the girl skipping to the father's walk, her long hair bouncing up and down on her back. They stopped and looked over the bridge. From the top of the stationary bus, Martha could see the low hulk of a barge disappearing under the bridge. The bus jolted forward. She looked back. They were walking again, the small girl running backwards and then twisting round, avoiding someone coming in the opposite direction. The father was grabbing her hand.

She remembered Daddy holding her hand in the Brecon Beacons, across the stream and up the hill through the bracken and the flowering rowan trees, away from Mummy and Philip. It was one of his happy times, early September before school started, sunlight through flickering trees, she his special, clever daughter. *Daddy, I'm going to be in the top group. I'm going to be head of the netball team; we're going to win all our matches...* He would smile and smile as he bounded up the hills and she would hang on to his hand panting behind him.

'*Daddy, Daddy, I can't keep up!*' Did she ever say that? When he was happy, his energy and enthusiasm were like a force that he poured into her, making her feel she could do anything. Other times, it was as if she let go his hand and slipped down those Brecon hills landing in the kitchen of their cottage with her mother and her brother. The trees and the fields lost their colour. The house became darker. They had to creep around. Daddy was upstairs. She could picture her mother now, sitting at the kitchen table with that tight, breathless look. She could picture her glancing up and nodding. That look. It was there at Daddy's funeral as they stood outside the church waiting to follow his coffin to the graveside.

Martha got off the bus and landed amongst the crowd of people getting on, and fought her way through them needing air. Bloody counselling. She walked in the road, cars and buses hurtling past her. Up a side street there was a steamed-up window of a café. Inside she made for the Ladies and turned on the taps into the sink wanting to cool down her face. But she switched off the taps and stared at herself in the mirror. She'd never thought about Daddy. She didn't have to think about him now.

In the Docklands Light Railway she checked her face in her small mirror. A low sun flashed through the window. She dabbed at the shiny end of her nose and gazed into her eyes. Ice blue eyes, someone had once called them, ignoring the yellow pigment spots. Scared eyes…? Grant said he loved her eyes. She reached inside her bag for the comforting hardness of her dark glasses case.

The glasses were still on her nose in the brightly-lit foyer of the building when Steve ran after her calling her name. There were tiny red blood vessels in the man's cheeks. She pressed the lift button hoping he would go away. One of the leader writers joined her. She smiled at him. 'Hello Robert.'

But Steve was insistent. 'Jon said you told him that he could have an office computer to take home.'

The left-hand lift had arrived. Robert moved towards it. He glanced back, holding the door open. She shook her head. 'I'll get the next one.'

The effort of reassuring Steve that there had been a misunderstanding and it was she who would give Jon a second-hand computer, not the office, made her forget what she'd remembered. And once back on the floor, the stories started landing on her desk and she gratefully became absorbed.

That evening she rang her brother, Philip. With him it was impossible to think anything might be scary. Philip made everything feel normal, ordinary. Younger than her, he felt older, reassuring. What she wanted to ask him would be unpopular, and maybe just talking to him would make her feel she didn't need to ask it. The idea was mostly Grant's.

But Philip was at a parents' meeting and Kathleen answered, and instead of waiting to talk to him later, she plunged straight in. 'Kathleen, would you mind if we didn't actually stay with you at Christmas?'

'Sorry?'

'Would you mind if we stayed at a bed and breakfast, this time. Grant and I are very tired.'

'A bed and breakfast…?'

'Well – a cottage perhaps.'

'You're staying with us.'

'We would come over every day, Kathleen. I'll bring the Christmas Pudding.'

'Where would you find a cottage?'

'There must be ones to let.' She was sounding bossy. Kathleen often had this effect on her. 'We're really looking forward to seeing you. It's just –'

But Kathleen was ringing off and telling her that she would get Phil to ring her when he got in.

Bossy, older, childless, career sister-in-law... that was probably how Kathleen saw her. Kathleen with her three children and her husband, the dependable Phil. Philip hadn't, as Daddy predicted, reached Martha's heights, but he'd made a family and was highly regarded in the teaching world and had now become head of Andover comprehensive.

She was asleep on the sofa when he rang an hour later. She clicked off the television and shifted herself up and wedged the phone in her ear listening to his slow sensible voice. It still had a faint lilt – from those years in the Brecon Beacons. 'Martha, you must stay. There's plenty of space. We've got the new room over the garage. Kathleen's parents can go in the room next to the girls. It's so easy.'

'Philip, we want to stay in a cottage.'

'Why?'

'We're tired. Grant's had a heavy few months. We want to be with you, but he's older, Phil. This is the best solution.'

'You don't want to come, do you?'

'Of course we do.'

'But Grant doesn't.'

'He does, Phil.'

'What is it, Martha?' There was a sharpness in his voice.

She flicked on the television, turning down the volume. Jeremy Paxman mouthed at his interviewee, a woman with pronounced lips and short, frizzy hair whom Martha didn't recognise.

'Martha, are you there?'

'It's alright, Phil. It really is.' How much easier if he knew. But if he knew, that would cut him off; he would be embarrassed about his kids. Jeremy Paxman was facing the camera. The interview had finished. There was a map of the Middle East behind him. 'Phil... all I'm asking is, could you find out if there is a cottage? Please.'

She pressed the off button and leaned her head against the sofa aware of the smell of the scented jasmine she'd bought last week and set in the fireplace. Grant was late coming home. She extinguished the silent figures on the screen. 10.54 glowed on her watch. Away, of course. Cambridge – a meeting or a conference. She reached for her bag to get his phone number thinking she might tell him she'd spoken to Philip.

The handouts from the counselling session had wrapped themselves around her diary. She discarded the leaflet describing the work of the Human Fertilisation Embryo Authority and picked up the single sheet entitled: 'Donor Information Regulations...' *The HFEA Regulations 2004 guarantee to donor-conceived people a right to receive identifying information (name, date of birth, address and appearance) about donors whose samples were used in their conception if those donors have registered with clinics on or after April 1, 2005....* Of course, there was all that, wasn't there? She lifted her eyes from the words.

The child would want to know who his or her father was. She stuffed the leaflets into her bag and zipped it up. Of course the child would. She sank back into the sofa and thought about Philip and her. And then she was thinking about Daddy again.

EIGHT

JON

Kingston was madness: canned carols, pedestrian precinct heaving, and Benthalls with its glass atrium and its escalators and its floors and floors that he couldn't get a handle on. And then there were all the other shops, and the banks and the building societies. Somewhere there must be an ATM to get some money.

He made himself stop and think. A present for Daisy... something silky and shiny... and sexy. M&S underwear? He was outside M&S now. Na... naff! He stared at the mannequin's legs in the shop window, shiny inside flesh coloured tights, feet almost vertical in red stilettos. He remembered his ma buying panties and tights in M&S when he was a kid. His face was thrust into a stand of white, slippery things. He hid in them, liking the darkness and the funny feeling of the slidey material. 'Get your face out of those petticoats, Jonathan!' No one called him Jonathan, except her. Not even her now.

He found a pub and downed a pint. He'd had the Christmas phone call from Dad. 'What are we going to buy your mother?' *We*? Why couldn't he buy it himself – she was his wife. Perhaps, if Monday worked and he managed to ask Daisy for a drink, he could say to Dad and Ma, 'I'm otherwise engaged. Christmas day is all I can manage.' Up yours to Dad and the bent Christmas tree, and Dad's *Christmas is family*. What family? Perhaps Daisy would be family... fuck it, whatever. He was going to spend time with Pete at Christmas, and Dave at his local.

He fetched himself another pint and remembered about the idea of the computer. Martha Morgan hadn't done anything, as she'd promised. And then Steve, when he'd asked him, had said, 'What do you want with one of those?' So he'd said, 'Martha Morgan told me to ask you.' Much good it had done him.

He needed a piss. There was one free urinal and he added his steady stream, holding his breath against the sickly, sweet smell aware of others aiming, yellow spits bouncing up. The feel of his fingers on his penis made him think of Daisy's fingers there; made it hard to pee. Someone farted. An old man kept stopping and then squirting more. One more pint, he thought, as his stream died away and he tucked himself in and zipped up his flies.

The bar was crammed, several people deep. The thought of Daisy's fingers continued to burn him. The pub door banged behind him, propelling him on to the pavement. He walked away from the crowds towards one of the roads that filtered cars around the edge of the town centre. There was a chemist – he would end up buying his ma some soap, as he always did… and now a camera shop full of cameras of every shape and size, and tripods and spools. When he was ten his dad had bought him a camera, a simple press-the-button camera that did its own focussing, but Dad fussed him and made it sound complicated and then told him he was clumsy. So he never used it. He found it a year later, very dusty on the shelf in the garage. While Dad was tinkering inside the bonnet of the car, not letting him touch, as usual, he removed it from the shelf and pinched a screw driver and went down to the end of the garden and sat amongst the dark needles from the tree and took the camera to bits. What surprised him was that he put it together again, and at some point took photos – pictures of the New Malden garden, the dark green tree, the place where he'd sat – a record of his achievement. He made a scrap book of the photos – one of the few things he remembered doing with Ma. They used glue, and Dad came along and told them they should have used *photo corners*.

Fuck Dad. But he felt lighter, remembering his achievement. He gazed into the glittery window of a jeweller's shop, his heart spinning at the rings – a whole tray of them, light sparkling in the different coloured stones. He passed by a card shop and thought he might buy one of the larger ones and frame it, make a picture of it. The photo shop in Surbiton had frames. There was a card with water and buildings, a sort of Docklands. Would Daisy like that? There was another one with a photo of Hampton Court. What did she like? At the NatWest he took some money out at the ATM.

A bit further on he paused outside a small shop, next to some tables containing bowls of stones and coloured pebbles. White, sharp crystals sparkled like the jewellery, making different coloured lights. *Crystals 3 for £2*, the label said. There were china eggs and candles. A woman stood in the doorway. She had black plaits with silver bows on the ends. She nodded at him, the bows doing a dance on her shoulders. 'There's more inside.'

It looked dark and cramped. There were the same bowls of stones and crystals, and fossils too. There were crusty chunks of rock with jagged green insides, and one with black insides labelled *jet*, the same black as the woman's black plaits with the stupid bows. Water trickled like the urinals. *Tumble stones – 60p. 2 for £1*. Black Plaits picked up a handful – all colours, white, black, green, red – and let them run through her fingers making a clacking sound. There were books for sale – tatty, second hand, with titles like *'World Environment'*, *'The Secrets of Tarot – Tarot cards, how to tell your fortune and predict the future.'* He took out the Tarot book, a small, blue hardback, and opened it at *The Hanged Man*, a picture of a man hanging upside down from the branch of a tree. He read: *The key to the figure lies in the man's expression, which is of pleasure...* New Age rubbish. He shoved the thing back.

Then, next to the crusty green rock in a bowl on a stand, he saw what he'd been looking for. They were stones, but they were round, shiny stones, and the one he liked was speckledy like a hen, brown and pale yellow. He picked it up and held it in his palm.

'Do you like that?' Black Plaits was staring at him from behind the counter. 'That's leopard skin.'

'Leopard skin...?' He looked down at the stone.

'It's made from volcanic lava. See the small brown circular marks in the pattern? Those are the explosions of the hot lava.'

'How much?' It was cool in his palm and smooth.

'£5. Shall I wrap it?'

He wanted to hold it. The blond part of the leopard skin reminded him of Daisy's hair, but as he fished in his pocket for some change, she produced a small box lined with white crinkly paper and he let her place the stone inside. Her nails were silver like the bows. She found more paper – a deep green, matching the outside of the shop – and wrapped the box, so that it became a present.

He wasn't sure he wanted that. Perhaps the stone was for him, not Daisy. He bought the book on Tarot cards. It was only £3.50. For Pete, he thought. He could imagine Pete getting into all that. Wouldn't like it for himself. Didn't like to think about the future. Happy where he was... mostly.

Black Plaits put the present and book into a bag and handed it to him. She had green eyes inside a ring of black eyeliner. 'Who's it for?' The bows bobbed. 'Someone's lucky!'

He smiled and saw the smile repeated on her face. She fancies me, he thought. 'Would *you* like it?'

'Get on with you. It's yours.'

'Come for a drink.' *Want a beer?* The refrain ran through his head – it seemed easy asking her. There was a pub a few doors down.

She shook her head. 'Got to mind the shop,' but she was putting out a silver nailed hand so that it nearly reached the patch on the sleeve of his leather jacket. 'Try me again. Sundays. Finish early. Five.'

He grinned and nodded and sauntered out of the shop, thinking of her hand inches away from his jacket and knowing she was looking at him. He bought soap for Ma, and Shirley (why not, he told himself?) and the usual bottle of whisky for Dad, and then on a whim – it was winter for fuck sake – bought himself a black coat from Oxfam.

Coats went into the Mail and Communications room but there wasn't a place to call your own, and nowhere to keep anything. Even the hook you hung coats on was shared by the other editorials. There was a message desk on each floor, but it was a public desk, a convening point as Steve called it. Steve had instituted trays for editorials. 'Not for rubbish. For information that I want you to read, learn and inwardly digest. But first you check in the communications book for priority messages!' How often had Jon heard him say that?

On Monday morning he stuffed the little square present into the depths of his Oxfam coat pocket and pushed his newspaper on top. Didn't put Steve past rummaging through his pockets. On Monday evening the present was still in his pocket. It had made the journey to the City and back on a special delivery job, and then done the sandwich trip at lunch time. He'd worn his coat as he pushed the trolley round the floors; his hand checking it was still there in the pocket. Sweat was breaking through his layers of clothes making him glad Daisy's desk was empty. He paused there a moment, imagining the little green present sitting next to her sandwiches, waiting for her return. Mid-afternoon, he saw her bent over her computer gazing into the screen, but by then his coat – and the thing inside – was back in the Mail and Communications room. She was tugging her fingers through her hair, pulling it into a knot, twisting round the yellow stretchy band. He could no more have approached her than written the thing she was typing. Her hands flew to the keys for a second, words growing on the screen, and then lifted and went back to her hair.

On Tuesday, making sure Steve wasn't lurking behind one of the machines, Jon transferred the present from his coat to his trouser pocket. Ready for the off. *Carpe diem*! Pete's face when Jon had used that expression. '*Carpe diem*, Jon! Anyone would think you had an education!' He loved it when Pete looked at him like that and said those things, and certainly wasn't going to tell him that he'd got it off the DVD of '*Dead Poet's Society*'. Seize the day! He glanced down at his bulging trouser pocket and fished out the present – it looked as if he was getting a hard on.

He stood over Steve as he sat at his desk in his little office off the main room. 'Steve, give me some typing to do.'

Steve's head jerked up, beady eyes under sticking-out eyebrows. 'What…?'

'I want to type.'

'You think you want a computer, don't you?'

'I didn't say that. I said...' Why did Steve make him feel small, even sitting down, even with his old man eyebrows.

Steve's head swung back to his PC 'Editorials don't type.'

'I could do things for you, Steve.'

'I'm paid to get the work done, not train you. It's that Martha Morgan, isn't it?'

'Wha– ?'

'She put you up to this.'

'It's nothing to do with her. I want to help.' The bugger was standing up and moving over to a filing cabinet and pulling out a drawer. Jon took a step nearer. 'I can type with two fingers. I can help you!'

Steve's stooped shoulders bent over the filing drawer. But now he turned, resting his arm across the drawer, and nodded. 'Alright. I'll try you. But you'll have to prove yourself. Prove you can save me time.' His eyes were looking in the wrong direction as if there was someone else he was talking to, and Jon nearly looked round to see who it was.

'Hey!' Steve patted Jon on the shoulder less than twenty-four hours later. 'You want to hang around today. Free drinks! Features floor. All your mates. Six o'clock.'

They had all had a few by then, the three of them, Steve, Gerry and himself, down in the pub at lunchtime, packed in with the docklands' office population getting pissed, the flashing lights on a miniature silver Christmas tree reminding Jon of his own success with the foyer Christmas tree lights. 'You an electrician?' Gerry had asked him, and Steve had congratulated him. He hadn't bothered to tell anyone that it was no more than a loose wire in an old plug.

'You up to typing the working rota for Christmas?' Steve stretched his hand towards the PC in the Mail and Communications room that same afternoon.

'Yeah, okay.'

'Right.' He lifted the cover off the keyboard and turned on the computer. 'First, you check each floor and find out who's covering, which day and when. Then you type the list which I'll want to check, then you make copies and then you circulate them. And when you're good enough you can circulate them by email.'

Patronising git, but at least he was letting him do it.

For the second time that day he felt his shoulder tapped and had Steve's red face grinning at him. 'You've got two hours. If you time it right you might get a free drink on the Features Floor.' It had to be the beer talking.

He started with the Features Floor and wandered about trying to find the right person to ask in *Health* and then in *Books*. No one seemed to be around. Doris in *Obits* told him to ask Martha Morgan's secretary. 'Always ask the secretaries. They do the lists.' But Martha Morgan's secretary wasn't at her desk – Sue her name was, wasn't it? He'd not had much to do with her. Luckily he didn't have to ask Purple Hair. She wasn't there either. Getting ready for the party perhaps. He moved down to the News Floor where a story was breaking. By the time he got to the PC it was nearly six. He'd done typing at school and had used a keyboard at Motsuki Pharmaceuticals to type out the orders but his fingers felt fat and clumsy. He hit the wrong keys and had to work out the delete button and where the cursor needed to be.

'This list's for Security, man! Names begin with capital letters!' Steve came behind him and put his hands over Jon's. 'See here – press that down. And now type the letter. Keep it pressed...!'

It was twenty to seven and he'd only typed the eight names from the News Floor and three from Features.

'Oh, forget it now.' Steve clutched the mouse in his hand. 'You've got the names from the floors? I'll type it tomorrow.' He closed the file and pressed *No* to the *Save?* question.

'I thought I had to circulate the list –'

'Too late.'

'I can type it tomorrow'.

'You'll have other duties tomorrow. We've got to sort out yours and Gerry's rota over Christmas. Hadn't thought of that, had you?'

He could have killed him.

They had turned off the lights on the Features Floor and he lingered by the photograph files in the darkness, hearing the buzz of voices in the distance while he tried to think of an excuse for being there. Any last minute errands? Any evening deliveries? Sod it. He got into one of the aisles and leaned his head against the cold metal partition between the hanging files.

'Is that Jon?'

He lifted his head and looked down the aisle.

'You're not still working, are you?' It was Matthew from

Obits. He liked Matthew. He always noticed what had been done for him, always turned his head away from the screen or paused in his conversation to thank him. 'I was just off for a piss. We're over in the Book corner. Go up there and help yourself.'

Jon emerged from the aisle and Matthew took his arm. 'Come on, I'll get you one.'

So many people... clatter of voices... shrieks of laughter. There was a table of empty bottles – wine, no beer – oh yes, a can on its side. Dirty glasses were everywhere.

'Hi, Jon!'

'Hello Liza.'

There was Purple Hair, and Sue, and Tony... Matthew was handing him a glass of wine.

'Thanks.'

Matthew smiled at someone else and glanced back. 'Plenty more where that came from. There's some crisps if you're hungry, or there were...'

Where was Daisy? He thought of what was still in his coat pocket. He could hear Martha Morgan's voice. It was boiling. There were too many people. He'd never get in amongst that lot. He gulped down some wine, concentrating on the effect – a sharpness raw in his throat. There was a bowl of crisps on one of the filing cabinets. He stuffed some into his mouth and swilled the bits round with another mouthful of wine.

'Enjoying yourshelf?' Purple Hair appeared in front of him, lifting her glass at a steep angle, wine slopping over the edge. 'Happy Chrishmash, Jon!'

He raised his own glass and laughed. Pissed – he could cope with that.

Her eyes quivered in their sockets. 'Daisy's shlipped out...' She tipped up her chin and then leaned away from him. 'I need...' He caught her arm before she toppled backwards. 'Toilet... I think...'

He removed her glass and shifted her round the edge of the

crowd to a chair against a filing cabinet and pushed her into it.

'Doing a good job there.' Martha Morgan was behind him.

He kept his hold on Purple Hair, gripping her shoulders. 'Would you like me to find someone who could take you to the toilet?' Purple Hair's eyelids were closing. Her head lolled back and hit the filing cabinet with a soft thud but her eyes didn't open again.

'She'll be alright. Where's *your* glass?' Martha Morgan was all in black tonight, the fitted V-neck top showing up her boobs.

'I'm OK.' He wanted a beer. He glanced over people's heads. Not a sign of a blonde head. She was blonde, wasn't she? She was the blonde part of the leopard skin lava stone.

'Jon, I don't think you'll get anywhere with Steve.'

'Wha– I mean, pardon?' He looked back down at her. There were beads of sweat on her forehead. His own head felt hot. He tucked his hair behind his ears.

'The computer – the PC you asked about.'

'Oh...' For a second he saw Daisy's long, pale fingers on the keys and words growing on the screen, and then his own when he got better at it.

'I don't think there will be any old ones that you could have free.'

'Actually, I think I'm going to be alright. Steve's letting me type–'

But she had her hand on his arm and then someone shoved past him from behind and suddenly he was up against her, his hair brushing the side of her face. He had to put his other arm round her, to stop her from falling... warm body, those boobs... several seconds like that, and then she stepped back, swaying a little.

He felt unsteady himself. 'Fuck – sorry...'

'It's alright...' Her hand clung to his and felt warm and quite large. 'What I wanted to say is that we have a PC at home. My husband's... you can have it.'

'Wha' – your husband's PC?'

She nodded. 'He's getting a new one. After Christmas I'll arrange for you to come and have a look.'

His hand was released and she swerved away pushing through the crowd. Martha Morgan's husband's PC... Over the heads he saw the unmistakable blonde hair pulled back into a red band. This was turning out to be his day.

'Hello Daisy.'

'Hi!' Light voice. She was pissed too.

'I've been looking for you.' *He* must be pissed, saying that. 'Want a beer?' He meant to say *want a drink*, but the other phrase had been so much in his head.

There were tiny wrinkles round her eyes. 'No thanks.'

And now – he couldn't believe it – her large eyes were swimming, the blue floaty in the white. Pieces of her hair had come out of the red band and looked darker where it stuck to her cheeks. Something about a story on child prostitutes... her voice kept breaking up. She clasped his arm, seeming glad he was there. 'Do you think I can really call it...' she sniffed, *'Christmas Presents?'*

'Wha'...?' He thought of the little box in his coat pocket.

'Christmas presents. The pimps offer them – these children, as Christmas presents...' He would have offered her his handkerchief if it hadn't been covered in newsprint and God knows what else. She grabbed a wine-soaked paper napkin and thrust it to her nose, her eyes looking at something behind him. He turned – Eva, from *Health* (veggie sandwiches and herbal tea) chatting to Peter from *Books* and not even looking their way – he turned back.

She blew her nose. 'What I'd really like...' The whites of her eyes were red – how long had she been crying? 'is... a coffee.'

A coffee? He'd only thought of a beer. 'Isn't it a bit late for a–?'

'In the kitchen. We can make some.' She grabbed his hand

and pulled him through the crowd. And then they were out of it and she was stopping at her desk, saying she needed to check her emails. She jiggled the mouse and bent over her computer, her sparkly, gold top riding up her back so that he could see her skin.

The screen lit up and she pressed the icon with her name on it. 'I hate you!'

He wasn't certain she'd said it. He was concentrating on her thin pale fingers on the mouse, her short rounded nails, and regretting the disappearance of her bare flesh as she sat down and pulled her chair up to the screen. He moved up behind her and saw the list of emails.

She clicked on an message from David Gould. Subject: Us. Her head was in the way. He couldn't read the words in the message, only hear her say, 'I hate you!' clear as a bell the second time.

In the kitchen, she let him make her a coffee and lend her his handkerchief; too bad whatever it was covered in. All that stuff about child prostitutes was crap. She was crying about David Gould, whoever he was. He banged his mug down on the draining board. Her hands clutching the mug gave a quivery jerk. He couldn't bear to look at her pale fingers round the mug. He hadn't asked her for that drink, dithering over a silly present he hadn't given her. She wouldn't want it.

Her eyes were wide, and swimming again. 'Put your arms round me – please...'

It was a shoulder to cry on, and fuck all else probably, but she was soft and warm, and her hair smelt of shampoo – the sort in the adverts that made him think of her. His arms were around her and he didn't want more. He wouldn't have known what to do with her. With Purple Hair, yeah... Or with Black Plaits from that New Age place. Or even with Shirley, bless her cotton socks. But not with Daisy. In this brightly-lit office kitchen with it's shiny, aluminium sink and draining board, better at the moment than any pub or café, this was enough, this and all the other things about today – keyboards, words, computers… Steve was letting him type… Martha Morgan was going to give him a computer. His future was spreading out in front of him – a future. This would see him through Christmas and right into the New Year.

NINE

GRANT

'Why aren't you staying with us? Will we see you and Grant?'

'We'll come and see you during the day.'

'Will you come for Christmas Day?'

'Of course, darling.'

The word *darling* seemed to come naturally, though Martha didn't use it for anyone else; certainly not for himself. He could see the child warming to the endearment, drawing nearer to Martha and reaching for her hand.

'You'll have to come, Martha, otherwise you won't have a Christmas tree.'

'Can we share yours, Becky?'

The child had been determined to accompany them to 'find their cottage', as she put it, jumping up and down in front of her mother and tugging at her jersey. 'Please, can I go with them? Please!'

Kathleen had pushed away the small hands. 'Becky!' She had handed over the keys, raising her eyebrows at Martha and himself. 'You sure you wouldn't like a cup of something first?'

'Please Mummy!'

'Shush Becky, you'll wake Will! Ciss is going to be home soon. Martha and Grant will be back for supper. You'll see them then.'

But Kathleen had glanced at Martha, and Martha had nodded, smiling. 'Let her come. That's fine.'

Kids. He wasn't sure he was going to stand it. They had avoided Martha's brother and family for the last few Christmases but for some reason had thought they could manage it this time. 'They're my nephew and nieces,' Martha had said. 'I want to manage it.' They were sitting at the kitchen table and he'd felt too anxious to say, why now, Martha? It makes no sense. It's just the time when we *shouldn't* be going. And then he'd thought: perhaps she's put it behind her; perhaps this visit is part of that. They never went for Christmas when they were trying for a child; now they had stopped trying she wanted to go. Thank heaven they were twelve miles away, though he didn't believe the story that there was nowhere to hire over Christmas except for a 'friend's' weekend cottage on an exposed part of the Vale of Pewsey, half a mile up the road from the canal and the railway line.

They could have had a nap or explored the narrow country lanes in the fading winter light or gone in search of the canal towpath, if Martha hadn't agreed to let her niece come with them. She was being pulled upstairs by her, to go and explore the bedroom. He couldn't remember them getting on so well.

'I'm not supposed to tell you,' the small voice echoed up the stairwell. 'We made some Christmas decorations for your cottage, but then you arrived a day early and we didn't have time to put them up.'

He moved into the kitchen and stared out of the window. A ragged lawn was scattered with dead leaves and bordered by a wooden fence. Beyond, lines of dark ploughed field sloped away to the west where a crack of yellow light gleamed through the grey sky. A swing hung from a branch of a tree – a beech tree probably from the smoothness of its bark; he wasn't good at identifying trees without their leaves. He turned away and opened the fridge, which was full of milk and cans of beer, a bottle of wine, butter, cheese, a sliced white loaf... clearly Martha hadn't told them they were bringing food. He banged the door closed and went out to the car to fetch in their own provisions.

A grey mist was lifting off the ground. He buttoned up his jacket and opened the boot, longing suddenly for the crisp, white winters of New England. He shivered as he got indoors and shut the door. He wondered if he could smell damp. He checked the radiators downstairs. Warm but not boiling. Pray it wouldn't get too cold. Poor insulation probably. Kathleen must have come over specially to switch on the radiators and fill the fridge.

It was meant to have been a couple of nights, and then Martha had come home saying she was going to take the week off and suggesting they spend four or five days in Wiltshire. She'd covered for the last few Christmases, she needed a break. Liza was in charge; it was easy to keep in touch.

He dumped the box of food on to the draining board. The crack of light in the west had vanished and already it seemed darker. There was a creak of boards from above and the murmur of his wife's voice. He couldn't hear the child's.

Two days earlier he'd rung the IVF clinic and asked about the procedures for couples considering donor sperm, and had been told there was a compulsory counselling session for both partners. He'd wanted to use the words *donor insemination*, but if Martha was secretly finding out about going ahead, it would be donor sperm that she would be requesting.

'You're married, are you?' came the voice, tactfully not asking his name for which he was grateful. 'Well then, the compulsory meeting with the counsellor would have to be attended by yourself, as legal father, and your wife, as recipient and legal mother.'

So couples would have to go together. Of course, they would. There were bound to be checks, legalities. There were huge issues. He should know this more than most. His anxiety had stopped him thinking. If, in the unlikely event, Martha followed this course, she would have to approach him first. They would have to go together.

Feeling easier, he'd switched off his phone and put it on answer, and attended to his next patient, Christine Mirado, arriving for her second appointment.

The older child had returned by the time they got back to Philip and Kathleen's house that evening and she stood in the doorway lit up by the hall light while they got out of the car.

'Ciss! Ciss!' Becky ran towards her. 'I've been to Martha's cottage!'

Ciss ignored her younger sister and walked sedately across the gravel, her shoes crunching on the little stones, holding her hand out to Martha as if that is what she had been told to do.

He watched Martha bend down and scoop the child into her arms. She held her tight and swung her round. He could see the child screwing up her eyes under her dark fringe, and once she was lowered to the ground she scampered away. He put out an arm to his wife wanting to protect her. But Becky had come back outside and was taking her hand, and Philip was in the doorway fielding his older daughter. 'Whoa, Ciss!' Philip caught her and she buried her head into his waist and he whispered something in her ear. Slowly she looked round and stared at the ground. 'Would you like to come and see the Christmas tree?' The shy one, Grant remembered, in spite of being the oldest. Martha should have remembered that.

Kathleen emerged from the kitchen with William on her hip and they went past the safety gate at the foot of the stairs and into the large sitting room to view the tree. All the decorations had been made by the children, including the purple and red tinsel. William had helped to make the play dough ball which the girls had sprayed with silver. A gold star hung over a crib on a table in the window. Philip had constructed the stable and the crib in his workshop. Kathleen and the children had rolled and shaped the clay figures on the kitchen table, and they had been fired in the primary school oven. 'Family enterprise,' Philip grinned at Kathleen and squeezed her shoulder. 'Our primary school teacher.'

Grant looked to Martha for her reaction, but she was kneeling by the table to inspect the crib, and letting Becky climb on to her back. He saw her arm reach behind and shift up the child, her broad fingers splayed across the small bottom. The gesture made him want her suddenly. 'Put your arms round my neck,' he heard her say. The small, fair-haired head nestled next to Martha's dark, grey-flecked one. Martha wasn't usually so physical with the children. She stood up, holding the child in a piggy back and twisted her round into her arms and tossed her on to the sofa. There was a pause and then the child burst into cackles of laughter. For a second he saw himself on the sands at Cape Cod throwing Christopher up into the air and catching him, up into the air...

'Martha...!' It was Philip.

Ciss had turned away from the crib and was running towards Martha. She stopped and looked at her father, colour seeping into her face.

Martha lifted her head to her brother, laughing. 'You don't mind, do you?'

'Yes. But you'll have to give Ciss one, and Will too probably.' He raised his eyebrows at Grant, his mouth smiling but not his eyes. 'What's got into your wife?'

Grant grinned at his brother-in-law, willing the man's expression to soften. The tension was probably about them not staying. The children were queuing up for the new game.

'Careful of the fireplace!' Philip placed his large frame in front of it although the fire wasn't lit and there was a huge fireguard. Eventually, Martha flopped on to the sofa and let them tumble on top of her, and he pulled them off. 'Enough now. Enough.'

'Tell you what,' Martha shifted herself to the edge of the sofa, panting. 'Why don't you all come over to us for supper tomorrow?'

Grant saw Kathleen look at Philip.

'Don't be silly, Martha.' Philip crouched down to pick up William without looking at her. 'Tomorrow's Christmas Eve.'

'Silly?' Martha blinked and flushed slightly.

Becky was grabbing her father's free hand, as he stood up.

'Father Christmas comes on Christmas Eve.'

Ciss hung back, glaring at Becky through her dark fringe. 'Do you believe in Father Chr–'

'Ciss!' Philip and Kathleen said it together and then looked at each other and laughed as if at a private joke. Philip handed William to Kathleen and spread out his arms. 'Bed, you lot!'

'No, Daddy! Please, no...!'

'Bed!'

'Come for lunch, then.'

Philip swivelled round and stood in the doorway, a big, easy-going man normally. 'Martha, it's all been organised!' He was shaking his head. 'You have no idea, have you? No idea the work that–'

'Phil...' Kathleen's hand caught his arm.

Kathleen sat down next to Martha on the sofa, holding the little boy like a barrier between them. 'It's very kind of you, Martha, but my parents arrive tomorrow.'

'They could come too.'

'Martha...' Grant heard his own voice. He spoke as gently as he could. Her eyes were filling although no one else seemed to notice. 'Let them come after Christmas day, huh?'

Kathleen kissed the side of the baby's head. 'My father's beginning to lose his memory. He gets confused. It's better if we stay here.'

Ciss stood by her mother's knee, steady eyes on Martha. 'Granddad can't remember our names. He even forgot Mummy's.'

Becky pushed in from behind Ciss, bumping against Martha's knees, to add her contribution. 'He called me *William*!'

The heating had gone off by the time they got back to the cottage. He switched it on again and followed Martha up to the cold bedroom. He closed the curtains and pulled her towards him and reached under her layers of clothes for her skin, wanting her badly now, wanting to soothe away the effects of her family – hoping that was what it was – but not certain that he was gauging it right. He slowed himself down and asked her if he should go and find a heater to warm her up – there surely would be one in that utility room at the back of the cottage. She shook her head and they undressed quickly and got in under the duvet. He turned her away from him – she seemed to want that, and she was quickly aroused. He went in from behind, going in deep, but then he withdrew and she lay back and he worked down her body with his tongue, taking his time. He sucked her away until her hips jumped off the bed in little tight leaps. Her back arched and she gave a long shuddering sigh.

He moved up on to her body for his turn, but now she was crying in heavy, jerking sobs. It made him go limp. He got up and fetched the box of tissues from the bathroom and tried to hold her. She was howling, worse than all those times with the IVF failures. Now we're going to talk, he thought.

She wiped her nose with the back of her hand. He gave her a tissue and propped up the pillows behind her. She dabbed at her nose and pressed the tissue against her mouth as if to stifle what might come out.

'Martha – what is it?'

'I – don't know.'

'You do.'

'My – my brother…'

'Your brother?'

'It could be… there's so much.'

'What for Christ's sake?'

'I – I don't know.'

'It's the kids, isn't it?'

Her shoulders lifted convulsively.

He removed the damp tissue from her hand. 'We don't need to stay. We can go home.'

Her head shook. 'I like them. I love Becky.' She took another tissue. Her head was shaking. She sniffed and swallowed. 'Normally Phil's so…'

'What, Martha?'

'Comforting.'

'Comforting?'

'He's the… only family… but today–'

'Today, he was verging on the rude.'

Her eyes filled again. He put an arm round her. She pulled away. 'It's the Christmas thing. They're done in with organising Christmas.' She blew her nose and took a deep breath. 'It'll be alright.'

'What will be alright?'

'Everything.'

'Everything?'

'Leave it, Grant.'

'I can't. You've started donor insemination.'

'What…?'

'That's what it is. Isn't it?' He knew it wasn't. They had to go together for the compulsory counselling session.

She leaned against the pillows her bloodshot eyes not focussing.

He wanted to shake her. 'Martha…?'

'No…' So quietly.

'You're going to, though?'

'No.' She pulled up the duvet. 'It's freezing. Do you think there will be hot water for a bath?'

'Martha, do you promise?'

She bent her knees to her chest and tucked the duvet round her shoulders. 'Oh, for God's sake… of course.'

TEN

MARTHA

He was looking at her across the small, round, wooden table. 'You okay?'

She nodded. It was odd sitting in the unfamiliar kitchen with its window looking out onto the bare, wintry countryside. She shivered, as if the raw, rainy day could get indoors.

He sipped his tea. 'Sure?'

Her eyes felt swollen and tight. He'd made such a fuss last night. As if her crying could be about one thing, as if it was as simple as that. She put down her mug of coffee, got up and went over to his side of the table and kissed the smooth, shiny top of his head. 'Thanks for putting up with me.'

His hand went round her waist. 'As long as you're okay.'

'Mmm...' The warmth of his arm radiated through her jersey. She leaned against him, feeling him there, solidly there, however she might behave.

He glanced up at her. 'Do we have to go to your brother's today?'

She smiled, happier suddenly. 'Oh, I think so.'

'Why?'

'You heard Phil on the subject of Christmas Eve!'

'We could have a day on our own. Go find a pub. Go find a country house, a country estate.'

She laughed. 'Country houses won't be open on Christmas Eve. We must go to Philip and Kathleen's.'

'Why?'

'We must...' She loosened his hand and walked over to the sink and stared out through the rain-spattered window. The clouds seemed to cut off the horizon, shortening the length of the ploughed field which stretched forever yesterday afternoon, the glimpse she had seen of it before being pulled indoors by Becky. She felt a wave of sadness from last night. She'd loved it that Becky wanted to come with them to the cottage. She'd loved all three children wanting to join in her game of being thrown on the sofa, in spite of Philip; loved all three of them wanting her to read them a bedtime story.

Grant was behind her. She concentrated on the feel of his lips and the scratchy feel of his chin against the base of her neck as he kissed her. An arm came round her shoulder and he squeezed her to him. She thought he might suggest they return upstairs.

'We shouldn't have come, Martha.'

She patted his hand. 'It's all right.'

'It's not.'

She removed his arm and turned to face him. 'Are you really suggesting we should go home?'

'God knows.' He shook his head. The deep line was in his forehead.

'Phil usually makes me feel okay.'

'What...?'

She nodded.

He stared at her. 'How does Phil make you feel okay?'

Her shoulders lifted. 'He's on my side, somehow.' She avoided his intense eyes. 'Yesterday he wasn't.'

'I'm on your side, Martha.'

Her hand brushed his arm. 'I didn't mean...'

He turned away and sat down again.

They compromised that day, phoned Philip and Kathleen and said they would join them in the early evening for drinks and Christmas Eve supper.

That night Martha woke from a dream.

She was in a car driving along a straight road, telegraph poles flashing by the passenger window. Daddy was at the wheel. She longed to slide along the bench seat so that there was no gap between them. The longing was like magic. The road curved and he turned the wheel. She fell against him…

The motion seemed to wake her. It was very black. There was something heavy. The duvet was over her face. She pushed it away, searching for light, the window. Grant was breathing next to her. The air in the room was cold.

But it wasn't a dream. She could remember driving with Daddy in the car with the bench seat, and the feeling. She could remember the pale square of the window in the darkened room, her hand in Daddy's.

Think about Becky, she muttered into the duvet, pulling it up around her. Ciss, William, Phil – no, not Philip… too close. Think about home. She mouthed the instructions to herself. Think about work – Tony, Liza, Jon… yes, messenger Jon. Think about the fact that you like him. He takes your mind off things. Makes you think he's looking after you. At the office party you were crushed against him and felt what it was like to have his arms around you. You wanted to stay there, not move. You held his hand. Warm, dry skin. Larger hand than Grant's. When did you last hold another man's hand? The next day you were on your way back from the Ladies and you saw him near the lifts. You chased after him to remind him about the computer, to remind him about the invitation to come to your house on a Saturday in the New Year…

Her mind moved on. She switched on her torch, wedged it under her pillow and reached for her book.

They had to have tea and cut the cake, Kathleen explained as they finished the Christmas Day walk along the top of the downs under grey, lowering clouds, and started to round up the children. Yes, in spite of the huge lunch. She pulled off her blue woolly hat – a present from one of the children – and stuffed it into the pocket of her fleece, and clicked the central locking. Thankfully it hadn't rained, and look, there was the glimmering of a sunset. It was so important to keep traditions for the children, didn't Martha agree? After tea there would be carols round the tree and one last present for the children, and then with this bribe, hopefully, bed. The adults could relax with the remains of the claret, or maybe a whisky or a liqueur, and flop in front of Christmas TV, or chat. Kathleen's parents, Lionel and Peggy, were sure to go up by nine-thirty. And then everyone could really relax. Kathleen seemed determined to stress the need to relax, in spite of her own activity, which hadn't ceased all day.

As they gathered in the kitchen to sit round the large rectangular table, Lionel pushed past his wife to claim a chair next to Martha.

'Lionel!' his wife grabbed his arm. 'Leave her.'

'It's all right,' Martha turned to her.

'But he–'

'It's all right.' The look on Peggy's face made her add. 'I like him.' She meant it, he had sat next to her at Christmas lunch with his bland, rather sweet face and disconnected chatter, a wonderful antidote to the precision of Kathleen's day.

'What do you do?' This question again. He stared at her through his glasses.

'I'm an editor.'

'An editor?'

She went through the routine. 'Of a newspaper.'

'The Editor?'

Kathleen's head lifted. 'Dad, you've asked that!'

Martha kept her eyes on his. 'No, the features editor.'

'Not in the hot seat?' It came out quickly.

'No...'

'Not responsible for crises.'

'That's right.' It hadn't gone like this before. He seemed capable of an ordinary conversation, his face alert. He was nodding, eyes on hers. She smiled at him. 'We interpret the crises. Find the interesting bits.'

97

'Analyse.' Again, the word was snapped out, as if he had to get it out quickly. Someone laughed. Ciss was saying something. William spat out his Christmas cake.

Martha bent nearer to the old man to try to keep out the interruptions. His hand was on her arm. She placed her hand on top of it. 'Not so much analyse, more... finding what's going to appeal, what's going to sell the paper...' But she'd lost him. His gaze turned towards Kathleen who was wiping William's face and lifting him out of the highchair. Becky clung to William's hand and looked up at her. 'Martha, we can get down now. Will you come with us to the tree? We've got one more present.' William slipped out of her grasp and landed on his bottom and started to cry. Lionel's head whipped round, 'What's that!' His head swung from side to side.

'Pick William up,' Philip called across the table. 'Pick him up!'

Martha lifted the small boy on to her lap and the crying stopped. She could feel damp coming through her skirt. The old man put a hand to his ear as if he couldn't believe the silence. He turned towards the two of them. 'Is he yours?'

She shook her head, catching Grant's eye for a second, and then Philip's. The child leaned forward and knocked the plate and half-eaten cake on to Lionel's lap. He whipped round and smacked the small hand. 'Bad boy! Bad boy!'

Kathleen was behind them. 'Dad, stop it!'

But it was too late. The child was bawling and the old man's face seemed to deflate into jagged lines of pain.

Martha heard Grant's voice instructing her to stand up and take the child away.

She moved out of the kitchen and headed for the sitting room, William squirming in her arms, the noise in her ears. The piles of opened presents had been cleared away and there was not a trace of wrapping paper – the room looked as if it had been hoovered. She made for the tree, thinking to distract him with the lights.

Becky followed her. 'William stop crying!' Her small hand reached for one of his and waggled it up and down. 'Stop it, William!'

Martha held the child tight. Left side, against her heart. Heartbeat and babies, wasn't that soothing? Not with toddlers perhaps.

Philip was behind her. 'Here let me have him.'

She turned slowly. 'I want to hold him.'

He laughed. 'You sure?'

'I wouldn't have said it if I didn't mean it.' She patted the child's back, rocking on her feet slightly. It seemed to quieten him. 'What's the matter, Phil?'

Becky was tugging at his arm. 'Daddy... Daddy, when are we going to have our last present?'

'The matter –? Shush, Becky –'

'But, Daddy...'

'Becky, I'm talking. Go and find out from Mummy.' He gave her a little push and she ran out of the room.

Martha swayed. The child's head rested on her shoulder. 'Is it the cottage?' She wished he would look at her.

He picked up a stray piece of cellophane from the sofa that had missed the clear up and scrunched it in his hands. 'You haven't been here for ages, and you can't even stay with us.'

'We thought it would make it easier.'

'No you didn't.' He chucked the cellophane into the fireplace. 'I'll take William.' He reached out his hands and the child stretched his arms to him.

She handed him over. 'We've been trying to have a baby!'

His head turned.

But she was out of the room, making for the stairs and heading for the loo farthest away from everybody. He was so harsh. The word 'harsh' made her blink. She sat down on the loo, tore off some paper and blew her nose. She mustn't cry.

Phil was usually so comforting, she'd said to Grant. Why did it feel so fucking sad? She tore off more paper, stood up and flushed the loo. Her face in the mirror as she washed her hands looked doughy, eyes pink. She rubbed her fingers over her skin and bent nearer her reflection. There were little lines where she hadn't seen them before – a small, bent one on her chin, and a faint vertical one running from the corner of her nose to her top lip. Philip probably thought she was too old to have kids.

When she came downstairs a candle was lit and placed on the mantelpiece. Lionel had fallen asleep on the sofa. The main lights were turned off and the rest of them circled the tree and held hands and sang *Away in a Manger* and *Once in Royal David's City*. William tottered round with them, giggling with delight. She could feel Philip looking at her. Don't get kind now, she thought.

She found herself in the kitchen and started to unload the dishwasher. He came through the door as she lifted out a stack of plates and took them from her, his eyes steadying on her. 'Martha…'

She bent over the machine. 'I'm all right!'

'Doesn't sound like it.'

What would you know? But she couldn't say it. She straightened up. He was piling the plates into a high cupboard, out of the children's reach; everything was child proof. His hands lowered. He seemed about to say something, touch her. She swallowed. Tears were coming again. But Kathleen appeared and told him she was going to take her parents upstairs and settle them for the night, and he followed her out of the door. 'Is the gate still across the stairs? Don't want your father kicking up about that.' They laughed. Martha heard them kiss and murmur something else, and then they both went away.

She emptied the rest of the dishwasher and placed the contents on the table: the smart plates, white with a gold rim, that Kathleen's mother didn't think should go in the dishwasher; the different sized glasses for the champagne and the red wine; the girls' china Beatrix Potter mugs that they had been allowed to have weak tea in; William's plastic beaker... she opened a few drawers looking for somewhere to put the knives and forks.

Once the children were in bed, Philip lit the fire and flopped onto one of the sofas, feet up on a stool. Martha curled up on the other sofa in the corner, Grant in the armchair opposite. Philip's and Grant's Port '98 shone in their glasses, a deep brick red. Martha sipped at a sparkling water and stared at the Christmas tree with its gaudy coloured lights chosen by the children. The fire heated the side of her face.

Grant's face looked flushed. He nodded and smiled at Philip. 'I'm really enjoying myself.' He made it sound as if he wasn't expecting to. 'It's been a great day. I want to thank both you and Kathleen.' His glass was raised.

Kathleen appeared in the doorway. 'You're not going yet, are you?'

He laughed. 'Not unless you'd like us to.'

'Of course not.' Philip lifted his feet off the stool and reached for the bottle. 'Have some port, darling.'

She was laughing too, reaching out to touch his arm. 'Not for me, remember?' They smiled at each other.

He turned towards Martha, grinning. 'Come on, Martha. Change your mind. It's delicious.'

She shook her head. He'd forgotten already.

The weather became colder on Boxing Day and on another walk the clouds split open into a crimson sky, causing Becky to run on ahead shouting that the clouds were on fire, Ciss chasing after her.

Martha felt a hand on her arm and looked round thinking it would be Lionel frightened by Becky's shouts. But it was Phil standing by William in his buggy, pulling up the collar of his jacket against the cold. He was a large man now, his face jowly – she could see he might have gravitas as the head of the comprehensive.

'Tomorrow I thought we might have a day together.' He nodded, his eyes kinder today. 'Visit Mum's grave. Go for a walk.'

'Visit Mum's grave?' She felt the urge to giggle.

'It's the anniversary. Remember?'

'Phil, I don't remember those things.'

'Of course, how silly of me.' He grinned and touched her arm, lighter suddenly, and started to push the buggy. The others were catching up with the girls, Lionel trailing behind. 'It would be nice to go together.'

'What about Kathleen and the children?'

'Peggy will help Kathleen.'

They've agreed to this, she thought. They know and feel sorry for me. Lionel was tottering back towards them. Peggy hadn't wanted him to go on the walk, suggesting a rest or a bit of telly. They reached the old man and Martha pulled his arm through hers and covered his hand with her own, surprised at the warmth through the thin skin.

Philip adjusted William's hat, pulling it round his ears. He glanced at her. 'Are you on?'

She nodded, her eyes filling, and looked down at her hand covering Lionel's, not wanting Phil to see. 'Lionel', she patted the old man's hand. 'Shouldn't you be wearing gloves?'

The journey was short. Only four miles, Phil told her the next day as they drove up hill from Ham past the sign to Ham Spray farms. Ham Spray House didn't have a sign but was at the end of the long drive vanishing towards the downs. She'd never got to it, in spite of her attempts to write an article for the series *Literary Gardens*. Mummy had just moved to Inkpen and she'd stayed with her, but the owners of the house weren't keen on their literary predecessors.

He parked the car in the road near the approach to the church. She remembered the tall Queen Anne House above the church with the Le Nôtre garden. She'd searched for a literary connection to that garden after her failure with Ham Spray House. A few years later they had walked down the narrow tarmac slope from the lychgate following their mother's coffin, the coffin tilting. They had worried that the pall bearers weren't going to make it, laughing after the solemnity of the funeral. Giggles had hiccoughed out of her as they had straggled up the road they were trudging up now. She'd forgotten there were trees around the edge of the field. It didn't feel like a cemetery in the sharp sunlight with the rooks calling.

Gravestones were dotted about: a shiny, sparkly black one with a picture of a cross on an altar: *In loving memory of Dennis Robert Edwards;* next to it a smaller, marble one, pale and milky: *Susan Welsh, I love you always.* Mummy's was in the top corner near a tall tree by the fence.

They stood with the winter sun on their backs, their long shadows spreading across the grave, their breath visible in the cold air. She had a sense that Philip might be closing his eyes, or worse, muttering a prayer.

Joan Morgan
1929 – 199...

Grey-green moss grew on the stone covering some of the words.

She glanced at him. 'Thank God it's not black.'

'Granite. The most expensive.'

'Hideous.'

He laughed. 'Mum's is York stone. A mistake perhaps. I'll need to come and scrub it.'

'Do you do that?' But she looked away not wanting an answer. It felt ridiculous standing round the grave. She stuffed her fists into her coat pocket and glanced along the rows of graves, the sun flashing through a break in the trees that bordered the road making the sparkly bits glint. Up the slope beyond the fence there was a house – a weekend cottage probably. Daddy had been cremated. Mummy wanted a cosy graveyard in the village where she'd chosen to live and forget about the unpalatable parts of life with Daddy. 'Do you really come every year?'

'I try to.'

'Why?'

'Why…?'

'What for?'

'I like to think about them.' He stared at the stone, at their mother's name and dates comprising a chunk of the twentieth century. 'Don't you think about them?'

'Not if I can help it.'

'I don't believe that.'

'I said, not if I can help it.'

'You're angry, aren't you?'

'No.' The low sun had pushed through a gap in the trees. She shielded her eyes trying not to look at him.

He bent down and pulled out a couple of stiff dead weeds and stuffed them in his jacket pocket. 'You knew Mum found someone else?'

'Of course I knew.'

He smoothed the grass where he'd lifted the weeds and stood up and banged his hands together loosening the grains of earth. 'I wasn't sure.'

'The famous church outing to Hereford Cathedral. Everyone knew about Peter, except Daddy.'

He looked back at the gravestone and brushed the last grains of earth off his hands. 'Dad had you.'

'Sorry….?

He turned to her. 'He did, didn't he?'

She pulled her coat around her and folded her arms. 'I'm not good at this. Come on, it's freezing.'

'No, wait.' He held her arm. 'I used to be scared of you.

You and Dad.'

She laughed. 'Scared?'

'I got over it. Felt sorry for you. Being the star. Must have been hard.'

'Not really.' But for a second she wanted to lean against him, be held. The rooks cawed. There was a faint drone of farm machinery. A couple was entering the cemetery. She felt his hand go through her arm and they started to walk towards them.

'When I was small we – Mum and I – we thought you could cure him.'

'Cure him?'

'His moods. That's why I felt sorry for you.'

'I didn't though, did I?' The couple had reached a gravestone, two rows away. The girl wore an orange woollen hat pulled over her ears and a matching scarf. Martha quickened her pace. 'Come on. I need a drink.'

They found an empty table at the local pub and ordered some lunch. Martha clutched her glass of Heineken and sat back into the corner of the long wooden settle, glad to be away from the bar; the place was filling up.

Phil swallowed a mouthful of Guinness. 'It was depression, wasn't it? Though no one called it that. They didn't know how to deal with it.' He wiped the foam from his mouth. 'No wonder Mum needed a friend. Did you ever talk to her about Peter?'

'Not much.' An elderly man was sitting down opposite the small table at the other end of the settle. His bony, veined hand touched his wisps of grey hair, brushing it away from his forehead. She lifted her glass of Heineken.

'They met on that outing to Hereford Cathedral. I think their choir was singing there. Did you know he was married with young children?'

The food arrived. She waited for the barman to lower the plates of sausages and mash in front of them and then placed her glass on the table. 'Do you think he killed himself?'

Phil stuck a fork into a sausage and cut off a piece with his knife. 'What...Dad?'

'Yes.'

He shook his head. 'Of course not. It was an accident. He was well. He'd been well for years.'

'I know.'

'Have you been thinking that?'

'Not often. Grant questioned it years ago.'

'What the hell does he know?'

'God knows.'

He put down his knife and fork and reached his hand to her arm, his jowly face looking into hers. 'Martha, it was an accident.'

She let herself be persuaded to go for another of his walks. He smiled at her as they plodded along the road towards Ham in the dazzling light of the bright winter's afternoon, and she felt her mouth stretch in response. This is it, she could say to Grant. With Phil, like this, I feel okay. Feet on the ground, anchored – all those clichés. Daddy killed in an accident, ashes safely scattered, Mummy dead too. They turned off and took the track between wide fields under a cloudless sky, heading towards the downs. He pulled an Ordnance Survey map from his pocket and pointed to the path climbing the hill past Little Rivar Copse and the dew pond at the top. They would turn left along Gallows Down and go and look at Combe Gibbet. There was a legend about the gibbet. Based on a true story. Someone had made an amateur film about it and then become famous.

His hand came through her arm. 'We haven't talked about you.'

'No need.'

'Isn't there?'

'Not this afternoon.'

'Don't you want to talk?'

'We can't make babies. And they can't find out why.' She glanced at him.

He was looking ahead. 'Is there anything we can –?'

'No.'

'I'm so sorry.'

'Don't be! I hate that.'

The good feeling of a moment ago was evaporating into the cold, clear air. Her legs ached. They passed through a tunnel of overgrown hedgerow as the path approached the hill. She panted after him up the steep incline, unable to think of anything except placing one foot in front of the next, the distance between them increasing. He waited for her at the top. A light wind blew against her hot face. She undid her coat and reached for his arm feeling better once they were linked and were walking the last few hundred metres to the gibbet.

Half-way along he stopped. 'I don't know how I'm going to say this.' They had passed the dew pond in the dip and climbed through the fence and on to the path up on to the ridge. 'You'll have to know soon and I would rather be the one to tell you, but I wish it wasn't today. It's been such a good day. Kathleen's pregnant again.' He clasped her hand. 'I'm sorry, love. Sorry to have to tell you this...'

But she thought he'd been going to say something different...

Boiled eggs and toast soldiers on the blue, Formica-covered table with Phil and Mummy. A game of whist she doesn't want to play. The Archers mumbling in the background. The noise – a thud.

'You go, Martha,' her mother looks at her with her hot flustered look. 'You go and check'...

She released her hand from Phil's. Below, the view stretched to the horizon, a patchwork of fields and trees, houses dotted about – Inkpen probably, Shalbourne somewhere. The sky was a pale turquoise, streaks of cloud turning inky purple as they stood there. 'It's all right, Phil. Let's walk on.'

ELEVEN

GRANT

The ridge became more dramatic the further east he walked. It was like New England, the marine blue sky, the razor sharp light. He stopped to look at the clump of beeches that tumbled down the north side of the ridge, their trunks bathed in light reaching up to a canopy of bare branches, and longed suddenly to climb over the fence and get in amongst the trees and gaze up into their branches. But he pressed on letting the relief of being on his own in this light soak into him, the relief of knowing where Martha was and who she was with, her being with Philip adding to the quality of his relief.

She seemed to need something from her brother he hadn't been aware of before. But he was always watching her, making sure she was okay, checking her out. Let Philip do it for a day. He was tired of watching. The beech woods on his left broke off, the hill dropping down on to a wide ploughed field and a house in the distance. She might spill the beans, of course. He hadn't thought of that. He pictured Philip encouraging her to go solo, have a baby at all costs if that was what she wanted. If that happened he would leave her, move out, sell the house, move back to America. Whatever… wait and see… he didn't know.

'I need a break!' He spoke the words out loud and watched his breath turn from white to blue against the sky. Perhaps he could trust her – trust himself to trust her. He couldn't go away during the treatment but now he could and maybe that was what he needed. He walked faster and broke into a run, feeling lighter. He'd stopped jogging several years ago, but he ran revelling in the scenery. This was not New England or California but the ridge became higher, bolder, the light even sharper. The path dipped so that the view was hidden, skirting round a pond – a dew pond probably; Philip would know – and then rose again so that it was on the apex of the ridge and there were views on both sides. He reached the gibbet on its mound and flopped down gasping for breath and then shifted himself nearer the odd structure and leaned his back against its vertical pole.

One thing he did want, which would unsettle Martha, was to get on with the book on fathers. He thought of his own father, lecturer of history rising to professor, taking the family from one university city to another – Houston, Denver, New Haven, Boston, New Haven again and finally the part-time, retirement job at Santa Cruz. Home had been a university campus and not a town or even a neighbourhood. But his father had shaped his life, made it possible to go and do things in the world, break the mould – study the psyche instead of history. He'd wanted to write about fathers in Boston long before anyone else, seeing it as pioneering work – the father's effect on the new born infant... himself and Christopher making sandcastles on the beach at Cape Cod. His interest on the subject had been born at that time. The time of Ruthie. He'd thought: if I can make people understand the importance of fathers. He'd travelled to England and met Martha and the book had never got written. Maybe it was too late. There was increasing material on the subject. What could he bring that was new, except his own despair at not being a father himself?

On his feet again, he looked at the wide view stretching to the horizon – fields, woods, scattered houses. He must not be put off. It was an exciting project. He wanted to do it. He would take time out, think it through, go visit Mom for a couple of weeks... Damn, he hadn't called his mom on Christmas Day. He pulled his wallet out of his pocket, looking for a piece of paper, but he had no pen. He extracted a £10 note and folded it into four and pushed it up one end of the wallet, hoping this would remind him.

On the way back he branched off on to a footpath to the left by the dew pond. The path kept high giving him a view to the south of hills and valleys sloping away, not a house or a person in sight. He walked down into the valley. A path forked off to the right along the edge of a wood, leading upwards and bending in a loop in what seemed the right direction to get him back to the path. He glanced at his watch. Two-twenty.

Not knowing who the father is. His reason for writing the book hadn't changed. Even more reason for writing it now. All those children being conceived by donor insemination, by anonymous fathers or mothers. Would it feel the same for those children wanting to trace their parents as for adopted children? Most of them would be tracing one parent. How would it be for a child with one genetic parent? Would there be a similarity to a child living with one step parent? He started up the path. A pheasant squawked in the wood. Out of the sun the air felt colder. He quickened his pace. He would ring Julia on his return. A chapter on these issues would need to be included.

'Good timing!' Philip slid down his window and laughed as their cars drew up together, their headlights beaming on to the front of the house. He got out and came over to Grant's car, his feet crunching on the gravel. 'Nice walk? We went for a walk too. Up to Combe Gibbet.'

Grant smiled. Over the few days Philip had become warmer. 'That's where I was.'

'Really?'

'Not when you were there, clearly!' He switched off the ignition and heaved himself out of the car feeling stiff. It had become dark and Martha had gone in ahead. He touched Philip's arm. 'Was it all right?'

'What do you mean?'

Perhaps he'd misjudged the friendliness. 'The visit to the grave.'

110

'Oh, fine. We decided to have a pub lunch, and then the walk.'

Grant followed him across the gravel and up the steps and into their wide hallway. Martha had vanished. The place felt empty. The door into the sitting room was closed and he was sure there had been more possessions before – coats on the chair, toys under the table. There was no evidence of the children or the old couple.

'Television,' Philip nodded as if reading his thoughts. He pulled off his coat and offered to take Grant's, and now Grant could hear the hum of voices and music of kids' TV. Kathleen padded down the stairs from tidying Lionel and Peggy's room – they'd left peacefully and arrived home safely. She lifted her face to Philip's for a kiss. Her skin was luminous almost blue under the eyes. No figure, Grant thought, but beautiful. Martha appeared from the back of the house, a toilet flushing in the background. Her skin seemed matt.

'I think we should go home, Grant.' She hadn't taken off her coat.

'Home?'

'To the cottage.'

He saw Kathleen turn from Philip to Martha. Her eyes looked tired. She probably wanted the place to herself. 'Do have some tea.'

Martha was right. The house had shrunk back to its family unit, everything tidy and back in its place, including the children. He glanced at Martha and felt a wave of sympathy. She probably would have liked more time with her nieces and nephew, help put them to bed, read them a bedtime story. But the family had closed ranks.

They returned to the cottage and made a cheese omelette in a heavy Le Creuset frying pan which they found under the sink, and then ate it on trays in front of the television in the sitting room. They consumed the bottle of wine that Kathleen had provided, a pleasant enough Sauvignon Blanc, and

111

watched an old French movie, *A bout de souffle*, Jean Seberg. He leaned his head against the back of the large sofa and fell asleep, Jean Seberg's face in his mind, and then Kathleen's. He could feel his feet plodding one foot after the next, as if he was still walking. The film had moved on to another film when he opened his eyes, and Martha had gone up. He rubbed his face and shifted himself to the edge of the sofa. He'd thought they would make love, hopefully without tears afterwards. But her back was turned towards him as he crept into the bedroom and he tiptoed out again, trying to avoid creaking floorboards, and got undressed in the bathroom and slipped into bed without waking her.

In the morning she told him she wanted to return to London. He looked through the kitchen window, thinking he might want another day's walking. Low clouds hung over the ploughed field, but it wasn't raining and the clouds looked paler towards the west. He wished it was yesterday with the prospect of the wonderful walk. Martha had seemed happy then as if looking forward to her day with Philip. 'Aren't Philip and Kathleen expecting us today?'

'They won't mind.'

'Won't they?'

She avoided his eyes. 'Please.'

They stopped off in Shalbourne to say goodbye. He shook Philip's hand, kissed Kathleen – one cheek and then the other, soft, young… Martha was already getting back into the car. The girls had gone to play with some neighbours' children. William was asleep. Philip and Kathleen smiled, linking arms as they waved. It was the right decision. Rain had set in. They got on to the M4 and he switched on a Brahms clarinet quintet, one of Martha's favourites, and accelerated, pulling out into the fast lane away from the spray being thrown up by the car in front. He thought of the things waiting for him at home: the chapter plan from Julia which she'd promised him before Christmas, the letter from the Institute of Group Analysis confirming a series of talks he was due to give over the next term. He felt a surge of energy. The small holiday had been a good break.

Martha turned down the volume. 'I'm going to ask that messenger over.'

'What messenger?'

'You know, the guy from work.'

He switched the windscreen wipers faster. 'Do I?'

'To look at your PC, remember?'

'Oh yeah.' He glanced at her, remembering now. Her eyes were staring ahead. He couldn't see her expression.

'He may need guidance.'

He nodded, wondering why she wanted to help the man.

His mood sank when he got home. There was no chapter plan from Julia or letter from the Institute of Group Analysis, and there were three messages on his answer machine, including one from his newest patient, Christine Mirado, cancelling appointments. He took refuge in his room and tried to call his mother and then his sister. Both of their answer machines were turned off. It was early morning their time; the thought added to his disorientation. They would be asleep, or away perhaps. It was mid-afternoon in Putney and through his rain-spattered window it was getting dark. Christine Mirado wouldn't return probably and he hated losing patients. He flopped on to the couch and sat in the semi-darkness. Twenty fours earlier he'd been on that walk striding along the downs in that ethereal light. He wished they'd stayed longer in Wiltshire, away from it all.

In the early evening he received a call from his sister, telling him that their mother had suffered a mild stroke.

'I'll come over,' he said immediately.

'No need, honey.'

'Of course, I will.'

'Grant, it was a TIA.'

'A what?'

' A transient ischaemic attack. A baby.'

'A baby?'

'The nurse called it that. Her way of – well, you know.'

'No, I don't know, Lani.' He felt hot with anger. He clutched the phone to his ear. Why hadn't he called Mom?

'Mom said she knew something was wrong. No more than that really. The words not coming out quite right.'

'Is her speech bad?'

'Fine now. She had no pain. All her limbs are working. She can walk. Just as good as before. They let her home the next day – she was that okay. She's at home with me. You don't need to come over. You don't, honey. Unless you want a holiday.'

Laughter echoed across the thousands of miles. And he'd thought he would go for a break. A baby stroke. Strange way of putting it. Babies grew, didn't they? The next one might kill her.

As the days went on patients trickled back from holiday. He debated whether to charge for the cancelled appointments – a gesture of Christmas good will; he might have to ask for their good will if he decided to visit Mom. He jerked out of his unprofessionalism and typed the invoices. He wasn't going to go.

Regular phone calls to Lani and Mom to monitor the situation, once – perhaps twice a week. That was the answer. Talk to Mom, gauge how she was. Talk to Lani. Agree with Lani a list of criteria to measure his need to be there. Go immediately if there was the slightest change in any of these criteria. He'd been bad about keeping in touch, sometimes leaving it months. Now he would diary times for these phone calls.

If he was not with a patient, he watched Martha's closed face as she left for work in the morning. The muscles in her neck seemed taut as she turned away from him to open the front door. She forgot things and had to go back upstairs. 'Don't wait.' A clipped order. If he said goodbye to her in their room or at the breakfast table he noted the flicker of her eye contact, the way she let him kiss her and pulled away. He ran after her one morning and took her in his arms, squeezing her to him, feeling the tension in her body. 'I love you.'

She leaned her head against the side of his. 'Thank you.'

I can't go to the States, he thought. I can't leave her.

He didn't want to. The letter from the Institute of Group Analysis had arrived confirming his talks, a meeting with Julia to talk about the book had been arranged, and later that morning Christine Mirado was returning to the fold.

That evening he rang Philip and Kathleen, wanting to thank them for their hospitality. He hadn't found time to write and he imagined explaining about his mother and then moving on to the subject of Martha and extracting a little more detail about the visit to the grave. He sat at the desk in his room with the door closed in case Martha returned home early.

But Kathleen answered the phone and once he'd thanked her was immediately into their 'exciting' news about her pregnancy. She broke off, stammering suddenly. 'Of – of course... you must know already. Phil... Phil said he told Martha on the walk...'

He pictured her dumpy figure – getting dumpier presumably – and her luminous skin flushing with embarrassment. He congratulated Kathleen and got off the phone as quickly as he could, and then sat back in his chair staring at the lecture notes that he'd started to assemble and that must be cleared away before tomorrow's patients.

Their infertility had become public. No wonder Martha had wanted to come home. She must have talked to Philip, and he'd rewarded her with this news.

TWELVE

JON

The rug covered the purple wall-to-wall carpet, leaving only a foot of purple border lengthways and about two foot widthways. There were bits of purple in the new rug... perhaps Ma had thought to match the purples – but it was mainly green and red, a nice green and red. It made the black leather armchair look as if it belonged, instead of being a copycat of Pete's. Pete's black leather armchair had been Shirley's idea, Jon had discovered after he'd bought his, which had made him want to send it back. But this new rug made him fancy buying another leather armchair, or a settee. It had made him want to spend the Christmas bonus that had caused grief with Steve, though he suspected Steve had something to do with it. 'Bonus, Jon? Better prove you deserve it!'

What was amazing was that Ma and Dad had bought the rug, made the one visit to his flat, noted the purple wall-to-wall, and bought it. Who's idea was it, he wanted to say? Who chose it? Dad had half an eye on the Christmas film as he undid the parcel, though he could tell by the way Dad kept twitching his head round that Dad wanted to watch. Ma got to her feet just as he was cutting into the masking tape that bound the brown paper, saying something needed seeing to. 'Stay Ma,' he called after her, but she vanished into the kitchen and clattered saucepans in the sink, and Dad's eyes stayed glued to the telly. Jon rolled out the rug and stared at it, in fucking tears almost. 'Hey, thanks!' Ma came to the doorway of the kitchen, her face hidden as she wiped her forehead with her apron. 'Do you like it?' 'Yeah,' he nodded, 'Yeah!' His dad grunted and shifted in his chair.

He dreamed about the rug, a day dream that must have come from a real dream – him on the rug, face downwards, the green and red colours up against his nose because he was lying on top of someone. It wasn't Daisy or Shirley (what put

116

her into his mind?). This was where he felt a real dream, dreamed at night, put the idea of Black Plaits into his head. She and him on the rug.

It made him think about returning to that New Age shop to search out another stone or another book about Tarot for Pete. Pete and Shirley weren't free over the Christmas break, but Pete had rung to thank for the gifts that Jon had 'so thoughtfully' delivered: they had arrived safely, in spite of being left outside the flat door. Shirley liked the soap and he looked forward to reading the book though he wasn't sure Tarot was his thing. Perhaps they could meet in the New Year – no, not New Year's *Eve*...

On New Year's Eve Jon got off work early and went home via Kingston to check out that shop. It was the same as before, stalls on the pavement full of old stones and a few white crystals, and the door into the shop wide open. He ran his hands through his hair and had a quick look at his reflection in the window before going in, but inside there was a different girl. She had short brown hair and small, tight boobs. He asked her if a woman with black hair worked there, and she nodded. 'You mean Carol?'

'Probably.'

'She's only here on Sundays.'

He knew that of course. Black Plaits – or Carol as she must be called – had told him. He glanced round the shop for the leopard skin stones. The one he'd bought was still in his trouser pocket. The girl was watching him. She had a sharp, boyish face and her small boobs were encased in a skimpy yellow T-shirt – he was surprised she was warm enough. Little smile now, only a kid. 'I can pass on a message.'

'Can you?' He smiled back, seeing colour flush into her cheek. 'Tell Carol I'll be here on Sunday afternoon.'

He phoned Ma and Dad and told them he wouldn't be there for Sunday dinner even though he'd said he would. Yeah, yeah, even though it was the first Sunday of the New Year. For some reason this was important to Dad. He must stop going so often. There was a time when they expected him every Sunday. At least he'd weaned them off that. He suggested they come to his flat for a change. On a Saturday. They could see the rug in situ. Find somewhere nice for Ma to have a cup of tea. Make an afternoon of it. But Dad said they couldn't do that. Too busy. Doing what, he wondered. Watching telly. His blood was boiling by the end of the conversation, Dad telling him he should keep his word. Get a life, he nearly said.

New Year's evening was spent at the *Spit and Polish* with the usual crowd. There were a couple of new people, Stuart, and Owen who was older and into computers. Owen leaned against the bar, in a shirt and a tie, his pot-belly pressing against the waist of his grey trousers, and told anyone who cared to listen that computers weren't rocket science – they were just ugly typewriters with extra buttons. He and Jon shifted along the bar to let in more people, and he turned to Jon and asked him if he could type. Jon nodded and signalled to the barman for more beers, liking what he was hearing. If Jon could type, computers were typing with a few extra tools. Nothing to be frightened of. They pushed their way through the crowd and found a small table. Owen removed his tie and undid the top button of his shirt as he talked about 'applications', and they moved on to vodkas and then chased those with more beers. By midnight they were raising their glasses to the great god computer and adapting the words of *Auld Lang Syne* to include a 'golden computer future'.

The phrase drummed a beat in Jon's head for the rest of that night and most of Saturday. He thought of dragging himself out to the *Spit and Polish* to connect up with Owen and get his phone number for future use, but his head ached. He woke late on the Sunday morning and remembered what he said he'd do that afternoon. It felt dark enough to be night. He pulled back his curtains and peered up to the pavement.

Rain had set in as he climbed up the steps from the basement a few hours later, and by the time he reached

Kingston it was sheeting down. He ran from the bus stop to the street and then found an awning to stand under to catch his breath. He brushed the wet off his corduroy jacket and flicked his fingers through his damp hair, wondering if he could be bothered with this visit. No stalls in the street, just puddles and a few sad people in anoraks. The shops looked identical with closed doors, as he wandered along. The windows were fugged up; he couldn't see in.

He pushed at a green painted door. A bell tinkled. The fug was inside the shop, clouds of it, a fog. Round the edges he could see the little dishes of coloured stones and a chunk of grey rock with jagged purple insides.

'Close the door, love. It's freezing!' There was a click and the fog began to disperse. Light glinted off the jagged purple insides. Folded tables were propped up against the counter, dishes of stones and crystals placed on top of it. Stuff everywhere. 'Just making some tea. Won't be a mo.'

'You want to be careful hiding yourself. I could've nicked things.'

Her head popped up from behind the counter. 'Got a gun under here.'

'Wha'?'

Her head vanished for a second and then came up again. She was holding a mug of tea. 'Kidding!' There were little semi-circles at the corners of her mouth as she smiled 'You left a message, didn't you?' No plaits this time, black hair scraped back pulling the skin at the top of her forehead. Her skin was white, like chalk.

'I came before... I bought a leopard skin stone.'

'No more of those, love.'

She was too old. He saw that now. That boyish girl in the yellow T-shirt was nearer his age. 'Any other things like that?'

She glanced towards a glass-doored cupboard on the wall. Her hair spread across the dome of her head, shining under the small lights that were dotted about the shop, and twisted into a knot at the back. 'Have you looked in the cupboard?'

He peered through the glass, ignoring his reflection – he didn't want to see what he looked like. More clutter. How had he ever found anything in this place?

'Did she like it?'

'Sorry ?' He turned back.

She laughed. He could see all her teeth. 'The leopard skin stone.'

'Who – oh…' he lifted his shoulders. 'Yeah…'

'You wanted to see me, didn't you?'

He remembered the feeling before, that she fancied him, that given the right circumstances women did fancy him. That was why he was here. With this woman… with this older woman, perhaps he could finally do it… he felt hot at the thought.

There was a noise from her throat, or somewhere deeper, making him feel hotter. 'Doesn't sound like she appreciated your present.'

He pictured Daisy's blue eyes, swimming, wet. Black Plaits had green eyes… pale – he fancied he could see right through them into her head. 'How about us having a drink?'

She said she couldn't shut up the shop until five and after that she was tied up but why didn't he join her now for a cup of tea. Did he want to make it another time?

Tied up… for a second the image of a black plait tied round his dick filled his mind. He spoke through the fallout, his head spinning a little. Yeah… yeah, he did want to.

They made a date for the following Sunday at five. She looked young when she smiled, even with the little semi-circles. 'You can come at four thirty if you like.'

Before he left, she put out a hand and stroked the arm of his jacket with her long-nailed fingers which had no colour on them today. There was a ring on her middle finger with a green stone. Green like her eyes, like the shop. Perhaps it was her shop. He could imagine her long-nailed fingers stroking the length of his dick.

Normally he liked Sunday evenings, even after a good weekend. It meant work and Daisy the next day. But today he hated the waiting. A whole week before he saw Black Plaits again. A whole week before he could start... start what? And what about Daisy? He kicked a plastic carton into the road and pulled up his collar shoving past two old ladies with umbrellas. He gazed into the window of a computer shop trying to focus. PCs were part of his future, weren't they, even if Martha Morgan hadn't come up with the goods? He'd typed up the Christmas rota, or part of it. He would suggest to Steve that he typed out the night rota, and the emails. His New Year resolution must be to *expand his role* as Pete would say. He could see his reflection mouthing in the window and looking... sod what he looked like; he would find out what Steve was always typing and make sure he typed it for him.

At home he slumped into his leather armchair and debated whether to nip round to the *Spit and Polish*. He clicked open a can of Foster's. By this time next week he and Black Plaits... he didn't allow himself to finish the thought. The magazines in his cupboard entered his mind. He heaved himself up from his chair and moved into his bedroom, and then the phone rang.

It was Martha Morgan. Could he come on next Saturday afternoon to look at her husband's computer? Could he come about three? She would send directions how to get there. Would he be coming by public transport? He wasn't good on directions. Where did he live? Could they come and pick him up?

So many fucking questions. He gave her his address, put down the phone and thought: Saturday Martha Morgan, Sunday Black Plaits.

THIRTEEN

MARTHA

She stood at the sink and filled the kettle. The oven clock ticked. Out of doors the light seemed to hover, hanging on longer than a week ago pushing away winter and darkness, letting in spring.

Across the hall, there was a buzz of male voices. It took time to hand over a computer, training someone to use it. Grant had got really into it. This was the third session. She liked knowing that the two of them were there. It filled the void of Saturday afternoon after the busy week. Through the window she watched a woman and two children walk along the pavement. A man ran after them and talked to them. All three turned back. Perhaps this was grief: this not knowing how to fill up space, this feeling all right only if she was absorbed in work. She'd finally given up the idea of having a baby and grief had kicked in. She plugged in the kettle and put her hands round it waiting for it to warm up. Grant had asked her what she felt about Phil and Kathleen expecting their fourth child. She'd told him she didn't mind. She'd begun to remember other things, though she didn't tell him that.

Soon they would emerge and the three of them would sit at the kitchen table over a pot of tea and something to eat. Jon liked marmite toast. Today she'd decided to try out a Victoria sponge from a battered pink Constance Spry recipe book belonging to her mother. The hardware shop had recommended a cake tin with a removable base and baking parchment to stop the cake sticking. The mixture had risen and turned into something that she could scar with a fingerprint. Making cakes, that was what you did with children.

She slipped off her shoes and padded into the hall, wanting to glance into Grant's room and watch them at the keyboard, the dark, thick hair next to the shiny bald head; join them perhaps. But the door was closed. It gave her a jolt. She was sure she'd heard their voices from the kitchen. No sound now. She hesitated by the door, but turned away and went upstairs.

In her bedroom, she dialled her brother's number and lowered herself into the rocking chair and faced the window, the ringing tone in her ear. The family would be back from a walk. Or coming indoors after an afternoon in the garden, the children leaving their red boots by the back door ready for tea and toast…

'Phil...'

'Yes.'

'It's me.'

'Sorry – who?'

'Martha.'

'Oh...? Oh hello.'A boat was chugging past, a light at its bow. 'I just rang to chat…'

'Martha, can I ring you back? We've got people.' There was a pause, and then as if he remembered. 'You okay?'

'Not really.'

'Oh love, I'm sorry.'

The endearment brought tears to her eyes. He was asking her what he could do. 'I'll ring you back.'

'Perhaps I could have one of your kids occasionally. Becky for a weekend.'

'Yeah… if that would help?'

The boat had disappeared. The bare branches of the poplar came into focus. Not a sign of a bud.

'Would that help, Martha?'

'I don't know.'

'She's not a baby.'

'I know.'

'Martha, you have tried everything, haven't you?'

'Yes.'

'Do you think you should talk to somebody? Try to come to terms with it. The sister of one of my –'

'It's all right, Phil.'

She pressed the off button and tossed the phone on to the bed, and sat rocking in the chair thinking he might ring back. The pragmatic, sensible one. The one who stayed downstairs with Mummy. The one who did normal, ordinary things. She rocked, trying to ease her heartbeat, rock, rock...

Boiled eggs and toast soldiers with Phil and Mummy. A game of whist she doesn't want to play. The thud from upstairs. 'You go, Martha. You go.'...

She leaned back in the chair and let herself remember...

Up the dark wooden stairs, away from Phil and Mummy. No light under Daddy's door. She taps lightly. 'Daddy!'

She takes the handle and pulls the door an inch towards her so that she can press the lever, soundlessly lift the horizontal bar on the other side and allow it to swing open. His room is black. She contemplates switching on the landing light, or the bathroom light. But the square of the window is emerging through the darkness; she can see the bulk of the bed. She steps inside and closes the door – a minute click. She bends down and unties the laces of her shoes, silently removes them and slips off her socks. Her bare feet feel for objects he may have chucked – books, loose papers, pens... Nothing has been thrown. The thud was not made by Daddy. It was the wind. Something banging outside. Mummy and Phil don't want her. This thought confirms in her mind that she should continue her journey.

Small creak as she slips into bed. Her head leans against the knobbly ridge of his spine. His back is bare, down to the waistband of his pyjamas. On days like this he doesn't get dressed, even when he gets out of bed to work at his desk, and some days he doesn't wear a pyjama top. She rests her face on the plateau under his shoulder blades. After a while, she reaches an arm over the side of his body and locates his arm.

124

She runs her hand down it, but his arm is too long for her to reach his hand.

'Thank you.'

'Shall I go?'

'Yes.'

'I can stay.'

'It's all right. I'm all right now.'

She hangs on to that 'now'.

Grant's door was open when she went downstairs, the room empty. There were no chairs by the computer. The computer sat on Grant's desk, the keyboard snug in its cover. Perhaps they had tidied up before they had gone, wherever they had gone. They wouldn't have sat on the couch.

In the kitchen the teapot was clean, the cake untouched inside the colourful tin that she had bought at the same time as the baking tin. She opened the front door and wandered down the tiled path to the pavement. There was a gap where Grant's car should be. Where could they have gone? There was a large removal van, a few houses along. A man in a green overall wheeled a tea chest on a trolley down the ramp. Behind him, another man carried the barred sides of a cot and a small mattress. She turned and went back indoors.

He returned about an hour later and told her that they had stood in the hall and called her several times. 'We thought you'd gone out. We were talking about pubs and decided to go and have a pint. Then I took him home. Of course, we would have asked you to come along. I should have left a note.'

'Pubs? I thought you were supposed to be talking about PCs.'

'It seemed a nice thing to do.' He dropped the car keys into the bowl.

'When are you going to take the thing over there?'

'What thing?' He hung up his jacket and glanced into his room, flicked on the light, flicked it off again, closed the door and came towards her.

'The computer.'

'When he's ready I guess.' His arm stretched out to put round her shoulder.

She moved out of reach, into the kitchen and looked out of the window. It was dark outside. A car was being reversed into a parking space, break lights showng red.

'Are you bothered about him being here, Martha?'

She pulled down the blind. 'Of course not.'

'Work and home, you know. Different status.'

'For fuck's sake.'

'What's the matter?'

She shook her head. 'Nothing.'

'You want me to help him, don't you?'

Her shoulders lifted. 'It's fine.'

'Hey, come on,' his hand brushed the top of her arm. 'You need a glass of wine.' He got a bottle of Chablis out of the fridge and took a couple of glasses from the cupboard.

She leaned against the sink. 'You closed the door.'

'What...?' He pierced the cork with the corkscrew and started drawing it out.

'The door to your room was closed.'

He glanced up. 'Was it?'

'When he was there! It felt unfriendly.'

He extracted the cork, put down the bottle and removed the cork from the corkscrew. 'I didn't mean to, honey. I didn't realise I'd closed it. It must have been automatic.'

She turned back to the teapot on the side ready by the kettle to make tea for the three of them. Next to it was the cake tin with its uneaten cake inside. 'Must it?'

After a break, it took a few days trawling through the papers, immersing herself in detail, before she could rise above it and see the big picture. She would touch base with the people who mattered, plug in to the office politics and slowly her energy would trickle back, stories would start to emerge, people to cover them evolve. The trickle would turn into current, a force inside her, pushing everything else out.

This time she floundered in detail. Tony didn't make eye contact, preferring to remove his glasses and rub his eyes or glance at other people rather than at her. She minded that he forgot to tell her that Peter from Books had been replaced by Brian; that *Fuzzy the Physician*, a tri-weekly comic strip had finally been accepted for the Health page; she minded that she had to find these details out from Sue. Liza made too much eye contact, her pleasant, irregular face dwelling on Martha's in a friendly but annoying way as if she knew something that Martha didn't. The dimple dented her cheek as she grinned over the success of the first in the series of *The Professionals* featuring Grant Weber, the psychoanalyst. At one of the weekly editorial meetings Tony glanced round. 'Did someone suggest a male *Bridget Jones*? Or did I dream this column? Sad, submissive man. Macho, self sufficient women *buying* their sperm. Bit passé possibly.' Martha kept her eyes on her notes and let it pass.

But these were small things and within a week her confidence had returned. Sue announced she wanted to leave by mid-February and it felt no more than an irritating detail. She wondered how she'd thought she could confide in the girl. Good job she never had.

'Have you got another position, Sue?'

'No…' she was staring in Tony's direction.

Martha followed her gaze and watched him approach Daisy: he was putting a hand on Daisy's shoulder and crouching down to look at her screen. 'Haven't you liked working for me?'

'It's not that, Martha. I need a change.'

Martha could see the silver, metal trolley, filled with the day's post, approaching Daisy's desk. A boy, barely out of school, lifted the packages out of the trolley. He said something to Daisy and Tony. Getting the sandwich order perhaps. A new boy presumably. That was why she hadn't seen Jon recently. She saw him every Saturday of course.

She took Liza out for a drink at lunch time and heard the rumour that Tony was leaving. The dimple was in Liza's cheek. Martha smiled back and poured more wine in to Liza's glass.

Liza fingered her packet of cigarettes. 'Only rumoured, Martha.''

The wine slipped down. Liza went out for a cigarette and Martha sat back against the red upholstered bench. Things were good between her and Liza. She knew little about her beyond the Features Floor, what her partner did, whether her work was her life, whether she wanted a family, but she could trust her. Unlike most of the others. 'Where does the rumour say he's going,' she asked on Liza's return.

'Editor of a tabloid?'

'Editor?' For a second she felt a twinge of envy – she'd thought he wanted *her* job. The two men at the next table were leaving. She took another mouthful of wine. Who would want to be an editor of a tabloid?

'You hadn't heard?'

She shook her head.

Liza placed the packet of cigarettes in her bag. 'I think it was Doris who told me.'

'How would she know?'

She was grinning again. 'I said a *rumour*.'

Martha forced herself to smile, pick up the wine bottle and fill Liza's glass. Liza wanted Tony's job. That was what this was about. Wanted *her* job probably. Sue was going. Perhaps with Tony. Perhaps Sue would stay if she was working for Liza. She probably couldn't even trust Liza.

That afternoon the alarm shrilled and the population of *The Chronicle* had to evacuate the building. Everyone streamed out, cursing that they had to leave their desks and one or two remembering how it was over a decade ago when they were doing this every other week. They huddled in groups on the pavement and then shifted along. Cars travelling in both directions slowed down to look. Martha pulled her cardigan around her against the wind coming off the river and felt a hand on her back. 'Okay?'

'Yes thanks, Tony.' The ringing was in her head. Too much wine at lunch time. She could see Liza and Daisy and a few others from *Weekend Travel* crossing the road into Cabot Square. 'I wish they'd turn that blasted thing off.'

'Perhaps this is a real emergency.'

She stepped off the pavement to get away from the crowds.

Tony grabbed her arm, 'Martha! Do you want to kill yourself?'

There was a rush of air as a car swept by. She steadied herself against him feeling shaky; she should have eaten at lunchtime. His arm supported her shoulder. They moved back on to the pavement, and the ringing stopped.

'Thank God for that.'

'You alright?' His eyes stared at her through his glasses.

'Of course I am.' A couple of secretaries she recognised from the Sports Pages looked towards them. He glanced at them and smiled, and looked back at her. 'We could probably go and have a drink, while we're waiting.'

'No thanks.' She looked beyond him to the building. Everyone must be out of it by now.

'We could be here for hours.'

'It's freezing. I'm going to find out what's going on.'

She walked back towards the building along the road, following a group of people doing the same. The traffic had been stopped. She should've gone for a drink with him, chatted, found out whether he was leaving. How much easier if he was. He'd been after her job from the moment he'd joined Features, and everyone knew it.

The group in front of her halted. Words were passing through the crowd: 'A suspicious parcel…a small fire…' She squeezed herself in amongst the people on the pavement and asked if it was a real scare. The young man next to her shrugged. 'They're not letting us in the building.' The woman on the other side of him laughed. 'Canary Wharf, isn't it? Oh hello, Martha.' It was Vi from Pictures.

'Anyone hurt, Vi?'

'Don't know. Hoax probably.'

They chatted and stamped their feet to keep warm. The echoing sound of pile driving boomed in the distance. The building work never ceased even as people tried to bomb the buildings, if that was what this was really about. She caught sight of Doris, who said she'd been meaning to talk to Martha about an idea for a feature. The two of them slipped away from the crowds and went off to Starbucks, Martha glancing round to check Tony wasn't looking. They sat on a sofa and clutched large lattes, and discussed obituaries and the fascination with dead people's lives.

After about an hour they were allowed back into the building and informed that there had been a suspicious bag left in the foyer, just inside the swing door. No one could confirm the exact details. All that could be certain was that someone – possibly one of the messengers – had removed the bag and raised the alarm.

Martha took the lift down to the ground floor. Jarvis, the security guard was chatting to Vi from Pictures and a couple of men she didn't recognise. She lifted her hand to Vi as she passed. She walked slowly along the passage, following the sign *Mail and Communications*.

Several people were at the entrance to the post room. She could just see Steve's head beyond them and hear his words. 'Jon to thank. I wouldn't have gone *near* the thing. Confidence of youth – or foolhardiness. A small bag – it was all right in the end. Followed the correct procedures – no, he's not here. I let him go home early, after the police had made sure it was okay. Bit shocked, even though it was a false alarm.'

She walked back into the foyer and out through the swing doors. The wind had dropped a little. The low grey sky was turning into night. Lights twinkled on the cranes and high buildings. She crossed the road into Cabot Square, took her mobile from her bag and dialled his home number, hunching her shoulders against the cold. It rang and rang. She walked on beyond the fountain towards the lights of the shopping mall. Eight rings, nine... There was a click and a pause... She felt a stab of disappointment as she heard his recorded voice: 'I'm not here at the moment... but please leave a message...' It sounded hesitant, shy. She waited for more but the long tone cut in. She heard her own voice lost in the space of Cabot Square. 'This is Martha – Martha Morgan... I think you're wonderful...'

She'd meant to say: I think that was a wonderful thing you did, are you okay? But it came out wrong. She switched off the phone and stared at the twinkling cranes.

The train rattled through the darkness between Waterloo and Putney and she sat in a corner seat and rested her head on the frame of the window.

'To be effective you can't try to do a thing. You either do it or you don't. Trying implies you won't succeed.'

Daddy's words...

They are sitting on the small bridge, across the stream at the bottom of their steep garden... you can do that: slip your legs either side of the vertical bars holding up the railing and dangle your feet inches above the water. Daddy tells her he has been trying to write a book, and the trying, the not being sure he can do it, the not believing in himself, is what causes

131

him to go silent and chuck it across the bedroom, scattering the loose leaf pages all over the floor.

Stars of light flash in the water. 'Is that why you go silent?'

His face is dark from the shadow of the trees. 'I think so.' He laughs and puts an arm around her, warm and firm. 'If I stop trying and just do it. Just write the thing. I think that might stop the silences.'

Fear spikes through her. She wants to keep being able to go into the dark bedroom and close the door, and bring him the cup of tea her mother insists she takes. 'Get out!' he shouts sometimes, and she thinks the lever arch file with all its pages will follow. 'Fuck off!' he once exploded. Her mother is outside. The door bursts open. He picks up the file and they both flee. It's when he is silent and still, and the steam is lifting off the untouched cup of tea, that she can lift the bedclothes and slip underneath and feel the rise and fall of his body and know that he is warm, alive.

The train was slowing down… stopping. Doors opened. Banged shut. She lifted her head and rubbed a hole in the condensation and peered through the window. Wandsworth. Between Wandsworth and Putney, she opened her bag and fished out her oyster card. Safer to do that in the train, Grant had told her, and she prayed Grant would be at home tonight.

They are in the car – not on the bench seat, separate front seats. They are in the Austin A40; the one he died in. He says teaching bolshy teenagers is too slippery a thing to hang on to, to hold. It won't last, whereas a book…

She never asked him what he wrote because she didn't really want him to get better. When it was too late to ask, she couldn't find anything he'd written.

She cursed their new security system which tonight appeared to have lit every room making her think Grant was at home. He must have heard about the bomb scare. It was a false alarm, but, Canary Wharf… tomorrow the department would be discussing a feature on bombs and false alarms and the threat of terrorism and the nanny state, and Tony would feed it into his project on conflict in the twenty-first century.

She flung her briefcase on the hall chair, went into the kitchen and sloshed some whisky into a glass, topping it up with sparkling water and ice. It slipped down her throat, reminding her of drinks in Fetter Lane pubs and the editors she used to chat up, passing herself off as the attractive journalist bitch that no editor could afford to be without. She drained the glass and picked up her bag and car keys.

The car headed up Putney High Street... she switched on the radio. 'You've just been listening to the slow movement of Mozart's twenty first piano concerto, the Elvira Madigan theme, followed by Albinoni's famous Adagio. Relax with Classic ...' Radio Three had a discussion on Schoenberg. Radio Four was in the middle of a play. She didn't want talking. She cruised down Roehampton Hill in silence, keeping to the 40 mph speed limit, no hurry. Cars overtook her up Kingston Hill. She hoped she could remember where he lived. She hadn't brought the A-Z. The speedometer crept up as she coasted down the hill into Kingston; no cameras about. She swung round the bypass along the empty, one-way system as though she was on a journey out of the city. People did that. Told no one, just departed. Further on a sign said Surbiton. She turned right at the traffic lights, drove along and then turned left.

There was a street name, high up on the side of a tall, white house. It seemed to be his street. She'd gone with Grant to fetch him the first time, but after that had let Grant go on his own. She remembered the tall, shabby Victorian buildings converted into flats and Grant's remark: 'Just a sad façade. What can they be like inside?' She saw the number now. There were railings to the right of steps going up to a large front door, and an opening in the railings to steps leading down.

She parked the car and switched off the ignition. The engine died away. She leaned her head against the leather-covered support. The street lights weren't too high, a friendly light – enough to see by but not glaring into his basement flat. Clip, clip – a woman was crossing the road. A siren wailed in the distance.

Her shoes echoed on the basement steps. There was no bell or knocker on his purple door. She wrapped hard with her knuckles. The siren was further away. More footsteps on the road.

After five minutes she returned to the car and sank into the seat. She pictured him lifting the small bag, cradling it perhaps in his large hands, and carrying it through the swing doors across the road to the water or to Cabot Square or to wherever he took it.

The feel of his arms around her at the office party. Her heart lurched. She and him – it was laughable. Her eyes closed... taller than her, warm... she remembered holding his hand... shit. She stuffed the key into the ignition and started the car, but still she didn't draw away, letting the engine idle for a few more minutes, in case he came back.

FOURTEEN

JON

'So you're a hero?' Her fingers had blue nails today. She laid them over the back of his hand.

He couldn't look at her. Warm pressure. Tingle of excitement. Fear too. He was glad they were in the café and not outside, alone, where he might have to suggest they go to his flat. It was too early for that, though he'd thought about it.

'A hero, Jon.'

He glanced up... black round her eyes, matching the hair. 'There was nothing in the bag.'

'Who dialled 999? Who got everybody out?'

'Steve made the phone call.'

'You removed the bag.'

'I didn't think there was anything in it!'

She laughed. 'You are funny.'

'Funny?' He could see right inside her mouth.

'Why can't you enjoy it?'

'Enjoy what?'

'The hero worship.'

'You sound like my ma.' She didn't, except that Ma and Dad used to tell him to enjoy himself when there was nothing to enjoy. He lifted his arm for another beer. Thank God this café had a licence. Black Plaits and her teetotal habit – he longed for a pub where he could go and order at the bar.

'I'm a mother.'

'Wha – ?' He lowered his arm.

She nodded. 'Is that a problem?'

'No...'

'A little girl. Opal. Her Dad has her on Sundays.'

'Today's not Sunday.'

'You're lucky, aren't you? Has her other days too.'

The day was going wrong. Everything with Black Plaits had gone so nicely up to now. He shouldn't be here. It was the wrong day. Just because he couldn't face going to work this morning. He'd felt sick in the darkness of his room. The idea of going back there after... what the hell had he done? Been a risky bastard Steve lost no time telling him. 'Reckless bravery' Steve had called it, but he had a look on his face Jon hadn't seen before. Perhaps he was a hero... Put it down to Martha Morgan's message on the answer phone. Put it down to that. Her voice fucking him up. Did she like him? He lay in bed knowing that the time to get out of bed and be out of the house had passed. The minutes ticked by. If he got up immediately, he could still get to work, maybe late but not too late to lose his job. He sat bolt up, sweating. He was ill. He had a fever. He was glad he'd had that thought. Glad he'd picked up the phone, had the stomach to ask for Steve and told him he needed a sicky. It was Steve who said, 'You're in shock. You may need more than a day off.' No, he'd wanted to say – wanted to shout it. No, don't encourage me. He wondered how he'd stopped himself from asking: will my job still be there? My job that now includes typing the rotas and the emails, the training of the new messengers, the running of the Mail and Communications room when *you're* having a sicky, will it all still...?

The phone back in its holder, he'd told himself to chill out. He was having a day off, a legit sicky. The job wasn't go to go away. It would be there the next morning. He peered through his window. Outside was a cold, blue day. He pulled on his clothes and went out to buy bread and jam for his breakfast, and fresh milk for his coffee. He dawdled in front of one of the cafés thinking he might take breakfast there. He was getting used to cafés with Black Plaits and her herbal teas, which was when he'd decided to go and find her.

He looked at her now. Too much black round her eyes today. Hair good though, in the one plait. 'Do you want another raspberry tea?' They were cheap, you could say that for them.

'You don't like it, do you?'

'Like what?'

'My daughter.'

'Don't know her.'

'I mean the idea of her.'

'Has she got green eyes?'

She laughed. 'I love you!'

'Wha'...?' Had he heard right?

She grinned. Pale green eyes that he could see through.

The waitress was coming towards them. He raised his arm.

Her hand pulled it down. She nodded slowly. 'Come on, let's go somewhere else.'

They got out on to the pavement and stood under a street light. It had got colder. The sky was dark blue. If they went and walked by the river away from the street lights, it would still be daylight – daytime, time to slow things down, time to sort out what he wanted. 'What about your daughter?'

'What about her?'

'Don't you have to –?'

'Jon, that's sorted.'

'Won't her Dad – ?'

'Jon, that's *my* business.'

'I just thought as Surbiton's quite a long –'

'Who said Surbiton?'

'That's where I live.'

Her arm jerked out of his. She strode across the road in her hard-soled boots, the noise of them soon lost in other sounds.

That was how you lost something. As easy as that.

He plodded in her direction, along the pavement, his reflection in the shop windows. It would lead him to the bus station. Get him home. Get him to the *Spit and Polish*. A bus trundled past and he got a whiff of petrol fumes. Maybe he would ring Pete. He needed a dose of Pete, needed to tell him he hadn't just laid in bed this morning, needed to tell him how his job was turning into something. He branched off on to the smaller street and stepped off the pavement getting out of the way of a crowd of people. He glanced at his watch. Five-thirty. Rush hour.

She was standing by the shop. It looked different with the door closed and no tables outside. He hadn't realised he'd crossed to that side of the street. She leaned against the door a cigarette in her mouth. 'Come inside a minute.'

'You're closed.'

She sucked on the cigarette. 'I've got the key, haven't I? I'll make you a cup of tea.'

A light in the corner threw shadows or sparkled in the glassy stones. She went through into the small room at the back, leaving the door open. The sink was like a doll's sink. He watched her from the other side of the counter. She tipped the kettle at an angle to fit it under the tap. 'I could get some weed if you want.'

'No thanks.'

'Don't you smoke?'

'That shit scares me.'

'It's nice.' She came through with the kettle and plugged it into a socket near the floor. She stubbed her cigarette in a small yellow dish on the counter and reached out her hand and touched his face. 'You're an innocent, aren't you?' The pad of her fingers was soft under the blue nails. 'Not used to women.'

He flicked his head away. 'I'm not a pouf!'

'Of course you're not.' She lowered her hand, her fingers trailing down the side of his arm. 'Who scared you?'

'Wha' ?'

'Someone's scared you.'

'I said drugs scared me…'

Her green see-through eyes rested on his. Her hand went back to his cheek, warm, nice – the whole of the side of his face glowed from the contact, and the hand stayed there; it didn't flinch, or go away. He remembered being in the bath, screaming in the bath. He was burnt… his ma was smacking his naked body…. he'd shat himself. No, she was washing him, she was soaping his body with her hands. It was Dad who was screaming. The feeling of his ma's hands was wonderful, the best feeling he'd ever had. The feeling of Black Plait's hand there now on his cheek…. But Black Plaits was lifting her hand away, and it was cold on his cheek. He opened his eyes. The interior of the shop seemed darker, the stones and rocks dull shapes. He wanted the hand to go back there.

'Don't worry yourself.' She patted his shoulder and let her hand slip down and squeeze his arm. 'Come on, let's make a cup of tea.'

The next Saturday, he noticed the lines round Grant's eyes, how they reached into his hair at the side of his head. He liked Grant's eyes.

On the previous Saturdays he'd looked at the grey letters on the white keys and stared at the grey words creeping across the screen as he'd listened to Grant's instructions, and the sound of his accent – he'd not got it at first, that Grant was American; it was only in little words like 'huh' and longer ones like 'insightful' that he could tell. He liked being on his own with Grant. On one of the Saturdays he moved from the swivel desk chair to the beige settee that Grant called a couch, and stretched his legs across the rug, which reminded him of his own rug though the pattern was different.

Grant's rug was new. He told Jon that he'd recently changed his mind about this room. Everything had been like a *tabula rasa* – Jon had to get Grant to tell him what the fuck that meant, though he didn't use the F word. 'A clean slate, Jon. No decoration. Nothing. Now I've got the rug. It's an experiment.'

'An experiment?'

139

'With my patients.'

'A sor' of magic carpet?'   Jon couldn't believe he said it.

'Yeah, Jon. Yeah...!'

'Fucking stupid!'

'No... quite insightful.'

'Wha – ?'

Jon couldn't believe Grant was being serious.

Grant would lean against the desk or sit on the swivel chair or the armchair, and they would talk about how Jon might improve his job.   Sounding like Pete in spite of the accent, Grant had suggested he set objectives. 'Write down a plan, Jon. Make an appointment with Steve, set an agenda...' It was like you were the only person he'd ever talked to in his whole life, and were ever going to talk to. It was like you were the most interesting person he'd ever listened to.

On one of his visits, Grant said. 'Whatever we talk about won't go beyond this room.'

Wow, Jon thought and had swirled round taking in the white walls, the magic carpet, the tree and the road through the window, thinking: I could stay here forever, bed down. He flopped on the sofa and leaned back his head.

Grant smiled. 'You can lie down on that if you want to.'

He'd laughed. 'Mind reader.'

'What would you like to do with your life? What did you enjoy as a child? What were the best moments in your life? If you had a magic wish, if a miracle happened...?'   Grant's questions were weird, but Jon wanted to answer them, wanted to tell him that he didn't know what he enjoyed, apart from drinking beer with Pete and, more recently, herbal tea with Black Plaits – and yeah, the sight of Daisy's hair did fill him with... well, all sorts of things, as did the memory of her crying in his arms.

The miracle was he talked. Talked about work and Steve. Talked about the flat and New Malden and his ma in the kitchen and the telly always on and his dad making him feel he couldn't learn anything.   He even mentioned Tracey at Motsuki Pharmaceuticals, though he didn't go into details. He could never see the point in things, but while he was talking to Grant he forgot that. 'You remind me of a friend, ' he said. He wanted to talk about the bit of Pete that was like Grant, the bit that made him want to shout, 'Eureka! This is it!' When we're nattering over a pint, just the two of us like this, it's here in this pub between us!   Excitement spurted through him at the thought of letting Grant in on this, but he got sidetracked on to Shirley and how he didn't see enough of Pete. And Grant said, 'You miss that,' and he was fucking nearly in tears.

He began to think he could talk to Grant about anything. He settled into the couch and let its firm shape hold him. But on that particular Saturday Grant started telling him about the different places he'd lived in as a child all over America. If Jon liked they could go up to the room where he kept his maps and he would show him a map of the States and all those different places. Jon shifted himself upright, thinking: how many more Saturdays are there? Will there be time to tell him all the things he needed to tell? Grant pulled up the armchair from the corner of the room. 'Before you go, huh?' and Jon sank back into the couch. The door was closed, they needn't go upstairs. He could talk to Grant, tell him anything. He just needed to think how to find a way in. Then he could talk about Black Plaits and Daisy.

But that was before the bomb scare and Martha's answer phone message and that visit to Black Plaits and that stupid memory. Today, as he noticed the lines round Grant's eyes – glancing round to make sure Martha wasn't lurking; the door was closed of course – he wondered why the fuck he'd arranged to see Black Plaits tomorrow. He needed to talk to Grant. It was Daisy he wanted to get off with. Not Black Plaits. He was heading along the wrong path.

'What's the matter, Jon?'

'Nothing.'

'Are you worried about something?'

He could feel Grant willing him to look at him, and nodding at him in the way that he did when was trying to get you to talk. 'Is it awkward seeing Martha here?'

'Not specially.'

'Do you see her much at work?'

'No...'

'Is that okay?'

'Yeah.' Why was he asking?

Grant's head was tilted, eyes nice and friendly. 'She won't bite, huh?' Ha ha, very funny, and now Grant's face was creasing into laughter.

He supposed he was meant to laugh too.

And then the door opened, no knock, and she was there in the doorway asking them if they would mind if she joined in, and Grant was getting to his feet. 'Hi honey. We've been talking about you.' The bugger, after that confidentiality crap.

She came and sat at the other end of the couch. 'I didn't want to miss out.'

Grant sat down in his chair. 'We were just saying, that it must be quite difficult for you two seeing each other here and then at work.' He smiled and looked from one to the other. 'What's she like at work, Jon? A bit of a tyrant?'

His shoulders lifted. He could throttle Grant this afternoon.

Martha kicked off her shoes and pulled her feet up on to the couch. 'I hardly see you, do I, Jon? When was it that you last got me a sandwich?'

Something strange happened then. She was about the same age as Black Plaits, same little lines round the mouth and at the corners of the eyes. Different colour eyes of course, and with the yellow bits, but something the same, the same look inside them, the same look looking at him. No need to be scared. Scared of me, more like. He sat back into his corner of the couch and put his foot up on to his knee and let his mouth spread into a smile. 'I don't do that now.'

'Don't you?'

'No.'

'Come up in the world.' She was nodding like Grant – ran in the family obviously – and smiling back, looking less... whatever it was – perhaps *scared* was the right word. 'You deserve it, Jon.' She glanced back at Grant. 'Did he tell you? He was the one who removed that suspicious bag at work.'

'No kidding?'

'I'm not.'

He sank into his corner of the couch and stretched out his legs across the colours of the magic carpet. It didn't matter that Martha was telling Grant that she'd phoned and left a message on Jon's answer phone, or that Martha was turning to Jon to check whether he had received the message. He nodded and repeated his smile and looked into her blue eyes with the yellow bits, amazed that he could do that. The arms of the upholstery curled round him. He wouldn't mind a settee like this in his flat. Wouldn't mind the carpet. Bit big. But perhaps not with him and Black Plaits, or Daisy, rolling around on it.

Later they sat at the kitchen table and had bread and butter and jam, and shortbread cookies, as Grant called them, made by the local cake shop. He wondered if he could ask for marmite. Grant talked about the different words for things in America, how they were simpler than the English, nearer the meaning. 'Like cookies. Or sidewalk. It's as if those Puritans were kids when they landed on the east coast of America and those words spread throughout the States.'

Martha filled their mugs with tea. 'Grant's father was a university professor and Grant lived in many different places as a child.'

Grant passed him the milk. 'I told you that, didn't I, Jon? I'll take you to my map room after this. Show you the places.'

Martha bit into a shortbread and pushed the crumbs off her mouth. 'Jon and maps don't go.'

He received the Grant grin. 'I know.'

He topped up his tea with milk and set down the little jug. It wobbled for a second. He steadied it with his hand. This was all right. This was how they were with the white jug and the white teapot and the mugs with the red flowers. They were proud of his action at work That was what the message on the answer phone was about. Martha had shared it with Grant. The three of them together were okay. He liked this light kitchen with its smooth clean surfaces and expensive units. He loved the hot tea and cakes and the cookies, although he preferred marmite toast. As he followed Grant up the red-carpeted stairs to look at Grant's map room, he wished he was climbing up the stairs to stay the night and get up the next morning for breakfast at that kitchen table and a chat on Grant's couch. They probably did eat breakfast. Then he could take his time finding his way home by train, if Grant didn't give him a lift, and after that he would go to Black Plaits.

FIFTEEN

GRANT

The lights turned green. The car safely in motion, Grant glanced at his passenger: pale profile against the window, dark brows, a set expression. He imagined saying to Martha, it would be dangerous to stop seeing him suddenly; and then remembered Jon wasn't a patient. He came out of the Robin Hood roundabout and moved from second to third as he started up Kingston Hill, feeling hot. How could he even consider going over that boundary? He hadn't, had he? Just offered him advice and a listening ear. He'd kept it strictly to that. Poor guy – he'd had little enough of it in his life.

He came out with a little, 'Uh huh, well...' All easy. 'I guess you're ready for the computer now.'

'Wha– ?'

The dropping of his 't's denoted agitation, Grant had noted early on in their – what could he call it; relationship? Not therapy; that must be clear. Friendship? They had got on very well today – all three of them. No harm there. 'Next Saturday, huh? I can bring it over. Help you set it up.'

'Yeah.... yeah, thanks.'

'Do you think you'll use it?' Grant could feel Jon turning towards him, although he made no reply. 'You'll get real fast at typing. Take over Steve's job soon.'

'Is that it then?'

'Is that – what?'

'No more Saturdays.'

He moved into the outer lane, his face breaking into a smile. He'd grown fond of the guy and would miss him when he stopped coming. 'Do you want to go on seeing me Saturdays?'

'Wha' about Martha?'

145

'What about her?' He glanced at him. 'Martha suggested it in the first place, didn't she? I'll bring over the computer next Saturday or the following one. It doesn't mean you have to stop coming to see me, if that's what you'd like.'

They had reached the roundabout about a minute away from Jon's flat. The street lights had come on. 'You do that, don't you?'

'Do what, Jon?'

'See people in your room. Ask questions – like you do with me.'

He parked outside the flat, switched off the ignition. That's my job he was about to say, but if you wanted to come and see us that would be friendship.

But Jon was lifting his head and putting out a hand to shake his. 'Thanks Grant.'

And that was it. Of course it was. Return the computer and say goodbye. Grant shook the outstretched hand with a feeling of relief. They had got too close, the three of them. He was nearly old enough to be the guy's father.

Jon's mouth was stretching in a grin. A tooth off centre had a chip that Grant hadn't noticed before. 'Next Saturday, can you teach me spreadsheets?'

Grant was smiling again.

The high, orange street lights formed vertical lines in the windscreen as the car climbed back up the hill towards the junction to Roehampton and made it across the lights. He liked him, and what was wrong with that? Martha did too. He'd seen that the moment she suggested giving Jon his old computer and now she looked almost happy on Saturday afternoons. 'Jesus', she called him.

He glanced at the signboard to Wimbledon and Putney and decelerated as he approached the next roundabout. Wimbledon Common… he slowed right down and joined a queue of cars, and turned his head to the right to catch a glimpse of the

Common, remembering that awful day in the rain when Martha had threatened donor insemination. He inched the car forward. Some days he thought she'd moved on. She said she didn't mind about Philip's and Kathleen's expected child, and he longed to believe her, longed to think she was more interested in work, and that when she looked sad, or seemed unusually interested in Jon, it was part of her getting over not being able to have a baby. He pictured her face at the bottom of the stairs about an hour ago as he and Jon came down from the map room; her look so bleak. She suggested she should take Jon home for a change. They both should have taken Jon home. But he'd wanted to have him on his own; had felt quite possessive as if they were fighting over him.

The queue was moving. He lifted the clutch and pressed on the accelerator, glanced once more at the Common, and then had to jam on his brakes as the car in front stopped sharply.

When he got home the door to his room was open. She was lying on his couch, her head resting on the arm, reading his notes, and he felt like turning round and going out again. He'd left out his notes to remind him to convince Julia that a chapter on donor insemination was important, and to finally face Martha on the subject. But he wasn't up to that now. He sat down in the armchair, his head pounding.

She shifted into a sitting position. 'You took a long time.'

'A lot of traffic.'

'I thought you'd skived off to the pub.'

'Of course not. Why are you here?'

'What…?'

'Why are you in my room?' But of course they had all been in his room, Jon with the computer Saturday after Saturday, Martha joining them sometimes. Only an hour or so ago the three of them had been here.

'I found these, didn't I?' She tapped the papers. 'What are these, Grant?'

'They're plans for a book.'

'A book?'

'Yes.'

'You're going to write a book about fathers?' She clutched the papers to her chest and shook her head.

He leaned back into the chair, tiredness sweeping through him. 'It's work. It's an important area. I've been wanting to write it for twenty years.'

'But – a book!'

'Martha…' His voice hardened. 'Perhaps I need to. Have you thought of that?'

'No… no, I hadn't.' Her voice quivered. She wedged herself into the corner of the couch and shuffled the notes on her lap, straightening them and shuffling them again. He had a strong urge to ask her to give them to him.

She glanced up. 'Is he coming back?'

'Sorry…?'

'Jesus?'

'Why do you keep calling him Jesus?'

'Why not?'

'He's very vulnerable, Martha.'

Her eyes were that pale blue. ''How can you bear to write a book about fathers?''

'Oh, for God sakes, Martha…'

They seemed to meet half way, her getting up from the couch, him moving towards her. He felt his arms go round her, surprised at the way she sunk against him. She was breathing quickly, sobbing he thought for a moment. He heard his own breath quicken. He buried his face in her short hair and encouraged her back to the couch. They sat there a moment. This was his workroom. His standards were shifting, tilting. The room had been sacrosanct until Jon had come along. He lifted her face to his and reached down to her jeans and unfastened the metal button and started to pull down her zip. She wriggled away. He thought she was going

148

to extract herself, but she was only easing herself off the couch and taking him with her on to the rug. He peeled off her clothes, rejecting the thought that they should find something to protect the rug.

Afterwards he went upstairs and brought down the duvet and pillows and they lay on the carpet hand in hand and stared up at the mouldings on the ceiling, and he asked her if she had read the notes, in a perverse way wanting her approval.

She told him she'd wanted to tear them up. But Liza had phoned needing her advice about something, and that had made her feel better. Then the doorbell had rung. It was the new neighbours coming round to explain about the skips in the road. She propped herself up on her elbows and looked down at him. 'I went round for a few minutes to meet the family. They had a baby in a Moses basket in the corner of the kitchen – a little girl, three months; eyelashes like doll's eyelashes. There were other kids running in and out. The husband asked me if I had kids. I didn't mind him asking me that. I told him I had a career. He offered to let me hold the baby, I laughed. No thanks, I said. I didn't want to.' She was laughing now as she turned to him, her face glowing as if she really meant it. 'I didn't want to hold the baby, Grant.'

On Sunday they got up late and walked along the river path to the River Café, high clouds scudding across a mild February sky, gulls squalling, the full tide water lapping over the towpath on the opposite bank. There had been a cancellation and they sat at one of the tables by the expanse of glass looking out on to the courtyard attended by a tall, white-aproned girl and took their time to plan their menu and choose the wine.

The restaurant filled. The light glanced off the chrome and reflecting surfaces. They prised open their warm crusty rolls and let the white butter melt into the dough.

Martha plunged her fork into a salad of radicchio and parmesan shavings. 'I wonder what he does?'

Grant watched her tongue pull a purple leaf into her mouth. 'Who?'

'Jesus.'

'Prays probably.'

'What?'

'It's Sunday, isn't it?'

She laughed. 'Have you been inside his flat?'

'Not yet.' His hand reached across the table. 'Smile again.' He pushed a fleck of green off her tooth.

Her lips closed round his finger.

A longing stirred, and then a hot fear. He lowered his hand. Her eyes flicked away.

The next door table were being advised on a particular year for a particular claret. She picked up her glass. 'We should take him out. Show him London.'

He pushed his fork into his wild mushroom risotto, wishing he felt hungrier. 'He probably knows it.'

'Show him what he doesn't know.

'I think we need to be careful.'

'Careful?'

'He could become dependent.'

Her hand was on her glass, lifting it to her mouth. 'You've been encouraging it.'

'Yeah… maybe.' He watched the movement of her throat swallowing the wine, the small bump a ripple under her skin. 'That moment just now… you weren't attracted to me because of him?'

'What…?'

'Jon… we were talking about him and then… I had this feeling that he was… I mean… for both of us.''

She put down her glass. 'What are you talking about?'

'You and I being affected by him.'

'That's ridiculous.'

'It can happen.'

'Sounds crass.'

There was burst of laughter from the next table. The tall attendant was hovering near their own table. She took the wine bottle out of the bucket and filled their glasses.

He waited for the girl to move on and placed his hand over Martha's and squeezed it. 'It does, doesn't it? Sorry.'

Her face coloured, water filling her eyes.

He put his hand on her cheek. 'It's alright, honey. We're okay. We really are okay.'

He woke in the night dreaming she wanted Jon's baby. The luminous figures of his watch told him it was four-thirty. He forced himself out of bed before the dream took a hold, then padded downstairs to the kitchen to make a sleepy-time tea. The dream was about his own insecurity, not Martha's. Both he and Martha had problems with infertility. Donor sperm was no more likely to work than his own. He shivered in the unheated house and fetched his puffer jacket from the cupboard under the stairs. Yesterday, she'd said she didn't want that baby next door. He sat down on the stool in the kitchen and sipped the herbal tea, and tried to believe that.

The following Saturday he drove in the hired car to pick up Jon, and decided that he must stop ferrying him backwards and forwards; the guy was perfectly capable of using public transport. They got back and he clicked on the Excel program, intending to introduce Jon to the concept and uses of spreadsheets, offer him an hour's good instruction followed by a quick cup of tea and then suggest they dismantle and deliver the computer to Jon's flat later in the afternoon.

He handed Jon a sheet of instructions and several copies of examples and left him in front of the computer to go and tell Martha the plans, but his arm was grabbed. 'Grant.'

He stepped back, feeling his arm released.

Jon was standing up. 'Can we talk?'

'Sure, go and sit.' Grant gestured to the couch.

'Do you mind?'

I do, he thought. He felt a pattering in his chest. No fool this guy. His face was taut as if he sensed they wanted to draw away from him. Hurt eyes. Seductive of course. Grant watched him settle into the couch, in the same spot as always, same posture, right leg across left thigh, and pulled up his chair ashamed of the tussle in his head. Choosing not to help him because of his fear of dependence or because of the rules of his profession, felt like turning his back on a child, just when the child wanted him. That was the trouble with his profession, it stopped you from offering ordinary kindness.

There was no stopping the guy, anyway. He'd uncrossed his legs and was leaning forward. He was making progress with an older woman, and he wasn't quite sure how far he wanted to go with this woman. There was someone else as well, at work, younger.

Grant folded his arms and let himself look at him. The guy had good features – broad nose, well set eyes, long thick hair… but they didn't quite add up. He was attractive to women probably and only just beginning to realise it. A virgin perhaps. He didn't seem gay. There were the awful parents, of course… There was also a deadness. If he was his patient, he would stick with this feeling, go deeper. But he wasn't his patient and he must stop slipping into analytic mode.

Jon grinned at Grant. 'I call this one Black Plaits. She wears them sometimes. I told you, she's older. She has a daughter.'

'So, a mother?'

'Wha –?'

'She's a mother.'

'Yeah.'

'Is she like your mother?' What was he saying?

'Grant, I wouldn't go with anyone like my ma. Dad doesn't go near her.' His head lifted. 'Do… do you and Martha…?'

Before he could stop himself Grant nodded. He could feel his shirt sticking to his armpits.

Jon was blushing, his hair flopping forward. 'Ou' of order, sorry Grant.' He tucked his hair behind his ears, glanced quickly and looked away again. 'Listen. Wha' I wanted to say – to ask you because I know you do that sort of thing – is about this memory I had.' He sat on the edge of the couch, leaning forward. 'It's me as a little kid, Grant. I'm screaming in the bath. The water's too hot or I've been slapped. It's a bad memory but good too.'

Grant rested his head into the corner of the chair and let the muscles in his back sag, wishing he could close his eyes and tell Jon to go away. 'What... triggered it?'

'Trigger – ?' Lines dug into Jon's forehead, and then he giggled. 'Bang, bang!'

Grant kept his face serious. There was a bird chirping outside.

Jon glanced towards the door. 'Her... touching me.'

For a second Grant thought he meant Martha. 'Sorry...?'

'Black Plaits. It wasn't that I didn't like – like her touching me. It was just – I had this – like a flash – the screaming bit... but there was a lovely bit too. I wanted the lovely bit to go on – her touching me to go on.' He tipped his head back against the couch. 'Yeah.'

The image of Martha and himself naked on the rug in this room snapped into Grant's mind. He shifted in his chair, aware that the bird had stopped chirping, and looked towards the window. The guy needed to talk to someone. In these last few weeks he'd wanted it to be him. His chest was pattering again. He must book an appointment with Neville and sort out his boundaries. Everyone in his profession had these little crises. It was the nature of the work. 'Jon...' he nodded, his eyes sliding back towards him. He would suggest a means-tested voluntary counselling service. Introduce him to the idea. Describe what it might be like. Give him a feel for it – he'd probably already done that.

Martha tapped on the door and invited them to come to the kitchen so that he didn't pass on any of these things. But he would, he promised himself.

They sat at the kitchen table and Martha told them she'd been watching skiing on television. Jon bit into a flapjack, crumbs clinging to the corners of his mouth and said he hated telly; watched too much as a kid, watched too much now.

'Skiing is the only sport I watch.' She poured out tea and offered bread and butter if anyone would like it; she'd just bought a fresh granary loaf. 'Grant and I used to go every year, didn't we? Verbier –'

'Martha, is Jon interested in skiing?'

She turned to him. 'Are you?'

Jon pushed his hair away from his face. 'Never tried.'

I mustn't leave it, Grant thought. I must persuade him to get support. Do that at least. He bit into a flapjack.

'Let's see if it's on now.' Martha was pushing her chair away from the table and standing up. She'd forgotten their conversation about dependency.

They followed her into the sitting room, taking their mugs of tea. Jon chose the armchair. Grant sat next to Martha on the sofa. The white lines of the football results filled the screen. Martha flicked the remote control, and for a few moments they sat silently watching the news on another channel and then thankfully Jon stood up.

'I'll get myself home.'

They both made to rise.

He put out a hand. 'I know where the station is. Grant and I pass it every time. One change at Clapham Junction. Even I can do that. I'll see myself out.' He lifted his hand in a wave. 'I'll look out for skiing.'

The front door closed, they flopped back into the sofa. Grant put an arm round her shoulder and heard the forced tone of his laugh. 'You mustn't encourage him.'

The next Saturday, they took the computer to Jon's dark basement flat. The place smelled damp. Martha went out shopping while the two of them installed the computer, and came back with Danish pastries and insisted she made a cup of tea in his sparse but clean kitchen. Everything was clean and tidy. Grant went in search of the toilet. The bathroom was on a small landing half-way up the stairs. He opened the frosted window and peered out onto a small garden. It backed on to another narrow garden, scruffy grass, tree at the end. There were outside steps descending from the ground floor. He went back down the gloomy stairwell with its dark wood and threadbare carpet. There was so little furniture in the guy's flat – a leather armchair, a table, the television – and no pictures or books, but the brightly coloured rug made it feel quite cheerful. The table which now held the computer looked new, possibly self assembled.

Martha was clutching her mug of tea and standing behind him as he stared at the screen. He was loading a game called 'Death Lottery'. Someone called Arthur had lent him the disc.

Martha took a step nearer. 'You must come up to the features floor sometime. I miss seeing you.'

His head turned, a flash of his eyes, and went back to the screen. 'Yeah... okay.'

Grant wondered about the forgotten memory and Black – whatever he called her. He didn't want to know about any of that, he reminded himself. He took Martha's hand as they said goodbye.

'See you next Saturday, Jon.' Martha said it, calling back to him like an afterthought as they climbed the steps to the road.

Grant opened the car door for her. She was smiling, mouth stretched too wide across her face. 'That may be the last we see of him.'

Her face was flushed. He wished she didn't look as if she wanted to cry.

The following morning they were woken at five-thirty by a phone call from Lani. Mom had suffered another stroke and this time it was a big one.

SIXTEEN

JON

Steve went through messengers like a dose of salts. Gerry, the new messenger, had moved on and now there was another, Max, who didn't know anything and thought Jon was the boss. Poncy name. He kept saying it was only a temp job before he moved on to greater things. It didn't bother Jon. There would be other messengers and the newer they were the more they looked up to him. 'Jon, which floor do I take these to? In what order do I …? What's the best way of getting to Aldgate… to Watford…?' He knew every inch of the way to Watford these days, from the bench on the platform at Canary Wharf so as to land opposite the exit to Bank to the coffee stall on Euston forecourt nearest the departure screens. If he was feeling kind he could tell him which trains past the hour coincided with the bus at Watford. The sweetest thing was sitting at the PC typing out a rota for the night shift, or updating the record of morning deliveries. Sitting there alone with the computer, Steve out of the room, Max on an errand. Sitting there when Max returned. Sitting there making Max wait while he tapped out the letters, Max waiting because he needed his help.

There was quite a gang at the *Spit and Polish* these days: Stuart and Owen – and he could hold his own now with Owen about computers – Dave, who could be counted on to prop up the bar on the bleakest of nights; Darrell from his Matt's Autos' days, who he'd got over from Ewell one evening early January as a consolation prize for the vanishing act of Pete, who was never available these days; and now Arthur who lived in Berrylands, and who'd dropped in on the *Spit and Polish* on his way somewhere and had decided to adopt it as his local though he lived at least two miles away.

'It's the company,' Jon would laugh. 'Can't resist us.'

Arthur was into computer games. He'd lent Jon the disc of *Death Lottery*. 'You can save it on to your hard disk.'

'Isn't that – illegal…?'

'Illegal? For fuck's sake, Jon! You'll love her.'

'Her?'

'Olga.'

He got dragged over to Arthur's place and shown how to load it and then given the disc.

Olga had a doll-like figure and was fucking life-like and sexy. Her black body-suited figure dodged lakes or traps or hidden dungeons, zapping monsters and sorcerers – ping! zap! bang! He and Arthur sat at the computer and roared as she defied death; groaned as death nearly got her.

Black Plaits wore black, like Olga. If he closed his eyes he could pretend she was Olga, pretend she was Daisy. Daisy was wearing black at the office party when he'd put his arms around her. So was Martha, but he didn't want to think about her. The memory of him and Daisy in that shiny office kitchen was like a distant dream – he couldn't believe he'd put his arms around her. David fucking Gould. Where was she at with him? Probably moved on to someone else. That was the trouble with sending Max on errands, he never got to see Daisy.

When he did get up there, she was usually chatting to Tony and leaning against his desk, or drawing up her chair next to Liza's, in with the crowd there and not needing him. 'Hi', she would lift an arm. Her long black skirt hugged her little bottom. Her jeans showed the divide between her buttocks. Sometimes, her hair was held up by one those clip things so that he could see the whole of her neck and think of his lips going there. That was as near as he was going to get, he thought too often these days. He could day dream about her in leather boots and skimpy flowery skirts half-way up her thighs, but they were the clothes Black Plaits was more likely to wear.

Sundays had become a regular with Black Plaits – four-thirty to five as she was closing the shop, sometimes earlier depending on whether he'd gone to Leatherhead for Sunday dinner. He had made it clear to Dad and Ma that he could only go there for dinner once a month. The trains were crap on Sundays and they could drive up to his place for a change. They never did.

The previous Sunday the train from Leatherhead was delayed at both Epsom and Wimbledon and when he reached Kingston he had to run to make sure she hadn't shut up shop.

She was on the pavement folding the last table. 'You thought you'd missed me. I'd have waited.'

'Would you?'

'Would you like me to?'

Her hair was loose and he couldn't decide whether it made her look younger. 'Yeah.'

She picked up the table. 'I could meet you at yours, but you don't want me to.'

He took the table from her and followed her into the shop. 'I never said that.'

'You don't.'

'You could.'

He passed her the table and she lay it carefully against two others, steadying the stack with her hands. 'Plenty of time.' Her head turned towards his.

That was what he liked about her, no rush as if there was all the time in the world. Everything nice and slow. The way her see-through green eyes paused on his and looked away. The way her hand lifted up her bag and her fingers with their long purple nails pulled back the zip to find her keys. He wanted her to come to his flat, but not yet, and he felt she knew that.

She didn't touch him that day or ask him if he was scared and that felt right too. Plenty of time as she'd said.

It was on the day after Martha and Grant had delivered the computer to his flat that he thought: I'm ready for her. He'd had to clean up the place and it seemed a waste of an opportunity. He hurried along the Portsmouth Road making for the river path, picturing Black Plaits in the flat. He hadn't bought that new leather armchair or settee he'd dreamed about. But he had the rug and the new computer table and chair, and he could see her sitting upright in the new chair, legs encased in thigh leather boots, one leg crossed over the other.

She'd touched his face and not removed her hand straight away, but it hadn't happened again. He'd had that memory flash. He'd talked to Grant about it, but couldn't remember what Grant had said. Didn't seem to matter after he'd told him. He just wanted to remember the feeling of her touching him.

His feet pounded along the river path as he ran towards the higher buildings of Kingston, towards her shop. He'd chosen to go there on foot because he needed to think how he would suggest her coming to the flat; how he would do it, the words. It felt easier in the open air. But he was going to be late, and he was sweating. His face would be scarlet. He slowed down once he'd swerved off the river path and was into the town. He leaned against a wall at the corner of the market, catching his breath, and then lifted the lapel of his jacket and checked his armpits.

She wouldn't have waited for him this time. He knew that from the way she picked up the bowl labelled *crystals* and *ammonites* and took them into the shop. She came out again and didn't look at him. That confirmed it. Her hair was pulled back into a brown slide – he hadn't seen that before. It made her look older. 'Can you bring in those bowls of Quartz.'

'I'll fold the tables up, if you like.'

'Thanks.'

She didn't want him there. *Plenty of time* was too slow for her. There was a limit to how long things took. They took the remaining bowls of stuff into the shop and put them on to the counter. They folded the tables and stands and lugged them in from the pavement and stacked and piled them into their allotted places. But then she closed the door with both of them inside, and leaned against it. 'Thought you weren't coming,' and he knew he was alright.

'Sorry.'

She moved nearer. 'I'd have missed you.'

He felt hot under his arms. He needed to take off his jacket.

She was looking at him. Her hand reached to his face... her fingers pushing into his hair. And then both her hands held the back of his head and brought it nearer to hers. Full works, he thought – his heart was thudding – but her lips just touched his, very gently lips to lips, mouths closed. She took a step back. 'I don't know what it is about you...' Her head shook. He could see the little semi-circles at the corners of her mouth, and her white teeth and her pink tongue.

He thrust his face into hers searching for her lips, hungry now. He heard her gasp as he squeezed her to him. His lips seemed too big for hers, too wet. He took them into his mouth, sucking at them, eating them.

But her face turned away. 'Jon, no... not here... not now...'

He clutched her head, turning it back.

'Jon, no...'

She was spoiling it.... just when he was doing it, just when it was happening... he wanted to pick up one of her rocks and make her let him go on...

She caught hold of his arms, slowing everything, and her warm, firm grip round his lower arms made things stand still for a second 'It's alright, Jon.' He could hear that he was panting. 'It's alright.'

And it would've been alright if she'd stayed slow and quiet and kept her hands on his arms while he caught his breath; if she'd told him there was plenty of time, no pressure, no worries. But she removed her hands and looked at him with those see-through green eyes and then smiled, her teeth and her tongue so expectant. 'Jon, we can go back to my place.' And he wasn't ready for that.

He shoved past her, fumbled with the door handle, and got the door open.

'Jon! Jon!' Her voice chased him, ricocheting off the buildings of the narrow streets, echoing, as his shoes thudded on the tarmac. He ran along the streets, thud, thud, into the wider shopping street. There were so many streets, and roundabouts now, and the fucking bypass. He preferred the river route – dark blue sky in dark blue river, lights coming on. They could have walked along the river, looked across to the open space, gone to their café, or a pub, done those sorts of things.

There was the large, pale building with tall pillars and huge glass swing doors that he'd noticed from the bus. The crown court. He stood at the bottom of the steps and imagined himself between two men in blue going through those swing doors; himself in the dock staring at the jury like on TV. Assault… murder! Black Plait's head done in with one of her rocks.

He turned back, knowing she hadn't called his name but crossing the four-lane road into the maze of streets because it was nearer to her, nearer to the shop. He strode with heavy steps straight on, turned left, turned right… thud, thud on the hard pavements… He cut through the covered shopping mall, circled the market place, skirted the church, and round again, on the same streets. She would have shut up long ago but his circlings moved him over to her side of town, the Ham side though he didn't know where she lived.

It was Grant's fault. Grant who'd put the idea into his head. Made him talk. Made him think he could have her. Made him think he was ready for her. 'Want to talk to me, Jon?' He fucking needed to talk to Grant now.

'Hello, darling.'

A Daisy look-alike was coming out of the *Horse and Cart* – he'd never heard of the place; he was on a main road, heavy goods vehicles rattling past. Tarty, long, yellow hair...

And now a Black Plaits – more or less... tight, black leggings and high heeled shoes.

He paused under the street light. His palm tapped against his knuckles. He could pull women. No doubt of it.

The yellow-haired one was looking at him, the dark one took a step nearer. 'Hello.' They spoke in chorus like twins.

The door banged behind them carrying a whiff of beer. He looked from one to the other. 'Want a beer?' That question with Daisy. Fucking memories...

'You all right?'

'Thirsty.'

'We've had ours.'

There was a whine of acceleration. He glanced up the road. Smell of exhaust. The traffic lights ahead were turning red. In the distance he could see the red glow of a further set and a lighted signboard.

'You lost, darling?'

In the yellow light he looked down at their made-up faces and felt his fists tighten. He swerved away and started to run, his feet thudding on the pavement again, back towards the centre of Kingston.

Mummy's boy Tracey had called him, all those years ago at the Motsuki Pharmaceuticals' office outing when he was barely nineteen. It was her fault too.

Back at his flat he lifted his overalls out of his bedroom cupboard and took out the magazines from under the overalls. Smooth, glossy pages... forgotten about for weeks. Hideous the girls inside, like those slags outside the pub... dumb faces, curvy painted-in lips.

Tracey had leaned against him as they queued to get on to the coach at the end of the office day outing, the worse for too

163

many gin and limes. He'd had to shove her into the seat by the window and then flop into the outside seat. Her head fell against his shoulder, her hair in his face, an arm across his thigh. The day's beer churned inside him. Over the backs of the seats he could see other couples snogging. He lifted her chin and searched out her tongue, got it in his mouth and sucked. She moaned like a baby. His hand reached the thick bits of her thigh, taut underneath the tight jeans. His fingers crept to the divide and found a hole in the crotch of her jeans.

They tumbled off the coach at Victoria bus station. She had to get back to Greenford. He said goodbye to her at the entrance of the tube station, and thrust his face in hers to give her his tongue.

'Don't, Jon. My head.'

'You going to be alright?'

She seemed to nod. He tottered off towards Waterloo to get some air, and clear his own head. He should have gone back with her, done it while they were both out of it. He wouldn't be flicking through these glossy pages staring at these slags now.

He'd got to know her when the original of page twenty-eight of a fifty-page document got stuck in the automatic feed in danger of being torn before it had made the required ten copies. Her dark brown eyes had filled with tears. It had been easy to touch her in the course of duty as he made her to sit down while he dismantled the flat panes of plastic and widened the slit so that he could release page twenty-eight. His finger had strayed to the skin at her wrist near the edge of the arm of her pink jersey.

After the day trip she came down to the post room nearly every day. She wore light coloured tops and black or brown skirts that stopped above the knee, and she had a way of opening her mouth and touching her top lip with the edge of her tongue. The post room was in a separate, low building away from the main office block and they would go out into the yard and lean against the wall in the sun for a mid-morning or afternoon smoke.

One evening he waited for her to come out of the main building and followed her to the pavement. She was wearing beige trousers that day and he could see the back of her ankles between the hem of her trousers and her brown heeled shoes. 'Like a drink?'

She turned and glanced at her friend, Maureen.

Maureen tucked her arm into Tracey's and eyed Jon as if they had never seen him before. 'The both of us?'

Maureen was in a red coat with a black fur collar and was a big girl, nearly as tall as him and certainly heavier – he had a feeling they were both older than him – but he pulled his hand out of his pocket and pointed to Tracey. 'Just you.'

A street light came on. Maureen removed her arm from Tracey's and stared at her. 'I thought we were going to the station, Tracey.'

Tracey lifted her shoulders. 'Well, we can.'

'What? With him?'

'Shut up Maureen.'

'Do you like him?'

All this, as if he wasn't there. He should have walked off there and then. But it was a good feeling when Tracey chose him. The two of them walked off under the dark sky, the streetlights lighting up. They chose a small pub a few streets away, and she ordered a gin and lime, and then another, and then a lager or was it lemonade? He matched each of her drinks with a half-pint. Her tongue flicked between her teeth. He reached out a hand and suggested they leave the pub.

They wandered through the streets back towards Motsuki Pharmaceuticals, arm in arm, weaving along the pavements, crossing roads, nearly going into another pub. They arrived at the post room and he unlocked the door and pressed the alarm number. He'd jerked himself off a dozen times thinking about the hole in her jeans. His hand shook and he got the number wrong. Tracey was leaning against the wall. The alarm ticked. He dialled it again, slowly – five, eight, three... the noise stopped. He didn't dare turn on the light. The photocopier loomed in the darkness. He pushed her up to the side of it and pressed himself against her beige trousers and yellow top, willing his cock that had been so alert in the pub to wake up. She squirmed against him. He wriggled and pressed... but she was slipping, her back was sliding down the shiny sides of the photocopier. He clutched her, and went down with her. They lay on the floor. He could smell the drink on her breath. Christ, would they stay here all night? People got here at sparrow's fart. But she was fumbling with the button on his trousers and pulling the button through the hole. Her fingers were on the zip.

'No...' The little bugger was asleep. He pushed her hands away.

'Wha'–?' She give a little groan and heaved herself up on to her elbow. 'I thought you wanted to.'

'I do.'

Her hair was all mussed and stupid. She stared at his crotch. 'What's the matter with you?'

'Nothing... if you put your – '

'Wha'?'

'It's alrigh' –'

'Wha...?'

'I said it was alright!'

'You can't do it, can you? You can't get it up!' She tottered to her feet and took a step back and leaned against the photocopier. 'You mummy's boy!'

'Oh, fuck off!' He stood up feeling dizzy and put a hand out to the photocopier to steady himself.

She wouldn't look at him. She was shoving her feet into her shoes and straightening her jacket which she hadn't even taken off, smoothing her hair, picking up her bag.

'Tracey...!'

Her head turned. 'Get off. Just get off me!'

She clip clipped with her brown heeled shoes round the end of the photocopier and clip clipped out the door.

He had to lock up – he didn't dare to leave it – and she wasn't there when he got to the road. He looked up and down. The street lights shone yellow. A car drove past. He turned back towards the building. She was probably at the station by now. He stared down the road again. Tracey! Tracey...!

In the morning he didn't go back. How could he work with that machine knowing what it had witnessed? How could he face Tracey? Career in the bloody post room. It was only meant to be temporary. He told his ma he'd finished with Motsuki Pharmaceuticals and not to answer any phone calls; he was going away for a couple of weeks. He bedded down with Pete and didn't return to New Malden for several weeks. Motsuki Pharmaceuticals sacked him for absenteeism. He signed on at the local job centre. Tracey didn't cry rape. For all he knew, she cried the opposite.

He pushed the magazines away. That was years ago. His hand clutched his tiny cock. Ancient history. If only it was. He tucked the floppy thing inside his pants and pulled up his zip. A mummy's boy. Who fucking cared? The younger ones were useless – Tracey, Daisy. He liked older women. He liked Black Plaits.

He doubled over with a groan. He'd fucked it up with Black Plaits. He'd fucked it up.

SEVENTEEN

MARTHA

Grant waved a hand through the open window and smiled at her. The taxi moved off and they didn't touch again. Martha watched the taxi turn left at the end of the road, aware of slowly lowering her arm as someone walked past. She put her hand on the cold metal of her gate and thought of him going all those thousands of miles away, and of the weekend they'd just had that seemed to be flying away with him: the three of them installing the computer in Jon's Spartan, but thankfully clean flat. She'd had a dread of the flat smelling, or of it being dirty. The dark interior with the barred window below the street made it feel like a prison. It had been a relief to come home to their own space and to smell Grant's skin and fall into bed with him. But now Grant had gone and there were going to be days to get through on her own, a week, weeks perhaps.

'Hello Martha.' The woman from the new family who had just moved in was standing beside her with a buggy, the baby inside. 'Barbara. Remember?'

'Oh... yes.' Martha tried to concentrate. A car drove past and turned left, like the taxi. There was a raw breeze. 'How's the unpacking?'

'Still in packing cases. No cupboards anywhere so we can't – excuse me.' Her head jerked away. 'Rory! Jane! Wait! Wait at the end of the road!' She glanced back. 'Sorry.'

'Don't worry,' Martha shook her head. She should welcome the intrusion. It felt like she would need distractions.

The woman laughed. 'It's half term.'

'Half term...?'

'Shoe shopping. They grow out of them so quickly...'

Philip had rung about half term taking it seriously that she might want Becky. She'd forgotten she'd asked him. He took

168

things so literally. I could do a long weekend, she told him, but I would need more notice; and he'd taken her at her word. Perhaps she should go back to him and say she would have Becky while Grant was away. Fill the time...

The woman was looking at her. 'Everything alright?'

'My husband's flying off to the States.'

Her head swung away again. 'Rory! Jane! Stop kicking that stone and come back here!'

The younger, higher voice of her son returned like an echo. 'You come here, Mum!'

'Rory, do as you're told! Both of you!' She turned to Martha. 'You were saying, your husband – '

'His mother's dying.'

'Oh, I'm sorry.'

'Mum!'

'Look sorry, I'll have to go.' Her hand touched Martha's arm. 'Come for a coffee later. We're just doing a bit of shopping. I'll be back in an hour –' she rolled her eyes, 'I hope.'

'I'll be going to work.'

'Work? Oh, of course...' She was pushing the buggy forwards. 'Drop in sometime. I'm always around.' She glanced back with a light laugh. 'I don't work, apart from this lot.'

Bundles in buggies grew up into shoe-shopping and kicking-stones monsters. They became Beckys, but only after years of hard work and the help of brothers and sisters. She pushed open the gate and walked back down the path into her empty house. Feel what it felt like. That had been the idea behind having Becky. Feel the experience of being with a child. Feel if that was what she wanted.

Work would fill the time. She could make it stretch and stretch. Once on the train heading for Waterloo and the Jubilee Line, watching the urban vista flash past, the sixties high-rise blocks scattered haphazardly under a grey sky, she reminded herself of that.

She'd asked Jenny, her new secretary, to get together a list of the regular contributors; she'd been relying on the regulars and needed new blood. This week she would search out new writers and do some networking, poaching even; meet useful contacts after work for a drink. She'd neglected these activities of late. She must decide the areas to focus on – not *Women*, but *Travel*, and *Business & Finance* maybe. Find out what Tony was really up to. Keep an eye on Liza. Liza had been writing. A story on children of asylum-seekers had been followed by another on refugee children and yet another on abused children. It had developed into a series called 'Marginalised Children'. Liza was digging in. It had comforted Martha – no plans for promotion presumably. Perhaps this week she might write something herself.

She attended a conference on the ethics of journalism and met useful people and came away with ideas to discuss at the editorial meeting. A piece on *The Chronicle's* record on ethics began to form in her mind. Tony sat at his desk; glasses pushed up on to his head. He was deep into an insider-dealing scandal and showed no signs of leaving. Liza had started her next story: 'The Only Child'. The days passed.

In the evenings Martha opened her front door to the empty hall, switched off the alarm, poured a glass of wine, stuck something into the microwave, and turned on the radio searching for news programmes, weather, arts stories – ideas for stories could come from the oddest sources, ideas for her to write about. These stories probably wouldn't get written, but the radio was company and the search for ideas filled her mind.

Grant phoned one evening and reported there was no change since his first call. His mother was semi-conscious and appeared to recognise him, but was unable to speak. Martha poured herself another glass of wine and lay on the sofa in front of *Newsnight*. Her gut ached, a low tugging feeling. She undid the waistband of her trousers and pressed her fingers into her stomach, recognising the pain. She shifted on to her side and dug her thumbs into the muscles round her hips, hating her body.

When the door bell rang she'd dropped off. She got to her feet and made for the hall, wondering whether she had really heard it – and turned away, remembering she was on her own. But it rang again. Her neighbour's face loomed through the security eye. She opened the door. The woman was standing on the doorstep holding her daughter, wrapped in a blanket.

'Barbara…?'

Her face was red and damp. The child's head rested against her shoulder. 'I'm sorry to bother you – but Michael's away.'

'Michael?'

'My husband. I don't know what to do.' She glanced down the road towards her house. 'I've left Rory and the baby. Emily's been crying and crying… her temperature…'

Martha steadied herself against the door frame, the cold air making her long to go back inside and up to bed. 'Come in. I'll ring the doctor for you.'

'No – I've done that. It's NHS Direct. They just tell me to give her Calpol. It's not working.' The child started to cry, a small sound like an animal. Barbara patted her head, pressing her lips into her hair. 'It's alright, Emily, it's alright…'

'I'm sure we can get a doctor.'

'They'll see her at A&E, but how can I with the other children…?' She looked down the road again. 'I suppose I could but – '

'I'll call an ambulance, Barbara.'

Tears welled into her eyes. 'Do you think we can?'

'Yes.' Martha nodded and touched her arm. 'Go back home, and I'll phone. What's the number of your house, so I can tell them?'

171

Within ten minutes the ambulance had arrived and Martha was walking beside Barbara as she followed the stretcher.

Barbara paused by the ramp and gazed into Martha's face. 'She was playing with her dolls' house this morning. It came on so quickly.' The paramedic's arm was round her shoulder. She glanced back at the house. 'Do you mind staying...? They're both asleep... if you could just check...' The paramedic encouraged her up the ramp and closed the doors.

Wide awake now, Martha folded her arms against the cold and watched the ambulance draw away and then ran back into the house. Thank God, it was warm. She went straight up the bare wooden stairs to check on the children. The landing was lit by a ceiling bulb and there were a couple of half-empty tea chests and screws of newspaper on the floorboards. Someone had scraped away a patch of wallpaper. She took off her shoes not wanting to wake the children. At least the bare light made it possible to see into the dark rooms. Three children, so two now. There were twin beds in the first room, heaps of clothes and toys in the corner, no carpets but plywood, ready perhaps for the carpet. She crept up to the mound in the nearest bed: tufts of brown hair stuck out of the top of a Spiderman duvet – the boy... where was the baby? She pushed the door into the next room – a large double bed, more heaps of clothes: their room obviously. No curtains in the window. She moved across the landing to the room opposite. A blanket hung across the window. The sheets were pulled back from the bed – the girl's room, of course. Was the girl going to die?

The house was chaotic. She put on her shoes and decided to have one last look upstairs and then... but she wasn't sure what she would do then. Could the baby be sleeping downstairs? Her shoes echoed on the floorboards as she went from room to room again – the girl's room... the boy's... but there was the cot in the corner of the parents' room behind the open door.

She flopped on to the bed, noises of relief escaping from her throat. Her shoes fell off and clattered to the floor. She held her breath and looked towards the cot. The shape under the white honeycomb blanket didn't move. She reached her bare feet to the floor and crept nearer. Tiny back of the head. Rise and fall of the small body. She sunk back on the bed and let out her breath.

Her gut ached and she needed a Feminax. She found the loo and sat on it, seeing the packet in the medicine cupboard at home, top left hand corner – blue lettering. Tension of muscles in the uterus – peeing wasn't helping. Labour pains were supposed to be like that, magnified, of course. She checked the loo paper for blood. There was some paracetamol in her bag. Better than nothing. She would lie down on the double bed and try to sleep next to the baby.

But she couldn't find her bag now, and she ran downstairs trying to picture herself locking the house and putting the key into her bag, and couldn't remember whether she'd put on the alarm and began to doubt that she'd locked the front door. She glanced into their kitchen and sitting room although she hadn't been near those rooms.

The bag was on the tiled hall floor, most finished part of the house, not dissimilar to their own tiled floor. She took it into the kitchen, filled the kettle and searched for some coffee, telling herself to calm down. If she could find a cafetière or an espresso machine and some real coffee, or – and this felt possible (the children wouldn't wake) – if she dashed back home and got her own cafetière and coffee, she would make herself a soothing, milky coffee. More than anything, she longed for the warm, milky taste in her mouth and the feeling of it going down into her throat. But there was no coffee, only a small jar of Nescafe next to some teabags near the kettle. The pain had worn off a little and she sat down at the table and delved in her bag for her diary.

However many times she counted – and she flicked through the pages several times, forgetting about the coffee – she made it five weeks. Even allowing for her irregular cycle it meant she must be two or three days overdue. Upstairs in the bathroom on the loo again she pressed down hard, wiped herself and stared at the loo paper. Not a speck of blood.

Back into the bedroom, she knelt down by the cot. Small mound rising and falling, white honeycomb blanket, downy back of the head. She pushed her face against the bars. She could hear the tiny breaths. Her longing for a soothing, milky coffee was suddenly relevant.

Only minutes later, it seemed, Barbara's face was level with hers, her breath hot and stale. 'It's alright. Emily's alright. It's not serious.'

The room was in semi-darkness, light coming in from the open door. For a second Martha wondered where she was, the duvet heavy on top of her, her clothes still on. Then she sat up and put her arms round the woman and clasped her warm, plump body, and remembered her own discovery.

EIGHTEEN

JON

They fancied him, those girls outside that pub in Kingston. That was what he told himself on the Monday and the Tuesday when Max didn't turn up and he was running his own errands, up and down to the floors all day long, and there was no time to work out how he was going to transfer the mailroom costs on to a spreadsheet like Grant had shown him. He could pull women. All sorts. And those ones were young, younger than Daisy even.

Steve stood over him half-way through the afternoon, just as he had a minute in front of the computer. 'This will have to go today.' He placed a brown envelope next the computer.

'Bit late, isn't it?' Jon guided the little arrow to the *Excel* symbol and pressed the mouse.

'*Today*, mate! It's only four o'clock.'

'Max'll be here tomorrow –' He clicked on *File* and then *Open*.

'Hand delivery.'

'Why can't it go special delivery?'

'What do you think they pay us for?'

The screen was clear. Of course it was; he hadn't made any files. He flicked the mouse on several exit boxes, hating to leave it.

'Don't switch it off!' Steve leaned against the computer table, eyes not budging until Jon had fetched his jacket and stuffed the envelope into the inside pocket. The address was in Soho.

'What happens if I lose it?' His blood was hot. Steve was already lowering his backside into the computer chair, taking his place. 'I might lose the way.'

'You'd better not. It's your job to deliver it safely.' Steve peered at the blank screen as if there was something to read on it and glanced back, stupid look on his face. 'Don't think I don't notice. Giving yourself airs and graces with Max and the others. But Max et al. move on. I don't mind you teaching the new editorials and typing the rotas and cost sheets. But if you choose to stay, your main task is delivery, Jon, job title *editorial*, and in this newspaper that means messenger, whatever the time of day.'

Fucking job. Fuck it if he lost it. And yet his hand crept inside his jacket checking the brown envelope as he descended in the lift, and did it again on the platform at Canary Wharf.

He surfaced at Tottenham Court Road and turned right into Oxford Street. A McDonald's packet bounced across the pavement, lifted and dived into a passing car. He turned left away from the crowds and the smell of hot dogs and onions. A plastic bag blew against his leg. Into Soho Square... over to the right... off to the right... with the help of his small A-Z Map, much less complicated than Pete and Shirley's *Greater London Street Atlas*, he could get himself anywhere. It wasn't Gerry showing him how to use the map – it was him having to show Max that had got it into his head. Finding places was simple now. He didn't know why it had been a problem. *Soho Street BW39 1*. He liked to find the page and trace his finger up and down the streets, and then go there and see what the place was like, though he hadn't done much of that recently with Max around. Perhaps that was how he could explore London – the important bits, the famous places. Take someone with him, Daisy, Black Plaits... sod, he hadn't thought about Black Plaits for at least an hour.

Number eight was a brown door with a peeling metal letterbox. He rang the doorbell and delivered the envelope to a tall, grey-haired woman who said she was expecting it. He strode away, thud, thud, down the narrow empty street, glanced at his watch, turned right into Carlisle Street and walked in the opposite direction from the way he'd come, searching for a quiet place to phone Steve and call it a day. But his mobile was out of juice. He wandered the length of Dean Street looking for a phone box, came back again. Someone told him there was one in Soho Square.

'How long will it take you to get back, Jon?'

'It's five, Steve…'

'Quarter to!'

'Steve, it's…'

'Alright! But get in early tomorrow. Nasty feeling Max has done a runner.'

No Black Plaits and now no Max. If he didn't watch it he would be running around at Steve's beck and call, fulfilling his job role as a messenger, being what he was a few months ago.

'Don't *you* let me down.'

'I won't, Steve!'

Bloody Steve. He replaced the phone and leaned against the door, only registering as he got out into the fresh air that Steve had replied, 'I rely on you.'

He found his way to Leicester Square station and got to Waterloo. At Wimbledon he took a Kingston train. The shop would be closed but she might be in the café, if the café was still open. He looked at his watch. Was today one of her days?

The worst was not knowing. Not knowing if he'd totally buggered it, not knowing if she wanted to see him again. She was old enough to be his mother… well, ten years difference… fifteen maybe. He should have got her mobile number. He didn't even know her surname. Could hardly remember her first name – Carol, wasn't it? He trod the familiar streets staring at his black work shoes, aware of other shoes passing his: trainers, leather boots, brown high heels. The stalls and tables would be inside by now. Would he go and check? He passed by their café and peered in through the window, his reflected face staring at him. He flicked his fingers through his hair and bent nearer the glass: single man in the corner, two women standing up… not her.

The weird thing was he didn't care about Daisy. It was like he'd left her behind, stranded on the Features Floor where he didn't want to go. He had to think hard to remember the jeans dividing her buttocks, or the long, black skirt hugging her bottom, and the picture in his mind didn't work.

He moved on from the café and got as close to the shop as he could, staring at the pavement as if his life depended on it, and then focussed upwards wanting to avoid the sight of the empty pavement and the *Closed* sign on the door. *Gem Universe*... curly, silver letters on deep green. He'd not noticed the name before. Gem Universe... those old stones and rocks. But then he saw that the door was open and the words seemed to blossom into the perfect name, and he made his way towards it.

A few minutes later with another envelope in his pocket, he headed for the river, cutting through the market place and looking at the sky, which had little pink clouds He plunged his hand into his jacket to touch – it was a white envelope. The blue of the sky was amazing. He'd never seen such a blue, such a deep, deep blue.

How did the girl in the shop know he was Jon? He'd stepped inside and seen her short-brown hair, his heart beat dropping. But then she'd given him the envelope, saying, 'From Carol,' and his heart had recovered.

That was why the heart stood for love – or whatever you called it. You became the heart. He could see that now. All that valentine's crap – sweetheart, heart's desire, broken heart... he understood it. That was what he was now: a heart pumping round blood, a small pulsing organ, a heart beat... boom, boom as he ran along the river path staring up at the sky searching for the special blue... thump, thump as he pounded the tarmac. He flopped on to a bench and looked at the river, the full fucking swell of it, so much water, so few feet away from him, flowing through London out past Canary Wharf to the sea. A dog scampered by and a moment later a couple talking quietly glanced at him as they followed. What he didn't understand was how this feeling, this boom, boom inside his chest, this thump, thump, had transferred from Daisy to Black Plaits; Black Plaits who was old and had chalky skin and had semi-circles at the corners of her mouth.

He pushed his hand into his pocket and fingered the envelope, feeling the point against his thumb. Inside it was a letter from Black Plaits, which he couldn't bear to open yet. The girl with the boyish face had smiled at him as she passed it over – cockier and sexier than the time when he'd seen her before – but that didn't mean that the letter would say what he wanted it to say.

Leopard skin stone. That was where it had started. Small round stone made from lava. Shiny yellow-blond with black spots. The spots, Black Plaits had told him, were explosions in the burning lava. He'd never given it to Daisy and probably never would. The person who deserved it was Black Plaits. He stood up and stuffed his hands into his pockets. The clouds were scarlet, the blue darker. He trudged along the path. Whatever the letter said, he would go to the shop and give the leopard skin stone to Black Plaits.

The white envelope was creased when he took it out of his trouser pocket as he undressed that night. He smoothed the envelope between his hands. *Jon*. His name was written in large, rounded, blue letters, matching that deep blue of the sky, which seemed a good omen. He laid the envelope on the floor by his bed. Her invisible words could sleep next to him. In the morning, whatever the words said, he had something to go to, and nothing must stop him from going to work.

'Dear Jon,

I don't know your address, and I don't have your mobile. I hope you come to the shop and if I'm not there Sue or Eric give you this note. I've tried to <u>say</u> it. Normally I'm good at saying

things. I've never met anyone like you. You… and please read on… you scare me, not because last time you came on strong and then left. You scare me because I want to go on seeing you, and I'm not a cradle snatcher, Jon. I'm older, much older, and you probably won't want to come back to the shop – it may be better that way. Take a lot of care.
Love Carol x'

Love Carol x… He was all heartbeat again, boom, boom, blood racing. He ran through the streets to the station, the tall, white houses shining like wedding cakes in the early morning sun – like *wedding cakes?* Fucking hell! But, yeah, from today, from six-thirty on this Wednesday morning under this yellow-pink sky that event was not an impossibility. Too old. Who cared? *I want to go on seeing you… love Carol… x…* He could cope with Steve bossing him and Max not being there. He would type the rota and create spreadsheets. He would wander up to the Features Floor, deliver the post, treat Daisy to a croissant and a latte, take the sandwich orders, and not mind that he was back doing that again, not mind that Daisy and David Gould were probably still an item and that he and she never would be.

He'd avoided the Features Floor the last few days. Just stepping in there felt like going backwards. But today he went straight there and pushed the trolley between the computer islands, voices calling to him: 'Hello stranger!' 'Haven't seen you for ages.' 'Thought you'd left!' Who would've thought that taking Max's place could be so good? Doris from *Obits* reached out her liver-spotted hand. 'Missed your handsome face, darling.' What was it with older women? He laughed. 'I'm standing in for Max. Don't normally do this.' Moved on to greater things, he wanted to shout.

He dropped off a heavy parcel in *Books* and wandered back through the women's section, and trailed his finger along Daisy's empty desk – no sight of her. It gave him a shiver, but made him know that Sunday he wouldn't go to Leatherhead to see Dad and Ma, as he'd promised he would. Sunday he would go to the shop to see Black Plaits.

NINETEEN

MARTHA

Each morning she got out of bed, rushed to the loo, and stared at the white loo paper. Excitement spiking through her, she paused at the window and gazed at the light making patterns on the river. It was high tide in the mornings that week. The water was as smooth as glass in places but there were areas where it was choppy, where the ripples made black shapes that moved and changed – like cells, it seemed to her, her cells, her fertilized egg cell that was hopefully growing and dividing. She would fling on her clothes, drink down a cup of tea, pick up her bags, and almost run in the spring sunshine up the hill to the station, and then stop at the flower stall to buy bunches of narcissi or freesia, a fresh bunch every day.

Head of little sperm penetrating wall of egg – such sexy language. The image of the cells in the river with their silver outline filled her head, making her laugh out loud and plunge her nose into the frilly petals. She stood on the platform and noticed women with children as if she'd never seen them before. Some were dressed in suits for the office – dropping off their kids first presumably; others in fleeces or anoraks, waving off older children and then returning home perhaps. There would be one – who would look like a girl – in stiletto boots with thick, long hair, holding a small child tightly by the hand – a nanny, she assumed.

She sat on the train and dreamed up titles: 'Men's jealousy.' 'Women in a unique time.' 'The potential for women to have a career and a family.' 'The history of the struggle for women to reach this potential, and the reasons for it taking millennia.' She would use herself, speak from the heart, contrast the sad place she'd been in for the last few years with the way she felt now. That was what had been missing in her job. *Not* writing enough. Not doing the thing that it was all about. She would get back to that part of herself, that skill. Write a seminal article, a series. Women would finally be convinced that they did have more than men.

'Lovely flowers, Martha!' Mark from *Travel* stepped into the lift on the first of those mornings. He was followed by Vi from *Pictures* who smiled at Martha and seemed to look at her as if there was already something visible. 'You're looking well.'

'Who's the admirer?' Tony asked her as she walked on to the floor clutching the flowers.

'Myself,' she laughed, looking into his pale eyes through the rimless glasses. 'Morning everyone! Jenny, would you find me a vase? And could you get me a latte? A weak one please.'

On these mornings she loved the quiet start of the day – people peering into their screens, sipping on a coffee or biting into a croissant. She loved knowing the activity would build up through the morning and the afternoon into the madness of the evening when fingers would fly across keys and people would shout down phones or call across to each other or jump up to come and see her. She loved Liza drawing a chair up to her desk, unwrapping a piece of gum, putting it into her mouth and twisting the paper in her fingers as if it was the longed-for cigarette, and then leaning forward to get down to business.

'Martha, what about a piece on only-children?'

'Yeah…'

'Famous only children.'

'Are there any?'

'Elton John, Robert de Niro, Iris Murdoch, Charles M. Schulz…'

'You have done your homework.' Martha sat back in her chair, clutching her latte and smiling. 'Are only children really *marginalised*?'

Liza grinned and chewed her gum. 'New phenomenon, Martha. Before contraception people couldn't *choose* to have

183

one.' She scrunched up the gum paper and dropped it into the waste paper basket by the desk. 'There's an American publication, of course. *Only Child News…*'

At the weekly meeting Martha congratulated Liza on her series and announced her intention to follow Liza's example and contribute more copy. People nodded. Tony folded his arms. Daisy clapped her hands. 'I so agree, Martha. We should never stop writing. That's what it's about, isn't it?' Doris from *Obits* banged her fat thigh with a hand. 'Hear, hear!' Even Tony didn't demur.

'Careful of the flowers!' she said to Daisy as the girl hitched herself on to the corner of the desk late one afternoon and pulled up a knee encircling it with her arms. The self-confidence was too much as usual, but even that seemed endearing.

'The professionals, Martha.'

'The what…?'

'Remember, we're going to finish off the series with 'The Features Editor'.' She lifted her hair off her shoulder, twisting it and securing it in a large black clip and smiled down at Martha. 'You!'

'Ah… okay.' And why not? Martha felt a glow of pleasure. People wanted her.

'Martha, are you really going to start writing more? I mean, how do you manage to write and do this job…? I mean, what's the right balance…?' She broke off and glanced upwards at the tall figure standing by the desk, spots of colour in her cheeks. 'Oh Jon, hi…'

Martha heard her own 'hello' superimposed over his words to Daisy. Not a spark of feeling though he seemed to be turning towards her. That had gone, thank God. No need now, she thought. He seemed young with his long dark hair and shy expression, a boy. There was something between him and Daisy – good luck to them.

'Martha? Grant doesn't have to pick me up from Surbiton on Saturday....'

'Sorry...?'

'I'll get myself to you.'

'Oh... fine.'

Daisy was looking down at her notes, colour gone from her face. Martha waited for him to move on, and patted the girl's arm. 'Make a list of questions and I'll do my best to answer them.'

Grant wouldn't be there on Saturday, she recalled later that day as she ran along Platform 18 at Waterloo with a minute to spare. How could she have forgotten when a few days ago she was wondering how she would get through a day without him? She stepped on to the train and found a seat and placed her hands over her stomach.

Tomorrow, she would search Jon out in the mail room and tell him not to come.

At home she opened a bottle of Macon Village, poured herself a glass, took a sip and dialled Grant's number. She hooked the phone under her chin, picked up her glass and the bottle, and made for the sofa in the sitting room and settled herself into it, exhausted suddenly. Staccato American engaged tone. She pressed redial. Same sound, getting inside her, making her long to talk to somebody. She pressed the off button and tried Barbara and got her husband who thanked her for her concern and kindness; the antibiotics had kicked in, Emily was much better. Is Barbara there, she almost asked, wanting to give them her good news – *I discovered on the night you took Emily into hospital*...perhaps she would call her Emily, if it was a girl. But she thought better of it and said goodbye.

Drinking and pregnancy didn't mix, she remembered. She put the glass of wine on the coffee table. No coffee either probably, or soft cheese. She hauled herself out of the sofa, returned to the kitchen, poured herself a glass of sparkling

185

water, shook some pretzels into a bowl and stuffed a couple into her mouth. Her face glanced at her from the small mirror in the hall as she moved back into the sitting room, pale in the bright light. She slid a Schubert quartet into the CD player, returned to the sofa and wedged a cushion into the base of her back. The sparkling water felt clean, washing down her throat. She ate another pretzel and poised her fingers over the dial buttons: Phil, I think I'm pregnant. Did Daddy kill himself? Why the two together? Her fingers pushed the digits for Grant's number, wanting to talk to him. She thought of them making love – nearly five weeks ago now. Presumably. She couldn't picture the night – or the morning. They had done it on a Sunday morning, but that was more recently…

'I'm afraid there is no one to receive your call at this time, but if you would…'

She placed her glass of water on the table. Next to it was the bottle of wine and the glass of wine she'd started. She took another pretzel and sipped more water. She went in search of her laptop, brought it back to the sofa and placed it on her lap. One new email:

'Honey, sorry we haven't spoken for some days. Mom is sinking. I would hate to leave her now, though the medics are saying this state could last for weeks. Keep you posted. Hope all's well. I'll try and call over the weekend. All love Grant'

The Schubert quartet had reached the slow movement. She moved the laptop on to the floor, picked up the glass of wine and pulled her legs up on to the sofa. One glass wouldn't do any harm. And now Daddy's face was swimming up from somewhere...

'I love you, Martha.'

Wide, windy beach at Pendine Sands, light bouncing off the waves. Mummy and Phil running towards the sea. His eyes zigzag over her face. For a moment she thinks he means it and she is back wanting to give him her face, give him herself.

He nods his head. 'You're going away from me, Martha. You must. I want you to go. I want you to go out into the world.'

High up, gulls cry. She sees him nudge the corners of his eyes with his knuckles. Her bare feet scuff the sand as she runs from him towards the sea...

I love you, Daddy. She never said it back. Too late by then; she'd learned her lesson.

She sank down into the sofa and put the cushion behind her head. Depression: Phil's word. Daddy was ill. She knew that. She'd been trying to make him better.

Another glass of wine. She shouldn't be drinking. The bottle was half-empty. But she was thinking about Daddy, Daddy and her, and she could only think about him if, like the baby inside her, she was swimming, floating.

TWENTY

JON

Surbiton to Clapham; Clapham to Putney and then the *A-Z* for the road from the station to Grant's house. He sat in his chair, the little book in his hands, knowing their page now and the look of their road so near the river. Grant normally picked him up two-thirty to three. No computer now. What would they talk about? Black Plaits...? Not Daisy. He'd seen her flick her head up at him when he'd told Martha he'd get himself to their house, hair pulled into that clip thing. She'd said, Hi Jon, and gone red and he'd thought, wow. But after that she'd not looked at him.

He chucked the *A-Z* on the floor and pulled the letter out of his pocket. *I've never met anyone like you...* the words still made him fizz. He spread the letter out on his knees, smoothing out the creases and wishing he'd kept the envelope, and noticed another sentence, as if he hadn't seen it before: *You probably won't want to come back to the shop – it may be better that way.*

He channel-flicked for a few seconds... Victoria Beckham showing too much leg, to kids – those sort of women had a lot to answer for... old Patrick what's-his-name spouting about the night sky in the southern hemisphere... the Welsh surf team competing against the Cornish. What was the use of black wetsuits on men? Saturday morning TV was crap. He switched it off. Perhaps he could still ask Daisy to come out for a beer, try it out, when he'd got more practise with Black Plaits. The one didn't have to rule out the other. He wandered up the stairs to the bathroom and stared at his face in the mirror.

I've never met anyone like you... I want to go on seeing you... You probably won't come back... He licked his finger and smoothed his eyebrows and leaned nearer his reflection until his lips were right up to the glass and he could kiss them as if they were hers – *love Carol x...* he mustn't be so hungry next time...

But should he go to the shop tomorrow? Did the letter mean that? He hadn't been to Dad and Ma's for several Sundays. Perhaps he would go there first – fill up the time so he didn't have to think about Black Plaits too much – and go to the shop on his way home. There was tiny spot in the crease by his left nostril. Tell-tale bump under the pad of his finger... shit. He distanced himself from his reflection so he couldn't see it, and moved back downstairs into the living room and pressed on the computer. A dose of *Death Lottery* to get him through the morning, and then Grant in the afternoon. Grant would know what he should do.

Clapham Station was the largest railway junction in Europe, if not the world, he recalled as the train climbed up the hill out of Surbiton. All those platforms and underground passages could do with a whole page in the *A-Z*. Simpler to travel to Waterloo and the familiar departure board, he decided, have a beer in the station bar and then catch a train out to Putney.

It was four-fifteen when he reached their small gate and he walked past it once or twice, glancing towards Grant's window to see if he could see him, and then hurried on and stood under the railway bridge. A car drove past. If he went home now, there was just the evening left, to be spent probably at the *Spit and Polish* – just those few hours followed by the night – and then it would be Sunday.

He went to their door, lifted the black metallic door knocker, peered through the patterned glass, and let it rap. A bird chirped. High up a plane droned. It would be nice to talk to Grant but if he wasn't home, he would make that trip to Kingston tomorrow. He would go to *Gem Universe*, whatever it was called. He would go there and see Black Plaits. He wanted to see her. The decision was made. One last peer through the glass – but the door swung open.

'Jesus, I'd forgotten about you!'

For a second he didn't recognise her. 'Sorry, Martha... sorry... bi' late...'

She was wearing some green thing and sandals as if it was summer. There was something funny with her eyes. 'You'd better come in.'

He closed the door behind him and glanced towards Grant's door. 'Is Grant...?'

Her head shook. She looked awful.

'I'll go, Martha.'

'No... no, don't.' And then she was crying and stepping towards him.

He'd done it before, of course. But Daisy had been soft and quiet in his arms and there had been layers of clothes between them. Martha made a noise and the green dress was a dressing gown and he wasn't sure what was underneath. He knew about crying. His ma was always crying. He would put his arms round her and his dad wouldn't like it. He stood now, his arms around Martha, trying to pretend it wasn't Martha. He could feel her breasts against his shirt. Over her head the yellow wall had paler yellow stripes.

And then she moved back. 'Oh fuck... fuck... sorry...!' He'd never heard her say the f word. She shook her head and sniffed and wiped her hand against her nose. 'Sorry... I shouldn't have done that.' Her head kept shaking. She pulled a crumpled tissue out of the pocket of her dressing gown and blew her nose, though the tissue didn't look big enough, and turned away.

He followed her into their big, light kitchen, wondering what the fuck he was doing.

She tugged at a roll of kitchen paper and blew her nose again, picked up the kettle and put it under the tap. 'He's away.' She dabbed at her nose. 'His mother's dying. He's in the States.' The kettle was placed on its stand. 'It's not *that*. Like some toast?'

Not what? He didn't want to know. Had Grant left her? He glanced at the chair longing to sit suddenly.

'Heart condition. Had to leave. Early Monday morning. Had to cancel all his patients.'

He would eat some toast – and marmite hopefully – ask no questions, and go.

She was lowering two slices of bread into the toaster. He could murder both. 'You like to talk to him, don't you? That's what he does, of course. Listens to people. All day listening, helping people to tell their story.' She reached for a container and took out a tea bag, dropped it into a teapot, lifted the kettle and poured in the water. 'Bugger!' She banged down the kettle.

'I'll – I'll go.'

She turned to him. 'No! No, please.'

'I can't help you.'

'The fucking water hasn't boiled, that's all!' She tipped the water out of the teapot and let it clatter into the sink.

He felt out of it. He'd hardly eaten since breakfast. A Mars bar half-way through the morning. It had been a long afternoon. He watched himself walk across the kitchen. It was easy to put his hands on her arms feeling that it wasn't him who was doing it, easy to guide her to a chair and make her sit at the table. He returned to the sink, found another tea bag, pressed the button on the kettle, waited for it to boil, and poured the water into the teapot which hadn't broken – and wasn't even chipped – in spite of the noise it had made when she let go of it into the sink. The toast popped up.

Her voice came behind him. 'Knives are in the drawer under the sink, plates in the cupboard. We keep the marmite in the fridge.'

He spread the butter into the hot toast. The marmite formed dark smears. Through the window, he could see their grey BMW parked near their gate. Pink petals from the nearby tree had landed on the roof and the bonnet. He cut the toast in half, put it on a plate and placed it on the table in front of her.

'No thanks.'

'It'll make you feel better.'

'I don't want it.'

She pushed it away. 'I said, no.'

He felt the same sensation of knowing what to do. He placed his hands on her shoulders and stayed in contact long enough to feel the warmth of her skin through the thin dressing gown, and see her stretched out fingers relax around the plate. It felt like it was with his ma, when he had to look after her when Dad wasn't there, when he could put his arm round her and they could sit together on the settee and talk a little, though Ma was never one for talking. He lifted his hands from Martha's shoulders and returned to spread his own slice – he was starving.

They moved into the large room where the three of them had sat before. He was happy to sit in that huge settee that she called a sofa with his third round of marmite toast, trying not to get crumbs everywhere, watching the tail end of *Grandstand* and following it with a repeat of '*Only Fools and Horses*', but after that it was time to leave.

She glanced up from her curled position in the chair. Her sandals were off and her bare feet poked out from under the dressing gown. 'You're not going are you?'

'Yeah, I will… thanks for the toast. And – and the computer.'

'You don't have to go. I'll take you out to supper.'

'I've had loads.'

'I would give you supper here if I had any food.'

'I don't need it.'

'I may not go in on Monday.'

'Wha' –?'

She picked up her cold piece of toast and bit into it. 'I may not go into the office.'

He shifted to the edge of the settee. 'I like my job. I have to go in – '

'I left yesterday. Late morning. I left the office and didn't go back. I rang Jenny. Told her I had a migraine.'

He should have stood up and gone. But she smiled suddenly with those semi-circles at the corner of her mouth like Black Plaits and tucked her bare feet under the green dressing gown, 'Stay a bit.' And it felt nice that she was more cheerful again. He didn't want to disturb that. It felt nice too going back into the kitchen and opening a bottle of wine and getting out the wine glasses and watching her pour in the dark red liquid, even if he would have preferred a beer. He drank one glass and then the next, gazing at the label on the wine bottle as she passed it to him, the words shimmering in front of him, foreign words followed by '1995'.

'Are you ill?' he asked back in their sitting room and into the second bottle, when he felt he could say anything. He was bigger and taller than her – he could leave when he wanted.

'Not really.'

'Wha's the matter?'

She shook her head. He could see the bump of her throat as she swallowed. He took another swig and stared at the large plant in the fireplace. It had white flowers.

'I want a baby.'

He looked at her. 'Wha' –?'

She nodded.

He clutched his glass. 'A baby?'

'Yes.'

'What do you want a baby for?'

'I do.'

'Why?'

'I don't know.'

'You've got everything, Martha.' He banged his hand on the arm of the settee. 'You just want more, don't you?' It was the drink talking. 'I never want a baby. What the fuck would you do with a baby?'

Her face sort of broke then – not crying but laughing. Her head tipped back against the chair and rolled from side to side... 'I don't know... you're so right... I don't know...' Give over, he wanted to say. That was what he would say to his ma. But then she stopped and sat up and smiled, sniffed and wiped her nose with her fingers, pulled out her tissue from the pocket of her dressing gown and blew her nose. 'I thought I was pregnant.' She nodded at him. 'For a few days I thought I was. But, you're right. What would I do with a baby?'

Her eyes – he couldn't tell whether she was crying or laughing. He looked away. If he didn't feel pissed he would have left, but his head hurt and he couldn't be bothered to get off the settee. He pulled up his legs and folded them against his stomach. The cushion smelt of material and was soft against the side of his face.

She put on a DVD she thought he would enjoy. '*Lock Stock and Two Smoking Barrels*' – had he seen it? There was shooting and drugs. Shouting too, which was noisy in his head. His eyes closed. The settee rocked. He was running out their door, Grant following him with a gun. Volley of shots. Loud...

She was sitting in the chair when he opened his eyes, closer than before, feet in her sandals. She asked him if he could keep the baby thing secret – he didn't know what she was talking about. He tried to wake himself up. She was sitting on the edge of her chair – that was why she was closer. She was getting up and switching off the TV. 'I don't want people at work to know. You won't tell, will you?'

She told him he could stay the night. There were clean sheets in the map room. He dragged himself up the stairs to the room with the big, high, firm bed and Grant's maps on the wall, which he'd liked before but which interfered with his eyes tonight. She hadn't touched him. She wouldn't, would

194

she? She wanted Grant, or a baby. There was no lock on his door. He put a chair against it.

Next morning his head felt as large as the globe in the corner and the daylight was too bright. He rolled out of bed, dying for a piss. The toilet and a shower were in the next room. His pee filled the toilet bowl. He plunged his hands into a basin of water, and nearly drowned his watch. He lifted out his hands. It was quarter past two. His head sparkled. He smoothed his hair. His scalp was tender. Quarter past two? It was Sunday, wasn't it? Sunday afternoon...? Fuck... no! Black Plaits...

Downstairs, Martha sat on a stool leaning over the kitchen table, the newspapers spread in front of her. A pink floppy jersey disguised her large boobs and had the words 'Sloppy Joe' written across it. At least she was dressed. The pink hurt his eyes.

She lifted a glass jug of dark liquid. 'Coffee?'

'I've got to go.' The words felt glued together. He passed his tongue between his teeth and lips and wished the room wasn't so light.

'Have some coffee first. I'll drive you. Toast?' She slipped off the stool and padded over to the sideboard and sliced the loaf. Not even sandals today, just large bare feet and the knob of her ankle sticking out of black leggings.

'No thanks.'

'Too much wine?'

He nodded – mistake.

'You must eat. And drink. Coffee's not so good.' She filled a glass of water and handed it to him. Her breasts lifted the letters on the pink jersey. 'I'll drive you.'

The toast popped up like a repeat of yesterday. 'One or two pieces? Marmite or marmalade? You made me feel better last night.'

'Wha –?'

The phone rang. She strode across the room. 'Don't go.'

'I must...'

She lifted the phone off its wall bracket. 'Grant, hi... how are things? It must be the middle of the night...' She walked into the hall. 'Six forty-five...?'

Her voice got fainter. She sounded as if she was going into the sitting room. He grabbed the toast out of the toaster, gazed at the butter and marmite for a second, picked up the knife and then sandwiched the dry toast together and stuffed it into his jacket pocket. He reached the door and glanced into the hall.

Grant's door was open; she was in his room. 'How's your mother...?'

The door chain hung loose. He turned the Yale knob and pulled gently. The door opened with barely a creak. Eyes slitted against the light, he crossed the street, left and then left again up the steps and over the railway bridge. His shoes thudded on the tarmac pedestrian path. Now that he was out of the house, he wanted to get away. Miraculously there was a station on the other side, taking him – he pulled out the *A-Z* to check – taking him straight to Wimbledon. And from Wimbledon, he had the choice: Wimbledon to Surbiton, Wimbledon to Kingston....

But it was three o'clock and the man in the next seat was getting up and moving away – he must stink, he needed a shower... no, the man was moving to the doors. Whatever, this afternoon was not the time. Black Plaits had told him not to go to the shop. He could see the long plait, the way he liked it, hanging down her back, and her white face and black eyelashes and her see-through green eyes looking towards the entrance of the shop or, if she was out on the pavement glancing up and down the street. He would make her wait, make her sweat a little. He would go next Sunday. Play her at her own game – write her a note.

The answer machine was flashing when he got in. He dived into the kitchen and pushed his face under the cold tap, rubbing the icy water over his burning forehead, letting it into his mouth and gulping it down his throat. He jerked open the fridge door and pulled out a Foster's, inserted his finger into the ring. One swig – what was he doing? He threw the tin into the sink and slouched back into his living room and pressed the answer machine and flopped into his chair.

Whirring sound, click, click and then Martha's voice: 'Thank you for staying. I would have given you a lift, but I understand that you wanted to go. You helped me. Thank you.'

He reached for the remote and pressed it on… *'Only Fools and Hors*es'… not them again. He switched it off. How had he fucking helped her? He shifted out of his chair and moved towards his bedroom. His ruffled sheets looked yellow after the smooth, white sheets of the map room, but the light was kinder. He closed the curtains and stripped off his clothes, got in under the duvet and sank into the valley of his bed.

Max's return and Steve's absence kept him in the Mail and Communications room most of the next day. At lunch time he found time to browse through Grant's notes on spreadsheets. He took out a clean sheet of paper and wrote *Mailing Costs*. He drew a grid: department costs across the top, days of the week down the side. Half an hour turned into an hour as he went into *Excel* and started typing on the screen, realising with a stab of excitement he could do it, he could make it happen.

At about five he wandered up to the Features floor and hit the end-of-afternoon frenzy: heads down over screens, Tony shouting from his desk, people rushing backwards and forwards. A page of copy had been lost; Purple Hair wedged a phone under her chin, fingers attacking the keys. He glanced towards Martha's desk. There was a tap on his shoulder.

'She's not here today.' It was Daisy, yellow hair loose on her shoulders, eyes looking into his.

'Isn't she?'

'Tony's on.' Her eyes flicked towards his desk. There was a little line in her forehead. 'Do you really go to her house?'

'Yeah.' Fuck it.

'Why?'

'Why not?' Someone pushed past, Doris waddling towards *Obits*. A phone rang.

'Seems...' Daisy's head tilted, her hair dipping over one shoulder. 'Do you know her?'

'No.'

'Did you know her before?'

'No... They gave me their computer.'

'Oh...'

'That's why.'

'Oh, right.' She looked round and then touched his arm. Everyone so busy the noise seemed to enclose them. 'I've been meaning to say...' she was back looking at him now, eyes medium blue that he remembered swimming with water, '...thanks for looking after me at the party.'

'The party...?'

'You know, before Christmas. You were really nice to me.'

'That was a long time ago.'

She laughed, teeth glinting between her lips. 'It was, wasn't it?'

'Has...has David Gould –'

'Oh God, he's off the radar.' She leaned nearer and he got the full eye contact. Whiff of her breath too. 'Someone else now.'

For a stupid second he thought it might be him.

She nodded, 'Yeah.'

He probably sounded too hopeful. Her face turned away and looked towards Tony. Tony was old enough to be her father – nearly. He tried to look as if he didn't care. He glanced round for his trolley. Purple Hair had stood up and was beckoning to Daisy.

198

Daisy's hand brushed his arm. 'Tell you about it sometime.' Her eyes were looking into his again. 'Better go. See ya. We should have a drink some time.'

'See ya...' He said it too, though he was never going to. Fuck you, he should have said. He pushed the trolley through the busy people, aware of her moving towards Tony and her desk.

He returned to the Mail and Communications room. Martha had said she wouldn't come in and she hadn't. The features floor was different without her, different with Tony in charge and Daisy running round after him. He sat in front of the computer and gazed at the blank screen and thought of the map room and the clean white sheets, and the large settee, and those times when Grant, Martha and he had all been there and they'd sat round the kitchen table. Even that had changed.

TWENTY ONE

GRANT

Mom lay in her bed in the hospital room, eyes closed but comfortable under a single, white, aerated blanket. Careful not to jog the transparent nasal tube, he stroked her forehead or rubbed her cool dry hands. Sometimes her eyelids flickered or her lips moved; an expression, almost a smile, crossed her face. He would bend nearer. 'Hey Mom, it's me, Grant. I'm here. I love you.' His lips brushed her cheekbone that pressed through her skin. She was all skin and bones now.

He tried to picture how she was two years ago on his last visit, but he could only remember how she made him feel. 'Don't worry about me dear, I have plenty to keep me busy.' She'd been saying that all her life, her wide-set eyes sparkling with energy, and all his life it had made him feel shut out. She might just have said, 'Go out and play, Granty, there's a good boy. Lani and Mom have things to do.' His father's work had taken the family from campus to campus but in each place his mother had made a home and been in charge. Women were in charge; that was the message when he was a child, in charge but not involved, and the feeling that gave him still made him burn.

He'd lost count of how many days he'd sat in the room, angry with her one moment, sad the next. Today he pulled his chair closer to the bed and lowered his head to her face. 'Mom? I want to tell you something.' He'd neglected her over the years and Lani would kill him if he prevented her from dying peacefully, filling her full of plans and changes she didn't need to know, but he needed to tell her. Hearing was the last sense to go and he was sure she could hear. 'Mom, are you listening? I think I may want to come home, back to the States. Martha and I…' But now his eyes were watering. 'Mom…' He swallowed. 'Mom, Martha, she wanted a baby.

200

We tried. It didn't work. She can't accept it. I can't accept her not accepting it. Do you understand, Mom? You never thought men counted. In spite of your clever husband, and your smart son – yeah, I've been very smart. I may not have had kids, but work-wise... This is difficult for me, Mom. I can't bear her not accepting. Can you hear? Can you hear me?' He fumbled in his pocket for his handkerchief and wiped his eyes and stuffed it back in again. 'So, I guess I may be coming home. And... ' He swallowed again. '... I need you to understand. I know what you're thinking. I should've realised this earlier. I should've come home to you while you were still alive, while we could still....' He clasped her bony arm. 'You are alive. You are!' But he'd implied she wasn't and he bent over her body sobbing, moisture pouring out of his nose. He stumbled up off his chair, tugging at his handkerchief again and blew his nose, trumpeting and hiccoughing, and moved to the other side of the room as if he might wake her, crying now for Martha, and for Ruthie, and for all the women in his life, and for baby Christopher too who must surely be fully grown.

He blew his nose and took deep breaths, and prayed a nurse wouldn't come, though he had every reason to weep. His breath jerked involuntarily. Through the window the flowering trees shone in the sunshine. A man was mowing the lawn. A woman stopped to talk to him and then crossed the tarmac driveway towards the entrance. His mother was dying. The word 'dying' made him want to sob again. She was going to die. He mouthed the word 'die' several times and took more deep breaths.

When he had rung her in California about Christopher, all those years ago, she told him he was young and there was plenty of time to start afresh. 'Granty,' she'd used the babyish name. 'Granty, you're well quit of her.' It's the baby, not Ruthie, he was unable to say for fear she might answer, 'what do you want with another man's baby?' The baby had still seemed like his.

The automatic gates opened to let in an ambulance. In the distance high rise buildings soared into a cloudless sky. He turned towards his mother. If he came back to live in the States she wouldn't be here. He moved over to her bed. Gentle up and down of her breathing under the white blanket. Still alive. He held her face in his hands. 'See you tomorrow, Mom. Love you.'

He hurried out of the building and made for the gates and waited for the porter to let him through. His eyes stung in the bright sunshine but outdoors he felt better. He reached the bus stop on Union Street. As on the other days a bus turned up within a couple of minutes. Transport worked better here in spite of the Bush administration. He climbed on to the bus and then instead of getting off at the usual stop and returning to his mother's apartment on Green Street, carried on to Columbus. He had a couple of hours to fill before meeting Lani for dinner and he wanted to drop in on the Museum of Modern Art. The bus slowed down past the City Lights bookshop and he jumped off at the next light, suddenly liking the idea of browsing through the psychology section and checking out new titles.

He landed outside a candy store selling newspapers and he pushed open the door. A bell sounded.

'Can I help you, Sir?' The man had black, shiny hair and dark skin. There was a smell of fried oil coming from the door into the back of the shop.

Grant glanced along the shelves of newspapers and magazines. 'Employment ads – which papers do you recommend?'

'Huh?'

'I'm looking for educational – university posts. Is there – an educational publication?'

'Now you're asking.' The man had a silver tooth when he smiled. 'I guess you better check. I won't charge. Just don't mess them.'

'That's kind.'

But he wasn't ready. And this wasn't the right kind of newsstand.

He grabbed a couple of papers, paid for them and got out into the fresh air, certain his clothes had picked up the smell in there. If he did decide to come back, he would need to call his friend Paula Schulz at Stanford, get a few contact names at Berkeley and possibly San Francisco State and maybe even Santa Cruz.

He bypassed the City Lights and found a café on Columbus, ordered a decaffeinated latte, and then located the separate ads pages. He folded back the paper and placed it on the table in front of him.

Teaching jobs, research studentships... no, the way in was through people like Paula; get a part-time faculty post and maybe look into hospital work. Over here he might write the book. He sipped at his coffee and ordered a croissant. A young man asked him if he could share his table. He turned his chair sideways to face the window and the pedestrians walking past it, trying to remain private. The book was defunct. Other people had probably written it. Even the issues about donor parents and the comparison with adoptive or step-parents didn't inspire him out here. If he was going to move back, he needed to make a fresh start. Teaching, but a different kind of teaching. Return to school himself, perhaps. Bone up on criminology. Work with the underbelly of society – there was enough material in this city. He could get to grips with the suicide factor, return to what had originally got him into this work: the need to understand through the individual. Did he still believe that through the individual you could understand groups, communities, nations? Returning to the States might give him the chance to test this out in a different context, give him a new purpose in life. But would Martha come with him? Would being here make up for not being able to have children together?

He got up from the table, his forehead tight suddenly. The bill paid, he walked on down Columbus in the direction of the Museum of Modern Art. But then he was in a cable car climbing up towards Grace Cathedral wanting something more amorphous than an art gallery where he could drift about and think.

Inside the canyons of masonry and the shafts of light there was a placard of information on ancient mazes. The cathedral had its very own maze. *Labyrinth… mazes…* he stared at the words and the diagrams and the pictures, not taking them in. He thought of finding a corner in one of the side chapels away from the tourists but he wandered outdoors into the sunlight. The maze was in the shadow of the high cathedral walls. Following the example of others, he removed his shoes and padded slowly after a white robed cleric along the paths of the labyrinth to its centre, trying to empty his mind.

'You could be here weeks, Grant. What about Martha and your work?'

He glanced through the window. The street lights were coming on. A tram slid past. 'They can wait.'

'What do you think she's waiting for?'

'Martha?'

'No, Mom.' Lani turned and lifted the empty water bottle to the waiter. 'Another bottle of sparkling, please.'

She reminded him of someone, the way her hair swung as she moved and then settled into an expensively cut shape an inch above her shoulders. The hair gene in the family had gone to her. It was a deep brown with the right variation of tint to make it look utterly natural.

Her eyes creased in tiny lines. 'I mean, I've told her everything she needs to know – you know, when she was awake…'

'Do you think she'd like to know I may come back to the States?'

'Huh?'

'I've been working it out with her. Talking it through.'

'You've been talking – with Mom, now? Are you crazy?'

The waiter had arrived with the iced bottle of water. He unscrewed the lid and poured it into Lani's glass and then offered to do the same into Grant's. Grant shook his head. Lani lifted hers. Who was it she reminded him of? He couldn't remember ever thinking Lani was beautiful.

'Are you and Martha splitting?'

'I didn't say that.'

She took a sip of water. 'Are you saying Martha's going to move out here?'

He wondered whether Lani had had a face lift? The thought made him feel like a stranger. 'I don't know.'

She put down her glass. 'I'm glad there are no kids.'

The waiter was back again with two large plates of food. Spinach and feta with noodles for her and something under a cheese sauce for him. He couldn't remember what he'd ordered. 'That's some of the problem.'

'Oh Granty…' Her hand came across the table towards his, her eyes trying to make contact. 'Didn't she want them?'

His head shook. Leave it like that. He couldn't bear to try and explain. For a moment, he'd thought he might be able to. He'd forgotten she would call him Granty and make him feel furious. He dug his fork into the thick sauce letting out a jet of steam and reached a firmness and then some meat – cannelloni, of course. Boiling – too hot to eat. He picked up the wine bottle. 'Come on, Lani. I can't drink all of this.'

'I don't normally.'

'Let go a little.'

She laughed. Beautiful white teeth. Capped of course. Women in London were in the cosmetic ark.

He forked the edge of his cannelloni and blew on it. Lani was Dad's favourite as well as Mom's. She'd followed in

Dad's footsteps and become a history teacher, and made it to professor once her kids had grown.

She was grinning at him with her beautiful teeth. 'So you're coming home? You'll be okay financially, even with alimony.'

'Alimony! Does that word still exist? '

'You'll have to support Martha.'

'Lani – Martha's very capable of supporting herself.'

'Whatever. There'll be Mom's legacy. Even split between us, you'll survive, even if you never work again. The apartment on Russian Hill should keep us in style.'

'Why would I never work again?'

Her shoulders lifted to the cropped edges of her hair. 'I don't know, Granty. Retire...?'

'I'm fifty one, Lani!' He put down his fork and picked up the wine and topped up his glass. 'Say nothing, huh? I've made no decisions.'

'I wouldn't.'

He swallowed some wine. 'I mean about moving back to the States.'

'Oh, that?'

'What else for God sakes?'

'You and Martha.'

'Lani, Martha and I are not splitting!'

An hour or so later he stretched out on the large double bed in his mother's guest room trying to ease his stomach. Too much gluten and dairy produce – and all that emotion earlier, of course. He breathed in and out, feeling his abdomen sink against the tightness. His patient, Christine Mirado – that was who Lani reminded him of. The dark, glossy, swinging hair.

He dug his thumbs into his waist muscles, and remembered the jealousy of his childhood. Poor little Granty. Mom and Lani both said it. Dear little Granty. Off you go, Granty. You're too little. You'll never grow up. Even now he wanted to show them how much he'd grown up, how much he'd done in his life.

When he goes there what will they do?

He woke with the words in his head, and the sound of sirens howling like wolves, louder and louder, and the thought: Jon was supposed to come over on Saturday.

He kicked off the duvet and reached for his watch and peered at the luminous hand. The sirens were yelping now – short, sharp shrieks. Five to eleven. He turned it the right way. Twenty-five past five. Add on eight hours – or was it nine? Did summer-time make a difference? Early afternoon. Perhaps he should call her and reassure himself. But the Saturday had passed, several days ago. He'd spoken to her on Sunday. She'd seemed fine. There had been no mention of the guy.

He switched on the light and reached for his book, *'The White Hotel'* by D.M. Thomas. He'd never read it and had taken it out of his mother's bookshelf surprised to find it squeezed between an Alison Lurie and a travel book about Peru. Had she read *'The White Hotel'*? He couldn't imagine it... the graphic sexual fantasies... but what child could contemplate their parent's sexuality? He glanced at the back cover... 'a dream of electrifying emotions and inexplicable violence recounted by a young woman to her analyst, Sigmund Freud...' Was Freud the attraction? Like the Alison Lurie, perhaps? An attempt by his mother to get nearer to her men folk, the Lurie a portrayal of her husband's university world, the D.M. Thomas a portrayal of her son's analytical world? Unlikely. The book fell open at the chapter, 'The sleeping carriage'. He hadn't got that far but it was the Babi Yar section and Lisa and Kolya were being herded along in a huge crowd, clutching their valuables, thinking they were catching a train to a better place, not able to believe there could be a more evil destiny. Compelled, he read a few pages. It was beautifully written. Spare, terrible. Out of the window another siren wailed. In the book the guards clubbed the young boy's groin, dogs barked. He snapped the book shut.

Why had they said, 'See you next Saturday, Jon?' *He* hadn't said it. Martha had. And yet she'd been the one to say, he won't come back. There had been tears in her eyes.

He leaned his head against the headboard, remembering a conversation…

'Dad was a butcher, all meat and knives. He'd be a cannibal if he could. But Ma's a vegetable.'

'A vegetable, Jon?'

'Yeah.'

'Dead?'

His eyes dart from side to side, skin colour up. 'Sor' of. As if there were a lot of life somewhere but not with us.'

'What do you mean?'

'As if she'd had kids in another life.' There are lines in his forehead. 'There should have been other kids.'

'Why, Jon?'

'Ma used to cry. I would put my arms round her, hold her tight, head against her boobs. Dad didn't like it.'

He'd encouraged him, hadn't he, wanting him to talk about his past, wanting to analyse him, when he should have been persuading him to see someone else? Depressed mother. Sadistic father. The memory in the bath. He'd been going to advise him to talk to someone, and then he'd had to come out here. He shoved back the duvet with a hot flush of shame.

Out of bed he moved into the darkened living room, past the furniture, and drew back the curtains. Street lights… lit windows in one or two of the houses across the sloping street… a boat winking in the Bay. He'd opened up something with the guy, and been thoroughly unprofessional. The dark sky was lightening. His hand shook as he held the curtain. They'd delivered the computer. Maybe they wouldn't see him again. He looked back into the room. Perhaps he would call Martha. Get her at work. Check everything was alright. Maybe if he got her now, they could talk. He could unburden, tell her everything. Maybe she could too.

He wandered into the kitchen and switched on the light and filled the kettle. Mug of tea first. The phone rang. Martha, he thought, realising how much he wanted to talk.

But it was the hospital. His mom had deteriorated. Yes they'd called his sister. Could he come straight away.

TWENTY TWO

MARTHA

The Sunday newspapers lay on the kitchen table. She lowered herself on to the stool. There was a whole page on war zones, European war zones versus third world war zones, the inconsistency of aid to these war zones... she'd seen all that yesterday. It tied up with the conference on Third World debt next week. There was a piece about "refugee" children and educational needs, which she needed to talk to Liza about; a voluntary organisation in the Midlands was working with the parents. Today was Monday. She closed her eyes and tried to focus on the beginning of the week's checklist: anniversary stories, time of year stories (spring-gardening stories), don't forget to book your summer holiday stories, sports stories in hotter parts of the world: cricket, sailing...

Her coffee had gone cold. She took the cafetière to the sink, poured away the remains and watched the oily liquid smear the white enamel, and then tugged at the plunger and tipped out the grains until they clogged up the plug hole. She just had to get in the train and go in. Or phone. She pulled on her jacket. The phone rang as she closed the front door.

She walked along the road and up on to the path that ran beside the railway bridge and stood at the railing looking at the low tide and the mud-coloured shingle. Like a dirty beach – old bottles and planks of wood and what looked like a shoe... like the wide, windy beach at Pendine Sands, light bouncing off the waves, Daddy's eyes on hers. 'I want you to go. I want you to go out into the world.'

A gull squawked and swooped over the brown slick of the Thames. What happened if she stopped wanting to go into work? A man ran past behind her, puffing, shoes thumping on the tarmac. Her stomach churned.

She rang Jenny on her mobile and told her she wasn't well. She would be back tomorrow probably, or the next day. Tony and Liza would be in charge. Over the bridge there were cafés near Putney Bridge Station and the river footpath to walk along towards Hurlingham. High, grey cloud... It wasn't going to rain. She could have a latte and plan what she was going to write – she'd told the editorial meeting she was going to write. She would write a series on infertility. Make something of it: 'The unbearable extension of hope'. A train was coming over the bridge. She turned back and went home.

Upstairs, she wandered into the map room. The duvet had been pulled roughly over the pillow. She puffed up the pillow, straightened the duvet and then pulled the duvet back. She could change the sheet. Jon wouldn't return. There was rain on the windowpane – no... just spots on the glass. The windows needed cleaning. Grant's nineteenth century map of North America stared at her from the wall, huge in its frame. She put out a hand to take off the sheet but then moved out onto the landing and into her room. She kicked off her shoes and flopped on to their bed. Later she switched on the radio and listened to 'You and Yours' and 'News at One'.

In the afternoon she walked up to the DVD shop in Putney High Street and fingered through the new releases, and landed up in the horror section. How had she got through life without seeing 'Silence of the Lambs' and 'Psycho'? She picked them out and took them to the counter. On her return, the answering machine was flashing. Two messages: Liza hoping she would feel better soon; Jenny checking if she wanted to go to the conference on Third World debt. She made some coffee and curled up on the sofa with FBI Special Agent Clarice Starling and Hannibal Lector.

The next morning she stood in the hall, the cold tiles under her bare feet. She just had to make herself open the front door, pick up the newspapers, and a headline would seize her attention; she would start flicking through the pages. Then she just had to get dressed and go out of the door.

A black bin bag filled as she sorted through the clothes in her cupboard and pulled out forgotten items. She knelt down and swept out a lot of dusty shoes she hadn't worn for years. The phone rang. Six rings. Clicked off. She stared at the shoes for a moment, stood up, and went over to the phone.

Tony's voice was on the voice mail, 'You're not coming in. Are you alright, Martha?'

'Alright' meant Daddy would be able to sleep that night. 'Alright' meant she could clomp down the wooden stairs back to Mummy and Phil and say could he have scrambled eggs for supper or some of Mummy's wonderful carrot soup if she'd made any. 'When does he think I've had time to make carrot soup?' But Mummy would be smiling because Daddy would be alright for the night. Daddy might be alright for the next morning. He would go to the school. He would come back in the afternoon, and if he was feeling bad, he could go back to his room and when Martha had eaten her tea and done her homework she could go up the stairs and cheer him up, and make him alright again.

Daddy jammed the accelerator on to the floor. She sat on the bed, phone in her hand, knowing it now. His car sped along the dark, narrow country lanes, headlights lighting the way, no fog. He put his foot on the accelerator, held the wheel and aimed straight for the telegraph pole.

The phone was ringing again. She let it ring and then dialled 1571. No new messages. Jon perhaps. She dialled 1471, pressed 3, and walked back round the bed to the shoes. Four rings and then a female voice 'Counselling Department.'

'You rang me. My name's...'

The voice told her that they were the counselling department of the hospital. They were going through their records. 'You're Mr Shorn's patient, aren't you, Mrs Weber? You have been to see one of our counsellors, Marilyn Phelps.

We were just checking if you would like come back and see her, or whether we can take your name off our books?'

'No...' She stuffed several dusty pairs of shoes into the black bag.

'I'm sorry?'

'I don't want you to take my name off.' She switched off the phone.

The cupboard floor was filthy. She would need the Hoover. The doorbell rang. She ran downstairs thinking it might be Jon, or Grant returned home suddenly. A uniformed man handed her a package, a special delivery for Grant. She signed for it, ignoring the bundle of newspapers on the doorstep. If Grant had been around, she would have talked to him. Told him things she'd never told him before; got it out of her system.

She closed the curtains in the sitting room and settled into the corner of the sofa to watch '*Psycho*'. Made before she was born. That was what people looked like when she was growing up – women in tight-waisted dresses and high heels, men in dark suits and ties – her mother, her father. Tears fell down her face as she watched Janet Leigh driving through the night towards Bates Motel. In the late afternoon she got dressed intending to return the DVDs and get more films to watch.

Out of doors the sun dazzled her. Perhaps she should take that walk, over the bridge and along the river path towards Hurlingham. A baby was crying. She wouldn't want a baby. She wouldn't be able to stop a baby crying. She turned towards Barbara's and the bridge. A train rattled over it.

But it was Barbara's baby. The pram was on the path the other side of their broken gate, the front door wide open. She stopped, expecting Barbara to appear in the doorway. A car drove by. She stepped on to the path. The baby was banging its head up and down against the mattress. She jiggled the handle of the pram and then lowered her hand to the blue and

213

white checked blanket and drew it back. Hot wriggling body in her arms. She pressed the small head against her shoulder and approached the front door. Silence now.

She twisted away and walked swiftly down the path, through the gate, along the pavement to her own front door. Key into the lock. She bent her head and sniffed the fuzz of hair. The hair was ticklish against her lips... warm scalp – there was whiff of scented washing powder. She turned the key and pushed the door.

There were shouts in the distance. A woman's voice. The baby's eyes gazed up at her, a deep blue.

'No o o o! No o o o!' The words were clear now.

Walk inside the door and close it. Lock it. Hide. Hide with the baby. Feel what it felt like. A little girl. Wonder what she might do. Take a train somewhere. Reinvent herself...

She ran back.

Barbara had reached the pavement and was looking from side to side. 'Emily, where are you? Emily...!'

Martha pushed the baby into Barbara's arms.

Barbara clasped the baby and rocked her, kissed her. 'Oh, thank God. Thank God.'

'You weren't there, Barbara –'

'What...?' Her head shook. A car was parking a few yards down the road.

'You weren't there –'

'I was.'

'Emily was crying. I... I went home to phone you.'

'But the door was –'

'I know. I'm sorry...'

'I only dashed in for a second. The phone was ringing – I was only...'

Martha's hand brushed her arm. 'It's alright. She's safe now.'

Barbara backed away, hitching the child against her shoulder. 'Why did you take her? Why?'

'I'm sorry –'

Her head was shaking again. 'I don't understand...' She closed her eyes as if she couldn't bear to look at Martha, and turned towards the house.

Jon arrived later and stood on the doorstep filling the doorway. She leaned against the doorframe, the incident with the baby washing through her.

'Martha, you haven't been at work?'

'Who sent you?' She wished he was Grant.

'No one.' He pushed his hair away from his face. It almost reached his shoulders. 'You weren't at work. On my way home, I just thought I would see if you were okay.'

'It's no business of yours whether I'm okay.'

His face flushed. There was the criss-cross of lines on the bridge of his nose that she remembered from a long time ago. She could see the beads of sweat on the edge of his hairline.

'Jon, I don't need anyone coming to enquire about me.'

'Righ' Martha. I should've thought of that.' He swung away and strode down the path and banged the gate behind him.

She closed the door, her hand quivering. Herself with the baby at her doorstep... the sound of Barbara's voice... She ached for Grant to be coming out of his room to ask when they were going to eat, or to be working on the other side of his closed door. A dark shape loomed through the engraved glass – Jon...? But it was the etching on the glass, the leaves and the thin stem stretching upwards to the flower. She yanked opened the door and ran down the path.

He was on the other side of the road, at the corner where the road turned left. 'Jon!' she cupped her hands round her mouth. 'Jon! Jon!' She walked across the road towards him beckoning with her hand. 'Come back, for God's sake.'

There was bacon in the fridge and a couple of onions in the vegetable rack. She chopped them finely and put them in a frying pan with oil and a splash of balsamic vinegar, and then found a dried-out bulb of garlic and managed to extract two useable cloves and crush them into the mixture. She cut the mould off a hardened square of cheddar and grated it, and cooked some fusilli. It was good to be doing something.

He laid the table as instructed and opened a bottle of wine. He said he would prefer beer. She told him to look in the fridge. 'You might as well stay the night.' She lifted the pasta on to their plates. 'You can sleep in the map room again.'

'I'll go home, Martha.'

'Why?'

'I got no clean shirts.'

'There'll be something of Grant's.' She placed the plates on the table and poured herself some wine.

He was staring at the Foster's can. 'Will you go to work tomorrow?'

'I don't know.' She pushed her plate away. She'd thought she was hungry.

He removed his finger from the metal ring of the unopened can. 'You don't want me here.'

'I do...' But he was getting to his feet. She took a gulp of her wine and stood up and gazed at the mound of shining pasta on their plates, the flecks of bacon and onion, the cheese melting over it in yellow streaks. 'Go if you want!'

'It's alright, Martha.'

She felt his hand on her shoulder encouraging her back to her stool. A firm, warm hand. Cold when it went away.

He sat down on his side of the table and clicked open the metal circle of the Foster's. 'You're not going to cry, are you?'

She shook her head. Her hand stretched across the table towards him – shit, what was she doing?

He was digging his fork into the pasta, head down.

'My dad couldn't stand it so my ma tried not to cry when he was there, which was why she cried with me.'

She watched her hand withdraw and glanced up. His skin had cooled down and looked pale.

He nodded. 'I hate that, Martha. Not knowing why. Dad didn't care, as long as Ma was busy. She didn't cry if she was busy. She washed everything: the floors, the cupboards, the shelves, the pots and pans, the bath, the sink – and clothes every fucking day; there was no machine. If she wasn't washing, she was cleaning, polishing...'

Her mother was always busy too. Busy with domestic chores while Daddy worked or languished in bed. Martha looked towards the window, aware of a car parking outside. Mummy never came on the walks in the Brecon hills because there was always something to do. What was she always doing, leaving it to her daughter to be with her husband? The question seared through her mind.

Jon shovelled in another mouthful of pasta. 'Never found out what was the matter.'

Martha stared at him. He was wiping his mouth with the back of his hand. *It wasn't my fault.* The idea held her steady for a moment. 'My father...' she nodded slowly, 'my father was a bit like your mother.'

He drained his beer can into his glass. 'You mean he washed everything?'

'No.' Laughter burst out of her, a kind of happiness flaring up. She stood up to get him another beer. 'I meant, I never – like you – knew why he was the way he...'

But she'd moved nearer and had stretched out her hands. His look made her turn away. He was not there for her. She gave him a can from the fridge and offered him tea or coffee when he'd finished the pasta, and some chocolates left over from Christmas and told him to help himself to the television; she was going to bed.

Upstairs, she remembered that he would need a shirt for the morning. She grabbed several of Grant's and took them to the map room and then returned to her bedroom, closed the door, tugged off her clothes and slipped in under the duvet.

Daddy has vanished. He's not himself. He's lost. He's in a kind of prison.

Her mother's words, her mother's phrases.

Phil looks up from '*The Famous Five*' or his Lego airport. 'He's only upstairs, Mummy.'

'Of course he is, darling.' Mummy pats Phil on the shoulder and gives Martha a look.

Now when she lies behind him, she presses the length of her clothed, eleven-year-old body against his. Now her head reaches the top of his back. She pulls down the collar of his pyjamas and touches his skin first with a finger and then with her lips. Sometimes when she goes up to Daddy her mother is out taking Phil to his violin lesson or going to choir practise.

One evening, Daddy takes her hand and strokes it, his fingers tracing the length of her fingers up and down, up and down. It is dark outside and cosy in bed. Phil is asleep, Mummy is at choir. Daddy's large hand is round hers. He squeezes her hand. She loves his hand round hers. She wants both hands in his. She wants to wriggle round so that she can face him. Daddy is breathing. He is alive – sometimes when she comes to his bedroom he is so still she thinks he is not. He is breathing loudly. She snuggles up as close as she can behind him, her hand in his warm against the soft bit of his tummy…

But her hand is free. Daddy has let it go. It floats, hovers – not knowing what to do. Does he want her hand back? He is shifting his body to the edge of the bed and telling her to get out. He is pushing her out of bed.

Her legs are wobbly on the floorboards. Her hands are waving about. He never tells her to get out. He says nice things when it is time to leave. Tears pour into her mouth.

'Daddy, don't make me go. Daddy, what's the matter? What's the –!'

His hand catches her face thwack! Her lungs leap up. Her breath is trapped. The walls turn.

But he has caught her. Her face is pressed into his warm chest beneath the pyjamas. 'It's alright, darling. It's alright. Now, shush, shush. It's alright. You mustn't cry. Calm down.' Her shoulders shake but his arms stay there. 'It's alright, darling. It's alright.'

His fingers lift her chin and turn it to examine her cheek. She loves the lines in his forehead and the look in his eyes. She loves it that they have made up. It will be alright. She will say she slipped and fell and hurt her cheek against the side of the bed. She will say that Daddy made her better and that will please Mummy because it means that Daddy must be feeling alright.

When she goes up to his room a few days later he is at his desk with his exercise books, dressed in his grey trousers and patched jacket.

She takes a step inside. 'Mummy's out.'

He gets up and puts an arm round her and turns her towards the door. 'I bet you've got lots of homework.' Her shoulder is given a squeeze. She feels his lips kiss her hair. 'Thank you, darling. I'm alright today.'…

In the early days, Grant used to ask, 'What was your father like?'

She could picture them leaning against the railing of the boat travelling from Kew to Hampton Court. The deep green of the tall trees along the towpath had given way to Ham House.

'Why do you want to know?'

'It tells me about you.'

Cars were parked by the river. A little kid waved. She lifted her hand. 'Nothing to tell. Just a father.'

He seemed too interested at the beginning. She could see them wandering along a wooded path in Richmond Park, sun flickering through the trees. 'Martha... do you think he took his own life?'

The way he phrased it annoyed her more than what he was asking. She moved out of the trees and started down a path in the middle of the bracken that led towards Penn Ponds. His hand reached for hers. She swung it away.

'Martha, it might help to talk.'

What annoyed her was that he made a thing of it when no one in the family had ever questioned how he died.

'Honey...'

She stopped in the middle of the path wanting to shove him into the bracken. 'I don't want to talk about it!' But that made it sound as if there was something to talk about and she strode on, pushing past an approaching couple, hating Grant.

Later – when she understood that probing and analysing was like a game to Grant and she just had to tell him to stop; and when he understood that her family history was mostly out of bounds – she did nearly talk. They were flying to America – their first trip – high above the world and normal self-censorship. She gazed out of the window at the clouds far below and rehearsed the words in her head against the hum of the aircraft.... During his bad times Daddy couldn't feel. His emotions were frozen. I got into bed to warm him up. When Daddy was well, he smiled and laughed, like he did with Phil or Mummy. He would clasp my hands and praise me for getting high marks at school. He was well most of the time. But I didn't want him to be well... She looked towards the rim of the sky, imagining she could see the curvature of the earth, imagining herself being able to say, *I didn't want him to be well.* She turned to Grant. But the air hostess had arrived with the plastic trays of food, and he was grinning at her, 'Hungry, honey?' and already lowering their plastic tables.

She rolled on to her back now and stared into the darkness, and tried to think of the nice things about the early time with Grant: Grant standing on her doorstep refusing to come up for coffee and sex but still wanting to see her. Getting the break on to the women's page at *The Chronicle*. Realising she didn't want to write articles on individual subjects, realising she wanted to see the whole picture, make the choices, become an editor. Grant seemed to enhance all that, made her think that was possible.

It was mid-morning when she got downstairs the following day. On the draining board a plate was propped against a mug. There were crumbs round the toaster. Jon had eaten toast before he'd left. The thought cheered her. Making himself at home as if he might return. She went straight to the front door to pick up the newspapers before the good feeling evaporated. A note had come through the letterbox.

'I think I overreacted yesterday. Do drop round. Love Barbara.'

She sat at the kitchen table with the newspapers and wedged the phone against her ear. 'No, Jenny, I'm not coming in.' She licked a finger and turned the pages. There was a feature on Third World debt. Tony had got a piece in the business pages...

'You sounded awful when you phoned. Are you better?'

'A bit... sorry to do this when you're so new. Are you coping?'

'Yes thanks, Martha.'

'Thing to remember about features is that we are reporting on the story behind the story, looking for the key... ' A thread of energy was returning.

'Martha...'

'Yes...'

'Liza needs to talk to you. About a profile on a journalist who was killed. Worked for one of the press agencies. Not

221

well known, but one of the best war correspondents – American …'

'Okay.'

'She said only if you're well enough.'

'That's fine. I'll talk to Tony too.'

Grant rang in the early evening worried that she wasn't at work. He'd tried to call her at *The Chronicle*.

'I'm not ill, Grant. I just a need a break…'

His voice was flat. 'She died.'

'What –?'

'Very early this morning.'

'Oh Grant! I'm sorry.'

'Thank you.'

'I'm so sorry… How… how did she…?' She couldn't think what to say.

'Peacefully. But sudden.'   He sounded odd, formal.

'I wish I was with you.'

'We're stunned, but you know all about that.'

'What…?'

'Your own bereavements.'

She lifted the phone away.   Bereavements – only Grant would use that kind of word. For several hours she'd pushed that stuff out of her mind. She'd spoken to Tony and Liza, told them she would be in as soon as she'd thrown off the flu bug, and had felt as she said it that she would; that within a couple of days she would be at her desk, working normally. She pressed the phone to her ear.

'… the funeral will be in about five days depending when we can book everything.'

She glanced round the empty, clean kitchen.   'Another week?'

'Probably.'

'I'll fly out.'

'Only if you want to –'

'Grant, I need you…' There was a crackle and a pause. 'Grant? Grant, are you there?'

'I'll call you again once I know the funeral date. You'll want to wire flowers…'

He hadn't heard. The spotless white walls of the kitchen swirled around her. Light glinted off the kettle.

'…Martha, I said you'll want to wire flowers, but if it's too difficult I'll do it… from both of us.'

She stared at the phone after it had clicked off – the little screen saying 'Down', the plastic numbered buttons, the green and red icons of telephone receivers. There had been a gap before he'd said 'from both of us' as if he hadn't meant it, as if he didn't want to share the flowers with her. Her shirt was pasted to her armpits.

She ran into the hall and pulled at the drawer in the small half-moon table. She must get back to him. His mother's number was in the card index in her study upstairs but it was quicker to find it in the old address book.

But now the doorbell rang. She prayed it wasn't the neighbours, or a delivery although that was unlikely at this time of day. Without checking the security eye she unlocked it and there was Jon, barely recognisable in a corduroy jacket and Grant's magenta shirt.

TWENTY THREE

JON

Martha was clutching a small green book and had that red, shiny face he never saw on her at work but was getting used to seeing here. 'Grant's mother's died.'

'Wha' –?' It sounded as if the old woman had died in Grant's room on his couch.

'I've got to get back to him.'

'Is Grant here?'

'Of course not! Come in, for God's sake, and shut the door.' She picked up the phone from the little table in the hall, punched a lot of numbers and put it to her ear.

No, why are you here again? Perhaps she didn't mind. The pile of letters on the little table was growing into a mountain. It was her fault anyway, inviting him to stay; he was getting used to the place – nice suppers and TV, stretched out on the settee. Upstairs in the map room were Grant's other two shirts: the green and the yellow one – shit, as long as she hadn't removed them.

This morning he'd picked the red one, amazed what it did for him, amazed what a colour could do – he wasn't sure what the colour was; *wine* probably – some poncy name. He'd gazed at himself in the mirror in the Men's room at work. It made his hair look darker, his skin paler, and the cut did something too. Trust Grant to have something classy. The Features Floor were all over him – 'Ooh, Jon! Ooh, aah! Like the shirt!' Only Liza kept quiet, staring at him from under her sticking-up fringe. Liza wasn't into personal stuff, and was the only one he could trust to ask about Martha, check for the umpteenth time she hadn't turned up. What's the matter with Martha, he'd paused by her desk wanting to ask? Liza looked as if she wanted to ask *him* a question, but then he remembered about the baby stuff, and whose shirt he was wearing. At lunch time he'd wandered into a couple of shops in the mall and glanced along

224

the rails. Shiny, fake material. Pale, nothing colours. Where the fuck did Grant buy his shirts? Perhaps he would keep this one...

Martha was hugging the phone to her ear and marching backwards and forwards between the kitchen and the hall. He leaned against the frame of Grant's door watching her sigh and then press the numbers again, and rested his head against the wood. After she'd gone to bed last night, he'd pretended the house belonged to him. He strolled into Grant's room and flicked through the books on his desk: *'The Father: Contemporary ...'* something or other... *'Terrors and Experts'...* *'The Symbolic...'* Grant was on another planet. He ran his hand across Grant's new computer, and sat on to the couch for a moment, though it wasn't the same without Grant, and then got up and felt the weight of the curtains, the heavy, quality material with its white lining. Nice stuff – he could live with it. In the hall he followed the pale, striped wallpaper up the stairs and saw that it reached right up to the ceiling above the landing. It made the downstairs and the upstairs look joined together, bigger. At New Malden every little room or passage had a different patterned wall covering, in Anaglypta, which grazed your knuckles. His fingers stroked the pale striped wallpaper. Everything was so fresh here: the clean, white poles of the banisters, the shiny dark wood of the rails, the thick red stair carpet. In New Malden the Anaglypta covered tat.

He'd started thinking: how had she and Grant got all this? This house? This space? These maps? What had they done to deserve it? It was like when Shirley moved in with Pete and they got more stuff. It moved Pete away from him on to another level. His hands had started to curl into fists. He got up to the landing wanting to know. It had been nice in the kitchen sitting there telling Martha about his ma. He'd wanted to go on talking, like he did with Grant. He missed Grant. He stood outside her door, tapping his fists against his thighs. Couple of steps and he would be in there. He stared at the keyhole. *In there…?* Fucking hell! He nearly laughed out loud. He didn't have to worry about *that* with Martha. He retreated a step or two, and then turned and went back downstairs past the striped wallpaper, across the tiled floor into the sitting room. He sank into the settee and turned on the TV, and after a few minutes went into the kitchen and found a can of Foster's…

And now here he was back the next day in this hall with Martha, and she was slamming the phone down on to the table. 'I don't know where he is!' She glanced around as if Grant might appear in a puff of green smoke, and then strode into the sitting room.

Jon moved away from the doorframe and followed her.

She sat down on the edge of the settee. 'I don't know where he was phoning from, Jon! I don't know what the matter is.'

He perched on the arm of the chair. 'His mum's died, hasn't she –?'

'I don't know whether I should go to the funeral.'

'Does he want you to?'

'I don't know!'

He tried to avoid her eyes. He could see his reflection in the glass doors at the end of the room, looming over her. He wanted to flick on the TV and get her off the settee and into the kitchen, so that she could cook his supper like his ma would. He wished she was his ma suddenly, and they were in the new bungalow in Leatherhead, without his dad. Him and his ma: Ma cooking bangers and mash or toad-in-the-hole, him making the gravy with her and chatting; or Ma frying the bacon to go in macaroni and cheese, him grating the cheese. None of that happened if Dad was there and Dad was always there now, in their retirement home, as he called it.

'He's had enough, Jon.'

He glanced at her, thinking she would be looking at him, but she was staring at the carpet.

'That's what it is.' She was up and walking towards the glass doors blocking the view of his reflection. She turned.

Her boobs were more prominent today under a white zip cardigan. 'We've been trying to have a baby. I told you that, didn't I? He's had enough.' She was back on the settee, the end nearest him. 'I'm sure of it. I could hear it in his voice.'

He slipped off the arm and on to the chair. She wasn't talking to him. She was talking to the carpet, working it out. That was how marriages ended, he supposed. Something was worked out and then people did things. Ma and Dad should've worked things out and everyone might have been happier. He sat back and dared another look.

Her eyes were on him. 'Perhaps you could give me a baby.'

'Wha'… ? Shit, Martha!' He pushed himself to the edge of the chair.

She put out a hand. 'It's alright. I didn't mean it.' Her hand lowered on to the arm of the settee.

There was a hot tightness inside him. He stood up.

'I was joking, Jon.' She pushed herself up to a standing position. 'Just hold me, will you?'

His head shook. 'I can't, Martha. Not what you want.' What the fuck was he saying?

She had that red, shiny face and was shaking her head as if she was going to cry. 'Sorry, Jon. Sorry… I shouldn't have said that. I don't know what's the matter with me....'

She wanted him to put his arms round her – no, she didn't… of course she didn't. She was walking past him and out of the room. He heard her steps on the tiled hall floor and then they went quiet.

Heart thumping, he listened. There was a whine of a plane. He tucked his hair behind his ears. Where had she gone? The heating clicked. He moved towards the door – no sign; walked through the hall not looking to left or right, opened the front door, closed it as quietly as he could and ran down the path out into the road.

TWENTY FOUR

MARTHA

For a long time her face stared at her from the glass oven door. She turned away and rummaged in the freezer for a packet of frozen prawns and then stood in front of the oven again holding them, shivering with the cold of them, unable to think what to do next… cut up an onion? Oil into a pan?

There was a footstep. She swivelled round. 'Jon…?'

But he'd gone, crept out; she'd heard the sound of the door.

In the hall, the drawer of the small half-moon table hung open as she'd left it, the address book on the chair beside it. She pushed in the drawer. Grant's letters were piling up on the table, hers as well. Next to the letters was the phone. She picked up the letters, thinking she might sort them, place Grant's on his desk, go through her own. She put the pile down, returned to the kitchen and stuffed the prawns back into the freezer. Asking him for a baby! His face as he'd looked at her. 'I can't. Not what you want…'

She fetched the phone and sat down at the kitchen table and tried Grant's mother's apartment again. The American recorded voice told her to leave a message and she did this time. 'Grant, are you there? Grant, you're not going to leave me, are you?'

She replaced the phone on its wall bracket, locked the front door, turned on the alarm and went upstairs. She ran a bath, and once undressed got in quickly and turned on the hot tap, needing to lie down. Perhaps she really was sickening. Something nasty she'd harboured and only now revealing itself. Illness affected your mood, lowered you. Her father was ill. Illness was an excuse for anything. The hot water circled round her body, not warming her skin. She reached for the hot tap, and twisted it on. Grant would come back after the funeral. Why did she think he wouldn't? Her face felt cold.

She swilled the water over it. How could she have thought Jon could help? But she had... right from the beginning, right from the first time she saw him when the computers crashed and he took her back to her desk. He'd held her at the office party, and in the hall here. She'd felt his arms around her.

She thought of all those men wanting her, saying she was sexy – Paul, Nigel, Richard, David... at university, in her twenties. Some of them had lasted several months. Paul was around for a year. She didn't have to do anything – that was what made it possible – just let them peel off her clothes, grateful that they wanted to do it, that they wanted to go inside her and deposit their sperm into her pill-protected womb. Paul thrust in and out, his strong body pressing down on hers, 'Please come. Please, please...' Sometimes her breath seemed to catch and she felt on an edge of something. 'Aah aah aah... ' her voice broke out of her. She groaned and moaned as if the noise might flip her out of herself.

Out of the bath, she rubbed herself dry and ran and got into bed. The sheet felt cold and slippery. She tugged the duvet around herself, longing for a hot water bottle. Grant would have brought her one. He knew what to do with her. He knew how to be with her. He couldn't not come back. She switched on the side light, and forced herself out of bed to turn off the main light and close the curtains, and then got back into bed and burrowed inside the duvet...

'Is it something I don't do?'

'No.'

'What then?'

'Grant, it's lovely. I love it.'

'Martha, I don't like not satisfying you.'

'You do.'

'Martha, what is it?'

Tears had sprung to her eyes. He was the first person to ask her that. She'd shaken her head. 'I love you. It's alright, I love you.'

She woke with the phone drumming in her head, wanting it to stop, and then reached for the phone thinking it might be Grant. A crack of daylight gleamed between the curtains. She heaved herself into a sitting position. Her watch on the side table said nine-fifty.

'Martha? It's Tony.'

'Oh... hello.'

'You sound awful...'

'I've just woken.' There was a pulse in her left temple. She leaned back against the pillows.

'I was going to run through the last couple of days but you don't sound up to it.'

'I'll be alright.'

'Nasty bout of flu.'

'I'm getting better.'

'You don't sound it.'

'You've said that already. Just give me a moment.' She pushed herself up a little and wedged the pillows into her back.

'We've had your messenger friend round.'

'What...?'

'That overgrown youth – you know, the one who never moves on; he keeps asking after you.'

'Sorry...?'

'Same again today. Thought you might not be okay. That's what he said to Liza. Got a crush on you. Doesn't like you being ill.'

Her hand was clamped around the phone. 'Don't be ridiculous, Tony.'

'Seriously. Are you alright?'

'I've got flu.'

'Not low or anything?'

'Why would I be low?'

'I don't know.'

She managed a laugh. 'For God's sake, I'm married to a shrink!'

'Sorr-ee.'

'I'll be back next week.'

'OK. So you are up to running through things?'

'Yes!'

'Hang on a minute –'

She heard him calling someone.

'Yes, I'm off the phone. Now!' His voice came back to her. 'Martha, I'll get back to you.'

She clicked the off button. Her smell wafted up from inside her nightdress. A muzzy, slightly sweaty smell. What had Jon been saying? The light shone through the curtains. Sunny day outside. She pulled on her dressing gown and walked along the passage to her study to find Grant's mother's telephone number. He must be there now. Too bad if it was the middle of the night.

She sat in the chair and gazed at her full pending tray, which needed to be taken to the office and sorted. Jon wasn't coming back. The thought overlaid the repeated note of the American ringing tone. That was what he was telling Liza, in so many words, making sure the department knew that their features editor was languishing at home because he, Jon, wasn't coming back. The odd notion made her eyes fill.

The American recorded voice cut in. 'There is no one to answer your call at this moment but you can leave a message....'

She clicked the off button. No one was coming back.

In bed and the pulse in her temple returning, she tugged the duvet around herself. You had to get a prescription for sleeping tablets. Was that why Daddy chose the telegraph pole?

Daddy is having a bad patch for the first time in – and Mummy always pauses before she finishes the sentence and encloses the word in a sigh – years. And it is years... Martha has forgotten, put it out of her mind. She is older now. Phil is at boarding school, Mummy is at choir practice. They are in a different house. She climbs up the carpeted stairs and pushes open his door.

His back is towards her, his head poking out of the sheet. It's a warm day, no blanket. He's her daddy and looks silly with his hair sticking up over the sheet. But he is still, not breathing almost... and she remembers that. 'Daddy, it's Martha.' She lifts the sheet, a little way... bare back, just pants... Replaces it.

He needs warming up, even though it's summer. Easy to get in. Easy to slip under the sheet like she did when she was younger. But she goes to the side he's facing and sits on the bed. There's a glass of water on his bedside table, and books: *'Mary Queen of Scots'*, *'Social History of Elizabethan England.'* Daddy, what's the matter? Why do you get like this? Pull yourself together. She's grown-up, nearly, and she can say these things, get to the bottom of it, snap him out of it.

'Daddy...?'

She returns to the other side of the bed and takes off her sandals and her skirt like she used to, and gets in under the sheet and moves up behind him. Bare back, the knots of his spine, his smell... her forehead rests against his skin.

No-one knows why he has gone downhill. Mummy sits at the kitchen table sipping a martini with lines in her forehead, and taps her cigarette ash into a saucer. Too long in the same job? No promotion to headmaster? No writing of the book? No writing of any book? She gets up and moves saucepans onto the stove, and tells Martha how she has discussed these questions with her friend, Peter, in the choir. She leans against the sink, smiling when she mentions Peter. He's a good listener, and very supportive.

Mummy goes to choir practice once a week and sometimes Daddy is downstairs and he and Martha have supper together, and he watches TV and she revises for her 'O' Levels. Other times he is in the bedroom and she goes and sits on the bed and asks for help with revision, or they lie side by side and look out the window at the oak tree in the garden and the hot sky beyond.

One afternoon she comes home early from school. Mummy has gone on a trip with the choir to sing Haydn's Creation in Hereford Cathedral. She goes up to his room. It's a hot day but he's lying on his side under the sheet, his face turned away from her. She takes off her skirt, her shoes, her blouse. It's so hot, she takes off everything and gets in beside him. And then she's on top of him, feeling burning out of her. His arms are around her, his face in her hair. He hugs her to him and kisses her forehead. She squirms and wriggles. And then suddenly there is his cock, huge against her thighs. She moves down. She knows how. She wants his cock to go to the place between her legs.

He's strong as he twists her over, heavy on her body. He gasps and sighs. She can hardly breath. She turns her head sideways, away from the muscle of his shoulders. '*Mary Queen of Scots*', and '*Drake and the Spanish Armada*' are on the bedside table. He presses and presses. He will crack –

But he has rolled away. There's air around her. It hasn't happened. She doesn't think it has – it couldn't be as easy as that. She has read about it in books. It hurts. He has to break the membrane.

She reaches for the sheet. It is at the foot of the bed. She tries to pull it up. Nothing has happened. They can go back to what it was before.

But he's curled up on the edge of the bed. 'Christ, Martha. Christ. Bloody hell!' His shoulders are shaking. She thinks he may be crying, and it's her fault.

She's shaking too, shivering. 'I'm sorry, Daddy. I'm sorry…'

'Go! Just go.'

'Nothing happened, Daddy. It's alright.'

233

'I said go.' The bed rocks as he turns towards her. There are yards of sheet between them. His eyes are tightly closed. 'I'm ill, Martha. Don't you understand?'

She slides backwards, wanting him to open his eyes, not wanting it – not being able to bear the look that will be in his eyes. Her feet are over the side of the bed, and on to the floor. Her pile of clothes are in the corner by the chair.

'I was just trying to make you better, Daddy.'

He shakes his head. Tears are streaming from his eyes down the sides of his nose. 'You're not to come back. Do you hear me? You're not to come up here again.'

Bang! Someone was in the house. For a second she thought: Grant, that's where he has been – on the plane, coming home. No mobiles on planes. She jumped out of bed, regretted it. Her head pounded. But, who....? Jon? She could hear someone in the hall. 'Who's...? ' Her voice broke through a whisper. 'Who's that!'

A female voice… 'Martha, it's me. Catrin.'

Martha moved out on to the landing and held on to the banisters. The pulse had moved from her temple to her eye. 'Catrin, I'd forgotten you were coming today.' She'd forgotten it was cleaning day. Forgotten what day it was.

Catrin was undoing the buttons of her jacket and glancing up. 'I didn't know you here. Are you ill?'

'It's alright...' Martha sat down on the stair and pressed her fingers into her forehead.

'You not look well.'

'It's a headache.'

'You have those a lot.' The jacket was being placed over the back of the hall chair, the trainers removed. Catrin pushed her feet into pink mules. 'You go to bed. I bring you coffee.'

'Just… water, please. Do you mind? There's a bottle of sparkling in the fridge…'

If Grant was there Martha might have got him to sit with her on the bed and talked perhaps, and waited for the pills to

234

take effect. She swallowed them and leaned against the headboard and held Catrin's cold glass of water against her forehead. Mummy used to press a cold flannel on her forehead, when the animal in her head refused to go away, and then Daddy would come up and read her a story and lie next to her on the bed, his warm side against hers, his arm around her, his voice bringing Ratty and Toad and Mole, or the Hobbits, into the room.

That was before he got ill.

'I love you, Martha.' Wide windy beach at Pendine Sands, light bouncing off the waves.'

That was after, when he was supposed to be well again, during the summer holiday spent in Pembrokeshire, the summer before she went to university. 'I love you, Martha.' His eyes zigzagged over her face, and perhaps he had meant it. She never went up to his room again. 'You're going away from me. You must. I want you to. I want you to go out into the world.' He made that gesture with his knuckle, nudging the tears from his eyes, and she'd stamped off across the sand away from him.

She placed her glass on the side table and forced herself out of bed before the pain in her eye spread to both or affected her vision. She walked over towards the window. Flat, brown Thames flowing out to sea. Dirty shingle. A barge now, keeping to the deepest part. She closed the curtains against the light and returned to bed and pulled up the duvet. Give herself a day or two to get over this headache and then she would fly out to America and Grant.

TWENTY FIVE

JON

The next morning at the station Jon's head felt thick. It was raining and people huddled under the platform roof, deep in their newspapers. He left the platform and picked up a newspaper from the guy in the station forecourt. The freebies never had anything in them and he needed to take his mind off things. He fished in his pocket for some coins and tucked the paper inside his jacket. Shit, she would go in today. Been away so long. And then she would tell everybody he'd been having meals there and staying, that she'd cried and he'd put his arms round her, that she'd told him she wanted a baby, that she'd asked him and… but she wouldn't say that. She wanted to keep the baby thing secret. She'd been away all week, she wouldn't go in. He was back on the platform, jiggling the change in his pocket, pulling the paper out from inside his jacket. He leaned against a pillar and looked down at his paper. A woman had got off from killing her husband and was standing on the court steps, linking arms with two women. He flicked through for the Page 3 girl.

He told Max he would do the Features Floor that day and pushed the trolley into the lift. His heart gave a little jolt like the lift as it started its ascent, and then began to patter as he approached the Features Floor. A few days ago and he'd wanted Martha to be there, not liking the place without her. Now he prayed she wasn't, although if she wasn't there he would have to decide whether he should tell someone. He'd been to her house. He knew she was still there. He knew what it was like when his ma had refused to go out of the house, and the trouble that had caused his dad.

The place was like a morgue this morning. Too early for most people. No Daisy. Perhaps she'd left – why did he think that? Just Tony lurking over in *Books* and Doris hunched over her screen writing about dead people.

Doris raised a hand. 'Hi, Jon.'

'Hi, Doris!' He waved back. Martha was in! No, she wasn't. It was her secretary, sitting in her chair, cheeky bugger. Purple-hair was looking at him over a coffee mug. 'I do like that shirt!'

There were more people than he realised. Across the desk Liza lifted her head. She had a dimple when she smiled and little crinkles round the corners of her mouth, like Black Plaits. Black Plaits... it seemed like he'd never known her. His heart went from pitter-patter to an ache. That was why they called it heartache. But he wasn't going to forget her. First things first. He pushed the trolley nearer to Liza, heart thudding again with the effort of having to ask the same question as yesterday.

'Is... Martha in?'

She turned her chair to face him. 'Jon, if you've got something for her I can get it to her. It's no problem.'

Heat rose underneath his shirt; Grant's red shirt. 'She's not in today?'

The crinkles had transferred to her forehead. 'Is there something you want from her?'

'She's not coming in.'

'What is it, Jon?'

He swallowed. 'I hope she's alright. That's all I want to say.' Heat was surging upwards again. 'I hope she's alright.'

Liza's eyes followed him as he turned and walked away. He'd done what he needed. Liza could take over. He discharged the packages and letters on to the correct desks, acknowledged Purple Hair's calls to send up fax paper, and pushed the empty trolley past the rows of metal photograph files. He stood at the lift doors, clutching the trolley handle. This Sunday he would go to Leatherhead, stick to what he was planning for last Sunday. He would arrive early, switch off the TV, sit down on the settee with Ma and make her talk, show

Dad he could make her talk. He would tell Dad about his job, make Dad listen. Make them both listen. Be assertive, as Pete so often told him. Then he would go and find Black Plaits and anything would be possible.

'Penny for them.'

The red, triangular down-light was pinging.

Doris nodded at him. She was fatter standing up, two lumps for boobs, and the lump of her stomach like a third larger boob. 'You should find yourself a good job.'

The doors were opening. 'I've got one.'

'Smart lad like yourself, you could do better.'

Oh get off, he wanted to say, not part of my plan; although he liked being called smart. What was it with these lifts? He remembered Martha saying the same thing, months ago now. He got back to the Mail and Communications room, checked the message book and the emails, updated the costs spreadsheet and sent Max on an errand to the City. This was his job and he liked it. He had a flat to support and rent to pay, a lifestyle. The flat might be dark and damp and covered in purple wall to wall carpet. The whole of it might fit into two of Martha and Grant's rooms, but he was going to keep the flat. He was going to go on doing the job and paying the rent.

The place stank when he got home. He wished he was heading down Putney High Street – no, he didn't. He left the door open. Newspapers were everywhere. Empty beer cans grew at the foot of his armchair. There was an old sandwich on the computer table; his trainers were underneath the table – perhaps it was his trainers that were stinking. He chucked them out of the door. The bin in the kitchen was overflowing. He lifted out the bag. The plastic tore spilling half a pizza bread. He found a new plastic bag and transferred half the rubbish into that and tied it tightly. He needed a beer. No cans in the fridge, just a carton of milk in the door. He took a whiff and poured it down the sink. Tap full on, he got out the mop he'd hardly ever used and sloshed water across the floor.

The sitting room was freezing. He slammed the door shut and gazed at himself in his bedroom mirror. The deep red shirt – *wine*, whatever it was called was still in good nick after two days' wear, and still making him look good. He wanted the other two – the green and the yellow one. He hadn't even tried them on – damn Martha. This one was the best, though. He would wear it for Black Plaits, on Sunday. He was ready for that now. He glanced at his watch. Seven-thirty... he needed a beer. Meet up with Owen and Arthur at the *Spit and Polish*. Invite Arthur back for a game of Death Lottery. The answer phone was flashing. Not a long wind-back. It was Pete, 'How are you, mate? Haven't seen you for a while. Give us a ring,' which lifted his spirits and seemed like a bonus.

On his return from the pub, the thing was flashing again. He pressed the button ... click.... whirr.... click... nothing. Someone who didn't want to leave a message. Pete? Na, he'd already left one; he must ring him back. Martha...? Christ, he hoped not. He'd done what he could for her, and now he must get on to the next thing. He would keep Grant's shirt – Martha owed him that. Show it off to Black Plaits. He stripped off and plunged the shirt into a bowl of Persil. So quality, the colours didn't run.

By Saturday the shirt was dry. Grant probably had it pressed by a cleaning woman or a laundry. Jon made do with the hanger over the bath – Black Plaits wasn't fussy. He inspected it for creases and slipped it on with his jeans... looked even better with the denim blue.

But Black Plaits wouldn't be at the shop today. He would leave a message with the kid with small boobs. He unfastened the buttons – even the buttons had class – and put on his black shirt that he saved for weekends. The red one was for Sunday and Black Plaits. He caught a bus into Kingston and ambled through the streets careful not to get hot and out of breath.

The letter had said it was better if he didn't see her. But she wanted to see him. He was sure that was what it meant and he wondered why he'd waited so long. Detained by the likes of Martha Morgan, going to her house to make sure she was alright – and what had *he* got out of it, apart from a shirt? She fancied him, didn't she? She'd wanted him to give her a baby. He shook his head and stopped for a second, aware of a woman in a grey suit and heels, glancing at him. He wanted to get to the shop now and make up for lost time. Make sure to leave the message. Make sure Black Plaits would be there tomorrow.

He checked his reflection in the window of *Focus Camera Shop* and was turning towards *Gem Universe*, when he saw Black Plaits on the pavement. He stepped back, his heart jerking. She was arranging the bowls of stones on the folding tables. Forget it. He didn't want to do this. But she was looking up, looking his way.

He lifted his arm, 'Hello!'

Her head twisted back as if she didn't want to see him. 'Oh – hello.' She picked up a bowl of fossils and put it on the other table.

He moved towards her. 'How are you?'

'Good.'

She didn't look good. The white stuff on her face looked like cement. The black hair was floating about on her shoulders; she should give the dye a rest.

'I didn't think I'd see you.'

'Sorry –?'

'Saturday's not your day, is it?'

'Bad luck.'

'Wha'?'

'You thought I wouldn't be here.' She emptied a bag of stones into a bowl.

'I… I came to see you.'

'Did you?' She flashed him a look. He'd forgotten the see-through green eyes.

'I was going to leave a message. Make sure you were here tomorrow.'

'I don't know about tomorrow.' Her head turned as a couple of girls stopped by the shop window and peered through the glass. 'I may have Opal.'

'Opal?'

'My daughter.' The girls moved on. She stepped inside the shop and picked up a cardboard box from the floor.

He'd forgotten about her daughter. It seemed brighter inside the shop. He could see right into the back behind the counter, to the little sink where she filled the kettle to make tea. Last time the door had been closed. He'd had his back against the counter. He'd had to push past her to open the door and get out.

The box was on the counter. She ran a knife along the tape sealing the box and lifted the flaps. 'I'm not here for much longer.'

'Wha' –?'

'I'm moving.'

'Moving –?'

She took some books out of the box.

His hands landed on the counter; he couldn't help it. 'When are you moving?'

She glanced at his hands and removed more books. 'Soon.'

It was like she didn't know him. Like they'd never touched. Maybe that was the trouble. They had touched and she hadn't liked it. The pile of books was rising. His shirt was sticking to him. 'Carol... I got your letter.'

'Why have you come?'

'I got your letter.'

She turned, her hand resting on the books. 'You thought I wasn't going to be here.'

'I told you I was going to leave a message. Say I'd come Sunday.'

'Were you?'

'Yeah!'

'Why didn't you come sooner?'

'Oh, fuck you!' He twisted away, out on to the pavement, past the stupid little tables, past the fossils and stones. He couldn't do things. He couldn't make things go right. A hot, sick feeling rose into his throat. He swerved back.

She was standing in the doorway, clutching a pile of books. 'I didn't think you'd come again.'

'Why not?'

'I told you not to, didn't I? It's no good.' Her head shook. She looked down at the stupid bundle of books. 'I shouldn't have written the letter.'

'Carol!' She was turning inside.

She looked back. 'I thought it might work.'

'Wha'…?' What did she mean?

'But it's no good, is it?'

She probably did this every morning – changed things, moved things, switched things on that made water trickle or lit up the pink and green rocks. He'd only been there at the end of the day. She had a job to do. Couldn't blame her for wanting to get on with it. The trouble was he didn't know how to stop her from doing things, how to stop her from getting on with her life. That was always his problem – people being busy… Pete, his dad, his ma even. He'd never learned how to tag on, get included. He'd thought Black Plaits might let him tag on. She probably wanted to close the door now, push him out, although that wouldn't be good for customers. He hung around unable to make himself shove off. He watched her make a space on one of the tables outside and fill it with the books that weren't selling. In the end he helped her, brought out more books, and then, as instructed, transferred the new books on the counter to the shelf near the door.

242

She started rubbing stones with a duster, breathing and rubbing on them, all chatty and matey – bloody women, he didn't understand them. 'Indian.'

'Indian?'

'I like stones, Jon,' more breaths, more rubs, 'but what I really like is Indian, Indian merchandise – all those colours and materials, and jewellery... I love that. We're going to find a house near the sea. Do you like the sea, Jon?'

'Don' know.'

'We're going to set up our own shop, me and my mum. We'll have money from our houses...' another breath. 'Jon, those books go alphabetically by title.'

He couldn't see the titles. The covers were a blur. A hot, gunky feeling was in his throat. He hardly knew her. She was a scrubber with dyed hair and white cement on her face. But he wanted things to stay still for one minute, one moment....

'I want to travel, Jon, and buy the goods. Mum can look after –'

'Why the letter?'

'What?'

He dropped the books and turned.

She was shaking her head. 'I'm sorry, Jon.'

'Why, Carol?'

'I shouldn't have written it, should I?' She stared at the stone in her hand. 'I didn't think you were going to come back. I didn't think you would want to.' She glanced up. 'I'm too old for you, darling.'

Sounded too old, the way she said it – the way she looked: cement face, dyed black hair. Perhaps he didn't want her. But she was putting the stone and duster on to the counter and coming round the counter and leaning against it, so that, though the gunky feeling was making him feel he might puke, he couldn't stop looking at her see-through green eyes and trying to understand.

'I've got this opportunity, Jon. Opal's Dad is going to Australia. He's a useless dad but I hung around thinking he should see her. But now he says he going, there's nothing to stop me. It's what I've wanted for years. There's more of a market in Indian than in stones.'

She wasn't saying the things he wanted to hear. She was avoiding his eyes, gazing at the little waterfall pouring down the gash of red rock. 'I couldn't see a way out of working here, Jon. And Stan, Opal's dad – he was never there for Opal. I was always having to leave her with my mum. And then, a couple of weeks ago, he tells me he's going off to Australia, and I think, even if he doesn't I'm not hanging about any longer.' She glanced up and put her hands to her face, smiling and nodding her head. 'I'm going to do it, Jon. I'm going to.' Her fingers were spread across her cheek. Green nails. He could remember them being blue when she put a hand on his and congratulated him on being a hero, and black and other colours too.

Her hands lowered and she took his hand now. 'You're lovely, Jon. If I was fifteen years younger –'

'Carol…' He had to push out the words as if the gunk inside him had to be forced out. 'Carol, I haven't got anyone.'

'You will, Jon –'

'I won't.'

Water was trickling somewhere. Her hand stroked his. 'Of course you will, Jon. You're an attractive man, and you don't seem to realise it.'

'Carol, I could help you. You'll need a helper.'

'You don't want to do that. You got your own life.' She patted his hand. 'You're a darling. But I'm okay. You don't have to worry. I've got Mum and Opal.' She was nodding again. 'Everything's going to be fine.' Her eyes looked beyond him as a customer came through the door. There was a last squeeze of his hand, so tight he was still feeling it hours later. 'Love you to bits, eh.'

He pushed open the door of *The Brown Cow* and struggled through a crowd to the bar. Kingston was a hole. *Budweiser* or *Holstein* or draught. No thank you.

Fuck, this was the place he came into before he discovered her shop and the leopard skin stone. He still had that, didn't he? In the pocket of his trousers. No, he'd put it in his drawer with his socks planning to give it to Black Plaits. He could still give it to her. She was the one who would understand the importance of being given a present like that. He would still give it to her, even if she was into Indian. Perhaps the leopard skin stone was Indian. Volcanic, she'd said. There were volcanoes in India, weren't there? He backed off from the bar and felt something wet on his shoulder.

'Hey! Watch it! That's my half!'

'Sorry, mate.'

'Mind where you're going!'

He would go back to her and tell her. It was only a few yards down the road. Tell her what? She wouldn't want to know. What would she care about a yellow stone with dark brown spots; she was into all things Indian. The spots were the tiny explosions in the lava, that's what she'd told him. She knew all about it. Did she know the history of all those stones or had her mind moved on to Indian stuff? He'd never thought about Indians. There were quite a few out at the print works at Watford. Dad sold his butcher's shop to an Indian. The man's wife wore a sari. Would Black Plaits sell saris?

He cut down a narrow lane with a sign that said *River Path*. A pub called *The Merry Juggler* with tables outside was filling up in spite of a raw wind. *Foster's*. Better than nothing. He downed a couple of pints and moved on. He would go home and ring Pete. Invite him over to the *Spit and Polish*. Introduce him to Arthur and Owen and the others. He hadn't seen them himself for a couple of weeks. But tonight was Saturday night, wasn't it, and Shirley would've organised something girly?

And tomorrow was Sunday. What would he do tomorrow? Black Plaits didn't want him. She'd said goodbye. Sunday dinner with Ma and Dad in Leatherhead. Couldn't wait. He was pissing himself with anticipation.

Love you to bits. He stamped down Putney Hill. Love you to death. He'd heard that one too. At least she hadn't said that. Fucking women. His dad was right. Shouldn't give them the time of day.

I want to go on seeing you... You scare me... You scare me because I want to go on seeing you... Stay... Stay in the map room... Have some toast and butter... Have some supper... Have Grant's shirts... Give me a baby...

He rang Martha's doorbell. Rapped on the wooden bit between the patterned glass until his knuckles hurt. Pressed the bell again. Martha wasn't fucking there. She should be there. He was going to give her a baby. He slumped down on to the step and leaned his back against the wall and closed his eyes. Cold wind. He folded his arms against his chest. Women screwed up everything. He saw that now. He understood Dad. Women were only fit for the kitchen. Give them an inch and they took a mile. Had to keep them on a tight rein. Had to hit them probably; whack them.

When he was a little boy in the bath, Ma rubbing his back, touching him, Dad had hit her, hadn't he? Slapped her – whack! Whack! Jon liked Ma rubbing his back. He didn't want her to stop – he was crying. Dad hit Ma, in the kitchen usually when he was in his bedroom, wondering what to do with himself, kicking the cupboard, not daring to go down and watch TV. Dad hit her because he knew it was the only thing to do to her.

Jon pulled his jacket tight around him and slumped down further...

'Jon! Jon...! Wake up! Wake up...!' Martha towered over him, her black zip shoes and jeans inches away. 'Jon, what are you doing here?'

He knelt up and gradually rose to his feet and steadied himself against the wall of the house. The wind blew in his face, his head spinning slightly. 'You asked me.'

'Sorry...?'

'You phoned me.'

'I didn't.'

'You left a message – !' But she hadn't, had she? That was another time. Sod it. He glanced around, remembering now what he thought he'd come to do. How the fuck did he think he was going to do that? A woman was walking on the other side of the street. The wind was blowing the leaves on the tree.

'You've had too much to drink.'

'I wish I had! Can we go in?' He moved nearer.

'Why are you here, Jon?'

'Martha please...' He glanced round again. Cars parked; not a soul now. Her hand was in her bag. He pushed her against the door. Her keys clattered on to the tiled path.

'Jon...!'

'I need to go inside.' He was surprised how important it was.

'Okay, but calm down...'

'Please...'

'Okay...! But you'll have to take your hands off me. One of us has got to pick up the key.'

He probably looked crap, but she was looking at him with her weird blue eyes, and if she would let him indoors, the light, clean house might stop him from remembering about Black Plaits. He released her arms and she moved round him and stepped on to the path.

But now she was the wrong side of him, and he leaned against the wall, flaked suddenly, the point of everything draining away.

'Jon, what's the matter? What's happened?'

He lifted his shoulders. The wall was hard against his back.

'Jon…? Look at me.' She came closer and put her hands round his wrists and held them tightly like handcuffs. The firmness felt nice. 'I'm going to pick up my keys and unlock the door. Then I have to switch off the alarm.'

He didn't like losing the feel of her grasp. The wind made his bare wrists feel cold. She got inside and the buzzing sound stopped. He closed the door behind them. The hall was dark and warm. The darkness felt good. It made him want to close his eyes into real darkness and forget everything and slip down again, go to sleep and not wake up. She reached out for the switch. He lunged forward.

Her hands were around his wrists again. 'Jon, it's alright. Come on, let's go and sit down in the sitting room.'

His wrists felt safe in her hands, like human handcuffs stopping him doing anything – he liked that idea. But her hands were loosening. She was turning away. 'No…' his arm reached out.

She turned back and laid a hand on his arm. 'It's alright.' Her hand was heavy, warm; it felt like he wanted it to stay there forever. She was saying things. She hadn't left a message, but she might have done, she might like to have done… she was sorry about last time… it was because she wasn't very…

Her hand rubbed his arm up and down. He wanted to strip off his jacket and feel her hand on his shirt – feel it through the shirt and on his bare skin. He closed his hand round hers and pulled it up to his neck, to the skin above his collar, to his face. He held it there and made it stroke his cheek, made her fingers rest on the bristly part of his chin and then ran them along his lips and into his mouth. His eyes were shut. His cock was moving inside his trousers.

He opened his eyes. Blue eyes, the yellow bits… he didn't need to see her eyes. She was telling him she was going to

America, going out to Grant. He didn't want to hear that. He flicked her head away with his hand. His fist caught the side of her face as she stumbled back. He grabbed her arms and shoved her in front of him into Grant's room and towards the couch. She fell into it. He tumbled after her. She tried to sit up and say things. He didn't want her to say anything. He pushed her face back. His fists landed on her shoulders and on the top of her arms – one, two, three... going away, fucking going away from him ... Black Plaits, Martha, Daisy... But this was Martha and she fought back. She caught his arms. They rolled off the couch on to the floor, on to Grant's magic carpet.

And now he'd got his trousers off and his cock was hard. That's what he should have done with Black Plaits – got cross with her, pushed her down. Martha was a tall woman but as his dad knew, you had to be stronger. And they let you. They opened their legs. They helped you. She was helping him. It was going in. It was so hard... nothing could stop it. Tomorrow he would go and find Black Plaits. At the end of the day when the shop was closing. He would give her the leopard skin stone with its black spots. The shop would close and then he would force her down on to the floor, whack her, hit her, show her how he could do it, show her how she wasn't going to go away without him, force her, fuck her, force her ... oh, oh, oh... he was rising, lifting, rising, peaking. Oh God, he was erupting. It was happening. He was exploding inside her. He was spilling deep inside her.

TWENTY SIX

GRANT

The cardiologist and a nurse spoke to him in the shiny, sterile corridor and offered quiet words of condolence. He could hear laughter back at the nurse's desk and feel the cardiologist's concerned look. The nurse's hand brushed his arm. He nodded a thank you and waited for them to move on in their soft-soled shoes, wanting to pause a moment before going into the room.

Lani was by the bed, dry-eyed but pale – she probably had a special make-up, he thought irrelevantly as she held out her arms to him. They hugged, her small, compact figure momentarily against his. He wondered whether she'd seen Mom's last breath or whether they had rung her on her cell phone as she drove to the hospital. He couldn't bear to ask. The white aerated blanket hung loose and was pulled up to the base of Mom's nose. No nasal tube now. One of them should have been there.

He watched Lani turn back to their mother and draw the blanket away a little. The mouth was open – a black cavity between the lips – but the rest was OK, a good, even colour tone, no lines, hair combed away from her face. At peace, he found himself thinking. Had she known they weren't there? He mustn't go down that road. Lani's long manicured fingers stroked the pale cheek. Still warm, she told him. 'Poor darling...' Her hand lifted the thin grey hair. But dead, he thought. She'd been dead for days... as good as – and yet he'd convinced himself she could hear him.

Lani took his hand. He pulled her to him again, his head turned away from the body, expecting tears. But neither of them seemed capable of it. The door handle was lowering. A nurse's bland face, 'Can I – ? Oh, I apologise.' The door closed. They withdrew from each other. Lani sat on the chair by the bed. He hadn't hugged his mother. The nasal tube might have jolted, might have hurt her. He must hold her before they took her away. Try and do that. He would come back later. Be on his own with her. Jacob, Lani's husband was coming through the door now, and touching his arm, squeezing it, and going straight to his wife. Their children would arrive soon.

As for his own wife, he thought after he'd got back to the apartment and called her with the news, she couldn't even get it together to send flowers, couldn't even make that personal gesture. Hadn't he gone to her mom's funeral? Hadn't he endlessly shown an interest in her parents? Should she fly out, Martha wanted to know. No, he'd felt like saying. He didn't want her if she couldn't make up her own mind about it.

Mom wished to be buried in the Napa Valley, Lani told him a day or so later at her large apartment in Pacific Heights. Mom went there regularly three times a year, and had told Lani that Calistoga was where she wished to be. 'Calistoga was home for her, Grant.' There didn't seem to be a trace of sorrow on Lani's face as she poured boiling water on to a herbal tea bag and pushed the china mug across the table towards him. Her hair swung beautifully as she placed the kettle on the side. American women washed their hair every day, didn't they? Lani's sort. She smiled and shook her head – crows feet at the corners of her eyes, he noticed with a tinge of pleasure. 'It was not the wine, honey. It was the mud baths that Mom liked.' As if that was a reason for burying her there. They had to make decisions about the transportation of the body and the funeral, and choose whether the funeral should be in her neighbourhood in San Francisco followed by a committal in Calistoga, or whether the whole thing should be in Calistoga, in which case many people might not make it there.

He returned to his mother's apartment to find a message on the answer phone from Martha. 'Grant, are you there?' A pause. 'Grant, you're not going to leave me, are you?'

He picked up the phone and stood in front of the bookcase, staring at the gap in the line of books where he'd taken out D.M. Thomas's *The White Hotel*. 'You're not going to leave me...' Had he made it that obvious? He put down the phone and went to the bathroom and took a long time before he could pee. She could be checking up so that she could go ahead with the insemination treatment. If that was what she wanted, he would return to the States. Decision made. He shook his head – she wasn't doing that. Her voice had sounded as if she needed him. He tucked himself in and pulled up his zip. The tap water flowed over his hands. He rubbed the soap between his palms, working up a lather, and tried to imagine life without her. He remembered the Boston flat after Ruthie and Christopher had gone, the view at the window through the high rises to the harbour, the sense of everything echoing. Nothing had felt right: the local café that always supplied a high chair; the wide streets to the bus stop on his way to work. He had not been able to go near the playground or look at toddlers in buggies.

Outdoors it was a grey, foggy afternoon, temperature drop of at least fifteen degrees. He stamped along Green Street, headed east up Russian Hill and crossed Columbus on Filbert aiming for the narrow streets round Coit Tower. Impossible to know what it would be like without someone, while that person was still around. His room in Putney, Martha returning from work... he couldn't feel what it would be like if she wasn't returning. The top of the tower was submerged in cloud. He turned back, swerving out of the way of a jogger pounding towards him. This town needed good weather. He climbed on to a bus on Columbus and got off at Market and made for the Museum of Modern Art.

There was three-quarters of an hour until closing time. The place felt empty, certainly less crowded than London or

European art galleries. People stood separately, space swirling around them, more interesting than the exhibits. A young, dark, short-haired girl – cut off T-shirt exposing inches of flat stomach and bony back – had placed herself in front of a Jackson Pollock, striking in her boyishness, beautiful. He should have phoned Martha. He stared at a Georgia O'Keefe, trying to concentrate. A blue mountain was reflected in a lake, a harmonious, symmetrical picture... wasn't Georgia O'Keefe attached to Diego Rivera? There was a mural by him at an art institute not far from Mom's apartment. He'd read about it in his guide book on one of those long days in her hospital room and had felt guilty because he'd wanted to get out of the room that day to go and see the mural – she wouldn't have been any the wiser if he had. He glanced round for the girl but her figure had been replaced by a couple linking arms. He looked back at the blue mountain, its graduations of blue reflected in the lake. Mom was dead. Georgia O'Keefe and Diego Rivera were dead. Jackson Pollock too probably...

He moved into the next gallery, and there was another Georgia O'Keefe: a large picture, the flowers bursting out of the frame. 'Black Hollyhock, Blue Larkspur' – folds of velvet black plunged into a pink centre, rich blue petals burst out from underneath... he laughed suddenly at the sexuality of the painting. An elderly woman swung her head round – heavy, handsome features, proper white hair. He grinned and nodded towards the picture, not caring what she thought. Further on there was another O'Keefe. Not flowers but hills in Mexico, layers of them cut through the centre by a valley, bare, exposed hills, the slit of the valley suggestive. He imagined slipping his arm through Martha's and getting her to really look. They used to go to galleries when they first knew each other. She wasn't a detail person and he used to enjoy slowing her down, tethering her. What could she see in an abstract – a Rothko, or a Pollock? Or an O'Keefe, he thought now, looking round for the old woman before laughing out loud again.

Those trips to the galleries had usually preceded sex. He stood back and gazed at the picture, and then moved to the leather covered bench and sat down, wanting Martha now.

There was a new message on the answer phone when he returned to the apartment, Lani asking him to drive with her to Calistoga to see the priest about the committal service.

He got a beer out of the fridge, opened it and took a mouthful from the bottle. It would be the middle of the night in England. Too late to ring. He looked in the fridge again: a thin packet of ham, one broccoli and half a packet of cheese. He would eat out tonight.

'You say Martha's flying over?'

He ignored the note of surprise in her voice. 'Yes, Lani.'

'You didn't tell me.'

'I didn't know until this morning.'

'Huh?'

'She only just called, that's why I'm calling you now. I'm not going to be able to come with you to meet the priest at Calistoga.'

'Well, no... if that's when she's arriving. If she really is arriving –'

'Yes.'

'I thought she wasn't flying over.'

'I didn't say that, Lani.'

'It's a shame. I wanted you to be with me, Grant, to meet Father Martin. Mom was fond of the man.'

'If it's so important, why don't we go Tuesday?'

'Don't you think it's important?'

'Yeah, so let's make it Tuesday.'

'No, I have to go tomorrow. Jacob will come with me.'

That was how she was when they were kids, always trying to get her way, to the last detail; and then when he did give in, on nearly every point, rejecting him. He wasn't going down that route now. Martha had to be met. 'You go with Jacob, Lani.'

'You're angry now.'

'I'm not.'

'You're apprehensive about Martha.'

'Lani... I'm in a strange place right now –'

'Aren't... aren't we all? I miss Mom so much.'

'I miss her too.'

'I called her every day, Grant. Every day since... I can't remember when. I know the last few weeks she was... '

Her tears came down the phone in halting sobs. 'We're... we're... never... never going to see her again...' He remembered this too. Her tears which were permitted when his weren't, and which in his mother's eyes put her in the right and him in the wrong. Tears that were probably glistening on her face now, when his used to be hot shaming things.

He burst out. 'Lani, you've got a family!'

There was a pause, and then a sound... he couldn't get it at first and then he realised she was blowing her nose. 'Your trouble is, Grant, you chose not to. And now it's too late.'

He sat on to the sofa, clutching the phone, and remembered the Sunday when Martha had talked about donor insemination. He'd left the house and run along the road and up on to the pedestrian path on the railway bridge thinking it could be the end of his marriage. There was the train to Wimbledon and the trudge up the hill through the rain to the common, fighting off the urge to call Dale. He hadn't talked to Dale in ages, but they always talked. A fellow American, he practically lived at her house that first, muggy summer in London; that was where he met Martha. But he plodded along a gravel path towards the windmill and landed up in the café drinking strong, milky tea in a plastic mug and thinking about Ruthie: Ruthie with her white teeth and her crusty eyelashes, and her red hair that cascaded over him and tickled as she lowered herself on to him. Ruthie who couldn't see what was wrong with fucking another man, who couldn't see it would make a difference if a child happened to be conceived.

The San Francisco Herald was spread across the low coffee table. He placed the phone on the editorial about a new initiative to clean up the Tenderloin district, and rubbed his hands together, the inside of his left hand where he'd been holding the phone damp with sweat. Had Lani ever considered he might like to talk to her? She'd not once asked him about his marriage to Ruthie, or about the break-up, or about Christopher. He wasn't sure she'd met Christopher. She was over on the West Coast by that time. Probably not. She'd certainly never been interested in him and Martha. He wiped his hands against his trousers. Martha would be here in twenty-four hours. He'd talked about her to Lani, and to his mom. Martha was better than both of them. She just wanted a baby, or thought she did. And he couldn't deal with it.

The place was a mess, books and newspapers everywhere. There was a dirty mug on the bookshelf. Junk mail and gallery leaflets were scattered across the mahogany table in the window. Mom's cleaning lady was ill and hadn't appeared while he'd been here. He dragged himself up and started to return the books to the shelves and gather up newspapers. The kitchen was horrible; he hadn't washed the dishes for days. He hadn't been like this since his student days, although things slipped after Ruthie and Christopher had departed. If Lani had visited he would have cleared up, but Lani said she couldn't bear to visit yet. How often had she visited when Mom was living here, he wondered, opening the fridge for a beer, snapping it open and taking a swig?

Underneath the sink there were plastic containers of scouring liquids and lotions, brushes, cloths, wire dusters, yellow rubber gloves – too small for him of course. In the cupboard there were polishes and yellow dusters and brass and silver cleaning fluid. He scrubbed and washed, and vacuumed and dusted until the apartment returned to a place Martha might recognise as his. The apartment was his now.

Already, Lani had told him she didn't want it. 'What do I want with another apartment down the road?'

Outside, the street lights glowed. Opposite someone drew a curtain across a window. He got another beer and turned on the table lamps planning to spend the evening with the movie channel. He sat down at Mom's antique desk and ran his hand across the dark, shiny, well nourished wood. Mom was into antiques, in spite of all their moves. Furniture used to get shipped back from Europe after the trips overseas. He pulled down the sloping lid curious to see what she kept inside. Writing paper, envelopes, stamps, paid bills in the little cubby holes – where were the important papers, he wondered. He drew back the chair and pulled out the drawers – packs of cards, unopened bridge packs, a box of scrabble, ludo. The bottom drawer was filled with loose photographs. He picked up one or two and held them to the light... Pop about forty years ago in baggy trousers... the four of them in Vermont – big sister Lani a head taller than him and Mom wearing a scarf gypsy style... his graduation picture – the one with his eyes closed that didn't get framed... and – yeah, yeah it was: Ruthie!

He tilted the picture to the light. Why had Mom kept this? Perhaps she hadn't. These were the duds. He studied the round, young, out-of-date face. Long hair, but bangs – he didn't remember those. He remembered her hair turning into corkscrews in the high humidity. He remembered escaping to Cape Cod and riding horseback on the sands, and seeing her hipsters sliding down nearer the saddle, her buttocks bulging over the top. He leaned back into the chair looking at the picture. She was wearing a dress – pink with white blobs, or flowers perhaps; difficult to see. High-necked anyway – she usually wore low cut T-shirts. Dressing up for his parents. She was standing by the front door of a small, ugly, brick house in bright sunlight – no sign of trees or shadow. That would have been his parents' house, that one year they had at Duke's University in North Carolina; the accommodation got meaner once he and Lani had left home. He ran his finger over the shiny celluloid and wondered what she would look like now.

TWENTY SEVEN

JON

He felt so cocky walking out of her house afterwards. Cocky...
ha, ha! He jumped on the train at Putney Station, got out at
Clapham Junction, got down into the long tunnel under the
platforms, checked the destinations at each stairway wondering
why he hadn't managed this before, got on to the right platform,
and arrived in Surbiton in no time. He stopped off at the *Spit
and Polish*, had a chat with Owen about the different uses of
spreadsheets, downed more beer, reached the flat, showered
and gazed down at his body – chest hair on pectorals (*pectorals*...
wow, the word burst out of him!), penis hanging nicely... and
felt he could do anything – move out to the country with Black
Plaits, get used to new streets, new roads, a new map.

But in the morning he woke thinking: How can I go back to
work and face Martha? And then: Black Plaits said she was
moving to the country but when and where?

He dragged himself out of bed and shuffled into the kitchen,
switched on the kettle, shook Nescafe into a large mug and
stood by the kettle with his eyes closed, trying to blank out these
questions. Mug clutched in his hand, he moved into the sitting
room and slumped into his armchair. Did he want to leave his
job? He didn't want to lose this chair. Didn't want to lose his
computer table and the chair that went with it. Or his computer.
Or the rug. He didn't want to leave the flat until he could take
his stuff with him.

The phone rang. Fuck, it was probably Martha. He shivered
wanting get back into bed and sleep. But it was his ma, and that
woke him up – she never rang. For a second he thought
something must be wrong.

'No dear, just wondering if you were coming down today.
It's Sunday.' Dad was out meeting someone, apparently, from

some club or other – Jon didn't catch the name; it seemed unlikely. Dad had met the person in the library. Did Jon know Dad had joined the library and went down there most mornings to read the newspaper. 'He likes the walk and the different surroundings. He still buys me my *Radio Times* and the *Sun* if I want it. Will you be coming, dear?'

'No, sorry Ma. Feeling a bit rough.'

'Next week, maybe?'

'Yeah… maybe.'

'I've got a little job, Jon.'

'A job?'

'In the Oxfam shop. Two mornings a week. I can still get home in time to cook your dad's dinner – well, not cook… no time for that. But I can get something cold… Dad saw it advertised in the library…'

What had got into her? Her voice didn't sound like hers but he hardly ever got her on the phone these days so he'd probably forgotten what she sounded like on the phone. 'See you soon, Ma.' They would both give him grief if he told them he might be leaving his job.

He pulled on some clothes and got out of the flat. His head felt better in the open air. Blue sky and little white clouds. The wind had dropped today. He stood at the bus stop and got on a bus going towards Kingston and got off after a few stops. He was outside the Crown Court and he remembered the other time he was outside it when he'd run away from Black Plaits after he'd kissed her and it had gone wrong and he'd felt too scared to go back to her place… better now than then. He caught a glimpse of himself in the window of a parked van – he could have worn Grant's red shirt. Today was the day when he was going to wear it… before all this. He glanced at his face in a shop window. Dark hair…eyes… shadow on his chin. The pedestrian precinct was too full of people. Someone was blasting an Oasis number from an old ghetto blaster. The side streets were quieter. He stepped out the way of a woman with a huge three-wheel buggy. An old man with a dog sat in a doorway next to a pile of *The Big Issue*. He didn't want to think about homeless people – might be there himself… he walked back and gave him a pound. 'Keep the magazine, mate.' The tables and stands were out on the pavement as he turned down the street to the shop. His heart was thumping now.

She was inside the shop behind the counter holding a mug of tea, her finger nails the colour of Grant's shirt. Didn't think you would be here, he just stopped himself from saying – he'd said that yesterday, for fuck sake. Where's Opal, he nearly said. He stood by the door not knowing what to say. He half expected to see the little girl at the back of the shop, a pretty little black haired girl with plaits.

'Can't keep you away, can we?' Black Plaits smiled, the semi-circles at the corners of her mouth.

Perhaps she was always going to be here today, but said she wasn't because she didn't want him to think that she would be… The place felt cold after the sunlight outside; dark. She normally had the light on, making the stones and crystals glitter. He could see why she wanted to leave.

She placed her mug on the counter and looked at him. 'You alright? Draw up that chair. The kettle has just boiled. I'll make you a cup of tea.'

She disappeared into the back. He'd not noticed the chair before. He lowered himself into it, but then stood up feeling that he wouldn't say anything if he sat down. He placed his hands on the counter. He could see her dunking a teabag into a large brown mug. She glanced his way. 'Sugar?'

He nodded.

'Opal's gone to Chessington zoo with a friend, so I thought I would come in today. More money I can earn at the moment the better.' She poured in the milk, fished out the teabag and chucked it into a small swing bin and walked carefully with it to the counter and handed it to him. 'Have a seat.'

He did sit down now. She came round the counter and leaned against it. Like yesterday, he thought, telling him he couldn't go with her, telling him he wasn't part of her life. But life had changed since yesterday and perhaps that was how change happened, not so you didn't notice, but suddenly with one thing. Like an accident you couldn't stop happening. Like falling off a cliff. You might as well shout. Nothing to lose. He'd always wondered what that meant.

'When you move...' His teeth felt as if they were stuck together. '... to your new shop. You'll need somebody. I want it to be me.'

'You said that yesterday.'

'I know.'

'You saying you want to leave your job?'

'Yeah.'

She stared at him, her see-through green eyes looking darker.

'You want to work with me?'

'Yeah.'

'It might happen quite quickly, Jon.'

'I don't mind.'

'But it might not. I don't know yet'

'Right.'

'Do you see?'

'Yeah.'

'I can't tell at the moment.'

He wished she wouldn't look so serious. He didn't want to think about it too much. Not the practical side. Just let the idea settle. He swigged back his tea. She would have customers soon. He stood up, and put his mug down on the counter.

She put down her own mug. 'I don't know what the money would be like, Jon. Hardly any to start. Nothing maybe.'

'Right...' Close up she didn't look too good. He liked her hair pulled back into the one plait but the semi circles at the corners of her mouth were digging into her cheek even though she wasn't smiling. His stomach tingled.

Her hand reached out and touched the sleeve of his jacket. 'Go away, Jon, and think about it. You could be giving up more than you get.'

That was what he liked about her. No pressure. No making him feel silly because he wasn't sure. Perhaps he was just scared of going back to the office and needed to ignore Martha and carry on with his job. He turned away. If he saw Martha, would he want to try and get off with her again? See if he... he could, though, couldn't he? He could do it with Daisy if she would have him, do it with Tracey of Motsuki Pharmaceuticals. Do it with Black Plaits.

'Where would you live, Jon?'

He was in the doorway. She'd switched on the light. The dish of stones on the counter next to her sparkled with little stars. 'Rent a room?'

'With me?' She said it, not him, laughing, her white teeth gleaming like one of the stones or crystals.

'Yeah. Or nearby.'

She nodded. 'Come to my flat. Next week.'

He caught a glimpse of his face in the glass door of one of cupboards, grinning and looking pleased with itself. 'Evening?'

'Day.'

'I'm working.'

'Thought you were going to leave.'

'Wha' –?'

'Only joking.'

'I will.'

But later, as he came out of the *Spit and Polish* after a couple of pints and a chat with Gail, the new bar girl, about how she was saving up to go round the world, he wasn't sure. Black Plaits had been like that before, smiling at him, wanting to kiss him, sending him that letter, and then when he thought he knew what she wanted, telling him she was leaving, telling him she didn't want him, didn't need him? Like all those others – Daisy, Tracey, Martha even...

263

TWENTY EIGHT

GRANT

Martha's thick, wavy, short hair bobbed over the heads of two grey-suited businessmen, as a crowd of people emerged into the large airport hall. Grant caught a glimpse of her face and remembered her expression outside their house as he'd left in the taxi – more than a week ago; it seemed longer. She'd stood on the pavement by their small black, wrought-iron gate, her hand raised, looking as if she wanted to cry, and he'd felt a flush of pleasure because it seemed to be about him.

She'd seen him now and his hand lifted in a wave, his face breaking into a smile. He pushed through the crowds and then stood by her trolley of luggage staring at her, surprised at how pleased he was to see her. 'Honey...' he held out his arms. It felt good to hold her, though she seemed thinner; he could feel her ribs.

They stood back from each other. She looked tired. There was a faint darkening near the corner of her left eye.

He nodded. 'Long flight, huh?'

A smile flickered on her lips. 'Here now.'

'Yeah, wonderful.'

He looked away, her words coming to him... *Grant, you're not going to leave me, are you?* He didn't expect to be reminded of them so quickly. They didn't seem to connect to the two of them here. The airport hall was emptying. 'Come on, let's get you home – I mean to Mom's apartment.' He glanced to see if she'd noticed the word *home*, but she was pushing the trolley and he took over, feeling her slip her arm through his as he guided it towards the glass door and the bright afternoon.

The taxi drove them in silence along the freeway through the sprawling, hilly suburbs. Every time he made this journey it took longer than he expected to reach the moment that he loved, the moment when over one of the hills the city exploded into view: the gleaming high rise buildings of downtown San Francisco, always taller than he remembered, always – in his memory of it – soaring into a flawless blue sky. Would he remind her of this moment? There were several inches of fake leather seat between them. She was looking out of the side window. She hadn't been to work, he remembered. But she wasn't ill. That was what she'd told him when he'd rung to tell her Mom had died. She didn't want to send flowers, and that had annoyed him. She'd said, I need you... he'd forgotten that until now. He'd ignored whatever was going on for her, taken up with his own stuff which was mainly about her but hadn't seemed like it. He should tell her about the funeral arrangements and the trip up to Calistoga. Last night after he returned Ruthie's photo to the desk drawer, he had the idea that the two of them might stay up there for a few days, make a small holiday of it. He'd fetched another beer and imagined her agreeing to follow him to the States. It had seemed realistic that she might agree.

He reached for her arm and took her hand. 'Okay?'

She turned, quivering slightly as she inhaled. 'I think so.' Their eyes met. She smiled and looked ahead. He could see the little cracks in her skin. The taxi was eating up the miles. He reminded her of the view. 'Any minute now,' he laughed.

They arrived at the apartment and climbed the steps up to the front door, and he held it open for her. It was clean inside and airy. Sunlight flowed in through the large living room window reflecting on the mahogany table. There were glimpses of the water of the bay through the gaps in the houses opposite. This could be a good pied-à-terre, and then they could buy something further out, something classy with the money from the Putney house. Martha was looking towards the bedroom. He took her case into the bedroom and suggested he put on some coffee. 'I've made space in the cupboard for you. Mom had so many clothes.'

She caught hold of his jacket, and he put his arms round her. She seemed to want him to undo the buttons on her shirt and slip his hands inside.

'You sure? Aren't you tired.'

Her head shook.

They undressed and got into bed and she slipped off her watch and reached round to put it on the bedside table. There was a dark smear on her thigh, blueish black like a brush stroke, and for a second he let himself dwell on it as if it was a part of her that he knew. He put out his hand. But then his heart jerked painfully. 'What is it, Martha?

She looked down. He saw the movement of her throat swallowing. 'I fell.'

'Fell?'

'Down a few stairs.'

'You fell downstairs?'

She glanced up. 'Only a few stairs.'

The shadow below the corner of her left eye was faint, spread over her cheekbone like a highlighter except that it wasn't matched on the other cheek. 'Is that what this mark is?' He touched it lightly with his finger, wanting to press it suddenly.

'I just slipped. Near the bottom of the stairs. It was nothing. I'm fine.' Her hand was reaching for his. 'Just love me, will you.'

I thought of leaving you, he nearly said. He would say it tomorrow or later tonight. Ask her why she hadn't been at work, and get to the bottom of what she'd been doing while he'd been away. Find out what made her fall downstairs, what she was doing before she fell downstairs. He pulled the duvet round her. She huddled up against the headboard. A hooter sounded in the bay. A car changed gear. Part of him wanted to wipe the slate clean, start afresh, not worry about complications that happened when he wasn't there. Putney was across a continent and an ocean. The idea of his room, his house, his work seemed lost in one of San Francisco's fogs. And yet now he was facing Martha – her eyes about to fill with tears; now she was sitting inches away from him, the image of the hall, the stairs going off to the left, his room to the right started to percolate through. He could see his computer, and the couch, and the Persian rug adding colour to the neutral environment. He could see the other thing he'd left behind: his computer protégé, that vulnerable, dark-haired man sitting at the desk, peering into the screen.

Relief flickered through him. They just had to work at it. It wouldn't be easy. Nothing was easy. But they mustn't give up. He drew Martha towards him, removed the duvet and carefully held her. A bird chirped. There were voices in the street. He lay back and held out his hands. 'Come on. Let's see how we're going to avoid the bruises.'

She climbed on top of him and he allowed her to slowly arouse him. He kept his eyes on her determined that she should come first. He waited for that familiar expression, that look of pain – eyes tight shut, cheeks pulled in – that always preceded what used to be such a hard thing for her to achieve. And then he let himself go.

TWENTY NINE

MARTHA

She seemed to swap one bedroom for another. Large double bed, view from the window, a feel of water nearby. The bedroom faced away from the Bay and looked down to a small paved courtyard dug out of the hill. The 'yard' belonged to his mom's apartment, Grant told her. A couple of trees on the other side of the wall made it quite dark but offered shade in summer. There were pots of flowers, and the paving had been cut away in one corner for a young tree with luminous, green leaves that dazzled Martha on her first afternoon after they had made love.

This wasn't his mom's bedroom, or more importantly, it wasn't her bed, Grant explained when he woke her with a mug of tea the following morning. His mom had kept the king size bed because she couldn't bear to get rid of such a good bed although she had never slept in it, preferring to sleep in the single bed that she'd slept in beside her husband, and had continued to sleep in after his death. Martha longed for him to put the mug down on the small side table and leave her to go back to sleep. She'd woken in the night, the image of Jon and herself on Grant's carpet flaring up into the darkness. Jon had left straight afterwards. She should have contacted him, come to some agreement. He might want to come back. He might have made her pregnant. These thoughts had invaded her in the Californian night. She'd glanced at Grant, very still on his side of the bed and thought: if I get pregnant it could be Jon's or Grant's. She was always irregular. How would she know?

She closed her eyes now and turned on her side, but Grant sat down on the bed and she was awake, suddenly certain he was going to say something. She shifted herself up and leaned against the quilted headboard and accepted the mug of tea – a weak herbal something or other. He told her that Lani wanted them to go over to hers for lunch in Pacific Heights. It was too far to walk. They would take a bus or a cab, but she would have to get up soon.

She'd forgotten how young Lani looked. Dark, glossy hair. Unlined, even-textured skin. Grant said that American women didn't do grey hair. They were either a real colour or snowy white. And had face lifts presumably. They sat down to a light fish mousse and salad served to them by a Spanish maid, high up on the fourth floor of the Victorian mansion block, the view through the window falling away to the Bay in the distance making Martha feel as if she was still airborne. She could hear the swishing sound of the aircraft in her ears. It mixed with the drone of Lani's slow drawl: the print sheet for the service would be ready by Thursday…. most people who would want to come had been contacted…it was such a pity Mom hadn't chosen her own hymns and readings… Martha held a mouthful of wine in her mouth, swilling it between her teeth – slightly sweet Californian Chardonnay but nicely chilled.

'Mom's apartment is yours, you know.'

It took a moment to realise Lani was talking to her. 'Mine?' She looked from Lani to Grant, wanting to laugh.

'Yours and Grant's. Although I might like some of the furniture.'

Grant had put down his fork and was staring at Lani.

Lani nodded at him. 'You'll be needing that apartment, Grant, if you're going to settle here.'

'Lani, all that's got to be decided.'

'Oh sure, I forgot.' Her eyes were directed at him as she lifted the bell for the maid.

'Martha and I haven't had a chance to talk.' Martha felt him turn towards her. 'Have we?' He reached a hand across the shiny dark wood table.

269

She clasped it, feeling too unreal to care. Everything could change. She could be pregnant by then. Grant might leave her. His mother's apartment might soon be theirs. She might get used to the hills, and the view of the Bay, and to spending holidays here or whatever Grant had in mind for them. His hand squeezed hers, lovingly it seemed. The meal proceeded into the next course of passion fruit salad followed by cheese. He glanced at her several times and became attentive, ensuring that she had the cream to go with the fruit, the butter and celery to go with the cheese; and then he appeared impatient to leave before coffee, irritated by his tiresome sister.

'The arrangements are all done now, right?' The line was in his forehead and he avoided Lani's eyes.

His sister's well cared for face looked as if it might crumple. 'Yeah... I guess so.' She sniffed and pulled a handkerchief out of her skirt pocket and put it to her nose. 'Don't... don't you want coffee?'

He got up and put his arm around her. 'Oh hey, I meant... the practical things.'

She dabbed her eyes with the handkerchief and blew her nose, but he insisted they leave and once outside in the bright afternoon said he needed to walk.

Their mother had died, Martha tried to remember as they wandered along the streets up and down past flowering trees and gardens, glimpsing blue water through the buildings, the sun pleasantly warm on their heads. Yesterday Grant had asked her whether she would like to see his mother in the chapel of rest. She hardly knew the woman when she was alive. Perhaps they would be going to see her now if she'd said yes. Perhaps Grant wanted to see her again; she hadn't asked him. And there was her apartment. What did Lani know that she didn't? They zigzagged down Lombard Street and headed for Telegraph Hill, out of breath by the time they had climbed the steep streets to Coit Tower, which they gave a miss in preference to the board walks and old houses of Filbert Street.

They sat in a café and he talked about how lucky it was that his mother had landed up in San Francisco which is a halfway decent city. They had lived in so many places when he was a child, she could have landed up in any city. 'Nowhere felt like home, Martha.'

He'd told her that often. She added hot milk to her espresso, bracing herself for what it might lead to this time. His mother had concentrated on the furnishings and artefacts so that there was a continuity, so that each place felt familiar even down to the coffee percolator... Martha hadn't heard this bit before. He wondered whether his mom had done this consciously to provide some security for her children, or whether it was just that she liked collecting things.

A temporary danger seemed to have passed. Martha added more milk – the coffee was strong – and glanced round at the other people, hearing their American voices. The tall girl with hair scraped up into a high pony tail, circulated the tables filling people's glasses with iced water. Service was good in this country.

'This baby thing. It has been tough, hasn't it?' He had his intent expression. The line was in his forehead. 'For the both of us.' His shoulders lifted.

She nodded, eyes stupidly filling.

He reached for her hand. 'We'll make it up to ourselves.'

She wished she felt strong enough to ask him what he meant, or find out what the hell he'd been talking about to Lani.

The street lights were blinking into existence as they emerged on to the street, the sky a deep blue, arcing over the high-rise buildings. They caught a bus back to the apartment and cooked themselves an omelette and ate it sitting on the sofa watching the movie channel. She fell asleep and woke to his hands lightly stroking her thighs. He'd pulled her legs up across his lap. They went into the bedroom and she let him take her clothes off and lie on top of her. He took her face in his hands and kissed it, his tongue going to places she'd not thought of before, the corners of her eyes, the soft skin behind the lobes of her ears. 'I want you, Martha. I want you.' Tears welled. He went into her and she felt the urge to choke and sob and turn her head from side to side and tell him everything.

Afterwards he got up while the room was still pulsing and went over to the window, and she thought he might never turn round. She sat up on her elbow, wanting him back, the white space of the bed expanding.

The next morning they got out his mother's wrought iron garden chairs and table and put them in the courtyard and sat down in the warm sunshine to toasted bagels, with cream cheese for him and apricot jam for her, and leaf Earl Grey tea, as if they were on holiday, and she wished there wasn't a funeral or babies or Jon or anything to worry about or explain. In two days, the funeral would be held in the crypt of Grace Cathedral followed by the committal in the chapel at Calistoga a couple of hours' drive away. Grant had suggested they might stay on for a night or two in the small town that lay at the foot of the mountain of St. Helena. They might try the mud baths, or take a hike up the mountain. They would taste the wine. She bit into her bagel and imagined them driving further north and taking a week or two to explore the north Pacific coast. The bagel had a distinctive, chewy quality she hadn't noticed before.

He lowered his mug. 'Martha, I've been thinking about returning to work here. I told Lani. That's what she was talking about yesterday. At lunch. I should have told you. I nearly did in that café.'

She nodded slowly. Next to his mug his fist was clenched.

He had lots of contacts, apparently, and might be able to shift the direction of his career, get involved in more teaching. He'd been thinking a lot and he knew it was a lot to ask of her but he needed a change. He looked down at his half-eaten bagel. High up a bird chirped in the tall trees in the garden above them. She could hear voices, children's voices. A school playground, perhaps. He seemed to be including her. It wouldn't happen immediately. With all his commitments it was likely to take up to a year before he could return and that would give her time to sort out whether she wanted to come...

She laughed, her heart pattering slightly. 'Are you serious?'

'I think so.'

'You really want to come back?'

'Would you come?'

She laughed again. 'How long for? A year? A sabbatical? For ever...?'

'That's the problem, isn't it?' He took a mouthful of tea.

'What is...?' She broke off a piece of bagel and put it into her mouth and wished she hadn't.

'You don't know.'

'How can I know? You've only just asked me...'

'You don't, though.'

'Grant, I have a job –'

'This baby thing has screwed us.' He banged down his mug. 'Even your messenger worries me. How sad is that?'

The bird was still chirping. The children's voices made an echoing sound.

He rubbed his hands over his face and stared at her. 'Did you see him? Jon, you know, your messenger. He was coming over on the Saturday.'

'Saturday...?' A horn started hooting.

'The Saturday I was away.'

'He didn't come.'

'He always came on a Saturday.'

'I know...' She took a sip of tea swilling down the remains of the bagel in her mouth and looked at him. She would tell him when she knew, if she needed to.

'Right.' He nodded and pushed the teapot towards her.

She shook her head.

He filled his own mug. 'I don't want it to be like this. I want us to be....' He glanced up, his face flushed. 'Do you want to be with me?'

The sun shone onto the little courtyard and the small tree with its pale leaves. The trees in the adjoining garden soared into the American blue sky. There would be the funeral and the committal and they would stay on in Calistoga and take mud baths, and walk, and drink the wine. She wanted to do these things with him and hope for the best. She wanted to talk to him about when to phone *The Chronicle*, and decide with him the best day to return to the UK. She wanted to keep her fingers crossed and plan the next bit of their life.

The car alarm had stopped but now a helicopter chugged overhead. She resisted the temptation to look up at the helicopter which seemed to be flying lower than helicopters over Putney and more noisily and might drown them out if it descended any lower, and put her hand across the table to his. 'I do.'

THIRTY

JON

Half-way through Monday morning Jon sent Max to the City with a parcel and then went up to the Features Floor without his trolley, pretending he was looking for Max. Martha's desk was empty. Her new secretary was sitting on a chair next to Tony with her pad taking notes. The Women's corner was deserted. No Liza, thank God. He didn't want her remembering he'd said he was worried about Martha. Doris was there, but she didn't see him and he retreated back to the ground floor.

The following day he made sure to sort out the letters. 'What do we do with Martha Morgan's?' He stopped by Steve's office, clutching the post trolley.

Steve's head lifted. 'Wha's that?'

'The Features editor's letters.'

'I know who Martha Morgan is.'

'I didn't say you didn't.'

'I beg your pardon?' Angry eyes under the sticking-up eyebrows.

'Sorry, Steve... didn't mean that. I just want to know what to do with her letters.'

'They go to Tony Walsh. Max knows that.'

''Course. Sorry.' Why the fuck was he apologising so much.

'She's away in America. I'm surprised you didn't know that. All her stuff has got to go to Tony until further notice.'

'Right.'

On the Wednesday he didn't go into work. He could have taken a day off. Been responsible. Booked it out. Or phoned and said he was sick. But he got to the station, picked up the *Metro* and walked straight to the platform going the other way as if that was the way he always went. He leaned against a pillar and glanced at the *Metro*, not reading the words, and when the train arrived climbed in. At Wimbledon he changed on to another train and got out at Leatherhead.

Dad would be at the library if what Ma was saying was true, and he should have gone straight to the bungalow. But he sat in a café and had a strong cup of tea, which made him think of Black Plaits and reminded him he was going to her flat this evening as if he'd forgotten. Perhaps he would drink his tea, return to the station and go home. He could go and see Black Plaits during the day as she'd first suggested. But he'd said he would go this evening, and that was what was stopping him from going to work. And he hadn't rung in. He finished his cup of tea and lifted his hand to pay. It was that kind of place. Just one other old lady, and no counter to go and choose from and watch them fizz the coffee or pour water on those herbal teabags. The girl came immediately.

Outside, he strode along the pavement towards his parents' bungalow and took out his mobile, turned down a side road so that it was less noisy, and dialled Steve's number.

'Wha' the hell's going on, Jon? Why didn't you phone?'

'I'm sorry, Steve. I don't know what it is. My head's... I think it's a...' he thought of Martha, 'a – migraine, maybe. A bad head –' pray Steve didn't know about Martha's bad heads... 'I feel so – sick... I couldn't ring until now... I'll try and get in tomorrow.'

'You better.'

Dad and Ma were both at the house when he got there. Dad had just got back from a morning standing outside the library rattling a collection box. 'Charity,' he lost no time in telling Jon. He'd joined Roter– something or other. Ma had been doing the weekly shop. She took up the commentary. Dad had dropped her off. She had done the shopping and then followed it with a coffee at the supermarket café where

Dad had joined her. They'd both had a bun, so neither of them were very hungry. If he'd only told her he was coming.

'I didn't come for food.'

He sat at one end of the settee and should have been pleased that Ma was sitting at the other end and not in the kitchen, but he'd imagined a nice cooked dinner which Ma would stretch to three: a roast with veg although that was Sunday of course, or just something hot like toad or macaroni and cheese. Plate on his knee, he bit into the soft white bread encasing one thin slice of ham. The soggy bread stuck to the roof of his mouth.

'So what are you up to?' It sounded quite friendly. Dad sat down in his usual chair and lifted the glass of beer that he'd poured from one can – more than half into his glass and the remains into Jon's – and twisted the wrist of his other hand to look at his watch.

Jon wondered what he would have to say to make Dad look at him. 'I've come to see you, Dad.'

'I can see that. Wednesday, isn't it? Holiday?'

'No.'

His dad stared at the glass of beer in his hand. His blazer with the brass buttons looked too warm. 'Why are you here then?'

'As I said, I've come to see you.'

'There has to be a reason.'

'Sorry –?'

He glanced up, his eyes looking towards the picture window. 'We haven't seen you. Not for weeks. Posh job.'

'Posh job?'

His dad's shoulders lifted, the glass shaking in his hand slightly. 'Don't ask me.'

Jon could hear his voice rising. 'You're always saying I haven't got a *proper* job.'

'You never come and see us.'

'That's why I've come.'

'As I said.'

'Wha' –?'

'Always for a reason.'

Oh fuck off, Jon wanted to say.

Dad lifted the glass and swallowed a mouthful of the beer, his tongue darting out to scoop in a few white bubbles caught at the edges of his mouth. 'Shouldn't you be at work?'

Jon took a swig of his own beer and clutched on to the glass. 'Dad, Ma told me on the phone, your life is changing. Well mine is too –'

'What makes you think that?'

'Wha' –?'

'What makes you think my life is changing?'

'Your… your library trips, Dad. And Ma says you've joined Roter… something or other – sounds good… and she says she's –'

'Rotary. You telling me you haven't heard of Rotary?'

Jon heard his own groan, outside of himself as if it was coming in from the garden through the gap where the picture window had been opened.

His father's head jerked round, his eyes momentarily meeting Jon's. 'Any self-respecting man has heard of Rotary!'

It was a sunny day, blue sky, clouds… they should have been outdoors, sitting on the white, plastic chairs Dad used to keep in the garden shed at New Malden, sipping the beer, looking out on to the square bit of grass and the fence, letting all the air in that wide space separate their differences.

Dad placed his glass carefully on to the centre of the mat on the small table beside him. 'Lost your job?'

'No.'

'What then?'

He tried to say it slowly. 'I haven't lost my job, Dad. I'm thinking of leaving it.'

'Same thing.'

Jon looked at his mother. She had been so chatty on the phone, and when he first got here today, in her white blouse with the yellow cardigan and the red skirt – very colourful for her. She was clasping her hands now, staring at the carpet. He wanted to see her eyes, try and make her look, make her hear – *communicate*, that was a good word, a Pete word. But her eyes were hidden by her lids, and he could tell by the way one hand pressed the fingers of her other hand that she wished he wasn't there. If only there were just the two of them, just him and his ma, because there were times when there had been just her and him. 'Ma, will you listen. I can't talk to Dad. He's like a brick wall, like… I don't know what like… but I'm going to say it. I'm going to tell you what I came here to do.'

Dad pushed himself to the end of his chair. 'Don't talk to your mother like that!'

'Like what, Dad?'

'Christ almighty!' He stood up, breathing heavily.

'I'm just trying to ask you to… to listen, Dad! I've listened to you. It's great you're getting out and going to the library and that you've joined Roter-whatever, that you stand outside the library and collect money for charity. I'm gobsmacked that Ma is getting out too. That is the best news I've heard in… but I need you to…'

Dad stepped towards him, his navy blazer puffing up as if his chest couldn't hold what was inside. 'Jon! If you don't stop shouting at your mother, I'm going to order you out of the house.'

'I'm not shouting at her…' But he was. He was screaming. 'Listen to me, Dad! Listen!' Nearly crying now, his eyes wet, tears wanting to choke out of him. 'You're… you're not listening to me. You never listen to me. You never fucking listen – !'

'Jon, leave the house!' He moved a step nearer.

Jon shoved his knuckles into his eyes. He mustn't look at him. He must turn and face his mother. He mustn't cry like a baby. 'Ma...' He reached for her hand, quickly before Dad would think he was going to attack her and do something stupid. He said – it burst out of him – 'Ma, I love you! Do you hear me? I love you. That's why... why I'm shouting. That's why Dad thinks... that's why I'm... I'm...'

Ma's face – he hadn't noticed what it had been doing. He'd been looking at his dad, as he always did if his dad was in the room. But Ma was looking at him, her eyes behind the large round glasses like saucers. She was staring at him, her yellow cardigan making the pale brown of her eyes look yellow too, but alive; and that was what was important, her eyes were alive, not dead, not crying, but looking at him with such surprise, and then turning and saying in a raised voice Jon didn't know she had. 'Maurice, sit down and for pity's sake eat up your sandwich, and let Jon get a word in edgeways!'

Jon kept his eyes on her. He wasn't going look up or indicate with a flicker of an eyelid that he feared Dad might come nearer and take Ma into the kitchen and hit her, though Dad probably hadn't done that since he was a boy. Perhaps Ma no longer feared that. It was a nice thought. He felt the movement of Dad's shoes on the carpet as he went back to his chair and his untouched sandwich, heard the faint whoosh of the upholstery and creak of the frame as he sank into the chair. His mother patted his hand. 'Now, Jon. What is it you want to tell us?'

He felt so proud of his ma for standing up to Dad, for being so cheerful in her clothes, her cardigan the colour of a canary, probably all bought from the Oxfam shop, probably got free. If he was not careful, Dad would become a blurred figure, sitting too upright, too stiff, seen through wet eyes. He wanted to say, take off your blazer, Dad, lean back, chill out. Go out in the garden, feel the sunny day on your shirt sleeves, sit on one of the white, plastic chairs that you can't have thrown out, have another beer. He focussed on Dad's knees that were pressed together showing up the outline of his legs: the straight line of the bone between his knee and his foot, and his thin thighs. What was he worrying about? He could knock him over so easily. 'Dad, I did take a day off. Specially to come and see you. I wanted talk to you. I wanted to get your opinion, your advice.'

In the train back to Surbiton he tried to remember what he'd said; whether he had really said it, Mum sitting in the settee looking at him, Dad in his chair, arms folded, looking as if needed that beer.

'I'm going to join a new business.'

Dad breathed in noisily. 'I thought you'd got one.'

'I'm going to move to the country. Go into retail.'

'In the country!'

'Maurice!' It was his ma again, clutching her hands together in her lap and nodding and smiling.

'An Indian shop. I'm going to help set up an import retail business.' It sounded good the way he said it. 'I'll rent a room. She needs a man. She needs someone who can work the till, someone who has a computer, someone who can do the paperwork, the electronic work – that's what it is these days, all electronic.'

He stood on the forecourt outside Surbiton station. A black taxi drew up as if he might take it. Didn't see many of those round here. Mostly mini-cabs, and you had to be careful they were legit, not that he ever took one. It was too early to go to Black Plaits. He crossed the forecourt, avoiding a car drawing in, and put a hand in his pocket for his mobile – luckily, full of juice. She'd given him her phone number and he'd added it to his list of contacts. Perhaps he would phone her and see if he could go there now.

THIRTY ONE

MARTHA

After the funeral they spent three days in Calistoga and then drove up the north coast and stayed in Mendocino for a few more days and browsed in the quaint shops and read about James Dean making *East of Eden* in the town back in the Fifties. They took walks in the pine woods and found a steep bank leading down to a small beach on the river, a water hole Grant explained, deep enough to swim. The word 'waterhole' appealed to her – their own pool, deep and contained, and very American somehow. The water shone brown and clear. He bent down to feel it with his hand. No one was about, and they stripped off and plunged in. The temperature took their breath away and made them shriek and laugh and swim back and forth until it started to feel warmer. They got out and ran up and down the beach, flapping their arms and hugging each other's wet bodies, and used his shirt to dry themselves. They held hands as they tried to find their way back to where they had parked the car; only a mile away they thought in a sandy clearing next to a couple of redwoods, but two or three by the time they found it.

The next day they strolled along the wide beach at the river mouth at Mendocino and dipped their bare feet into the icy ocean, and collected logs stripped clean of bark, like bones, and made a wood house and sat in it, sheltering from the wind. They wandered into a second-hand bookshop and bought an ink-stained copy of *The Grapes of Wrath,* which she'd never read, and a clean blue Penguin edition with the phoenix rising from the ashes of *The Death of a Salesman,* which he'd never seen or read, and sat reading for hours in the two armchairs in their hotel bedroom window. In a small store on Main Street they found two large blue and white swimming towels and returned to the waterhole for another swim.

The thought of returning to San Francisco seemed premature and they stayed on another day. They agreed not to talk about the last few weeks, or the future, or the possibility of coming to live in the States. The deal was to be together and to do enjoyable things. 'Let's wait until we're home,' Grant said. She hoped 'home' meant the same place as it did for her.

Now, three days later they had driven back to San Francisco and were on the plane flying back to the UK.

She clipped her table into the seat in front and leaned her head against the seat rest, the drone of the plane in her ears. The in-flight evening meal had taken an age to arrive and even longer to be cleared away. She shifted over to her right side and slid the stiff white plastic blind half way up the window. Beyond the broad beam of the plane's lights, the sky was black, the silver wing just visible.

'Jon!' The palm of his hand had pushed her face, pushing her back against the couch. 'Jon, it's alright. I want to...'

They had tumbled off the couch on to the floor. She'd tried to help him, pulling down her trousers, but he pushed her hands away, hitting her thigh, tearing at her clothes, needing to do it himself.

She closed her eyes, remembering that she'd climaxed almost instantly once he was inside her. He'd taken a few moments longer. He'd shouted; such strange words... 'India! Oh India, I'm coming!'

Her heart pattered. She pressed her head against the seat rest and glanced across the empty seat towards Grant.

His eyes were open. 'Alright?'

'Yeah.' She reached for the air control, feeling hot. 'Good sleep.'

'I wasn't sleeping.'

'Weren't you?'

'No…'

'Right.' Behind him a grey-haired woman padded along the aisle.

'Get away from a place and you get a different perspective.'

'Sorry…?'

'About the States. I'm not going to know if I want to work there, until we've been back several weeks – months maybe. Let alone whether you want to come.' He turned to her. 'I won't go without you.'

She laughed, dizzy almost. 'Won't you?'

He shook his head. 'No. I may not *want* to go. Do you see? It may just have been the fact that Mom was dying, and all the baby stuff…' Their eyes met. 'You left that message, didn't you?'

'Message –?'

'On the phone… remember?'

'Oh, yes…'

'I did thinking of leaving you –'

Shush, she wanted to say.

He reached his hand across the empty seat for hers. 'Sitting by Mom's bedside I formed the idea about coming back to the States and thought if you didn't want to come with me it wouldn't matter. But it would.'

She nodded. It had been good after the funeral in Calistoga and Mendocino. They'd made love on the night of the funeral and twice in Mendocino and she'd not felt once like crying. Swimming in that clear, brown water in the woods… sitting in the window of their hotel room with their books, the light bouncing off the ocean she'd thought: *everything will go on being the same.* She tried to remember now when she'd left the message; the feeling that made her leave it. When she couldn't make herself go to work, probably; when Jon had left her after one of his overnight stays in Grant's map room; when everyone seemed to be leaving her.

Grant was clasping her hand. 'Mendocino was like a holiday. It was probably what we needed.' He grinned and took her cheek between thumb and finger. 'I'm not going to leave you, whatever we do.'

She managed a laugh. 'I hope not.'

He shook his head again and leaned over and kissed her.

She put on the earphones and checked the list of films : George Clooney in a thriller.... a Harry Potter film... the Simpsons movie – nothing she hadn't seen or wanted to see. She switched to the classic music channel and closed her eyes. For a few moments she seemed to drop off. When she glanced at Grant he was asleep, eyelids like a child's under the thick eyebrows. 'Grant,' she mouthed. He was probably only lightly asleep and perhaps she could talk to him now. But the lights were being turned down and she thought of Jon.

He could have slunk off once he'd got off the floor, or made a run for it, that was what it felt like he wanted to do, but he waited for her to pull up her trousers and stand up and then put his hands in his pockets and glanced round with what seemed like a last look: Grant's desk with the new computer and keyboard – replicated in his own flat; the couch that he'd sat on, that he'd pushed her off; the blank walls; the Persian rug. He moved towards the door and turned back, glancing in the direction of the front door as if he needed to check his escape route. 'You alright?'

She had made herself stand where she was in Grant's consulting room where neither of them should have been. She could feel the tasselled edge of the Persian rug between her toes and sense the empty walls around her. Pale skin, dark long hair, eyes she'd thought offered some kind of calm but which were often agitated, moving from side to side, unable to focus, unable to look at her. There was something she loved about his face. 'I'm fine, Jon. You go.'

THIRTY TWO

GRANT

The first morning he woke to the sound of American automatics accelerating up Green Street and the whine of sirens, and took a few moments to realise that the noise was the drone of the planes heading for Heathrow and that he was in his bed in Putney. The small bedside clock said 10.50 am. Light streamed through the curtains. It would be three in the morning in San Francisco. He glanced over to Martha's side. Her back was turned to him, thick, short hair bunched against the pillow; not a movement. He got out of bed, walked to the window and carefully drew back the curtain. River in full tide, glittering under a medium blue sky, not as intense as a Californian sky but good enough, he thought, loving suddenly the sight of a dinghy with a man and a dog, chugging past the end of their garden making for the next bridge.

Lifting his dressing gown off the hook on the door he went down to the kitchen, brewed himself some tea and made for his room. Martha had organised for Catrin to clean the house the day before their return and the sun shone through spotless window panes, bringing out the colours on the Persian rug. His armchair wasn't in the right position and it looked as if the couch had been moved. He shifted it along, pushing it right up to the skirting board, and then scanned the room again, everything as he liked it, clean and uncluttered. He sat at his desk, sipping his tea, and gazed at his screen. All the patients he'd emailed from California were looking forward to starting again. He had a full list of them the next day. There was the Institute to phone and the book to think about. It was two o'clock when he next looked at his watch.

Martha was lying in bed on her side, eyes closed, as though she hadn't moved since he got up. He touched her shoulder

286

and she shifted on to her back and asked him to put the tea on the table. He thought of the other times he'd done this – San Francisco on her first morning; here months back on that awful Sunday; here last year, and the year before, when she lay there because she had her period again and hadn't fallen pregnant.

He placed the cup and saucer down, noticing that it was now two-thirty. 'You'll never sleep tonight.'

Her lids lifted. 'I will.'

He leaned over and kissed her. 'You alright?'

'Yes.'

'One of your headaches.'

'I don't know.'

'Do you need your pills?'

She shook her head.

He helped her to sit up against the pillows and passed her the tea cup and saucer, and sat down on the bed making sure she kept awake. He thought of his words on the plane. *I'm not going to leave you. Whatever we do.*

The next day was Friday and she stayed in bed all day. She seemed better and he liked the idea of her being up there while he sat with his patients, and felt almost disappointed as he climbed the stairs to hear her voice on the phone planning to return to work on Monday, the newspapers spread out on their bed. She got up mid-morning the next day and sat at the kitchen table flicking through the film guide and drinking green tea, the tension in her face smoothed away, and beautiful it seemed to him as she looked up to suggest a walk in the afternoon and maybe a film early evening. Jon didn't turn up – and wasn't expected to, of course – but after lunch before they went out, Grant stood at the window in his room half expecting to see him loping along the pavement from the direction of the station in his scruffy leather jacket and faded jeans. He felt in his pocket as if he might pull out his car keys and drive to pick him up from Kingston. Jon hadn't come when Martha was here on her own, and that was a good thing he reminded himself. She would see him at work presumably.

He turned away from the window and went to find his jacket and they walked from Putney Bridge along the towpath south of the river towards Barnes, rowers in their boats rowing against an ebbing tide, the coxes shouting encouragement. In the warm sunshine Jon felt like a figment of their imagination. They stopped to let a group of joggers overtake them and he glanced at her.

'Looking forward to going back?'

'It's been weeks.'

'I know.'

They skirted round people coming from the opposite direction.

He reached for her hand. 'Why did you stay away?'

'I couldn't get out the front door.'

'Couldn't you?'

'No.'

'Will you tell me about it?'

Her hand held his very tightly. 'Soon, I promise.'

A cyclist with a megaphone sped past them issuing orders to the rowers. A couple had taken their dog on to the shore and threw a stick into the water. They were opposite the River Café now. There was the little wall; and the tables outside probably, though it was too far away for him to see. He remembered their lunch. They seemed to have come a distance since then.

He looked at her, laughing and wanting her to join in. 'I'll keep you to it!'

THIRTY THREE

MARTHA

The features floor seemed low-ceilinged and stuffy on her first day back at work. Scruffy too with its pitted lino floor and worn surfaces and debris round the desks. She stopped at the water fountain and filled a plastic mug wanting to slip in unnoticed, and glanced round for Jon with the early morning deliveries. She couldn't think how she was going to deal with seeing him. How did people manage infidelities – though this wasn't really that? The iced water made her shiver. A one-night stand... the phrase seemed old fashioned. Would he need to tell somebody? It seemed only now she realised this part of the risk.

'Welcome back!' Liza shouted. 'Be with you in a sec.'

Doris heaved herself off her chair in the Obituary corner and came and gave her a bear hug and then everyone else was doing the same.

Her desk was piled high with mail and newspapers. She'd rung Jenny and asked her to prepare a précis of all that she'd missed. 'Main stories, who's been doing what, any surprises, anything you think I should know? Try and postpone any meetings in the morning.' She sat at her desk feeling strange. It would be about one in the morning in California.

Jenny rushed in apologising, 'Sorry! Northern Line's on the blink. How are you? Good to see you.' Her coat was off and Martha was handed a wad of stapled notes. 'Hope it covers everything.'

The delivery trolley had arrived, pushed by the young boy with spiky blond hair.

Tony was away for three days in Canada in discussions about his new appointment as editor to one of the main Canadian dailies, so it was Liza who took her through what she'd missed, and at the end of a long list of events, which included details about Tony's new job and the pending resignation of Eva in Health – there had been ructions over the cool reception of *Fuzzy the Physician*, which was Eva's baby – she told Martha that her messenger friend had left. 'You know the guy with the long, dark hair.'

They had taken themselves over to the sofas in *Books* and Martha had sat back with Jenny's notes on her lap occasionally adding her own notes. 'You mean Jon?' She scribbled his name illegibly.

'I think that's what Daisy said. You could find out more from her. I got to know him a little. He kept coming over and asking after you. Unusual guy but rather endearing.'

Something high up in her rib cage seemed to drop. 'We gave him our old computer.'

Liza grinned. 'No wonder.'

Martha placed the notes carefully on the low table and leaned back against the sofa. Across the floor she could see Daisy at her desk. Liza's purple-haired secretary was getting up and going towards her. 'He came to our house.' She could tell Liza now. Make it sound plausible. Position herself back where she should be, leading the features department with no odd history behind her. 'He wasn't exactly computer literate. Grant had to show him the rudiments.'

The dimple was in Liza's cheek. 'Daisy took a shine to him too, when she wasn't hankering after Tony.'

'Tony...?'

She rolled her eyes and nodded at Martha. 'I don't think she'll stay once he's gone. You okay? You look spaced out.'

'Jet lag.'

'You should have waited a day or two.'

I did, Martha almost said. Lay in bed. Let Grant look after me. Tried to read *The Chronicle*. Tried to ignore the spikes of nausea and odd taste in my mouth... She couldn't believe she was here now, sitting on the sofa with Liza, looking down at

Jenny's notes on the table to hide what might be in her eyes, glancing up, talking about work. She couldn't believe Jon might have gone.

Liza grinned. 'We can manage without you, you know.'

She shook her head, and smiled. 'No, you can't.'

A week went by and she woke from a dream. Grant was away on a two-day conference, and the whole bed was hers.

In the dream she was on the chalk downs near Phil's on a beautiful summer's day. A small boy held her hand and they walked along the ridge to have a picnic in the clump of beech trees, a warm wind blowing on their faces. When they got there the boy ran off to find a tree to climb but the branches were too high. He sat astride a fallen trunk and asked her if he could run to the bottom of the hill. He'd hardly gone, zigzagging through the trees and out into the open, when she saw a figure. He emerged from behind a tree. She walked beside him into the sunlight and looked across the grass down the hill towards the boy scampering away from them. 'You know, don't you? You know that he's ours.'

She turned on to her back, wishing she could conjure up the face of the figure. It felt like Jon's. But it could be Grant's. Little sperm and unpredictable egg. Either of them. Light seeped through the curtains.

Downstairs she made herself some tea and sat down at the kitchen table with a bowl of cornflakes, ate a mouthful and then pushed it away, and went to look for her diary and Jon's number. It was in her bag hanging over the back of the chair in her bedroom. She picked up the phone and dialled his home number and sat on her bed and listened to the ringing tone until it cut out. She tried his mobile and that rang and rang too.

On her way to work she tried both numbers again, staring at the blue and orange pattern of the seat cover opposite as the train rumbled out of Putney. Perhaps there had been a row and he'd lost his job. Perhaps he'd shouted it around the Mail & Communications room that he'd had it off with the Features Editor. He was out there now without a job, evicted from his flat possibly, discarded by *The Chronicle*, Grant and herself. She thought of going down to Mail and Communications and asking Steve outright, but news stories broke early that day. A teenager had vanished, walking through a park two hundred metres from her home. A meeting had to be called to decide whether *The Chronicle* was going to join the paparazzi outside the parents' home, or whether to take a more ethical approach.

Towards the end of the day the spiky-haired messenger wheeled his trolley around the floor distributing late deliveries, and she glanced up from her screen and asked him about Jon. He leaned against his trolley, a gap-year, public school boy, and looked down at her computer and her post-it notes, and then at her. 'He got a job in a shop. Didn't sound much to me.' His mouth curled into a smile, eyes too confident for her liking. 'Some woman or other!'

He pushed his trolley on towards Obituaries and she drew back her chair and hurried to the Ladies. Two of the doors were engaged, the small red bar glaring at her. There was a sound of urine trickling into water. She made for the furthest cubicle, clanged the door behind her, and retched into the white bowl.

On the train home she tried his numbers again. The last time, she told herself as the train drew out of Waterloo. No reply from either. At home, she poured herself a whisky and then tipped it away and went out and got into their car to drive to his flat. There was a woman. All along there may have been a woman. It didn't make sense. He was lonely, dependent. But he'd slept with her. Maybe he'd slept with other women. She knew nothing about him. He could have a sexually transmitted disease. He could be HIV positive. She pressed her foot on to the accelerator up Putney Hill to Wimbledon roundabout, along the edge of Wimbledon Common, down

Roehampton Hill to the next roundabout. She'd done this journey before and he hadn't been in his flat. He wasn't going to be there now. He'd got another job. He was happy. He'd gone. She circled the roundabout and came back up Roehampton Hill towards Putney.

She could talk in confidence to Anne in Human Resources. Get an address, his parents' address maybe, their phone number; ring them, talk to them, find out exactly what had happened. She parked the car outside their house and turned off the ignition feeling sick – she needed something to eat. Human Resources would keep the details on record for at least a year if she wanted to contact him; and she could keep trying his mobile and hope he hadn't changed the number.

Grant's patient intake seemed to increase. He appeared to get up at six every morning for one of his early seven a.m. appointments. By the time she was standing in the kitchen downing a mug of tea, and as the days went by a piece of toast to stop the queasy feeling, he was well into his second if not his third patient.

'Don't be ridiculous, honey,' he laughed as he pulled on a shirt in the dim, curtain-drawn bedroom, and as she turned on her side and sunk her head into the pillow. 'I've taken on two more that's all, and they're not the early morning slot.' He'd taken on an extra evening class at the Institute of Marital Therapy too, and was involved in setting up a conference on relationship guidance. 'I'm not going to write the book on fathers. You know that, don't you?'

She nodded, feeling her eyes close.

'I haven't completely given up the idea. A paper perhaps, if I can find the right co-writer.' He bent over and kissed her cheek. 'Love you.'

She felt light-headed with his busyness. They hadn't talked about moving to the States since their return, although it was on the agenda. He seemed happy in his work and confident of her, forgetting perhaps she had something to tell him.

One morning on the train into Waterloo, she nearly vomited. She stared ahead of her between two people's heads to the door between the carriages, sweating with concentration, praying the carriages wouldn't sway too much and not daring to look down at her paper or out of either of the windows at the moving houses and buildings. At Waterloo she got out of the train and stood on the platform taking gulps of fresh air as everyone rushed past her. The newspaper stall had a small packet of biscuits. She paid for it and went and leaned against a wall and extracted a biscuit from its cellophane. Her period was two weeks overdue. She ate the biscuit, carefully, one mouthful at a time and returned to the stall and bought some water. She took deep breaths, and walked slowly towards the tube entrance to continue her journey.

Tony's departure left a hole in her team and she found herself, reluctantly now because she'd lost the urge to write, writing a feature on press censorship and pornography. She worked late most nights and then ate a sandwich or stopped off at a café or a wine bar before starting the journey home, which seemed to claw at her energy and make her long to lie flat. At least she got a seat at that hour on the Jubilee line and on the train. The worst was the wait on the forecourt at Waterloo gazing at the departure boards. At home she would collapse on the sofa in front of *Newsnight* and let Grant bring her a glass of wine and hope he wouldn't notice that she didn't drink it.

'You alright, honey?' he said more than once.

She expected him to remember their walk on the towpath and ask her what she'd said she would tell him. Her eyelids drooped. 'Just tired.'

Her brother rang one evening and apologised for not ringing before to find out how they were after the funeral. Kathleen had had a scare. There had been a show of blood which had involved a couple of nights in hospital but all appeared to be well and the scans revealed a flourishing baby boy.

'Come down for a day, Martha. Both of you. It's so lovely down here in early summer. I won't ask you for the weekend. It's a bit much for Kathleen.'

'Of course, Phil.'

'But do come.' He sounded as if he really meant it. 'The girls and Ben would love it. Becky's been asking why we haven't seen you. We haven't forgotten that you want to have her to stay for a weekend. It could be very useful in the future.' A burst of laughter. 'We might ask you to have both girls. No, I'm not serious. I know how busy you are.'

A week went by, and then another. A Saturday arrived and she considered doing nothing for a further week. Nothing until he noticed – that would be one way. Grant was working in his room and she walked up Putney High Street along the crowded pavements to the local Boots. She wandered up and down the aisles looking for the Family Planning section which seemed to have moved since she'd last had to buy a pregnancy testing kit. That was before the IVF treatment; one of the many times she was late with her period. Grant had been with her and they had nervously returned home and put off trying it for a few hours. She found the right section now and there was the same choice of brands in blue and pink and white packets with names like *Predictor* all promising 99% accuracy.

Neil Meredith had been their G.P. for years, on first name terms and almost a friend, and her news brought a flush of pleasure into his lined face. He removed his glasses and sat back in his chair, smiling. 'So, it's worked!'

'Sorry?'

'The IVF.'

She felt a wave of sickness and wished she'd managed a piece of toast before she'd left.

He replaced his glasses and glanced at the screen. On his desk was the framed photo of his wife Deidre, and on the shelf above a photo of his grandson. 'With Mr. Shorn, aren't you?'

'I was.'

He looked back at her.

Her heart pattered. 'I stopped.'

He took off his glasses. 'Of course you did! I'm sorry, I'd forgotten.'

'We stopped the programme months ago.'

'So it was without in vitro fertilisation?'

'Yes.'

'And you've done the test, more than once?'

'Yes.'

'And you're pleased?'

'Yes.'

'Well, well.' He gazed at her as if it was his own wife giving him the news, his mouth stretching into a smile again. 'It does happen, you know. More often than you would imagine. But I expect it feels like a miracle. People give up too quickly these days. Try for a few months and when it doesn't work get themselves on to a fertility programme which doesn't do their bodies any good. That's marvellous, Martha. Congratulations.' He leant forward so that she could see the emotion in his eyes.

'Thank you, Neil.'

'Is Grant pleased?'

'I haven't told him yet.'

He nodded slowly. 'You wanted to be certain.'

She returned his nod.

He looked at the screen. 'We must make certain we look after you.'

It was a relief to get through the practicalities – he took her blood pressure and told her to pop on to the bed so that he could give her a quick external examination – and get out into the street with her prescription for iron tablets and her appointment for a scan.   There was not a breath of air. Summer had arrived early.   She plodded up the street towards the station. A coke tin lay in the gutter. A Burger King packet had been chucked into one of the front gardens, the half-eaten burger landing about a foot away at the base of a miniature cypress. She sat down on the low wall bordering the garden and wiped the cloth of her shirt against her armpits and under the line of her bra and up between her breasts, and then pulled out her mobile and stared at the small screen. *Liza, I may not be in today. Something's happened, something very good...* A woman clipped down the hill towards her. She stuffed the phone back into her bag without sending the text.

The woman passed by and she followed her down the hill, waited for a space in the traffic and crossed Putney Bridge Road.   The petrol fumes tasted in her mouth.   Everything tasted now.   Her heart pumped.   She was in their road, the other end of it... Grant would be working in his room a few hundred yards away, listening to a patient with his full attention, letting nothing distract him; or writing a lecture for his new class; or planning his next paper, or thinking about America.   She turned into Wandsworth Park and found a bench under the trees and let her heart slow down – two heart beats in there now.

A jogger skirted the trees and headed towards the path near the river.   Over by the entrance a dog scampered in circles. *Some woman or other.* That was what the spiky-haired messenger had said. He'd gone to work in a shop with a woman. In Kingston if she cared to look, or Surbiton, or anywhere quite nearby. Or India, she thought. Those strange words, *Oh India I'm coming*. Maybe that was where he'd gone. Maybe she could allow herself to think that was where he'd gone.

The bench shuddered.   Someone had joined her.   She glanced quickly – an old man... grey hair spread in lines over a balding head... a matted brown and black dog with its nose on his lap. She got up and wandered towards the river where the jogger had run. The tide was coming in. Mud-coloured water seeped up the sides of the banks. She leaned against the railings. For a second she looked for the cells in the ripples of water, black shapes darting away in the sunlight, joining up, dividing... She didn't want a vulnerable young man. She wanted this baby, whoever the father was. In a minute she would turn away from the railings and start for home. Then she would try and tell Grant the whole story, and hope they could bring up the child together.

THIRTY FOUR

GRANT

Half-way through the morning, in a break between patients, he got up to stretch his legs and clear his head, and went to the window and saw her about twenty yards away walking along the pavement towards the house from the direction of the bridge, her light summery skirt swinging as she walked, her yellow T-shirt bright in the sunshine. He took a step back, as if she might stroll on past the house, his heart slipping a beat. She'd left for work at least an hour ago and should certainly not be coming from that direction. He looked again, wondering whether it really was her in that yellow T-shirt which looked a bit tight. She was crossing the road, heading towards the house, and now she'd seen him and was lifting her arm.

He waved back and watched her reach the pavement and in a few more steps their gate. She was carrying her work bag, and as she came up the path she looked up and smiled. He turned away from the window. A patient had cancelled and he had an hour before the next one. He puffed up the cushions on the couch, rubbed a hand along the top of his armchair, glanced around his room, determined that by the time he'd walked into the hall and opened the front door he would be ready for whatever she was coming home to tell him.